THE PLACE OF THE SKULL

THE PLACE OF THE SKULL

Chingiz Aitmatov

Translated from the Russian
by Natasha Ward

GROVE PRESS
New York

Published by Grove Press
a division of Wheatland Corporation
841 Broadway
New York, N.Y. 10003

Library of Congress Cataloging-in-Publication Data

Aitmatov, Chingiz.
    The place of the skull.

    I. Title.
PG3478.I8P54   1989   891.73'44   88-34758

ISBN 0-8021-1000-2

Manufactured in the United States of America

This book is printed on acid-free paper.

First Edition 1989

10 9 8 7 6 5 4 3 2

MAN

Daylight brought a slight thaw, brief and elusive as the breath of a child, on the south-facing slopes of the mountains; then, imperceptibly, the weather changed: the wind blew down off the glaciers and a penetrating darkness stole up the ravines, trailing behind it the cold pearly-grey of a snowy night ahead.

Snow was everywhere. The whole length of the Issyk-Kul ridge lay buried by the blizzard that had swept through a couple of days before with the wild rage of a forest fire. Such storms could be a terrifying thing, as the snowy darkness swallowed up mountains, sky and the whole of the visible world. Later the raging ceased, and a clearer sky broke through. Since then the mountains had stood in frozen silence, imprisoned and isolated from the rest of creation by a mantle of ice.

The only sound was the growing roar of a heavyweight helicopter, cutting up through the canyon of the Unzun-Chat to the frozen wastes of the pass at Ala-Mongyu, half visible in the evening light and the curling wisps of cloud; closer and louder it grew, until at last, triumphant, it filled with its thundering clatter the ridges and peaks, the untouched snows where the only trespassers were light and sound. Echoing off the rock-face and the screes, the sound grew with such inexorable power that the mountains seemed poised for a repeat of the recent earthquake, remembered with horror by all in those parts . . .

Suddenly something cracked and a stony slope, denuded by the winds, directly beneath the path of the helicopter, started to move. Shuddering as the sound-wave reached it, a bank of scree ran down but was quickly stilled, like the flow of blood at the utterance of a charm. So unstable was the surface, how-ever, that even this small movement was enough to send a few of the heavier stones crashing down the slope, gaining speed, raising dust and chips in their wake, until they burst at the foot like cannon-balls through the bushes of *krasnotal* and barberry, and tunnelled through the deeper drifts to thunder down on to the roof of a lair which the grey wolves had burrowed out in a cleft beneath the overhang, tucked between a thicket and a small, half frozen but gradually thawing spring.

Akbara, the she-wolf, backed away from the stones and snow that rained down from above, backed into the darkness of the cleft, coiled like a spring, hackles up, eyes burning with a phosphorescent fire, ready to strike at a moment's notice. However, she had nothing to fear. It was out in the open steppe that a wolf could find no hiding place from a pursuing helicopter, from the deafening whine of the blades and the flash of machine-gun fire; no clefts in the steppe, where a wolf could save its ill-starred hide from a helicopter; no hope out there that the earth might open to shelter her fugitives . . .

The mountains were different, for here there was always a chance of escape, a chance to hide and wait till the danger should pass. Here, a helicopter was no threat: up in the mountains, the threat was to the helicopter itself. But the fear was an instinctive one, reinforced by experience. At the helicopter's approach Akbara whined loudly and crouched back in a ball, shoulders up; then suddenly her nerve broke and she howled at the top of her voice, seized with a blind, impotent fear, before crawling shivering on her belly towards the opening, her teeth chattering in anger and despair, ready for a show of strength as though she hoped to put to flight the metal monster that clattered through the ravines and tumbled the very stones, like that other time during the earthquake.

Akbara's cries of panic brought into the lair her he-wolf, Tash-Chainar, the Stone-Crusher, whose powerful jaws had earned him his name from the shepherds in those parts. Since the start of her heaviness, he had spent most of his time just outside the lair, in the quiet of the bushes. Now he crept to where she lay with a soothing growl, as though to shield her from attack with his body. Cringing close to his side, the she-wolf continued to whine and howl, calling, perhaps, on an inequitable heaven, or cursing her fate or something else, and trembling still long after the helicopter was gone beyond the great glacier of Ala-Mongyu and its sound swallowed up into the clouds.

4

Then suddenly the mountain silence reigned anew, and in that soundless interstellar clarity the she-wolf felt within herself, within the depths of her womb, a living movement. She remembered the time at the start of her hunting life, when she had brought down and strangled a fat she-hare; within the she-hare's belly had been the movement of some invisible beings, hidden from view, surprising and intriguing the inquisitive young she-wolf as she stood there, ears pricked, sniffing diffidently at the corpse of her victim. So strange and marvellous was the sight that she even tried to play with the invisible bodies, as a cat will play with a half-dead mouse. And now she discovered the same living burden within her own body, as the first signs of quickening came from the cubs who would, if all went well, be born in another couple of weeks. For the moment, however, the unborn cubs were still a part of their mother's body, a part of her being, and so they too suffered in the pre-natal mists of their inchoate consciousness the shock and despair that invaded the mind of their mother. This was their first, still indirect, contact with the outside world and the inimical realities that awaited them. Their way of responding to their mother's suffering was to squirm within her womb.

As she concentrated upon the independent movement within her quickened womb, Akbara was filled with foreboding. The she-wolf's heart beat faster, with courage and resolve to foster and cherish at all costs the cubs she bore within her belly. She would attack anything that lay in her way. She was in the grip of Nature's great instinct to preserve her issue. Suddenly, Akbara felt herself engulfed by a great surge of tenderness, by the need to touch and warm the unborn cubs, and to give them her milk, as though they had already arrived. It was a foretaste of the happiness to come. She closed her eyes and groaned with pleasure, with the expectation of the milk that would fill the two swollen rows of rosy nipples on her belly, then stretched languidly (as far as the size of the lair would allow) and, happy again, moved closer to her grey-maned Tash-Chainar. He was a powerful beast, with a coat that was warm, thick and springy. Even he, gloomy Tash-Chainar, was somehow aware of what the mother-wolf was

5

feeling and of the processes taking place within her. They must have touched him too. Ears pricked, Tash-Chainar raised his heavy square head while across the steely depths of deep-set eyes flitted the shadow of pleasant anticipation. He gave a discreet growl, as though to show his readiness to honour and obey the blue-eyed she-wolf, and set to licking Akbara's head, especially her shining blue eyes and her nose, with tender, thorough strokes of his short, warm, liquid tongue. Akbara loved Tash-Chainar's tongue when he played and frolicked with her, trembling with impatience, and his tongue, hot and turgid with blood, was stiff, swift and full of energy as a snake (although she always started by pretending that she, at least, was indifferent to his advances). She also loved it when, in the peace and well-being that followed a good meal, her he-wolf's tongue was soft and wet.

Of the pair, it was Akbara who had the brain; she had the right to instigate the hunt, while he was her faithful muscle-power, reliable, tireless, the unswerving instrument of her will. Their relationship never changed. Just once there was a strange, inexplicable occasion when her he-wolf disappeared all night and returned at dawn with the traces of the scent of another female, the disgusting smell of a young she-wolf who had been tempting males for miles around; filled with rage and irritation, Akbara rounded on him and plunged her fangs deep into his shoulder, then made him trail behind her for days over the mountain tracks to punish him thoroughly. She made the fool keep his distance, and however loud he howled, she never responded, never stopped, as though Tash-Chainar, far from being her he-wolf, had nothing to do with her at all. If he had dared to come close in an attempt to seduce himself back into her affections, Akbara would have gone for him in a serious way: not for nothing was she the head and he the legs of their strange grey partnership.

But now Akbara, after calming and warming herself at Tash-Chainar's broad flank, was grateful to him for sharing her fear and so for giving her back her faith in herself; she therefore did not resist his caresses, but licked his lips a couple of times in return and, controlling the shudders which still ran through her body now and again, turned her attention to the disquiet of the cubs within her, and came to terms with life as it was, with

6

the lair, the winter in the mountains, and the gradual deepening of the frosty night.

And so finished that day of terror for the she-wolf. Completely under the sway of her maternal instincts, she was afraid not for herself, but for those who soon would fill the lair, for whose sake she and Tash-Chainar had sought it out and made it theirs, in the deep cleft beneath the overhanging rock, hidden by the bushes and the fallen stones, this wolf's nest that gave them a place which belonged only to them, and where they would rear their young.

Akbara and Tash-Chainar were new to those parts. They even looked different from the local wolves. The manes of hair on their necks, framing their shoulders like thick silvery-grey capes from the chest to the nape, were lighter, like those of the steppe-wolves. The *akdjaly*, the silver-manes, were also taller than the usual Issyk-Kul mountain wolves. Anyone who came close enough to Akbara to see her eyes would have been astonished at their brightness and blueness: she was very probably the only wolf with eyes of that unusual colour. The local shepherds had christened her Akdaly, 'White-Back', which had gradually mutated into Akbary, as names do, and from that into Akbara, 'The Great', without realizing how apt their name for her would later seem to be.

The silver-manes had been in these parts only a year. They still kept themselves to themselves. At first they avoided confrontations with the local wolves by keeping to the paths that were in no-man's-land as far as wolves were concerned, living from hand to mouth, sometimes going for food as far as the fields and valleys where human beings lived, but never becoming a part of any local packs. Akbara of the bright blue eyes was too independent a creature to join with others and live in subjugation.

Time is the great tester. In time, the silver-maned newcomers had established their place in the world and through a series of deadly dog-fights had captured a territory for themselves on the slopes above the Issyk-Kul where they, the newcomers, were masters and the local wolves no longer dared to trespass. The silver-maned newcomers were now well established, but there is a story behind every successful conclusion, and if animals could remember the past then

Akbara, with her subtlety and her intelligence, would have had to live with the memory of those events that even now filtered through her consciousness every so often in the shape of a tear or a deep sigh.

That distant, other world, the world of the Moyun-Kum savannah, was a hunting world, endless chase over the boundless Moyun-Kum after the infinite herds of saigak, the steppe antelope. The saigak had lived since time immemorial on the steppe which they shared with the dry *saxaul* bushes. They were the most ancient of the cloven hooves, tireless in flight. Their aquiline profiles with the broad tubular nostrils pumped air through their lungs with the energy of a whale gulping great draughts of the ocean, thanks to which they could run without resting from morning till night. Wherever they moved, the wolves moved with them; one jumpy herd would infect the next with panic, then a third, and a fourth, then the stampede would pick up more herds, great and small, that grazed in its path. The saigak would gallop across the Moyun-Kum like a great flood across the hillocks, plains and sands, the earth rushing beneath their drumming hooves like a storm of hail on a summer's day, and the air would be filled with eddies of movement, of flinty dust and sparks from beneath their feet. The smell of their sweat mingled with the smell of the race to the death, while the hunting wolves, running close to the ground, ran behind and beside them, striving to turn the herds into their ambush where the most experienced of the wolves lay in wait to spring up at the fleeing saigak; then the two would plunge together to the ground, and in an instant the wolf would tear out its quarry's throat and plunge back into the chase. Often the saigak seemed somehow aware of where the wolves were waiting and shied off to the side; then the hunt would begin again, with even greater passion and speed, and hunter and hunted (linked together in the chain of cruel existence) took to their heels anew, blood pounding in a death-agony, to kill or to survive. Only God himself could have halted either pursuer or pursued, for it was life and death for both antelopes and wolves. Those wolves who could not stand the pace, those who were not born to wrest their existence from the chase, fell and were left to choke in the dust raised by the cloven hooves as they swept away like a sandstorm. Even if they survived, they slunk away to distant places where an easier living could be made by robbing the flocks of harmless sheep where none ever dreamed of running away. True, there were other dangers for them, the worst of all possible dangers: with the flocks lived men, both gods and slaves to their sheep, men who lived but did not let live, especially those beasts that were free and independent of the human race . . .

Men, men, the human gods! Men also hunted the saigak of the Moyun-Kum savannah. Once they had been on horseback, wearing skins, armed with arrows; then they had noisy shotguns and galloped hither and thither, popping away, while the saigak rushed from side to side, safe in the shelter of the *saxaul* thickets. Later, however, the time came when the man-gods learned to stampede the saigak, exhausting them in the chase just as the wolves did and shooting them from their moving vehicles; and now it was helicopters. They would spy the herds from the air and surround them, co-ordinating their movements, while the snipers on the ground, directed from above, made speeds of a hundred kilometres and more to reach the saigak before they could hide. Jeeps, helicopters, repeater rifles . . . life in the Moyun-Kum savannah had changed beyond all recognition . . .

Blue-eyed Akbara was still only half grown, and her future mate Tash-Chainar a little older, when the time came for them to learn the ways of the great stampede-hunt. At first they could not keep up with the running, so instead they tore at the fallen antelopes and killed those which still lingered, but in time they surpassed many experienced wolves, and especially those who were growing old. If everything had gone as Nature intended they would soon have been the leaders of the pack, but this was not to be.

Years differ, and that spring the saigak were particularly fertile, with many of the mothers bearing twins. The previous autumn the dry grass had greened again twice after copious rains that came while the weather was still warm. A lot of food meant a lot of young. The females removed in the early spring to the snowless sands at the very heart of Moyun-Kum. It was too far for the wolves to follow, and anyway no wolf was a

9

match for the saigak, even in foal, over the sand dunes. The wolves were more than compensated in autumn and winter, when the seasonal migrations drew countless numbers of saigak on to the semi-arid desert and the steppe. This was the time for the hunt! In summer, especially when the heat was greatest, the wolves preferred to leave the saigak in peace, especially as there was enough easier prey to be had, like the thousands of marmots which covered the steppe, making up for all they had missed through their winter hibernation. They had to do in the summer months what the larger animals could spread out over the whole year, so they bustled busily, ignoring the danger. Every beast in its own time, and there was no preying on marmots in the winter: they simply were not there. Other birds and animals, too, especially partridges, varied the wolves' diet in the summer; but their main prey, the saigak, was hunted from the autumn and right through to the end of winter. Those were the Nature-given laws of life on the savannah. Only some elemental catastrophe or human inter-vention could change the way things had always been on the Moyun-Kum . . .

2

By dawn the air over the savannah would cool, and its living creatures could breathe more freely. This was the joyful time between the coming day, already heavy with the approaching heat of noon that beat mercilessly down upon the salt-marshes of the steppe, and the arid closeness of the passing night. The perfect yellow sphere of the moon sailed above the Moyun-Kum, flooding the plain with blue light. No start, no finish was there to this earth: on every side the dark horizon merged with the starry sky. The silence was full of life for all the denizens of the savannah; all of them except the snakes hurried to enjoy the cool, to live. The early birds chirped and rustled in the tamarisks, hedgehogs bustled noisily from place to place, the cicadas (tireless singers of the night) found their second wind, and marmots peered warily out from their holes before embarking on the gathering of their food, the seeds which fell from the *saxaul* bushes. A family of screech-owls was out on the wing, the flat-headed parent with five flat-headed young: ruffling their new feathers, they were trying out their wings on a haphazard course, crying out every now and then to keep within earshot of one another. All the creatures of the dark-dawn savannah were out and about . . .

It was summer, the first summer shared by Akbara and Tash-Chainar who had already proved themselves tireless hunters of the saigak and taken their place among the leaders of the Moyun-Kum wolves. It was their good fortune (for we may presume that among animals, too, there are lucky and unlucky individuals) that both of them possessed those God-given qualities so essential for predators of the steppe and the semi-arid savannah: quick reactions, a prescience in hunting, a kind of 'strategic' imagination and, of course, the unlimited physical strength that gave them speed and stamina in the chase. Everything augured a great future as hunters, and a life filled with well-being and the beauty of beasts living as Nature intended. They could rule unchallenged in the Moyun-Kum, since man's only incursions at the time had been few and far between and neither wolf had ever come face to face with a human being. That was to come later. Another advantage, privilege even, of all animals, since the beginning of time, has been the fact that beasts can live from day to day, knowing neither fear nor concern for what tomorrow might bring. Nature, so rational in all her manifestations, has not burdened the animals with consciousness in the way that she has man, although this merciful fact bore the seeds of the tragedy that was later to strike the animals of the Moyun-Kum. None of them had any inkling of what was afoot. None of them could imagine that the seemingly endless savannah, however great, however broad its sweeping expanses, was no more than a tiny island in the Asian sub-continent, a thumb-nail printed yellowish brown in the atlas, nibbled away from year to year as the virgin lands were put to the plough, trampled further and further in by the countless herds of domestic animals which roamed where artesian wells had gone before them, opening up new areas of grazing. The savannah was under attack from canals and roads built on the periphery because of the huge gas pipe-line that passed close to the edge of the savannah; and, finally, there were more and longer visits from men with more and more technology at their disposal – men on wheels and men with motors, men with walkie-talkies and water-tanks who could penetrate any desert or semi-desert, including the Moyun-Kum. The men were not scientists dedicating their lives to discovery, to be venerated for their selfless search by future generations; no, they were ordinary men doing ordinary things, bearing no stamp of the heroic . . . How were creatures of the unique Moyun-Kum savannah to know that in the ordinary deeds of men lie hidden the sources of good and evil on this earth? And that everything depends upon the men themselves, on how they direct these ordinary deeds, towards good or evil ends, to build or to destroy? No idea had the four- and two-legged creatures of the Moyun-Kum savannah of the complexities crowding in upon a humanity that had been struggling to understand itself since the moment when man became a thinking animal, struggling in vain with the eternal riddle of why evil almost always triumphs over good . . .

In logical terms, none of these human matters could have touched the lives of the beasts of Moyun-Kum, for they lay outside the nature, instincts and experience of the animal world. For the most part nothing had ever seriously disturbed the pattern of life of the great Asiatic steppe that spread over the hot, semi-arid plains and uplands with their unique strain of drought-resistant tamarisk, and the *saxaul* of the sands, half grass, half tree, hard as stone and twisted as a sailor's rope, the springy grass underfoot, and most of all the arrow-sharp reeds of the *chiy*, pride of the semi-desert, shimmering like a ghostly golden forest in moon- or sunlight, like a shallow lake in which any creature larger than a dog could lift its head and see or be seen far around.

This was the land where the new wolf pair was to live its life. By then Akbara and Tash-Chainar were already (an important moment in the life of an animal) the parents of their first litter, three cubs born to Akbara that same spring in the Moyun-Kum, in the lair which they had chosen in a hollow washed out by the rain beneath an old *saxaul*, by a half-dried thicket of tamarisk near enough at hand for the cubs to be taken there for their first lessons in life. The cubs' ears were already standing erect and their different characters beginning to show (although they reverted to lop-eared babies as they played together), and they were now steady on their feet. They tagged along with their parents on expeditions great and small.

One such expedition, lasting the whole day, had nearly ended in tragedy for the wolf family.

Early that morning Akbara had led her brood to the very edge of the Moyun-Kum savannah where the deserted gullies and hollows were overgrown with a tall-stemmed grass whose languid, captivating smell was unlike any other. The longer you wandered through the tall grasses, sniffing the pollen, the lighter your movements felt, until you drifted along barely touching the ground. This feeling then gave way to torpor and sleepiness, and weakness in the legs. Akbara remembered the place from when she was a cub, and made for it once a year at the time when the *durman-trava*, the trance-grass, was in flower. Catching a few of the small steppe creatures on the way, she liked to feel her head spinning in the long grass, to lie

13

in the essences distilled by the heat, to run until she was exhausted and then to fall to sleep.

This time Tash-Chainar and she were not alone, but accompanied by the three gangling, long-legged cubs. The young wolves had to travel as much of the territory as possible to have it firmly imprinted on their young minds. The fragrant meadows towards which the she-wolf led them lay at the very edge of wolf country: beyond them was an alien world where humans could cross their paths, from where the long howl of a steam engine, like the autumn wind, blew in to remind them of the enemies of wolves. Akbara led them across the savannah to the edge of the world she knew.

Tash-Chainar slunk after Akbara, while the cubs gambolled along, bundles of energy, for ever trying to overtake their mother who kept them firmly in check. Nobody was allowed to step in front of her. The terrain was sandy, and as they passed through the thickets of *saxaul* and desert wormwood the sun rose higher and higher, promising (as always) a clear, hot day. By evening the wolf family had arrived at the edge of the savannah. They arrived just in time, while it was still light. The grasses were high that year, almost up to the backs of the fully grown wolves. Still full of the heat absorbed from the sun over the course of the day, the inconspicuous clusters of flowers on the hairy stalks were giving off a strong smell, particularly in the places where the grass grew especially thick. Here, in a small gully, the wolves rested after their day's journey. The tireless cubs preferred rushing about to resting, sniffing and inspecting everything that caught their attention. The family were fed and watered: a few fat marmots and hares had passed their way on the journey and there had been several nests to rob; their thirst they had quenched in the spring of a gully across which they passed. They might have stayed there the whole night had not an extraordinary event forced them to leave immediately for home, for the lair in the middle of the savannah. The journey back took all night.

What happened was that at sunset, when Akbara and Tash-Chainar, drunk with the scent of the wild hemp, were resting in the shade of the bushes, there could suddenly be heard the sound of a human voice. The first to see the man were the cubs, playing at the top of the gully slope. The cubs had no inkling, indeed could not have realized, that what had appeared on the scene was a man. An almost naked being – in swimming trunks and trainers, a once white Panama on his head – was running through the same grass. The path he chose was strange: he picked the thickest growth and ran back and forth between the plants, as though finding pleasure in the process. At first the cubs froze, puzzled and wary, for they had never seen such a thing in their lives. The man ran back and forth through the grass, grinning like a madman. The cubs grew bolder, driven by curiosity, and wanted to play with this strange new naked biped running about like a clockwork toy. At that moment the man noticed the cubs. The strangest part of it all was that, instead of pulling back with the thought that cubs must mean grown wolves in the vicinity, the man went straight up to the little wolves and held out a friendly hand.

'Just look what we have here!' he murmured, panting and wiping the sweat from his face. 'Wolf cubs, eh? Or is it a hallucination? No, cubs, three of them, three beautiful big wolf cubs! Well, well, you little beauties! Where are you from, and where are you off to? What brings you here? I know what brings me here, but what would a wolf want in the evil weed? Come on, come on, don't be shy! Come on, you silly little things!'

The inexperienced cubs were captivated by the gentleness of his tone. Tails wagging, clinging playfully to the ground, they crept towards the man in the hope of a game of tag, but at this point Akbara leapt out of the gully. In a split-second she had evaluated the situation. With a growl she rushed at the naked man, pink with the rays of the setting sun. She could have slashed him, throat or belly, with one sweep of her fangs. The man was completely mesmerized at the sight of an angry, charging she-wolf; he sank to his heels and grasped his head in terror. It saved his life . . . As she ran at him, Akbara for some reason changed her tactic in mid-stride. She jumped straight over the man, naked and defenceless, whom she could have felled with one blow. As she jumped, she had time to see his features and the eyes, transfixed with terror, and to smell his body. Then she turned and jumped back in the opposite direction, rushed to the cubs and hustled them off, nipping them painfully in the heels and pushing them back towards the gully. Here she came face to face with Tash-Chainar, bristling strangely at the sight of the human; him too she nipped to turn him, and they all tumbled together over the edge of the gully, to disappear in the twinkling of an eye.

Only now did the naked madman come to his senses and run for his life . . . He ran for miles over the steppe, never once looking back or pausing to draw breath.

So passed the first unexpected meeting between Akbara's family and a human being. Who was to know what lay in the future?

The day was coming to an end, with the last hot breaths from the setting sun and an earth that had baked all day. Sun and steppe are eternal invariables, for the sun gives its measure to the greatness of the steppe and the vault of the sky is determined by the height of a kite's upwards swoop. In that evening hour a whole flock of white-tailed kites was circling high above the earth. They flew smoothly and aimlessly, simply for the joy of it, in the faint haze of the cool, cloudless heights. Round and round they circled, as though to symbolize the eternal stability of the land and of the sky, silently observing the life down below them on the earth. Thanks to their exceptional, omnipotent vision (their hearing is vastly inferior), these aristocratic birds of prey live their whole lives in the heavens above the savannah, descending to the sinful earth only to eat and sleep.

From that height they must have been able to see the he-wolf, she-wolf and three cubs as they lay on a small hummock among the scattered tamarisk and the golden *chiy*. Tongues hanging out with the heat, the wolf family had no inkling that it was being observed from the sky. Tash-Chainar lounged in his usual pose, front legs crossed and head raised high, standing out from the rest with his thick mane and his heavy, muscular body. Beside him, her short, bushy tail beneath her, motionless as a statue, lay Akbara. The she-wolf's straight, wiry forelegs lay directly in front of her. Her whitish chest and concave belly, whose two rows of nipples had lost their rounded fullness, emphasized her lean and powerful haunches. The three cubs frisked further off. Their playful demands for attention in no way irritated their parents; the latter watched indulgently as the three gambolled together . . .

16

Still the kites circled, and still they observed dispassionately all that passed beneath them on the Moyun-Kum at the hour of sunset. Saigak were grazing not far from the wolves and their cubs, hidden in the tamarisk thickets. Further away grazed a larger group, on the edge of the tamarisk, and a large herd beyond those. If the steppe antelope had been of the slightest interest to the kites, they would have seen that the beasts were numberless in the broad sweep of the savannah, for they increased and multiplied in the perfect conditions of the semi-arid plain. When the heat of the evening was over, the saigak sought out the rare drinking-holes to slake their thirst. Small groups were already hurrying in the direction of water. The distances involved were enormous.

One of the herds passed so close to the wolves' hummock that they could not help but see them through the transparent veil of the *chiy*, backs and sides passing swiftly by and the males' heads crowned with little horns. They always move with their heads down to minimize the wind resistance, for they remain ready for flight at any and every moment of their lives. So they have evolved by the laws of nature, and that is the chief advantage of the saigak; they can run from any danger. Even if nothing has startled them, they usually move at a steady gallop, tireless and unswerving, giving way to no one but the wolves, secure in the strength of their countless numbers . . .

And so they moved past Akbara's family as it lay hidden in the bushes, a galloping mass that raised a wind filled with the scent of the herd and the dust from their hooves. The cubs on the hummock stirred instinctively, sniffing the air, ready to set off in the direction from which the scent was coming. They wanted to rush off into the *chiy*, through which they could make out galloping bodies as they flashed past where they lay. Neither Akbara nor Tash-Chainar moved or even changed position, although a couple of bounds would have brought them to the side of the galloping herd, where they could drive them on into that race to the death where heaven and earth are turned upside down and where a sure foot on a sharp turn could bring down a couple of antelope at one throw. On the other hand, they might be unlucky and fail to catch up with the prey. Akbara and Tash-Chainar, however, had no intention of

17

starting a chase: even though their prey seemed to be falling into their lap, they did not move from where they lay. They had their reasons: their bellies were full, and chasing saigak in that heat, on a full stomach, would be madness. The main reason, however, was that the cubs were still too young to learn that kind of hunting. It would break their nerve if they ran out of breath and fell behind, and they would lose their will to win the prize. Next winter would be the time, during the great hunt; then, nearly a year old and almost full-grown, the cubs could try their strength and hunt as part of the pack. That would be their day!

Akbara detached herself from the cubs who strained for the fun of the chase, and sat down in another place. She continued to observe the movements of the antelope as they made their way to the water-hole, moving flank to flank through the silvery *chiy*, like spawning fish moving upstream through the current, identical and united in their goal. Akbara's thoughts flickered in her gaze: today they might be passing on, but the time would come when she could have her pick of anything in the savannah. The cubs had diverted their attention to their father, and were vying for the attention of gloomy Tash-Chainar.

Suddenly Akbara thought of winter, of how one fine day the great semi-arid steppe would wake up with new-fallen snow that never lasts more than a day or a half, but shows the wolves that the time for the great chase is ripe. From that day on, the hunt of the saigak would be the most important thing in their lives . . . The day would come! Mist in the dips, hoar-frost on the sad whiteness of the *chiy*, tamarisks bent beneath the weight of the snow and a hazy sun high above the savannah . . . The she-wolf could see the day so clearly that she suddenly shuddered, as though she had breathed in a gulp of frosty air, as though the hard pads of her feet were already trotting over the snow and she could see her own tracks grouped like the petals of a flower, and those of the cubs, larger now, stronger, more clearly differentiated (it would show, even in the footprints), and beside them the largest prints, Tash-Chainar's, the claws massive as fangs. Tash-Chainar was healthy, heavy-chested and powerful; he was the quicksilver knife at the antelopes' throats. Any saigak that he reached would stain the savannah snows with a fountain of crimson blood, spraying out like the bright wings of a red bird breaking cover, one blood spilt for the sake of another – the blood beneath their grey coats – for their blood preyed upon the blood of others, as decreed by the foundation of all foundations. This way it should be, and no other, and none to stand in judgment, for there was no right and wrong in this equation. Any guilt lay with the One who had created one blood to feed another. (Mankind alone has a different way, to grow his bread and breed his meat and by his own labours to create unto himself Nature.)

The prints in the first snows of the Moyun-Kum, two large sets and three smaller, would move together through the low-lying mist and would come to a halt in a hollow amidst the bushes, where the wolves would watch and wait for the beasts to run into their trap . . .

That hour of joy would soon be upon them, when Akbara would creep as close as possible on her belly in the snow, crouching behind the frozen grasses, close enough in the breathless silence to see the saigak, see their eyes still calm and unaware of the danger as they grazed, then – pounce! The hour of the wolf! So vividly could Akbara imagine the first winter lesson for her cubs that she suddenly cried out and almost leapt in the air.

Oh, the first winter chase over the savannah! The herds of saigak stampeding as from a fire, their hooves scoring black scars in the white of the ground, Akbara pounding behind them, the cubs hard on her heels, her first-born, her children, born for the hunt, and behind them Tash-Chainar, their mighty father, tireless in the chase, single-mindedly dedicated to the task of driving the saigak into the trap in order to teach the cubs how to hunt. What a chase that would be! Akbara was thinking less of the prize than of the joy of the hunt, when they would fly over the steppe like swift-winged birds . . . There lay the whole meaning of the life of a wolf . . .

Such were the dreams of the she-wolf, dreams which she had learned from Nature, dreams which would linger on as bitter memories, like a knife through her heart . . . Long would she howl in payment for those dreams. All dreams are the same: at first they emerge in our imagination, then for the most part they wither away in punishment for the fact of having grown without roots, like some flowers and trees . . . All dreams are thus, and therein lies their tragic necessity as we learn the knowledge of good and evil . . .

3

Winter came to Moyun-Kum. Snow had already fallen once, relatively thick for the semi-desert, and whitened the whole savannah, which woke revealed as a boundless white ocean, frozen in waves, open to the winds and to the tumbleweed. Now all was silence, like the silence of the stars and the silence of eternity. The sands and the stiff *takyr* had soaked up the extra moisture, and softened. The flocks of honking geese had already crossed the savannah, flying down over the Moyun-Kum from the northern summer on rivers and seas, over the Himalaya to the waters of the Indus and Brahmaputra. Had the other creatures of the savannah wings, all would have answered the same call. But every heart has its own heaven . . . Even the kites, floating at the same altitude, gave no more sign of recognition than a slight deflection of their course to one side . . .

By winter Akbara's cubs had indeed grown tall and lost their indistinguishable childish looks. All three were angular year-lings, but each an individual. Of course the she-wolf could not give them names – no beast may overstep the limitations ordained by God – but her sense of smell, which man has lost, meant that she could easily distinguish between and summon individually any of her children. The largest of them had the father's head, so was thought of as the Big-Head; the next, also large, had the longest legs and was evidently destined to be a runner, so he was thought of as Swift-Foot; and the third had eyes as blue as Akbara's own, loved fun and was her favourite, so in Akbara's wordless mind she would have been the Favourite. Great would be the fighting among the males, once the time had come to win her . . .

The first snow, falling unnoticed in the night, made a holiday of the morning for them all. At first the cubs grew timid at the sight and smell of something so unfamiliar that transformed the world around their lair; then they grew to

love it, and frolicked in the cold delight, snorting and barking with joy. And so began the winter at the end of which
would come the time of parting from their mother, their
father and each other, each of them to begin a new life, all
alone.

More snow fell by evening, and the steppe was bright and
luminous before dawn the next morning. Peace and quiet
reigned supreme, along with the sharp pang of hunger that
winter knows so well. The wolves were listening hard, for the
time had come to get to work, to hunt for food. Akbara was
waiting for other wolves to join them before instigating the
hunt . . . So far there was no sign of what everyone was
waiting for. Big-Head sat tense, as yet unaware of the hardships of the hunt. Swift-Foot sat ready, too. Favourite sat
looking with courage and devotion into the she-wolf's eyes,
while beside them paced the father of the family, Tash-
Chainar. All were waiting for the sign from Akbara. Higher
than she, however, there was another authority, King
Hunger, the king of satisfaction for the flesh.

Akbara rose and trotted off. The time had come. They all
followed. It started more or less as she had imagined on that
summer's day when the cubs were still small, before the time
was ripe for the great chase through the steppe. Soon the cold
would drive the independent wolves into groups, and they
would hunt together until the end of the winter.

Akbara and Tash-Chainar set off with their first-born for
their first taste of the hunt.

On they trotted, keeping to the contours of the steppe,
leaving on the untouched snow their five-petalled prints like
an emblem of strength and concentrated will, trotting proudly
through the bushes or slinking over the open ground like
shadows. Everything now depended upon their own efforts
and upon the luck of the chase . . .

Akbara jumped on to a hummock for a better view, and
froze, searching the horizon with her blue eyes and the scents
on the wind with her keen nostrils. In the dawn light the great
savannah was strewn with herds of saigak, the young year-
lings who were due to separate off into new herds at that time
of the year. A good year for the wolves as well . . .

The she-wolf did not hurry down from her viewing point.

She had to be sure of her choice, and sniffed the wind to decide the direction for a faultless start to the hunt.

At that moment a strange clatter rang out above and to the side, and a roaring that was nothing to do with thunder rang out over the steppe. The sound was completely unfamiliar and grew louder and louder. Tash-Chainar jumped up to join the she-wolf and together they cringed in terror at what was happening in the sky. A strange bird, rattling monstrously, was sweeping across the savannah in lop-sided flight, its nose dipping wildly, followed at a distance by another of the same. Then they moved away and gradually the sound subsided. They were helicopters.

The two helicopters crossed the Moyun-Kum sky like fish that leave no trace behind them in the water. No trace either in the air or on the ground, except for the fact that they were on a reconnaissance trip and were reporting back over the radio all they had seen, giving exact information and map co-ordinates of possible routes for jeeps and container lorries to travel into the Moyun-Kum.

And the wolves? As could be expected, once they had got over the shock they soon forgot the helicopters and trotted away again over the steppe after the saigak, unaware (for how could they be aware?) that all of them, all of the creatures of the savannah, were already marked down – in an organized way, on maps with numbered squares – for a massive culling operation, that their death was planned and co-ordinated and moving in on them already on dozens of wheels and engines . . .

How could the steppe-wolves know that their natural prey, the saigak, was needed to make up the figures in the state plan forecast for meat production, that since it was the last quarter of the last year in the Five-year Plan the economic planners for the district were getting jumpy – 'We're not getting the production figures we need' – until some bright spark in the district management committee had suggested 'tapping' the Moyun-Kum's meat resources. The idea was that the meat production figures could be overlooked as long as the meat deliveries were at the levels set by the plan, and so the district could save face in the eyes of the people and of the higher

23

reaches of the organizational ladder. How could the steppe-wolves have known that telephones were ringing in all the district offices, with urgent messages from the central authorities that the heat was on and by hook or by crook, in this last year of the five, something had to be done, otherwise what could they say to the people? Where were the figures? Where was the meat? Where were the promises they had made at the beginning of the planning period? 'The plan will be fulfilled, without fail,' answered the district management committee, 'within the next ten days. We have further reserves forthcoming at the local level, we'll get them moving and out of there . . .'

The steppe-wolves, unwitting of all these developments, were creeping carefully up by a roundabout route to their prey, still led by Akbara, moving noiselessly over the soft snow towards the last of the cover, clumps of tall *chiy* into which they blended, looking for all the world like brownish hummocks of grass and soil. The *chiy* gave Akbara and her group a perfect view of the countless antelopes with their eternally unchanged markings, white sides with a chestnut ridge down the back. They grazed, unaware as yet of any danger, in a broad valley of tamarisk, greedily tearing at the feather-grass, peppered now with snow, that lay at their feet. Akbara knew she had to wait, had to wait until the whole group was prepared to leap as one from the cover and then burst into action. Then she would see the way the case went, which should be their next manoeuvre. The young wolves wagged their tails and pricked their ears impatiently; even the reserved Tash-Chainar felt his blood rising and his fangs itching to plunge into the prey – but Akbara, eyes aflame, was waiting for the exact moment to give the signal to jump. Only then could they be sure of success, for the saigak can leap without a moment's hesitation, so far that not a single beast could catch them. She had to grasp the moment.

Suddenly, thunder from the sky: the helicopters were back. This time they flew fast and threateningly low over the terrified saigak, as they galloped in flight from the monstrous attack. So fast and unexpected was the approach that hundreds of shaken antelope, their leaders and sense of direction forgotten, flew in disordered panic. The harmless

24

creatures were no match for flying machines. The helicopters were working according to plan: pinning down the fleeing herd and rounding on it in a pincer movement, they drove it towards another, equally large, that had been grazing near by. More and more of the herds were drawn into the stampede, the cloven-hooved creatures losing their heads completely in the panic of a catastrophe the like of which the savannah had not seen before. Not only for the cloven-hooves; the wolves, too, their inseparable companions and hereditary enemies, found themselves in exactly the same trap.

When the helicopter attack took place before the very eyes of Akbara and her group, the wolves at first shrank back into the roots of the *chiy*; but then their nerve broke and they leapt in terror, rushing to escape from this accursed place. Their instinct was to disappear, to reach a place of safety, but this was not to be. No sooner had they taken to their heels than the earth behind them thundered and shook, as in a storm, for the multitude of saigak, driven through the steppe in the direction chosen by the helicopters, was galloping behind them at an incredible speed. The wolves had no time to turn aside or hide: they were directly in the path of the living, pounding stream that galloped forward like an enormous, advancing cloud. To stop for a second would mean death beneath the flying hooves of this close-packed mass of elemental animal panic. Only the fact that the wolves put on a terrified spurt of speed saved them. Now they too were surrounded, a part of this fleeing herd where predator and prey (had they not been planning to tear the saigak limb from limb?) ran flank to flank from the common danger, equals now in the face of a merciless turn of fate. Never, even in the great steppe-fires, had the Moyun-Kum savannah seen wolves and saigak running together like this.

Several times Akbara tried to leap out of the galloping stream, but found it impossible. She would have been crushed beneath the hooves of the antelopes as they ran, shoulder to shoulder, in a solid wall. For the moment, her wolves were running all together and she could see them from the corner of her eye, close to the ground, gaining ground, eyes wide with terror: her first-born, Big-Head; Swift-Foot, fading fast; Favourite too; and together with them her Tash-Chainar,

25

terror of the steppes, running in panic with all the rest. How different from the dreams of the blue-eyed she-wolf! Instead of the great hunt they were running with the herd of saigak, powerless to act, carried away by the antelopes like wood-shavings in a river . . . The first to perish was Favourite. She fell beneath the flying herd, her scream drowned in an instant by the thunder of thousands of hooves . . .

The hunting helicopters, flying on both flanks of the stampede, communicated by two-way radio, co-ordinating their movements and making sure none of the beasts could escape out to the sides and force them to start another round-up. They kept up the pace, forcing the saigak to flee faster and faster. Excited voices crackled in the headsets: 'Number twenty, hey, number twenty, listen! Bring up the speed! Come on!' The helicopter pilots had an excellent view of the black river of terror as it roared over the white snows of the steppe. Back came the cheerful answer: 'Aye-aye! Speed increased! Ha, ha, look! There are wolves in there, running with them! Now there's a thing! The old grey-coats are trapped! Curtains, brothers! No more "Three Little Pigs" for you!'

They were driving the stampede to exhaustion, according to the calculations of the plan, and the calculations were accurately computed.

Once the wave of antelope broke on to the plain, it was met by those for whom the helicopters had been working since early morning. There stood the hunters, or, rather, the executioners. They took over the chase in open jeeps, shooting with machine guns at point-blank range, scything down the beasts like hay in a summer garden. Behind them moved open trucks with men who gathered in the cheap-won harvest, throwing the trophies one by one into the backs of the lorries. They were bright lads and soon got the hang of this new type of work, slitting the throats of those saigak that were not dead and chasing the wounded ones to finish them off as well. Their main job was to heave the bloodstained carcasses by the legs up and over the sides of the trucks. The savannah was paying a bloody price to the gods for daring to remain savannah: mountains of saigak carcasses steamed slowly in the backs of the trucks.

The slaughter went on and on. Driving into the very thick of the now exhausted beasts, the gunners brought down saigak to right and left and increased even further the panic and despair of the survivors. In the apocalyptic terror Akbara, deafened by the shooting, imagined the whole world deaf and dumb and the sun itself, floating soundlessly above her, also pursued in this frenzied stampede, rushing and seeking escape. Even the helicopters suddenly seemed soundless, circling silently above the vast expanses of the steppe like gigantic silent kites . . . The gunners were soundlessly raking the stampede from their jeeps; the noiseless vehicles flew over the ground as the exhausted saigak sank silently beneath the piercing bullets, spilling forth their blood . . . In this great apocalyptic silence, Akbara saw a vision of the face of Man. It was so close, so vivid and so clear, that she was filled with terror and nearly fell beneath the wheels of the jeep that was running close beside her. The man was sitting in the front, leaning out of the vehicle. He was wearing glass goggles, his purple face whipped by the wind, a microphone to his black lips into which he yelled at the top of his voice, rising from his seat, though no words could she hear. He must have been in command of the cull, and if the she-wolf could have heard or understood the speech of humans, she would have heard him shout into his walkie-talkie: 'Shoot to the sides! Get the edges! Don't shoot into the thick, they'll trample the carcasses, you useless so and so's . . .' He was worried that the trampling hooves might ruin the quality of the carcasses in their path.

At this point the man with the microphone suddenly noticed that right by the side of his jeep there ran a fleeing wolf, with a small group of wolves behind it. He twitched, roared something with a cruel smile upon his face, threw down the microphone and grabbed his rifle, reloading it as he moved. Akbara did not understand that the man with the glass goggles was aiming at her, and even if she had understood there was nothing to be done. Trapped by the stampede, she could neither turn nor stop. The man was still looking into his sights, and this is what saved Akbara. She felt a blow beneath her and turned a somersault, but was back on her feet in an instant to avoid being trampled. The next moment she saw Big-Head, the largest of her first-born brood, fly into the air, shot as he ran, then falling slowly back to earth, rolling slowly on to his

27

side, stretching, reaching out, perhaps crying out in the pain of death, but she heard nothing. The man in the glass goggles shook his rifle in triumph over his head, and the next moment Akbara leapt over the lifeless body of her Big-Head. Now the sounds of the real world returned to her awareness: the voices, the stampede, the ceaseless rattle of the shooting, the penetrating hooting of the jeeps, the shouts and cries of men, the death-agony of the antelope, the clatter of helicopters above . . . Many of the saigak lay jerking their legs, past all hope of ever running again, their hearts and lungs bursting from the strain. The carcass-gatherers cut their throats with a sweeping slash as they lay, grasped them by their shuddering legs and threw them, still half alive, up on to the backs of the trucks. The men were a terrifying sight, their clothes stained with blood from head to foot.

If any eye were watching the earth from the heavens that day, it would have seen the stampede and how it ended for the Moyun-Kum steppe; but even such an all-seeing eye could hardly have known what else was to come and what plans were afoot . . .

The cull lasted until evening, when all, hunters and hunted, were exhausted and the steppe night started to close in. The plan was for the helicopters to go back to base, refuel, and begin again in the morning. According to calculations, there was enough work here for three, even four, more days, especially since the preliminary reconnaissance flights by helicopter had shown that the western, sandiest parts of the Moyun-Kum steppe contained many more herds of saigak, as yet untouched by panic, officially labelled 'undisclosed regional reserves'. Since undisclosed reserves existed, it followed inexorably that they, too, should immediately be included in the statistics for meat delivery (in, of course, the interests of the region as a whole). Such was the official justification for the Moyun-Kum 'campaign'. However, we all know that behind every official decision lies a particular set of circumstances, defining the course of history. Circumstances, in their turn, boil down to a particular set of people, with their desires and passions, their vices and virtues, their incalculable complications and contradictions. In this respect the tragedy in Moyun-Kum was no exception. The people who spent that night in the savannah were, willy-nilly, the instruments of this evil deed.

Akbara and Tash-Chainar, the only wolves from the group to survive, trotted in the darkness through the steppe to move as far as possible from the place where the stampede had taken place. They found it hard to travel: the fur on their bellies and right up to the base of their tails was soaked in mud and sleet. Their bruised and wounded feet were burning as though on fire, and pain shot through them every time they touched the ground. More than anything, they longed to return to the lair they knew, to sink into oblivion and forget the catastrophe that had overtaken their ill-starred lives.

Again, luck was against them. They had almost reached the lair when they suddenly ran into another group of men. Directly beside their lair, right in the thick of the tamarisks (which hardly came to the top of the wheel), towered the bulk of a huge truck. In the darkness around, they could hear human voices. The wolves stood listening for a moment before turning silently back towards the open steppe. For some reason, just at that moment, the headlights sprang into life, searing through the darkness, and although they were shining in the opposite direction, that was more than the wolves could take. Limping and hobbling, they took off as fast as their legs could carry them. Akbara's front paws were particularly bad. To cool the burning pads, she chose places where the morning snow still lay. Sad and bitter were the limping petals of the prints which now led over the snow. The cubs were dead. Behind them lay a lair to which they could no longer return. Humans had moved in . . .

The humans were six, including Kepa, the driver, six of them brought together by fate to collect the carcasses of antelope and remaining to sleep out on the savannah so as to start again as early as possible at the job which had turned out to be so profitable: fifty kopecks a carcass. Even though they had already filled three trucks, the light had not lasted long enough for them to collect up all the saigak killed by bullets or trampled underfoot in the stampede. In the morning they would find the rest and throw them in to be sent off and reloaded into articulated lorries, lorries that would take them out of the Moyun-Kum, well hidden beneath tarpaulins.

That evening the moon rose early over the horizon, a great full circle visible from all sides of the pale steppe where the snow still lingered in parts. The moonlight laid a pattern of light and shadow over the trees, gullies and hummocks of the savannah. The fear generated in the wolves by the towering silhouette of the truck, such an unusual sight in these regions which humans never visited, pursued them for miles. Every now and then they glanced fearfully behind and hurried on, their tails between their legs. One last time they stopped, however, and stared back as though straining to understand what was happening, what men were doing beside the old lair, why they had stopped there and how long that great vehicle would stand there rearing threateningly into the darkness. It was a 'MAZ', a war-time four-wheel drive with tarpaulin top and tyres so thick they looked as though they would last a thousand years. In the back of the truck, among the few antelope carcasses that they had left to dispatch in the morning, lay a man with wrists bound as though he had been taken prisoner. He could feel the carcasses cooling and hardening. Even so, were it not for the warmth from their coats, things would have gone ill for him. Through a gap in the tarpaulin he could see the moon. He stared at it as a man stares into emptiness, and suffering was stamped on the pallor of his face.

Now his fate depended upon the men with whom he had come here, men who assumed that, like them, he was here only to earn a fast rouble in the Moyun-Kum stampede . . .

The six – or, rather, the five, since Kepa, the truck-driver to whom they had been assigned, kept himself to himself (besides, he was the only family man of them all, which set him apart, however close in essence and meanness of spirit he might in fact have been to the rest) – were all strikingly two-dimensional as people, at least when they arrived at the Moyun-Kum . . .

First, they were all homeless, rolling stones, except, of course, for Kepa. Three of them had wives who had left them, and all were losers to a greater or a lesser degree and therefore men with a chip on their shoulder. The only exception to this was the youngest, the one with the strange Old Testament name of Avdiy – Abdias – like the Abdias who is mentioned in the Third Book of Kings, a deacon's son from somewhere near Pskov who joined the seminary after his father's death as the promising scion of a clerical family and was expelled two years later for heresy. And now he lay, wrists tied, in the back of the truck, in expectation of retribution for what Ober himself described as 'attempted mutiny'.

Apart from Avdiy they were all hardened or, as they would have put it, 'professional' alcoholics. Kepa again was something of an exception here. After all, he had his licence to hold on to (his wife would go for him if he ever put that in jeopardy). That night in the Moyun-Kum, however, he took quite a bit on board, no less than the rest; the real odd man out was again Avdiy, that rootless wanderer, who had refused to drink, which earned him an even bigger dose of hatred from Ober.

Ober had told the men who worked under him in the collection of carcasses to address him as 'Ober' for the sake of brevity, implying as it did an element of seniority. In fact he had indeed been senior lieutenant in a disciplinary battalion before he was eventually cashiered. At the time well-wishers had interpreted his problems as stemming from over-scrupulousness in the discharge of his military duties, and he too had been deeply wounded at the injustice manifested by his superiors; he preferred, however, not to go too deeply into the real reason why he had been discharged from the army. Anyway, what was the point? It was all so long ago. Ober's surname was in fact Kandalov, but nobody gave it a moment's thought; Ober was an 'ober' in every sense of the word.

Second-in-command in the junta was Mishash. 'Junta' was the name they all agreed upon for their team. (The only one who objected, weakly, to the word was Hamlet-Halkin, formerly an actor at the local theatre: 'Junta? Stuff it, I don't like juntas, lads! It's a safari we're off on, let's be "The Safari".' But nobody agreed with him. Perhaps the exotic overtones of 'safari' lost out to the raw energy encapsulated in the word 'junta'.) Mishash's full name within the group was Mishka-Shabashnik, Mishka-the-Fixer, a fiercely violent man ready to lash out with his tongue even at Ober. Effing and blinding were as natural to Mishash as breathing. It had been his idea to tie up Avdiy and throw him in the back of the truck. And with the junta, no sooner said than done.

Lowest of the low in the group was the actor, Hamlet-Halkin, whose career on the stage had come to an abrupt and premature halt once he took to drink. He worked now and then, when the opportunity presented itself, at whatever came his way – like now, chucking saigak or antelope or whatever they were called (who cared?) by the legs into the back of a lorry and earning the equivalent of a month's wages plus a bonus from Ober (albeit paid for out of the group's earnings), a case of vodka to share between them. And finally, there was the gentlest and best-natured of them all, a local boy who grew up on the edge of the Moyun-Kum, Uzyuk-Bay or, as they called him in their straightforward way, 'The Aborigine'. The finest quality of Uzyuk-Bay the Aborigine was his complete and utter lack of pride. He would agree to any suggestion and was prepared to go anywhere, even the North Pole, for the sake of a bottle of vodka . . . The short life-story of Uzyuk-Bay the Aborigine can be summed up as follows. He had been a tractor-driver until he reached the stage when he existed in a permanent alcoholic stupor. One night he abandoned his tractor in the middle of the high road. A passing car crashed into it and a man was killed. Uzyuk-Bay spent a couple of years in prison. When he came out, his wife and children had left him and he remained in town as a casual workman, loading and unloading at the food shop and drinking in doorways, where he was discovered by Ober. Uzyuk-Bay followed Ober without a backward glance (precious little to glance back at . . .). There was no refusing Ober-Kandalov: he really did have a nose for finding just the type of person that was needed . . .

And so Ober-Kandalov brought them all together, and the stampede brought them all to the Moyun-Kum savannah . . .

While we are on the subject of life and fate and how circumstances determine events, God is our witness that Ober-Kandalov would never have had to struggle with our unsuccessful seminarist, Avdiy, if the latter had completed his course and eventually been received into the relevant degree of Holy Orders. Avdiy's one-time classmates, previously as frivolous as any other students, once they had chosen their path through life turned out far more sensible and (even more to the point) prudent than Avdiy himself, even if he was the son of a deacon. Since graduating from the seminary they were pursuing successful careers up the ladder of the hierarchy. If Avdiy had remained among their number (and at the start he had been considered one of the most gifted and enjoyed the favour of the good fathers and theologians), then he and Ober-Kandalov would have had very little opportunity ever to meet, especially since Ober-Kandalov sincerely believed priests to be a relic of mistaken times and would never in his life have crossed the threshold of a church, even out of curiosity.

Ifs and buts . . . Who could have known what was to happen? If we could see ahead . . . But nobody writes out a c.v. when they are signing up for a single trip, to go off in a group and earn a little spare cash. Students go every year to help out with the potato harvest! Instead of digging up potatoes they were rounding up saigak, into trucks rather than sacks . . . If Ober-Kandalov had known when he met the wandering Avdiy at the station that he was round the bend, he would not now be racking his brains out here in the Moyun-Kum sands over what to do with him, how to get rid of this crazy Avdiy at no cost to himself, for Avdiy had almost succeeded in spoiling all his carefully laid plans to rehabilitate his past. Who could have thought that things could come to such a strange and unexpected, but ridiculous, pass? The thought was enough to drive Ober-Kandalov to drink, to a real bender (his speciality): half a tumbler at one go, then another, and another, till all sense of restraint was completely subli-mated . . . And then let the lads lay the boot into Avdiy . . . But he was afraid to, for he knew how dear it would cost him afterwards . . .

What was he doing here, this Avdiy, messing things up? But while we are on the subject of life and fate, of circumstances that are revealed to be the causes of subsequent events, we should know that it all started long ago and far away . . .

After he was expelled from the seminary as a heretic and innovator, Avdiy worked as a freelance for the regional Young Communist newspaper. The editorial board had shown a lot of interest in the ex-seminarist who wrote so passably on topics which the readers liked to see. Anathematized by the Church, he was an excellent subject for anti-religious propaganda. For the failed seminarist, on the other hand, the interest lay in the possibility of publishing articles on the moral and ethical subjects that were dear to his heart in a newspaper read by young people. The unusual ideas which he succeeded in getting on to the pages of the newspaper did indeed attract a lot of readers, and not only young ones, especially when contrasted with the dreary, didactic slogans and social exhortations to which the regional readership was normally accustomed. For the moment the interests of both sides were served, but few knew (or rather, with one exception, no one knew) the ambitions that were cherished by this young but budding reformer. Avdiy Kallistratov was hoping that with time, if he could consolidate his journalistic reputation, he would find an acceptable form, perhaps a marginal area of the ideological field, where he could express what he saw as his timely and seminal innovatory views on God and man in the contemporary world, in counterpoise to the dogmatic postulates of an archaic faith. The ridiculous aspect of his situation lay in the fact that before him stood two absolutely impregnable and totally indestructible fortresses, whose strength resided in their individual stability and total incompatibility. On one side stood the millennia of religious thought, impermeable to the action of time, zealously guarding purity of dogma from any, even well-intentioned, innovation; on the other, the mighty logic of scientific atheism, negating religion in its very essence. To fall between them was to fall between two millstones, but still his light burned brightly. Possessed by his ideas of 'the development over time of the concept of God as a function of the historical development of the human race', the heretical Avdiy Kallistratov hoped that sooner or later life would give him the opportunity to reveal to his fellow-men the essence of his conclusions, for (as he saw it) the time was coming when men themselves would want to learn of their relations with God in the post-industrial age when the power of the human race had reached its most critical phase. Avdiy's conclusions had still not stabilized, but were open to discussion; even so, they revealed too much free-thinking to be acceptable to official theology, and when he refused to repent of the heresy of innovation, the diocesan authorities expelled him from the seminary.

Avdiy Kallistratov had a high, pale forehead. Like many of his generation, he wore his hair down to his shoulders and sported a thick dark beard which, even if it could hardly be said to ornament his face, gave a prepossessing expression to his features. His grey, protruding eyes had a febrile glitter that expressed the agitation of his mind and thoughts, so much a part of his nature; it was a mind which gave him much joy from his own ideas and much suffering from the people around him, in spite of the spirit of good will in which he approached them . . .

Avdiy mostly wore a checked shirt, sweater and jeans. When it was cold he added an old coat and a fur hat that had been his father's before him, and it was thus arrayed that he appeared on the Moyun-Kum savannah . . .

The fact that at that moment he was tied up in the back of the truck gave rise to various bitter thoughts. This time the most stinging blow was the loneliness. He remembered a half-forgotten line from one of the oriental poets:

> And in a throng of thousands – you're alone
> Alone with yourself – you're all alone . . .

It was even harder for him when he thought of the one who had become his closest friend in all the world, the constant companion of his thoughts, the underlying substance of his very being. In his hour of need he could not separate her from his own self, could not help directing towards her his thoughts and feelings; and if telepathy really does exist as suprasensual communication between individuals who are close at moments of stress, then she must that night have been experiencing a strange weariness of spirit and premonition of disaster . . .

Now at last he understood the meaning of the paradoxical words of that same oriental poet, words at which he had always laughed before:

> It were better not to love for him whose
> nature is to love . . .

'Rubbish!' he had always thought. But now he sobbed silently, thinking of her, aware that were it not for her existence and his desperate, undisclosed love for her, like a daying man's love for life, then he would not lie in the grip of this unrescinding hurt, this lonely sadness, this insuperable, mad, tormenting desire to tear free and run, run to her through the night and the savannah, to the little station of Zhalpak-Saz, alone on the great trans-continental sweep of the railway, so as to stand, like that other time, even for half an hour, beside her door in the little house by the hospital, where she lived on the very edge of the great desert . . . Unable to break free, Avdiy cursed his (useless?) devotion. After all, it was for her sake he was here, for her sake he had come back to these asiatic regions, to this Moyun-Kum where he lay bound, humiliated and insulted. He was tormented by the impossibility of seeing her, and by his loneliness. But these feelings also revealed to him the beauty of oneness with God, for now he realized that God, in manifesting Himself through love, makes humankind a gift of the greatest happiness in life, and that in this, God's generosity is as infinite as the flow of time. He also understood that the purpose of love is different each time and for each new individual . . .

'Glory to God in the highest!' he whispered, looking at the moon, and thought: If only she knew how great is God's mercy, when He puts love into our hearts . . .

Suddenly he heard footsteps beside the truck and the sound of puffing and belching as heavy bodies heaved in over the tailboard. It was Mishash, closely followed by Kepa. They seemed to have made a good start on the vodka, judging by the smell which filled his nostrils.

'Lolling here, eh, you? Come on, get up, you son-of-a-bishop, Ober wants you on the carpet, he's going to teach you a thing or two,' said Mishash, picking his way through the carcasses like a bear lumbering about its lair.

Kepa, giggling, added his contribution: 'No carpet, just your own bum, you've got all the sand of the Moyun-Kum to sit on.'

'Carpet! Huh!' belched Mishash again. 'It's Siberia you need, you bastard, not carpet! Thought he'd pull one on us, did he? Thought he'd make monks of the lot of us, eh? Not bloody us, mate! Got your sums wrong there!'

4

Avdiy Kallistratov had sent several letters to Inga in Zhalpak-Saz. She had answered them poste restante at the town's main post office, since by then he no longer had a permanent address. His mother had died while he was still a child and his widowed father, Deacon Kallistratov, had devoted all his warmth and considerable erudition, both theological and secular, to his son and daughter (who was three years older than Avdiy). The sister, Varvara, had gone to study in Leningrad. She had hoped for a place at teacher training college, but was refused because she was the daughter of a clergyman and therefore not suitable to be let loose in a school; then she passed the examinations for the Faculty of Engineering and settled in Leningrad for good, getting married, having a family and working as a draughtswoman in some design institute. Avdiy's chosen path lay in the spiritual sphere; it was his choice and supported by his father, especially after Varvara was refused entrance to the teacher training college. When Avdiy started his studies at the seminary, Deacon Kallistratov was happy and proud that his dream had come true, that all his efforts and exhortations had not been in vain and that the Lord had heeded his prayers. Soon, however, he died; perhaps it was a blessing in disguise, for he would never have survived the heretical metamorphosis that took place in his son once he developed an enthusiasm for innovation in a field that should have been as unchanging as the world itself, in theology, revealed once and for all in the infinity and invariability of the power of God.

Once Avdiy Kallistratov was expelled from the seminary and started to write for the local youth newspaper, the small flat in which Deacon Kallistratov had lived with his family for so many years was needed for the replacement deacon; it was put to ex-seminarist Avdiy Kallistratov that since he no longer had any connection with the Church it would be expedient for him to vacate the flat.

At this Avdiy summoned his sister Varvara so that she could choose what she needed and wanted of their parents' things, particularly the ancient icons and other paintings, and take them back to Leningrad as her share of their memories and their legacy. For himself, he took his father's books. That had been the last meeting between brother and sister, for although they had not quarrelled in any way, they each had their own life to lead. Since then Avdiy had always been a tenant, at first renting a whole room in someone's flat, then a corner of a room when he could no longer afford more. Which was why he had to use the post restante address.

It was during this period that Avdiy travelled for the first time to Central Asia on behalf of that local Komsomol newspaper. The immediate reason for the trip was Avdiy's idea of researching and writing about the ways and means by which the narcotic *anasha* hashish was finding its way into the lives of young people in the European part of the country. *Anasha* is a plant which grows in Central Asia, in the steppes around the Chui and Moyun-Kum deserts. It is closely related to the famous marijuana, a particular type of wild hemp whose leaves, flower-clusters and especially pollen contain fast-acting intoxicating substances. When smoked, these produce euphoria and the illusion of well-being. Increasing the dose brings on a phase of depression and later on of aggression – a loss of control that is dangerous for other people.

In his articles Avdiy Kallistratov gave a detailed description of his journey. He also described his unexpected meeting with the family of wolves in the steppe and everything else that he had experienced. He described his pain and anxiety, as an eye-witness and as a citizen concerned at the spread of the narcotic. At first the editorial board was delighted with the articles; then publication was postponed, at first temporarily, and then permanently.

Avdiy Kallistratov wrote to Inga of all his failures and sufferings. For him she was a gift from fate, the closest friend in all the world; like a river of healing water she could give him new life and resurrect him to continue on his everyday path. It did not take him long to understand that this correspondence with Inga was the most important thing that had ever happened to him – perhaps the reason for his being born at all, the thing which justified his very existence.

Once he had sent off a letter, he would think of nothing else but would recall every word he had written, going over it in his mind and adding his own comments for the next letter, each of which became an expansion of the previous one. It was a strange kind of long-distance communication, a series of continuous emissions through time and space from his suffering spirit:

Then I wondered for days whether I had not shocked you with the first words of my last letter: 'In the name of the Father, and of the Son, and of the Holy Spirit!' I used them because I grew up in that tradition, and they ring out for me like a kind of tuning fork before any serious talk, attuning me to a prayerful attitude of spirit; and I do not want to betray that rule, although I know it is superfluous for me to remind you yet again that I am from a religious background and was once a student at the seminary. My feelings for you do not permit me to hold back on any subject affecting me in this way. Are we fated to meet again? My secret and most cherished dream is that we should be. My dreams are like children; I nurture them and cannot live without them. I can imagine what happiness it must be to love one's children, if one loves them, as one's dreams. My dreams came into being as the spirit's striving for divine perfection in all its glittering infinity. It is thanks to those dreams that, without being aware of it, I have resisted the threat of annihilation. Perhaps it is because love is the antithesis of death that it is revealed as the key aspect of life, after the mystery of birth. I repeat all this as a charm, to ensure that we should be fated to meet again. But there's so much more to say . . .

Inga, I hope you remember our agreement that as soon as my newspaper published the articles I came to your part of the world to write, I would send them straight to you by airmail. Unfortunately I am not at all sure that my articles on the adolescent *anasha*-runners and all the rest of this sad reflection of the times we live in will be printed at all in the very near future. The reason why I say 'the times we live in'

39

is because although *anasha* has been growing as a weed in these parts since time immemorial, it so happened that about fifteen years ago . . . Though why tell all this to you, who are a specialist on the subject? But no, I'm sorry, Inga, I am going to tell you, because that is the only way to make sense of this whole enterprise . . . So, fifteen years ago, the locals assure me, nobody would have dreamed of collecting the horrible stuff, or 'herb' as the kids call it, whether for smoking or for anything else. This is an evil that attacked very recently, and to a great extent it was under the influence of the West. Now the newspaper is suggesting that I limit my action to sending some kind of private report to 'the proper authorities' – it's incomprehensible! I understand their point, their spurious fear that sensational material about drug-addiction among adolescents (sorry; let's qualify that for the sake of accuracy), among certain irresponsible adolescents, will supposedly strike a blow against our prestige and make us a laughing stock throughout the world. Real ostrich politics! Who needs prestige if the price is so high?

I can just imagine, Inga, the condescending smile at my naïve indignation with which you read those lines. Or perhaps you were frowning, which suits you so well? When you frown, your face becomes pure and profound like that of a young nun seriously broaching the task of apprehending the essence of the divine. The true beauty of the brides of Christ lies in that inner light in their faces. If I said that aloud, or in the presence of other people, it would look as though I were trying to flatter you. But as I have already said, there is nothing in my attitude toward you that needs to be changed in any way. If your worried brow reminds me of the Mother of God in Renaissance pictures, you can regard it as being, at worst, a result of my very limited knowledge of art. Anyway, I have every hope that you are convinced of my sincerity. After all, that was how it all began; you believed me from the first, and opened up a new era in my life . . .

Went into the office again today about my articles. No change. Nobody can explain to me why my articles were initially greeted with such delight, but now there's such a total lack of enthusiasm. Everyone had so much to say on the issues I confronted! Now the editor is avoiding me. I can't get through to him on the phone, his secretary just says he's awfully busy, a meeting, or a planning session, or else he's been summoned by 'higher', as she loves to stress, 'authorities'.

And so I wander alone about the streets I know so well, as though I were an outsider, here completely by chance, rather than born and bred in these parts, so empty and alien does everything feel. Some of the people I know turn away when they see me: for them I'm an excommunicate, a heretic who was expelled from the seminary and so on. Only one thing warms my heart, only one beloved concern is with me all the time: my letters. As I walk I think of what I'm going to write, of how I'm going to tell you everything I think you'll find interesting and everything that gives me ideas to share with you. I never imagined that loving a woman, thinking about her and writing her letters, would ever become the reason life was worth living! I'm waiting to pounce on the slightest provocation to come back to where we met. Roll on the day! I'm sure other people have had days when they were happy to see the meaning of life in love, but unlike them I shall love to my dying day and see in that my whole *raison d'être*.

Leaves are already falling on the boulevard. Just to think that what I wrote about happened at the beginning of the summer! At that time the newspaper was welcoming my idea with open arms! How could I know that when it came to the crunch they wouldn't want to know? How could I understand the strength of the strange principle that we're allowed to print only what is favourable and prestigious?

At the time I was caught up in the prospect of the journey to the southern regions that so attracted me, a provincial northern Russian. The idea was to go not as an outside observer but as one of the *anasha*-runners, to worm my way into their group. Of course, I'm older than they are, but not so much older as to make it look suspicious. At the paper they decided that in old jeans and down-at-heel trainers I could still look the part if I shaved off my beard, which I did. I didn't take along any notebooks, but relied on my memory. The important thing was for me to break into their circle, to find out what it was about these particular kids that attracted them to this kind of thing, what was motivating them apart from the lure of profit; I wanted to study it all from the inside, to find the personal, social, family and especially psychological background to all of them.

And so I made my preparations. That was in May, when the *anasha* begins to flower. And that is when the people who come to the steppe around the Moyun-Kum desert and the Chu river specially for that purpose start to gather the flowers. I learned all this from Viktor Nikiforovich Gorodetsky, a local history teacher whom I knew. When we were alone, talking about anything and everything on earth, he used to call me Father Avdiy for a joke. He was relatively young, the same age as my sister Varvara. His nephew Pasha was later discovered to be in with one of these *anasha* gangs, but Viktor Nikiforovich did not know about it at the time.

Pasha asked his parents if he could go to Ryazan to see his grandfather, whom he often visited. Five days or so after he left, Viktor Nikiforovich had a telegram from an examining magistrate of the Transport Prosecutor's Office, a certain Djaslibekov, sent from some distant station in Kazakhstan – a long way from Ryazan. The telegram informed him that his nephew was being held under arrest for illegal transportation of narcotic substances on the railway system. It was immediately clear to Viktor Nikiforovich why Djaslibekov had sent the telegram to him rather than the boy's parents. Pasha was afraid of his father, a stern man with a sharp temper. Viktor Nikiforovich flew immediately to Alma-Ata, from where it took him another twenty-four hours to reach the small wayside station in the steppe. He found Pasha in a state of total despair. Hanging over him was the threat of an immediate trial with the sentencing guidelines amended to allow a sentence of at least three years in a 'strict regime' camp. A trial was inevitable, since he had been caught red-handed. Viktor Nikiforovich tried as hard as he could to make his nephew realize that there was no way out, that in law crime is followed by punishment. He gave him advice on how to behave in court, what to say, promised to explain to his parents and to visit him in the camp. All this in the presence of Djaslibekov. Suddenly Djaslibekov said, 'Viktor Nikiforovich, if you will act as guarantor that your nephew does not repeat any such crime, I will exercise the power invested in me to let him go. Something gives me the impression that you would be able to put this young man back on the right path. If, however, he's caught carrying *anasha* again, then he'll be tried as a second-time offender. You decide.'

Of course Viktor Nikiforovich was overcome with relief. He immediately signed as guarantor for Pasha. When he wondered how he could thank the investigating magistrate, Djaslibekov said, 'Viktor Nikiforovich, there is something you can do. You're a teacher. When you get back, try to get the press to take a serious interest in what's happening here. We're fighting against crime at the stage where it's already been committed, or is in the process of being committed. What we don't know is who or what drives these . . . these boys out into the wildest steppe, forces them to mix with down-and-outs, even with hardened criminals. We put them on trial, these adolescents; we have to. I was very impressed at the way you reacted instantly to the telegram. It helps us a lot if someone comes at once. Many parents – most of them, actually – don't come at all. And so you get fifteen-year-olds pitched straight into a "strict regime" camp. And what happens to them there? Useless, and crippled in spirit: that's what they'll be like by the time they get out. No need to tell you what prison means. Viktor Nikiforovich, it breaks my heart to see it. Last season alone, we tried more than a hundred boys, just from this stretch of the railway alone, and goodness knows how many more got away. And still they keep coming, from all corners of the country, Arkhangelsk to Kamchatka, like fish to the spawn. How long can it go on? We can't put the whole lot in jail! They have a whole organized system . . . There are people, local and others, who guide them to the places where the *anasha* grows. We put them on trial as well. And if only you knew the havoc they wreak with the trains! They stop goods trains out in the open steppe (they wouldn't dare to travel by passenger train, they'd be caught

43

at once). Somebody's supplying them with a chemical, some kind of powder, that you can put on the rails and in the light of the train's headlamps it looks as though the sleepers are burning. Of course, the driver stops the train, anything can happen out in the steppe, and runs forward along the track – he has to check that it's not really a fire. The *anasha*-runners have time to climb into the goods wagons with their bags and suitcases. Goods trains are so long these days, up to a kilometre in length, and there's no way you can keep checking all the time. They travel to the main junction, and there they buy a ticket. So many people travel by train, they just manage to disappear in the crowd. Although these last few years the police have started using sniffer-dogs, trained to the smell. It was a dog that caught your nephew . . .'

There were lots of other things that Viktor Nikiforovich found out about while he was out there. He taught me all I knew. But I had been looking for something like this for a long time. I had long been obsessed with the idea of finding a way to the minds and hearts of my own generation. I saw leading them to the right path as my true calling. Of course, it was somewhat presumptuous of me to see that as my destiny, but I was sincere in my desires and I think it probably has a lot to do with my background. I had already made general references in various articles to the pernicious hold of alcohol on young people and said much the same about drugs, quoting the bitter experience of the West in that respect. However, all my knowledge was at second hand. What I needed was vivid and striking material which would give my own ideas and my own reaction to all the cases of drug-addiction that were known about but mention of which was superstitiously avoided amongst teenagers, cases which led in some instances to collapse of the personality and in others to sadistic murders. To make it vivid and personal I needed an inside view of the problem and first-hand experience of the realities. And just then Viktor Nikiforovich Gorodetsky, with his personal experience of the matter, decided to share his thoughts and feelings on the subject with me. Pasha's family, father, mother and all the children, exchanged their flat for a smaller one in another town and moved away. They had to, to get Pasha away from his old cronies and their traffic in *anasha*. Viktor Nikiforovich told me all this with great sadness and bitterness.

And that was the event which prompted me to get moving with the idea I had conceived.

I went to Moscow. The trains for the hemp-bearing steppes leave from the Kazan station, where the group of runners, as they call themselves, first joined up. I later learned that the runners come from all over the Baltic states and the north, with the liveliest cities being Arkhangelsk and Klaipeda, probably because of the resale value of *anasha* passed on to sailors setting off to sea. To get in touch with the runners I had to find a porter with a badge saying 'No. 87', nicknamed 'Utyug' – 'The Flat-Iron', and say that I brought greetings from one of the former friends whom Pasha had mentioned. Utyug had a friend in the ticket-office, so for a small consideration he dealt with the matter of acquiring a ticket. I never succeeded in finding out exactly how; evidently there was someone well concealed in charge. Utyug fixed it so that a group travelled together – that is to say, all in the same train, but with reservations in different carriages. Once I got to know the runners better, I learned that their first precept was to protect one another; if any one of them was caught, they were not, at all costs, to give each other away, and therefore they talked as little as possible in the presence of outsiders.

And so I stood on Moscow's Three Stations Square, where I had stood so many times on visits to the city. The crush was terrible, especially in the Metro and at the stations. Thousands of people from all over the country, whirling along like twigs in a whirlpool. But I still loved visiting Moscow, loved wandering about the less crowded central streets and looking in all the second-hand bookshops, lounging by the posters and advertisements and, if possible, revisiting the Tretyakov and Pushkin Museums.

This time, as I left the local train at Yaroslav station and followed the crowd over the square to Kazan station, I found myself thinking how carefree my life had been before, when I was my own master and could roam as long and as

45

far through the streets of Moscow as I wished. Now I had to plunge into the giant ant-hill of the Kazan station and try to find Utyug, the link-man, with his badge saying 'No. 87'. If mine was number eighty-seven, there must be at least a thousand of them in the whole station, or so it seemed as I looked about me. Finding him turned out to be much harder than I ever expected. I wasted half an hour looking around all the places where the porters gathered, only to find him at last on the platform by a train leaving for Tashkent. He was loading boxes and cases into the carriage from his trolley, exchanging jokes with the attendants. I waited to one side for him to finish, for the travellers to get inside and the people seeing them off to range themselves down the side of the carriage. Suddenly he got out, panting, putting his tip in his pocket. He was a gingery cat of a man, with cunning, shifty eyes. I almost made the mistake of begging his pardon for disturbing him.

'Well, hello there, Utyug, how's things then?' I asked, as hearty and casual as I could make it sound.

'Same as ever, the one with the trolley gets more of the lolly!' he answered as though we had known each other for years.

'Oh, so you're in the lolly then?' I asked, pointing at his trolley.

'Huh! We know who's in the lolly, don't we. Anyway, what can I do for you? Need something moved? Happy to oblige!'

'No, I can move anything I need to move,' I answered casually. 'There's something else.'

'Well? Out with it!'

'Not here. Let's go over there.'

'All right, let's go over there.'

We walked down the long platform towards the station concourse. The Tashkent train moved off, a long line of windows with faces pressed against the glass. Another train arrived on the other side. The trains stood several deep, people fussing and hurrying around them, while above the concourse the announcer's voice crackled the numbers and destinations of the incoming and outgoing services.

When we reached the station concourse, Utyug stood his

46

trolley in an empty corner and there, after a quick glance over my shoulder, I passed on the greetings from Pasha's friend. The friend was called Igor, but for some reason the runners called him 'Morzh', and 'Walrus'.

'What's Morzh up to these days?' asked Utyug.

'Not much,' I answered. 'It's his ulcer.'

'I told him so,' cried Utyug, slapping his forehead, the sympathy in his voice mingling with pride in his own diagnostic skill. 'I told him, last time I told him, watch out, Morzh! Watch out, I said, don't go over the top! Always was one for the extra, Morzh, and I could see it was getting out of hand. Led straight to an ulcer, then, did it?'

I arranged my features in an expression of sympathy, although quite frankly I hadn't the foggiest what he was talking about. I presumed that 'extra' was a make of vodka, but had the sense not to ask stupid questions. It turned out that I was completely wrong and that 'extra' was what they extracted from the 'plasticine' (the brown pollen paste that looks like a slab of children's plasticine, the most expensive part of the narcotic substances produced, on a par with opium). In the laboratory, 'extra' could be processed into a powder for injection, like heroin. Of course, the likes of Morzh had no access to laboratory equipment, so they took it by holding it under their tongues, chewing it, downing it with a gulp of vodka or eating it in bread. They called taking it 'a thump on the head'. The easiest way and the most common was, of course, smoking the unprocessed *anasha* in tobacco. The effect was just as good as the 'thump on the head', although in smoke it was over a little faster than with the other ways.

I learned that and a lot more about the lives of the runners during the journey to 'Khalkhin-Gol', which was their word for the places in which the *anasha* grew. That was another word over which I nearly gave myself away.

'So, lad, it's off to "Khalkhin-Gol", is it then, for you as well?' asked Utyug, off-hand.

Initially I was stumped by 'Khalkhin-Gol', but recovered enough to mutter: 'Er . . . Well, yes, of course, otherwise . . .'

'Right then. Don't worry about tickets. I'll do your ticket.

47

As for the rest, once you're back with the stuff, Dog will sort it out. That's up to him, not me.'

Who 'Dog' might be, and what part he played in tickets and 'the rest', I never did discover. I did gather, however, from what Utyug said, that we could not leave for Khalkhin-Gol until the next day, when all the runners would have reached Moscow: two were coming from Murmansk on the night train and another from somewhere else on a train that arrived in the morning. I was perfectly happy to have the extra day in Moscow.

Utyug told me what time to come back the next day (although I had nowhere else except the station to stay the night) and checked that I had a rucksack and plastic bags for the plants, which I had, in my suitcase. He also recommended that I buy a sealable glass or plastic container for the 'plasticine', the paste of pressed pollen.

'You never know, you might be lucky and get some plasticine, though it's not that easy,' he explained. 'I've never been down there myself, though I've heard all about it. You know Lyokha? In two seasons he got enough to buy a car! Drives around Moscow now, cocky as can be . . . Can't have taken him more than ten days in all, all told . . .'

At that we parted. I put my scruffy little case into the left luggage and set off to wander the streets.

It was the end of May, the best time of the year in Moscow, when spring is just turning into summer. Autumn is lovely, too, when the air is pure and the leaves are golden, the magic reflecting in the face of every passer-by – but I prefer the beginning of summer, bright by day and even by night, when the evening twilight lingers in the stars until it meets up with the morning in the east.

I was keen to get out into the open air, but the quickest way to travel in the centre of Moscow is by Metro, so I plunged back down into the swirling crowd and travelled to Sverdlov Square through a rumbling succession of light and darkness. The evening rush-hour had not yet started, so the trains were not crowded. Once in the centre, I went straight to my favourite city garden, green and bright with flowers, an island of peace amidst the traffic and buildings that pressed in upon it from all sides. At first I let the crowd sweep me towards the Manège, hoping to find an exhibition on, but the Manège was closed so I wandered past the old university, the Pashkov house, on to the Volkhonka and from there to the Pushkin Museum. I don't know why I felt so calm and happy; perhaps outside the rush-hour the streets of Moscow exude this feeling of peace, or perhaps it was the brick silhouette of the Kremlin, towering over this part of the city with the stability of a mountain range. What sights these walls had seen! As I wandered along, deep in thought, I forgot that I had shaved off my beard and kept touching my naked chin with my hand. I also forgot for a while that I was trying to worm my way into the little nest of evil that had established itself at the Kazan station.

You know, fate *does* exist, for better or for worse. I never expected a lucky stroke of fate as I set off into the Pushkin Museum. The most I was hoping for was some interesting new exhibits, although I would have been quite content to wander about the halls renewing my acquaintance with the old ones. But right by the entrance, in the gardens, a couple who were on their way out stopped me.

'Hey, you! Want a couple of tickets?' The boy had a bright green tie and his new brown shoes were obviously hurting his feet. The girl with him was bored and dying to get away, to judge by the look on her face.

'Aren't they selling them at the entrance?' I asked. I hadn't seen any sign of a queue.

'Not for the museum, for a concert. Only you've got to take them both.'

'What concert?'

'Oh, just some concert, some church choir or something.'

'In the museum?' I was surprised.

'Do you want them, or don't you? Look, two for the three roubles. Take them.'

I grabbed both tickets and hurried into the museum. I hadn't heard that there were ever concerts in the Pushkin. When I asked, however, I was told that the museum had a regular programme of classical concerts, mostly chamber music played by well-known performers. Amazingly enough, this time it was a concert of ancient Bulgarian choral music, to be given in the museum's Italian Court. Could they really be giving the work of Ioann Kukuzel, father of the Slavonic liturgy? The administrator to whom I was talking said that she was not sure of the details, but that they were expecting all sorts of important guests, up to and including the Bulgarian ambassador himself. I was more interested in the programme than the guests, for my father had talked to me a lot about Bulgarian choral music, and as a prelude to my risky journey, it was all I could have hoped for. There was half an hour to wait before the concert started, so instead of looking at the museum I went back outside to get some fresh air and calm my spirits.

Moscow! A May evening on one of the seven hills along the Moscow river: a joyful order seemed to reign within the city, and harmony triumphed within my untroubled soul. I breathed freely and deeply, the sky was clear, the earth was warm, and I walked up and down by the iron railings of the garden in front of the museum.

It seemed a shame to be alone – perhaps because I had two tickets. I imagined waiting for someone, seeing her on the other side of the street, trying to cross the road, afraid she was late, and I making frenzied signs to her not to get herself run over, afraid that she might rush impetuously into the stream of traffic. Of all the people around us, she would be the only one to bear a happiness I could share. She would smile at me, guessing from the look on my face what I was thinking. I imagined running over to her side of the street (I would be better in traffic than she) and taking her by the hand to look into her eyes. All these images were running through my mind when I suddenly stopped and felt so lonely at the thought that life still had not brought me together with the woman whom I was destined to love. Was I destined to love anyone? Perhaps I was just over-complicating my life with such a fanciful idea? I had thought about it so many times, and every time I came to the sad conclusion that it was all my own fault, that either I was expecting too much, or else I was just not the type that girls were interested in. Whatever the reason, other men of my age were much more successful. The only excuse I could think of was that the seminary had cut me off from the rest of my age group, although leaving the seminary had not brought me any more success. Why not? If she really did turn up out of the blue, the girl I was all ready to fall in love with, I would start by saying, 'Let's go and listen to the choral music, lose ourselves in it in order to find ourselves.' But I would be tortured by doubts. What if she found it boring and monotonous? Or incomprehensible? Liturgical music in a church is one thing, in a secular building in front of an audience it is quite another. Might it not turn out like playing Bach chorales during a display of gymnastics at the stadium or for parachute regiments more accustomed to military marches?

Shiny black cars and even a bus full of foreign tourists were drawing up at the gates of the museum. It must be time to start. People were already crowding around the entrance to the Italian Court. People were asking whether anyone had a spare ticket. With a pang I gave one to a short-sighted student who seemed to be wearing the wrong glasses. He got out his change to pay me and dropped it; I told him not to bother, that I had been given the tickets and therefore didn't need the money, but he insisted and put the coins into my jacket pocket as I went through into the auditorium. Of course I needed the money, I was living from hand to mouth, but still . . . I was embarrassed by the elegance of the Moscow audience compared with my worn old jeans and open jacket, my clumpy boots and the naked chin to which I just couldn't get accustomed, all of them carefully chosen for the long journey to the far-away steppes with a group of 'runners' I had never seen before in my life. Although none of it mattered . . .

All the exhibits remained in the Italian Court. Rows of chairs had been placed in the centre, and on these we took our places. There was no stage, no microphone, no curtains. Where one might have expected a platform, there was a small music-stand at the side. In a couple of minutes all the seats were taken and there was even a small crush of hopefuls by the entrance. A lot of the people seemed to know each other and were talking animatedly. Only I sat silently alone.

Two women emerged from a side door. One of them, a

51

curator at the Pushkin Museum, introduced the other, a Bulgarian colleague from the Alexander Nevsky Cathedral Museum in Sofia. The audience fell silent. The Bulgarian, a serious young woman with hair smoothed severely back, had good shoes and good legs (for some reason I noticed this detail). She peeked at us through a pair of large, tinted glasses, said, 'Good evening,' and gave a short lecture in perfectly acceptable Russian. We learned that along with priceless examples of church architecture, ancient manuscripts, icons and books their museum also exhibited what she called with a smile 'its living treasures', medieval liturgical music that was sung at evening concerts in the crypt of the cathedral. And now their choir, called 'Crypt' after their usual auditorium, was here at the invitation of the Pushkin Museum to share its music with us.

The singers came in. They must have been waiting right outside the door through which the audience had entered. There were only ten of them, all young, my own age. They were in evening dress, black bow ties and starched white collars, and shiny black shoes. No instruments or microphones, no loudspeakers, not even a platform to stand on, let alone lighting. They simply dimmed the lights slightly in the part of the court where the audience was sitting.

Although I was sure that everyone in the audience understood what choral singing meant, I was suddenly afraid for the singers. The audience was so large, and young audiences these days are so used to amplified sound, that the choir looked like unarmed soldiers on a battlefield.

The singers stood shoulder to shoulder in a semi-circle. There was calm and concentration on their faces, with no trace of the consternation that I was experiencing. At moments like this all the other, normally so important, concerns of a man's life are completely excluded from his thoughts, in the way that before a battle the only thought is of how to win the day.

As the singers took their places, the serious Bulgarian in the tinted glasses gave us a short account of the history of the Bulgarian Church, with its Byzantine roots but its own national traditions and its own liturgy, and after a few details about Bulgarian choral music she announced that the concert was about to begin.

The singers were ready. For a few more silent moments they adjusted their breathing, moved even closer together, and the court was as silent as if it had completely emptied. Everyone was waiting to see what this small group could do, what they were hoping to achieve. Then there was a nod from the third from the right, who must have been the leader, and they burst into sound. The voices flew up . . .

In the silence the music swelled like a rising chariot, glittering in waves of invisible sound beyond the confines of the court. The solemn and jubilant spirituality of the voices lingered in the purity of the air. The ten singers sang as one, an instrument so flexible and so polished that any accompaniment would have been superfluous. From their singing you had the feeling that the ten of them had been born for each other, born for the things of the spirit, born to keep alive that which had inspired their fathers and grandfathers before them: to keep alive Him whom they had invented to symbolize the spiritual heights for which man reaches instinctively out. That was the power of their singing, a passionate marriage of sound and feeling where the liturgical texts addressed to Him were merely a pretext for the celebration of the human spirit, striving to reach the heights of its own greatness.

The audience sat spell-bound, each thinking his own thoughts, each seeking in his own way that which men have sought for aeons in tragic error and in enlightenment, seeking themselves outside themselves; at the same time together they heard the Word, as repeated by thousands of tongues throughout the ages, and this increased tenfold the power of the singing to affect them. Each of them was drawn in imagination into that shadowy world that consists of all dreams, memories, longings and pangs of remorse, all the joys and sorrows, gains and losses that make up the individual on his path through life.

I did not stop to think of the effect upon myself of the singing of those ten men. They looked like ordinary men, like me, but the anthems that they sang seemed to come from my own heart, from the hurts and fears and joys to which I had never been able to give expression. By cleansing me and then filling me with new light and feeling, the art of those singers brought to me the true essence of liturgical singing: the cry of life, the cry of a man with his hands raised aloft, of man's eternal thirst to assert himself, to lighten his load, to find support in the boundless wastes of the universe, in the tragic hope that besides himself there are powers in the heavens that will come to his aid in all this. Magnificent delusion! How vast is the human need to be heard from above! How much thought and energy have we put into persuasion, remorse, praise and forcing ourselves, in the name of this desire, into humility, obedience, and resignation, despite our mutinous blood and our elemental thrust for revolt, for negation and for innovation. How hard it came to us! Psalms, charms, the *Rig-Veda*, hymns, the mutterings of shamans! A flood of prayer and utterance over the centuries, that if it were a physical thing would have drowned the world like a bitter-salt ocean overflowing its banks. How hard won was the 'human' element in our humanity . . .

The ten of them sang, brought together by God, so that we should all be drawn within ourselves, into the deep waters of our subconscious minds. They brought to life in us our past, the spirit and sorrows of departed generations, for us to arise and soar aloft, to triumph over ourselves and the world and seek out the beauty and meaning of our own purpose in life. Since we are a part of life, we should know and love its pattern and meaning. So selfless and inspired was the singing, more so, perhaps, than the singers themselves were even aware, that in the hearts of their listeners they awoke the kind of feelings that normally lie dormant beneath the cares and troubles of everyday life. A wave of emotion passed through the faces in the court, some of which were even glittering with tears.

I was so happy and grateful to fate for bringing me here, for presenting me with this opportunity to escape from time and place into all that I had ever known or felt, my memories of the past, my knowledge of the present and my dreams of the future. Among all the other thoughts was the awareness that I had never been in love, and the desire to

54

love that burned in my blood and awaited its hour I experienced as a gripping pain in my chest. Who was she? Where was she? When and where would it happen? Several times I found myself glancing at the door – perhaps she was here, standing there, waiting for me to notice her? What a pity that she was not there beside me, to share all my feelings and longings. I prayed hard that when it came I should avoid making a spectacle of myself, should not have to think back afterwards with shame . . .

Suddenly I remembered my mother from my early childhood. I remembered a clear winter morning with snowflakes falling here and there on a tree-lined avenue; my mother looked with smiling eyes into mine and started to button up my coat. She said something, I laughed and ran away; she ran smiling after me and we heard the bells ringing out over the town from the church up on the hill, the church where my father the provincial deacon was serving at that moment. He was a fervent believer but (as I now see it) perfectly understood the artificiality of all that man has created in the name and on behalf of God . . . In spite of my sympathy for my father, I have chosen a different path, not the one for which he hoped. It is hard for me to think that my father passed over into the next world in harmony with himself while I waver, negating the past, although revering the greatness and the magnificent expression of what was once an all-powerful idea, an idea which grew from century to century in the attempt to convert unconverted souls on all the continents and islands so as to assert itself for all time in the world, in the succeeding generations and their minds, containing and diverting into the depths of resignation the eternal call of doubt in the mutinous human spirit, as a lightning conductor diverts the electric charge from the clouds into the depths of the earth. We should be grateful to them, to Faith and Doubt, the two forces of being that move our lives.

I was born at a point when the forces of doubt had the upper hand, giving birth in their turn to new doubts. I am the product of that process, anathematized by the one side and unaccepted, with all my complexities, by the other. Never mind, history plays tricks by throwing up just such as me, when it needs to unburden itself . . . Such were my thoughts as I listened to the Bulgarian liturgical singing.

They sang the anthems one after another, sang them in the court like an echo of past days. The 'Evening Sacrifice', 'Smiting of the Innocents' and 'Angel Announced' were followed by the severe melodies of anthems to those who had died for their faith, and although much of it was familiar to me, I was captivated by what I was hearing, by the way in which the ten members of the choir made magic with their material, transforming what I knew into truly great art, whose strength was a function of the stamina and absorbing power of the spirit of a people, throughout history, since suffering brings knowledge in its path.

As I listened to the choristers from Sofia, inspired by their own singing, as I searched the expression on their faces, I suddenly realized that one of them, the second on the left, a surprisingly fair man amidst the dark Bulgarians, looked very like me. It is strange to see someone who looks so much like you. The grey-eyed chorister also had hollow cheeks, a Roman nose, two long furrows across the forehead, and – what I noticed first – a beard exactly like mine had been before I shaved it off. As I nervously touched my naked chin yet again, I was reminded that the next day I was to set off with the *anasha*-runners. Suddenly I was horrified by the contrast. Where was I going? Why? Here in the museum we were hearing a concert of divine music, and there at the station reigned the dark passions of the likes of Utyug for the evil smoke from an evil weed. But after all, human life with its good and its evil had always run its course outside the walls of church and temple. Especially in our time . . .

After I noticed the coincidental likeness, my eyes never left my double's face. I watched him singing, watched his face stretch when his mouth opened wide as he took the highest notes. I felt for him and felt with him, as though we were one flesh, and the feeling seemed to give me a part in the singing. The whole of me sang, I was a part of the choir and filled with a burning brotherhood, moved to tears by the feeling that we seemed to be reunited after long years of parting, to raise again our strengthened voices to the heavens while our feet stood firmly on the stable earth. Together again to sing for ever . . .

The anthems they sang were the work of men, men who called in exalted and even frenzied voices from the dark of ages upon an Almighty whom they themselves had created, upon something which had no reality in itself but made a spiritual reality; men convinced that in the loneliness of this world only in song and prayer could they find Him.

As I watched the righteous devotion and inspiration in the eyes of the choristers from Sofia as they sang their age-old anthems, sweat pouring from their tense faces, I was filled with envy: I wanted to be among them, I wanted to be the one who was my double.

On the wave of enlightenment, I had another thought: why does man feel the call of music, of song, of prayer? Why is it that he needs them, and has always needed them? Could it be from the subconscious awareness of the tragic nature of his passage through the whirlpool of life, which ebbs and flows, flows and ebbs, an awareness which makes him strive to express himself, to give his life meaning, to give himself permanence? When it is all over, when in millions of years the end of the world is here and our planet dies, dark and cold, some cosmic consciousness (perhaps from another galaxy) will hear our playing and singing amidst the silence and emptiness we leave behind us. That is what has been inextinguishably programmed into us from the moment of our creation: life after life! How essential it is for every man to know, to be completely confident, that in principle it is possible for him to continue to exist in some way. One day, presumably, men will invent some kind of everlasting automatic unit, a kind of musical *perpetuum mobile*, an anthology of all that is best in human culture of every successive age; and as I rejoiced in the singing of the choristers I firmly believed that in the far distant future anyone who heard their words and music would have the key, through understanding or intuition, to the contradictory creatures, creatures of genius and of suffering, that were the human beings who inhabited the earth and were the only ones of her denizens who enjoyed the gifts of reason and awareness.

Life, death, love, sympathy and inspiration – it will all be expressed in music, for in music we have achieved the highest freedom, that freedom for which we have fought throughout our history from the first awakenings of reason in man, but which we have never achieved except in music. And only music, triumphing over the dogmas of all ages, has always striven towards the future, which is why it can express that which we ourselves are incapable of expressing . . .

A glance at my watch told me that the concert in my beloved Pushkin Museum would soon be over. I thought with horror of going back to Kazan station, a different world, the eternal world of hustle and bustle, where divine singing is never heard and would be meaningless if it were . . . In that, however, lay the very reason why my return there was so vital . . .

5

It was gone midday, and the train was already passing through the Volga region. In the compartmented carriages people were settling down to spending several days in each other's company, in groups as stable as any that form during a journey. The cheaper carriage in which Avdiy Kallistratov travelled was not compartmentalized, and the life the passengers led therein was therefore a more communal one. All sorts of people were travelling, each with his own reasons for taking to the road. All normal enough – people need to go somewhere, so they get on a train. Some of them were the *anasha*-runners travelling with Avdiy. He guessed that there were at least ten of them in the train, though he had met only two, introduced at the station by the chirpy Utyug. They were the lads from Murmansk, an older one, Petrukha, who was about twenty, and a younger one, Lyonka, a boy of only sixteen, although it was his second expedition. That fact was enough to give him airs, for it gave him an aura of experience. The pair from Murmansk were at first very restrained, although they knew that Avdiy was one of their own and was starting his career as a runner on the recommendation of people whom they trusted. The only communication they had was half-hinted remarks exchanged where two carriages linked and where they went out for a cigarette, since smoking was not tolerated in the carriages themselves because of the numbers of travellers and the air that was already stifling. The link was a good place to meet and have a smoke and a chat. Petrukha was the first to notice that Avdiy did not smoke in the way that they did.

'Hey, Avdiy, never smoked before or something? You smoke like a little old lady! Afraid to inhale, are you?'

Avdiy had to lie. 'I used to smoke, but gave it up . . .'

'Well, I can see *that*. Been smoking since I was so high, myself. And as for Lyonka, smokes like a chimney, drinks like a fish as well, ha-ha-ha! Not now, of course, must keep our noses clean now, eh? But afterwards . . .'

'Bit young, isn't he?'

'Who, Lyonka? Ha-ha-ha, young, but not backward, eh? Your first time out, isn't it? No picnic this, you know! Now our Lyonka, he knows all the ropes, don't you, Lyonka boy, knows his stuff does our Lyonka.'

'And does he smoke the *anasha*, or just run it?' asked Avdiy.

'Lyonka? Of course he smokes it. Everyone smokes it, these days! But you have to know what you're doing,' added Petrukha judiciously. 'Some people go over the top, they're no good for the run, of course. We call them the "rotters", one push and they're over, like a rotten tree-stump. That sort can give the whole game away. That's what it's like, the weed, heaven on earth, fill your soul with joy, take you out of yourself . . .'

'What kind of joy?'

'Well, joy, like, imagine a little stream you could step across, spit across if you like. Well, to you it's a river, an ocean, paradise. There's the joy! Joy, I say – where else could you get it from, joy like that? Well, I mean, bread you buy, clothes you buy, shoes you buy, everyone drinks vodka, that costs money too. But the grass, although that costs you, too, of course, it's a special, a different kind of feeling; it's like you're living in a dream, like – like it's all on film, you're watching as it takes place before your eyes. Only with a film, there's hundreds and thousands of other people sharing it, while with this, it's up to you, and everyone else can mind their own business, or get a fist in the nose for minding other people's. Yeah, that's the way!' He made a crude gesture and squinted over at Avdiy. 'Like to try it, Avdiy? Try a little taste of heaven, eh, just for starters, I can spare you some from my personal supplies . . .'

'Oh, I'll wait and try my own,' Avdiy declined. 'When I get my own portion, that's when I'll try it.'

'Yeah, perhaps you're right,' agreed Petrukha. 'Something special about stuff you've picked with your own hands.' He fell silent for a moment, then went on. 'Main thing, Avdiy, with this stuff, is: keep your eyes peeled! Remember: they're all after you! Every grandma you see, every old soldier with his medals on his chest, every old geezer with a pension-book, not to mention the rest! They're all out to get us, have us put away, hard labour and out of sight of the likes of them! That's why the rule is, sit in the corner, quiet as a mouse, head down, till you've made your pile, then whoosh! Then you can really let rip, once the money's in your pocket, and let them all go off themselves. And listen, Avdiy, if something goes wrong, you can croak but you can't grass on your mates, OK? That's the rule. If you grass, you can be sure they'll get you sooner or later. Even in prison, they'll find you and get you. It's not a kids' game you're playing now, you know . . .'

Avdiy gradually learned that Petrukha worked through the winter at various building-sites, and once summer set in he would be off to the Moyun-Kum steppe where he knew all the best places for *anasha*. He knew places, especially in the valleys and gullies, where the *anasha* grew so thick you could pick as much as you wanted. All he had at home was his old mother, who drank. His brothers had both left home, one for the far North, the other to work on the gas pipe-line. Poor guys, hard way to earn their bread: if the frostbite didn't get you, the insects would. When it came to making money, Petrukha could make one trip out to Asia, out to the land of the slitty-eyes, and spend the rest of the year sitting on his butt spitting at the ceiling, so long as he didn't run out of spit. As for his mate Lyonka, his family circumstances were even more lamentable. He never knew his mother. He started life in an orphanage. When he was about three, an ocean-going captain from Murmansk, working mostly on the Cuba run, turned up with his wife and filled out all the papers for an official adoption. They didn't have any children of their own. Five years later it all fell apart. The captain's wife ran off to Leningrad with some fancy-man; the captain took to drink, and was transferred to shore-work. Lyonka just about kept his head above water at school, living first with the captain's aunt, then with his brother, an accountant, who had a real harpy of a wife, so things went from bad to worse and the boy was soon completely out of hand. He left the captain and moved in with a disabled veteran, a former submarine man, who was kind and lonely but had no influence on Lyonka at all. The boy did exactly as he pleased. If he felt like disappearing, he disappeared. If he felt like coming back, he did so. This was

Lyonka's second season on the *anasha* run; he was obviously heavily involved with the stuff himself, and there he was, only sixteen, still on the threshold of life . . .

It was all Avdiy Kallistratov could do to stop himself reacting to all these sordid details, but he had set himself the task of studying from the inside whatever it was that drew more and more young people into its tentacles. The more he heard of their depressing stories, the more firmly he became convinced that it was like a strong undercurrent beneath the superficial calm of a sheet of water. Besides the personal reasons that might incline this or that individual to the vice, there were obviously weighty social reasons which allowed, or gave rise to, this disease which was attacking the youth of the country. The reasons would not be easy to determine at first glance; they resembled interconnected capillaries, carrying a disease in the blood until it infected the whole of the organism. However deeply you went into the reasons at the personal level, they were meaningless without the context and the overall picture. The minimum that the situation demanded of Avdiy was a complete sociological investigation; it would be even better if he could open up the topic for discussion, either in the press or on television. That was what he wanted, and what he hoped for with the naïvety of an alien from a different planet . . . Which is exactly what he was, if we bear in mind the limitations of an education received within the walls of a seminary and his lack of knowledge of the everyday world. Later he was to realize that he would find nobody prepared to support open discussion of such topics; refusals would always be justified with vague references to the necessity to preserve the prestige of our society, whereas the real reason was of course a desire at all costs to do nothing which might have an adverse effect upon the position and situation of the individual concerned, since these depended upon the whim and opinions of other, more powerful, people. Evidently the courage and confidence to take steps which might rebound upon you yourself was a prerequisite to any attempt to raise the alarm over problems in some particular sector of society. Luckily or unluckily for him, Avdiy Kallistratov was free of the burden of any such secret fear for his place in society or for his career. For the moment, however, he was nowhere near making all these discoveries. He was only starting out along the road, only making his first contacts with that aspect of modern life which, out of sympathy for those who had gone astray, he desired to experience from the inside so as to help albeit even a few of the victims. He wanted to help them not by lecturing them in print, not with reproaches and accusations, but by taking their part for himself and showing them, by his own example, that the only way out of the morass was through a personal rebirth; each of them was faced with the prospect of a revolution, at least a personal revolution at the level of the individual. For the moment he had no idea of the high price he would have to pay for his selfless and grandiose ideas.

He was young. And not only young . . . While at the seminary he had studied the story of Christ with such fervour, become so much a part of it, taken His sufferings so much upon himself that he had sobbed as he read of Judas's treachery in the Garden of Gethsemane. To him it seemed the end of the world that Christ was crucified on that hot afternoon at Golgotha the Place of the Skull. He had not the experience to think that perhaps there is some law according to which this world reserves the greatest punishments for those of its sons who express the purest notions and the finest strivings! Perhaps he should have asked himself whether maybe such was the natural form in which such notions existed, and in which they triumphed? Or what the implications of the fact might be, were it so? Could it not be that here, he could have put his finger on the very price of victory?

The subject had been touched upon in conversation with Viktor Nikiforovich Gorodetsky, before Avdiy finally decided to break off his studies at the seminary.

'What should I say? You see, young Father . . . Please don't be offended if I call you "young Father" now and then, Avdiy, the two words go so well together . . .' said Gorodetsky thoughtfully, as they drank tea together in his room. 'If you leave the seminary, I think you're very likely to find yourself excommunicated. I'm sure that your teachers will not allow you to fling down the gauntlet and flounce out with impunity. Especially as the reason for your leaving is a rare and very unpleasant one for the Church; after all, you're not leaving because you think someone's been unfair, not because you've been offended or discriminated against, not because of some row with a church official. No, young Father, you have no axe to grind with the Church itself . . . Your objections are purely ideological.'

'Yes, Viktor Nikiforovich, it's true. There's no direct reason. It's not me that's the problem, it's the fact that the traditional religions are hopelessly obsolete for today's world; there's no way you can be serious about a religion that was designed with the collective consciousness of the barely awakening masses in mind. You can see for yourself that if history can come up with a new central figure on the horizon of faith, the figure of a contemporary God with a new conception of the divine that is relevant to the needs of today's world, then there is hope that faith still might be worth something. That's why I'm leaving.'

'I see, I see,' smiled Gorodetsky indulgently. Taking a sip of his tea, he went on. 'It all sounds world-shaking. But before we go on to your theory, there's one thing I ought to say to you, and that's how glad I am as we sit here drinking tea and enjoying ourselves that we're not living in the Middle Ages, you and I. You can be sure that for such unprecedented heresy somewhere in Catholic Europe, in Spain, say, or in Italy, you and I, young Father, would have started off by being quartered, then burnt at the stake for good measure and finally ground into powder and thrown to the four winds. In your case, for daring to say all this, and in mine, for listening to you! Oh, the Inquisition would have loved to crush us, would have really gone about it with gusto! Just think, if the Holy Inquisition burnt one poor wretch at the stake just because it was stated in an anonymous denunciation that he permitted himself a mysterious smile at the mention of the Immaculate Conception, then . . .'

'Viktor Nikiforovich, I'm sorry, but I've got to interrupt,' laughed Avdiy, nervously playing with the buttons of his seminarist's uniform. 'I do understand that what I say amuses you, but seriously, if the Inquisition still existed and if I was threatened with burning at the stake tomorrow for my heresy, I wouldn't retract a single word!'

'I believe you,' nodded Gorodetsky.

'I didn't come to this by chance, you know. I studied the history of Christianity and observed the life of today. And I shall search for a new, a contemporary God, even if I never succeed in finding one . . .'

'You're right to mention history,' interrupted Gorodetsky. 'But now, listen to me. Your idea of a new God is abstract theory, however fashionable it might sound in intellectual circles. It's your own ideas, your own "calculations" as they used to say. You're programming for God, but God can't be calculated to order, however attractive and convincing the idea might seem. Don't you understand? If Christ had not been crucified, he wouldn't have been the Lord! That unique individual, possessed of the idea of the triumph of a kingdom of justice, was first put to a cruel death by His fellow men, then revived, lauded, mourned, and finally fully experienced through human suffering. It is a marriage of worship and self-condemnation, repentance and hope, punishment and mercy – and love for the human race. I know that later it was all distorted and adapted to serve the particular interests of particular power groups, but that is the fate of all universal ideas. Just think for yourself: which is more powerful – which is stronger and more compelling, and closer to our hearts – a Victim God, who submitted to execution, to crucifixion, for the sake of the Idea, or some completely superior being, an abstract idea, however contemporary the approach of that Being might be?'

'I've thought of that, Viktor Nikiforovich. You are right. But I cannot forsake the idea that the time has come to review the old idea of God, however stable it might have been, for it has long ceased to keep pace with the new discoveries we have made. That's obvious. Let's not quarrel. You may well be right that I'm working from an abstraction and searching for that which cannot be sought. So what? So what if my ideas are incompatible with the canons of theology? I can't change the way I am. I would be only too happy if someone could convince me otherwise.'

Gorodetsky shrugged understandingly.

'I understand you, Father Avdiy. But I do feel I should warn you that "God-seeking", as the Church authorities view it, is the worst possible crime against the Church, to be equated with an intention to turn the whole world upside-down.'

'I know,' said Avdiy calmly.

'And "God-seeking" is even more frowned upon in the secular world. Have you thought of that?'

'How paradoxical!' exclaimed Avdiy.

'Just wait and see . . .'

'But why? You mean they agree on this, at least?'

'It's not that they agree, just that for each of the sides it's something totally irrelevant.'

'Really? Then the only thing that has any relevance to our life is something regarded as completely irrelevant by both sides?'

'You're going to have a hard time of it, Father Avdiy. I don't envy you, but I won't try to stop you,' was Gorodetsky's final parting remark.

He was right. Absolutely right. It was some time later that Avdiy Kallistratov had the opportunity to convince himself of the fact.

The foregoing scene took place a short time before he was expelled from the seminary. That day an important figure, one Father Dimitriy, Patriarchal Co-ordinator for Educational Establishments, arrived at the local station to be met with great pomp by a delegation from the seminary rectorate. The seminarists knew him as Father Co-ordinator. As kind and sensible a middle-aged man as could be hoped for in such a position, Father Co-ordinator had come on this visit to sort out an extraordinary situation: one of the best of the young seminarists, Avdiy Kallistratov, had turned heretic, openly revising the Holy Scriptures and advocating some suspicious notion of a contemporary God. Of course, the Father Co-ordinator had come as mentor and peace-maker, to use the power of his authority to return the straying youth back into the bosom of the Church before news of all this spread beyond the seminary walls. In this respect the Church is very much like secular institutions, for whom 'keeping up appearances' is the first priority. If in Avdiy's place had been someone more experienced in the art of living, he would have perceived the Co-ordinator's fatherly intentions in this way; Avdiy, however, really, sincerely, did not understand the attempts of the distinguished churchman, which of course was hardly calculated to lighten the latter's task.

Avdiy was summoned to an interview with the Father Co-ordinator in the middle of the afternoon and spent at least three hours with him. At first the Father Co-ordinator proposed that they pray together at the altar of the college chapel, built in one of the halls of the main building.

'My son, you must have guessed that I have come for a serious talk with you. But let us not hurry; be so kind as to lead me to the altar of God,' said he, peering at Avdiy with his reddish, bulging eyes, 'for I feel that we should start by praying together.'

'Lord bless you, good Father, of course,' said Avdiy. 'At once. For me personally prayer is the counterpoint to my constant meditation on the Almighty. It is as though the thought of the contemporary God never left my mind.'

'Let us not be hasty, my son,' murmured the Father Co-ordinator discreetly as he rose from his chair. He even ignored the daring phrase about the 'contemporary God' and counterpoint; as an experienced cleric he wished to avoid starting off in a state of conflict. 'Let us pray together. I must say,' he continued, 'that the longer I live, the more I am convinced of the goodness of God and the infinite nature of His mercy. And I am grateful that the awareness of it is granted to us in the grace of selfless prayer. The forgiveness of the Lord is infinite. And truly, the Almighty is infinite in His love for us. Maybe for Him our prayers are but a frivolous murmur of sound, but for us they are our indivisible unity with Him.'

'You are right, Father,' murmured Avdiy, standing in the door.

And then, since he was young and green and impetuous, he did not leave the pause in the conversation which propriety would have demanded but played at once his trump card.

'I would, however, make so bold as to note that though God is infinite in our understanding, ideas on earth develop from perception to perception – which must, in its turn, lead us on to the idea that in God, too, there should be the perception of a development. What do you think, Father?'

At this point the Father Co-ordinator could not avoid an answer.

'You are very impetuous, my son,' he murmured, coughing drily and adjusting his heavy cassock. 'It is not for you to discuss God in this way, even taking into account your youthful fire. No man can know the pre-eternal Creator. He exists outside our being. Even materialist philosophy recognizes that the world exists independent of our awareness. How much more is that true of God.'

'Forgive me, Father, but it is better to call a spade a spade. There is no God independent of our awareness.'

'Are you convinced of that?'

'Yes, otherwise I would not be saying it.'

'Well, let's not cross all the "t"s and dot all the "i"s right from the first moment together. Let us instead hold a short academic discussion. We will return to it after we have prayed. But first, would you be so kind as to lead me into the chapel?'

The very fact that the Father Co-ordinator paid Avdiy the compliment of praying together in the college chapel should have been perceived by the latter as a sign of the former's good will; one would have expected a seminarist, threatened with expulsion, to make the most of this positive aspect of the situation in which he found himself.

They proceeded along the corridor, the Father Co-ordinator in front and Avdiy Kallistratov half a pace behind and to the side. Avdiy looked at the priest's upright posture and confident step and at the swinging black cassock that fell freely to the very floor and gave a special dignity to his figure, and could feel emanating therefrom that force, built up over the centuries, which in all human affairs (while protecting the canons of the faith) was first and foremost protecting its own narrow interests. It was this confronting force with which he would have to grapple in his search for truth in life. For the moment, however, they were both on the way to communion with the one in whom they both believed in their own ways, and for the sake of whom it was their duty to instil in others a shared approach to the world and the place of man therein. Both placed their hopes in Him and His omniscience and mercy. And so they advanced . . .

The college chapel was empty at that moment, and therefore seemed larger than it was. It was a chapel like any other, except perhaps for the image of the face of Christ in a frame of dark hair at the back of the darkened altar, whose penetrating, steady gaze was lit up in the gloom by the light of a small spotlight. The two kneeling men directed their eyes and their thoughts in His direction. One was the pastor and the other the young student, not yet relieved of the freedom to serve here. Each of them had come in the hope of personal communion with Him, for He could converse at any time of the day or night simultaneously with an infinite number of those desiring His presence, if necessary with the whole of humanity at any point of the globe and at any one time. Such was His omnipresence.

And so it was here: as they prayed, both of them strove to express their anxiety and their sadness, and to justify their actions as resulting from faith in Him. Both tried to place themselves within the universe as they perceived it, a universe in which they occupied such a tiny space for such a fleeting moment of time, and each of them, as he made the sign of the cross, thanked the Creator for giving him life and sought the grace, whenever the end should come, to die with His name on their lips . . .

Then they went back to the study, and had an open talk, man to man.

'Listen, my son, I do not intend to lecture you,' began the Father Co-ordinator, settling comfortably into the leather armchair opposite Avdiy Kallistratov who sat meekly on an upright chair, hands on the bony knees that poked upwards through the grey material of his seminarist's suit.

Avdiy was prepared for a stiff chat, and was somewhat startled by this approach. In the eyes of the Father Co-ordinator he could discern neither anger nor any other unkind motive; on the contrary, the Father seemed on the surface of it to be a picture of calm.

'Yes, Father,' said the seminarist dutifully.

'So, as I said, I do not intend to scold you or tell you off. Such primitive methods of getting a reaction are not for the likes of you. But we cannot help being disappointed in the utterances which you are allowing yourself to make, less from frivolity than from an impetuous nature, I feel sure. You have probably noticed that I am speaking with you as with an equal. Moreover, you have a fine mind . . . I will be open with you: it is in the Church's interests that this fine mind of yours should work not against the Church's teaching, but as one with her for the fulfilment of God's will. I will not try to conceal that fact. Of course I could simply have boxed your ears in fatherly affection, since I was an old friend of your late parent and we loved and understood one another. He was a man of true Christian virtues, and an educated man as well. And now fate has brought me together with you, Avdiy, son of the late Innokentiy Kallistratov, for many years deacon of the Church, to put it officially. And why? To be frank, I heard a lot of positive things about you at first, but (as you must realize) it is alarming circumstances that have brought me here today. So you've set out to revise the tenets of the faith although, if we examine your status, you are only a student of the Church. From the few things you happen to have said to me, I have already realized that your mistakes are a function of your youth. Or so I would like to think. The fact is that for all sorts of reasons youth goes hand in hand with a kind of presump-tuousness that comes out in different ways with different people, depending on their temperament and the way they were brought up. Have you ever heard of an elderly man, one who has known his share of life's torments, losing his faith in God towards the end of his life or starting to reinterpret the concept of Him in his own way? No, for if it ever does happen, it happens extremely rarely. Age is the key to a deeper and deeper perception of the essence of the divine. All those European philosophers, like the so-called "Encyclopédistes" in France, who started in their troubled pre-revolutionary times the atheistic movement that was to take religion by storm and that has been on the attack for almost three hundred years by now – were they not all, by the way, young men?'

'Yes, Father, they were,' agreed Avdiy.

'So you see, then! Doesn't that prove that it's natural for the young to be what I believe is fashionable to call extremists, simply because that is one of the attributes of youth?'

'Why yes, Father, but is it not also true that those young people whom you have characterized as extremists could be said, in all fairness, to have held convictions that were not ill-founded?' insisted Avdiy.

'Most certainly, most certainly,' the Father Co-ordinator hastened to agree, 'but that's another question. In any case, they were not priests. Their attitude to religion was their own business, whereas you, my son, are a future priest.'

'Then it's all the more relevant,' interrupted Avdiy, 'since people will be expected to have total confidence in me and my knowledge of things divine.'

'Don't hurry,' frowned the Father Co-ordinator. 'If you have no intention of turning to your own advantage the sense of what I was saying, for your own good I might add, then let us look at it another way. First: you are neither the first nor the last to be seized by the spirit of contradiction as you tread the path that leads to faith. Doubters like you are no novelty to the Church. But what of it? There are costs to be borne in every great undertaking. These transient moments, these chances of fate, have always been and will always be. The important thing is that the outcome is always inexorably the same: either the doubter puts his doubts decisively behind him and turns with even greater zeal and fervour to the strictest acceptance of the one true faith, from which follows the forgiveness of the Fathers Superior; or, if he persists in his dissent, then he is ejected as a heretic from the bosom of the Church and anathematized. Do you see that there is no third path, that any possibility of a third path is totally excluded? Your innovations could never be accepted. Do you understand that?'

'Yes, Father, but as I see it, it is not me, but the Church itself that needs a third path.'

'Well, well!' the Father Co-ordinator shook his head with a mocking smile. 'What rubbish you are talking!' Then he added maliciously, 'Then perhaps you would be so kind as to tell us what sort of a third path you have planned out for the Holy Church? Some sort of revolution, I suppose? Never heard of such a thing in my life . . .'

'It would involve overcoming her long-standing ossification, freeing her from dogmatism, offering the human spirit liberation in the knowledge of God as the highest essence of its own being . . .'

'Stop, stop!' protested the Father Co-ordinator. 'Your amateur theology is making me laugh, dear boy.'

'Well, if you discount all independence of thought *per se*, Father, then I'm afraid there's no point in our continuing.'

'I quite agree – no point at all!' stated the Father Co-ordinator hotly, and rose from his seat. His voice was booming. 'Come to your senses, young man, and reject your pride!

71

You are on the road to perdition! You imagine, wretched creature, that God is but the fruit of your imagination, thereby making man a god over God; in fact our mind itself is created by the power of heaven. Give rein to innovation and you will negate thousands of years of commandments and prohibitions, so dearly paid for in insights and suffering, so as to pass divine principles down from generation unto generation. That's the way you're going with your demands for liberation from dogmatism, when dogmas are given us by the grace of God. The Church can continue to stand perfectly well without innovation, but without dogma there can be no passing down of the faith. If it comes to this, remember: dogmatism is the primary support of all regulations and all authority. Just you remember that. While trying to improve God by your innovations, you are in fact ignoring Him. And you are prepared to replace Him with yourself. However, since God's treatment of the human race does not depend upon you and the likes of you, your blasphemy will destroy no one but yourself. The Lord will remain unchanging and eternal! Amen.'

Avdiy Kallistratov stood white-lipped before the Father Co-ordinator, tormented by the indignation which bubbled within him. Even so, he did not retreat.

'Forgive me, Father, but it's wrong to ascribe to the powers of heaven that which proceeds from us ourselves. Why should God have created us so imperfect if He could have prevented us, His creation, from combining simultaneously within ourselves two opposing forces, the force of good and the force of evil? Why should He need to make us so prone to doubts, to vices and to perfidy, even in our dealings with Him Himself? You call for an absolute in the dogmas of faith, for a view of the essence of the world and of our spirit that is settled once and for all, but that's illogical – can it really be that after two thousand years of Christianity we are not capable of adding a single word to what was said in almost pre-biblical times? You call for a monopoly on truth, but that is self-delusion at the very least since there can be no teaching which shows us the truth, once and for all, and the whole truth – even if revealed by God. And if there were, it would be dead dogma, not the living Word.'

He fell silent, and through the windows came the sound of

the bells in the town's church. The sound was so distant and so close to his heart, the symbolic link between man and God, that Avdiy wanted to float away, to fade and disappear, like the sound of the bells, into the infinite . . .

'You're going a bit too far, young man,' said the Father Co-ordinator in a cold and distant voice. 'I was wrong to enter into a philosophical discussion with you, for your knowledge is immature and even somewhat suspect, since I cannot help wondering whether perhaps you aren't speaking at the insti-gation of the enemy of the human race, the Devil himself. One thing, however, I will say in parting: you're going to come to grief sooner or later with those ideas of yours, because in the secular world too they have no truck with those who question and doubt the principles of any teaching from whatever sphere. Every ideology claims to have the last word on truth, and that's a fact you're bound to come up against sooner or later. Life out in the secular world is much harsher than you might think: you'll yet find yourself paying for your stupidity and then you'll remember what I said to you. Anyway, that's enough. Get ready to leave the seminary, you're going to be excommunicated from the Church.'

'The Church will be with me always,' answered Avdiy, insistent to the last. 'My Church is my own self. I don't recognize the stones and mortar that call themselves churches, and I certainly don't recognize the clergy, especially in the state in which we find it today.'

'Well, boy, pray God that all will be well, but one thing you can be sure of: the secular world will teach you obedience, for out there you have to deal with the vital necessity of earning your daily bread. It's that necessity that up to now has ruled the lives of millions like you . . .'

Later Avdiy did indeed have occasion, and more than once, to remember these warnings, but each time he was convinced that the purpose to which he had been born, the higher meaning of his life, lay still in the future, like the line of the visible horizon; that all his troubles and adversities on the way to it were temporary and that the day would dawn when many would follow his example, as was surely the object of his existence.

During those days, as he travelled with the *anasha*-runners

73

towards the hemp-fields, staring through the windows of the train from morning till night at the empty wastes of the steppe, he told himself: Now, you're on your own, nothing to tie you down but your instructions from the newspaper. As far as everything else is concerned, you're free to do exactly as you wish. Well, what have you revealed in your road to Calvary? Here's life as it really is, and you're sitting face to face with it. This scene can't have changed much in a hundred years, people travelling across the country in a train; you're just one of the thousands of passengers. And so are the runners, passengers like any others, though potentially they're desperate men, for after all they're living like parasites on one of life's most terrible vices. That bitter smoke may seem innocuous, a passing sweet intoxication, but it destroys the human in a man. How are you going to help them, when they willingly sacrifice themselves? Do you know what the causes are? Why they do it? Haven't got an answer, have you. You don't even know where to start, how to explain it, what to do. Weren't you desperate to escape from the seminary into the rapids of life, to do your bit and change things for the better even in the smallest way? But now you're wondering whether these runners really do need your help, need you meddling in what they're doing. What can you do for them, anyway? Change their minds, make them live their lives some other way? And while you squirm here, wondering what to do and how to do it, they're travelling east with a firm purpose in mind, thirsty for success and convinced that when they achieve it, they'll find happiness into the bargain. How can you change their minds, how can you make them see the truth? If you don't interfere, if you don't help, they'll end up in prison camps sooner or later and see it not as a punishment they deserve but as bad luck for getting caught. It would be different if you were able to turn them away from evil, to purify them with repentance and persuade them to renounce for themselves this criminal way of earning a living and find happiness in something else. Wouldn't that be wonderful! But where are they supposed to find their happiness? In the values we proclaim from every rooftop? They've all been devalued and debased! In God, who since childhood has been nothing more to them than a fairy-tale, something to laugh at the old people for? And what can you do with words

74

when you're up against the possibility of big money, easily earned? The money earned by the runners probably includes money coming in from abroad, to judge by the number of runners from the ports, from Murmansk, Odessa, the Baltic, even the Pacific coast, so they say. Where does it end up, the *anasha*, the products of 'plasticine' and 'extra'? And anyway, the point is not where it ends up but why it's happening at all, how such a thing is possible in a society like ours which has announced to the whole world that under a socialist system vice becomes an impossibility? If only I could write something, something that would get a reaction from thousands and thousands of people, people who would treat it as something of intimate concern to them personally, as a fire in their own house, a misfortune affecting their own children, only then could the Word, caught up by thousands of people, none of them indifferent, overcome the power of profit and triumph over vice! God grant that it should go that way, and His words not be in vain: if it is true that 'In the beginning was the Word', then let the Word retain its primeval power . . . That would truly be something to live by . . .

But, God, I turn to Thee again: what is the Word, when pitted against the jingle of money? What is my call, when pitted against a secret vice? How can the Word overcome material evil? Lord, give me strength, do not desert me on the way. I am alone for the moment, alone, while they, obsessed with the chance of turning a fast rouble, their name is legion . . .

Leaving behind Saratov, the Moscow–Alma-Ata train was into its second day of travel through Kazakhstan. Avdiy Kallistratov, in the Turanian region of the continent for the first time in his life, was amazed at the size of this country that had once been left as an empty space on the maps of the old Russian Empire. The distance stretched away as far as the eye and the imagination could see: taken together with Siberia, he thought, it's almost half a world of land . . . The settlements were so few and far between . . . Towns, villages and *auls*, stations, junctions, the odd barns and houses, clung to the railway, like isolated brushstrokes on the endless canvas of the steppe, a canvas just touched by colour here and there, but for the most part left the monotonous grey of the raw surface . . . The open steppe stretched in all directions, covered at this season with the grasses, great and small, that flower to perfection, transforming the face of the earth for a few days, to wither beneath the merciless sun and spend the rest of the year awaiting the return of spring . . .

Through the open windows of the carriage they could smell the strong scents of the flowering steppe grasses. These were especially powerful when the train stopped at some tiny halt, open to the steppe on all four sides; you wanted to leap out of the airless carriage and run free through the grass, so unimportant to look at but so heady with the smell of sap and the dryness of the earth. Strange, thought Avdiy, can it really be that the accursed *anasha* also grows so freely and smells so tempting? Even stranger, they said, though the main thing was that the *anasha* was tall-stemmed, growing almost to waist height. It did not grow just anywhere: you had to search it out – and thank God that was so, thought Avdiy . . . And so the runners travelled from the distant coastal cities, from one end of the world to the other, mesmerized by their search for the intoxicating grass . . . They were still nowhere near their objective, and there was no telling what success they would enjoy, what would become of them.

Sometimes Avdiy forgot for a while the purpose of his secret journey and sat imagining the time when men first settled these parts, remembering all that he had read in books and seen in films as a schoolboy; each time he saw evidence of a vanishing age, his heart leapt, be it a herd of brown camels, cemeteries with domed tombs scattered over the steppe like abandoned cities, small *auls* and nomads' tents, now and then even a real yurt, all alone as far as the eye could see. He shuddered at the thought of people living so isolated in this ancient form of habitation. Sometimes they saw horsemen, alone or in groups, some of them in pointed hats as in days of old, their horses still wearing the ancient harness . . . He found himself thinking: How could people have lived here for so many generations and not died of loneliness and drought on these enormous plains? What is it like in the dark? What does a man feel when face to face with the universe at night? He must tremble at the awareness that he is completely alone in these untrammelled wastes and find the sound of passing trains a comfort rather than an annoyance as it is in the big city. On the other hand, the grandeur of the night in the steppe might give birth to poetry, for what is poetry if not the self-assertion of the human spirit in the vastness of our world?

Such considerations did not distract him for long from the thought that he was travelling on the *anasha*-run, consorting (from the legal point of view) with criminals and having, for the sake of the ethical and sociological report that he wanted to write for the newspaper, to tolerate their life and the evil which they bore within them. He suddenly felt a sinking feeling in the pit of his stomach, a vague sense of alarm, as though he really were one of the runners himself, one of those who were caught up in this criminal venture. Now at last he understood the inner state of those who live with a secret burden on their soul; he realized that however vast our earth, however joyful new impressions, none of it has anything to offer either our minds or our hearts if there is even the slightest ulcer on our conscience, for it will gradually poison both our attitude to ourselves and our relationship with the outside world. When he studied the runners whose journey to the hemp-steppes he was sharing and tried to draw them out into frank conversation, Avdiy could see that in spite of their seeming self-assurance each of his companions must be to some degree oppressed by his way of life and by the constant fear of inexorable retribution. Avdiy was sorry for them. Only thus could he explain their bravado, their aggressive and exclusive slang, their cards and vodka, their 'all or nothing' daring, for there was no other way that they could possibly live their lives, given the circumstances. Avdiy longed to liberate them from the power of vice, emancipate them, open their eyes to what they were doing to themselves, free them from the eternal persecution of fear that poisoned their lives like some venom released into the air. He summoned up all his knowledge and extensive, if hardly rich, experience and strove to find a way to achieve his lofty aims. Only now did he understand that although he had left the seminary and broken with the official Church, in his heart he still wanted to preach (in the sense of bringing to men the word of truth and goodness as he understood it), and that this was the greatest good he could ever achieve in his life. He did not need Holy Orders for that; he simply needed to be faithful to that which he worshipped. He still did not completely realize what his mind and his heart were drawing him into, led on by the best of intentions. It is one thing to have noble dreams and in them to save others from vice, and quite another to do good amongst actual people, people who have no desire to be shown the way of virtue by some Avdiy, just another runner doing the steppe trip, just like them, to make a quick rouble. What was it to them that Avdiy Kallistratov was obsessed with the noble desire to transform their lives by the power of the Word – for he firmly believed that the Word was God and for the Word to fulfil its divine function, it must issue forth from a truth that is authentic and irreproachable? He believed that to be a universal law, but one thing he did not yet understand: evil will resist good, even when good is trying to come to the aid of those who have embarked on the road of evil . . . That he had yet to learn . . .

6

The humped flanks of snowy mountains that appeared at dawn on the fourth day showed the train to be nearing the steppes around the Chu river and the Moyun-Kum desert. The mountains were only a milestone on the way; they, too, would sink back beneath the horizon once the train was out in the spacious steppe that was their ultimate destination. Now the sun was rising on the edge of the world, illuminating the scene with peaceful light as it did every morning, and the train, a glittering necklace of carriages filled with so many different kinds of people, turned on to the plain, pushing on through the heat mirages until the mountains could be seen no more.

At a station called Zhalpak-Saz the runners had to leave the train and make their way further as best they could, each one for himself but working as a team. A team . . . That was what occupied Avdiy's thoughts most of all. Who was the one they called 'Sam', 'himself', the leader of all these gangs, the unblinking eye that followed them all the way and of whom they rarely spoke and always in a half-whisper?

There were about three hours left to Zhalpak-Saz. The runners were beginning to pack their things. Petrukha annoyed the other passengers by monopolizing the washroom for a long time while he eliminated the traces of last night's session with the vodka before going off to Sam for last-minute instructions. The session had begun for him and his friends with champagne, drunk by the tooth-mug full as though it were lemonade, and gone on to vodka. The effect was tangible. Young Lyonka had been completely overcome, and it was all Avdiy could do to get him back on his feet. Only the fact that they would soon be in Zhalpak-Saz made Lyonka pull himself together and sit up on the wooden seat, his unkempt head lolling on his weak and dirty neck. Nobody wold have thought that this young lad was earning his big money illegally, or that his life was already stamped with the seal of perdition.

The train was travelling smoothly and easily through the flat, featureless steppe, and somewhere, in one of the carriages, sat Sam. Petrukha, still wild-eyed from the night before, swilled down a glass of tarry black tea as a final measure for sobering up and hurried off for instructions. Evidently Sam had little sympathy for those who drank. Since Moscow Avdiy had not succeeded in catching so much as a glimpse of Sam, even from a distance, in spite of their travelling in the same train. Who was he? What did he look like? No way of guessing, out of the hundreds of passengers. Whoever he was, he was as wary as a reed-bird, lurking in the thickets, never giving himself away at all throughout the journey. Soon Petrukha returned from his interview with Sam, tail between his legs, silent, snappy and looking much less cocky. Somewhat naturally, Sam had come down on him with a stream of strong language for getting drunk the very night before they were due to arrive. Of course, he was right; the real work would start the moment they reached Zhalpak-Saz, and that blockhead Petrukha had drunk so much that it would take him a week to get over his hangover. Glancing automatically at Avdiy as though it were somehow his fault, Petrukha growled, 'C'mon out, I've got something to say.'

They went to the end of the carriage and lit a cigarette. They could hear the sound of the wheels below.

'Right, then, you, Avdiy, listen here, and just remember this,' started Petrukha.

'Yes, right . . .' frowned Avdiy.

'And you can take that stupid look off your face,' snarled Petrukha. 'Who are you, anyway?'

'Hey, come off it, Petrukha.' Avdiy tried to calm him down. 'Why take on like this? OK, so I don't drink and you like a drop, but is that the end of the world? You'd do better to tell us what the plan is.'

'The plan is whatever Sam says.'

'That's what I mean. What does Sam say?'

'That you're new, so you don't have much to do,' answered Petrukha brusquely. 'You'll go with Lyonka and me, the three of us together. The others'll go in ones and twos.'

'Right. But go where?'

'Don't you worry yourself about that, you'll go with me. We'll get off at Zhalpak-Saz, then it'll be up to us. We can hitch rides as far as the Moyun-Kum state farm, and from there it's entirely uninhabited – you'll have to go the rest of the way on foot.'

'On foot?'

'Well, what were you expecting – a chauffeur-driven Lada or something? Oh, no, friend! Out there, anyone they notice they might nab, and if you've got a car or a motorbike you stick out a mile!'

'Well, well! But what about Sam? Where'll he be? Who'll he go with?'

'What's that to you?' interjected Petrukha indignantly. 'Why d'you keep asking about him? Where'll he be, who'll he go with . . . Maybe he won't be there at all! Have you been told to keep tabs on him or something?'

'Of course not. But since he's the boss, we ought to know where to find him, just in case.'

'That's just what you don't need to know,' announced Petrukha, lapsing into a significant silence as he evaluated the effect of his words; then he looked straight into Avdiy's eyes with a steady gaze still glazed from last night. 'Sam had a special message for you, Avdiy: if you work well, then you can become a permanent member of the team; but if you're going to let us down when the going gets tough, then you'd better quit now. Got it? When we get out at the station, you can slink off, we won't come after you; but if you're in this with us, that's it – no going back. If you let us down, we'll get you wherever you try to hide. Got it?'

'Got it? Of course I've got it. What is there to get?' answered Avdiy.

'Right, then, just for the record: I gave you the message, and you heard. Just so there's no mistake, no "Sorry, I didn't understand, please forgive me just this once" and that kind of thing.'

'All right, Petrukha, that's enough,' interrupted Avdiy. 'No need to go on and on. I know what I'm getting into and I know what I'm doing. Now this time, you just listen to me. Give it up, now and for ever, and stop teaching Lyonka to drink. He doesn't know any better. Why do you drink? Here we go, off into the heat of the day, open country and a splitting hangover – what kind of runners will we make in this state?'

'OK,' said Petrukha roughly and he smiled with relief, a grimace on his wet lips. 'You're right. OK, Avdiy, I won't touch a drop more and I won't let Lyonka either. That's it. Finito!'

They stood silent, both gratified that their chat had shown sense to both sides. The train rumbled on towards the junction of Zhalpak-Saz, where it would have a change of locomotive and drivers. Many of the passengers were due to leave it here, and they were already packed up. Lyonka glanced worriedly out to where they were sitting.

'What are you up to out there?' he asked, frowning at his splitting headache. 'You ought to be packing up. We'll be there in an hour.'

'Don't worry,' replied Petrukha. 'We haven't got much to pack. No ten dozen travelling trunks for us, eh, Avdiy? Rucksack on your back, and you're ready for off!'

'Lyonka . . .' Avdiy called the boy over. 'Come here a minute. Head ache?' Lyonka nodded sheepishly. 'Petrukha and I've decided that from now on, not a drop. Agreed?' Again Lyonka nodded in silence. 'Right, then, off you go and we'll be right with you. Don't worry, we'll be on time.'

'There's still loads of time,' said Petrukha, glancing at his watch. 'A whole hour and more.' Once Lyonka was gone, he said, 'You were right, there, about Lyonka. It's him, he's the one who wants it, but once he's had a glass or two he can't keep on his feet. Anyway, it's all off now. Business is business. That was just a little indulgence for the road. And don't worry, I wasn't letting Lyonka pay for any of my drinks, I don't know if he . . . But I pay my own way!'

'No, of course not, that's not the point at all,' answered Avdiy bitterly. 'It just seems a shame that he's so young . . .'

'You're right,' sighed Petrukha judiciously. This frank exchange must have brought to mind for Petrukha some idea that had been at the back of his mind for a long time. 'Hey, Avdiy, before, like . . . I mean before us, what did you do for a living? I mean, where did you work? Maybe you were buying and selling, speculating, like? Don't be shy now, you know from now on it's either celebrating together at the same table, or sharing the same toilet bucket in a prison cell, eh? Doesn't worry me what you did before.'

Avdiy didn't try to conceal the truth.

'No, I wasn't speculating. I'm not shy. I was a student in the seminary before.'

Petrukha was presumably expecting nothing of the sort.

'What? What? The seminary? You mean, like, you were learning to be a priest? Incense, cassock, all that stuff?'

'Yeah, that's just about the size of it . . .'

'We-ell . . .' Petrukha's eyes bulged and he gave a fatuous whistle. 'Why did you leave, then? Or were you kicked out?'

'Both, really. But mostly the former.'

'But why? Wouldn't they give you a big enough slice of God, or something?' joked Petrukha. 'Well, there's a laugh and a half!'

'Yes, I suppose that's just about the size of it.'

'Well, since it seems you're in the know – is there a God, then?'

'Well, that's a hard one to answer, Petrukha. There is for some, but not for others. It all depends on the person. But for as long as man exists, he's going to wonder if there's a God or not.'

'Well, Avdiy, suppose there is: where is he, then?'

'In our thoughts and in our words.'

Petrukha fell silent, digesting what he had heard. The wheels clattered louder and more insistently through the door between carriages which some passenger had left open. Petrukha closed the door and listened to the deadened noise, then said at last, 'So I suppose there isn't for me. What about you, Avdiy? Is there or isn't there?'

'I don't know, Petrukha. I'd like to think there was. I'd like there to be . . .'

'So it's something you feel the lack of. . . ?'

'Yes, it's something I feel the lack of very badly . . .'

'I don't understand you, then,' grumbled Petrukha. Evidently something was bugging him. 'What effing business have you got coming out here with us if it's God you're looking for?'

Avdiy decided that this was neither the time nor the place to go deeper into this matter.

'Well, everyone needs money,' he said placatingly.

'Ah, so that's it, is it? This way God, that way easy money. The money seems to be getting the upper hand!'

'Yes, it does for the moment,' Avdiy had to admit.

This exchange gave Avdiy a lot of food for thought. In the first place, it was now quite clear that Sam, who kept the runners' journey under his personal control from start to finish, was extremely suspicious and cautious. He was obviously ruthless as well, and if he had any reason to suppose all was not well with some link in the chain of the operation he was managing, he would stop at nothing to inflict retribution or to assure the safety of himself and those whom he protected. What else would you expect from a drug-running organization? The second thing which he had understood from conversations in the train with Petrukha and others was that there was some hope of acting upon the runners by means of the Word. The way to 'preach' to them was to talk his way into their confidence, without a thought for the danger to himself in this. After all, selfless missionaries had taken the Word of Christ to the wild tribes of Africa, risking their lives, and who knows? The saving of souls at the price of his own life might turn out to be the final reckoning, the fate determined for him, the *raison d'être* of his journey through life . . . his way of saving his own soul.

They reached Zhalpak-Saz at about eleven in the morning. It was a junction where many people changed trains on to the two lines which led away in the direction of the distant snowy mountains they had glimpsed in the light of dawn. For that reason there was always a big crowd at the station, an extremely convenient circumstance for the runners since they could lose themselves in it all the more easily. Avdiy was amazed how little time and effort it took for them to penetrate the canteen beside the station, even though it was the start of the lunch hour. There seemed to be about twelve of them, including Avdiy, all ready to set off into the steppe in search of *anasha*. They sat at different tables, in ones and twos, but within sight of one another although they did not speak openly together and were indistinguishable from the rest of the crowd – there were several boys like Lyonka and older ones like Petrukha as well. The place was full of other travellers, at the height of the season, a typical mixture of Asiatic and European faces . . . Although every now and then a policeman would glance to make sure all was in order, and although the station itself was crawling with policemen, no one seemed ruffled by the fact. They ate fast, for there was a long queue of others keen to sample the dishes of the day, and then at some subtle sign they melted away, each with his own piece of luggage: one a soldier's kit-bag, another a briefcase, all containing bread and tinned food and the other things they would need. And so the runners dispersed into the infinite distances of the Moyun-Kum steppe.

Petrukha set off with Avdiy and Lyonka, as decided and sanctioned by Sam (whom Avdiy had still not seen). He did know now, however, that Sam was invisibly directing the whole of the operation. Petrukha's little group had the furthest distance to go, almost all the way to the actual desert which gives the Moyun-Kum steppe its name. For twenty-five roubles, paid by Petrukha out of the money issued to them by Sam, a passing truck took them to the Uchkuduk state farm. They made up a story, in case they needed a cover: they were to be labourers looking for casual work on the farms thereabouts. Avdiy was a carpenter, the most useful of all trades in these parts, and indeed there was some truth in his cover: he really was a passable carpenter, for his father had taught him to work in wood from the time when he was a very small boy. Petrukha placed in his kit-bag some simple instruments – a plane, an axe and a chisel – which he had brought from home for the purpose. He and Lyonka were painters and plasterers, supposedly on holiday from training school and looking for seasonal work at the Uchkuduk farm in the Moyun-Kum steppe, hoping to make some money on the new houses that were being built. It all sounded very convincing.

The noon heat was up, but in the open back of the truck they were better off – not so hot, and a cool breeze on their faces. The road, like every country track, was all pot-holes and cracks.

When the truck slowed down to negotiate a particularly

large imperfection in the surface of the road, the wheels threw up dust in such quantities that they flapped their arms about and coughed for long afterwards. The only thing that made the journey a pleasure was the landscape around.

'What's the vital need,' thought Avdiy, 'that sends people seeking out poison for themselves and for others? What prompts them to it? And what are they left with, if they renounce their own higher selves?'

In the distant and God-forsaken Kazakh village of Uchku-duk, they did indeed find work, and straight away. They signed on for a couple of days as carpenter and plasterers in an unfinished house that a herdsman was having built for himself. The herdsman himself was away with the flocks at the summer pastures, his family with him, and a neighbour who was also related had been charged with the task of hiring casual workers to carry on building if any should turn up as they had the previous year. The three young runners, Petrukha, Avdiy and Lyonka, fitted the bill exactly.

They lived in the house they were helping to build, since the roof was already on and the weather was hot. They built a fire in the yard and even did some cooking. There was no pretence when it came to hard work. Petrukha rose first and woke his 'colleagues', Avdiy and Lyonka, and they worked right through until darkness fell, when they dined by the light of the fire. Only then did Petrukha allow himself to relax and chat a little.

'Hey, Avdiy, I can see that you're happy doing this kind of work. Of course, we'll get something for our work, the going rate. But for guys like us, you know, money like that is peanuts. We're just doing it for a smokescreen. As soon as we get going, find a good place where you can gather it in hand over hand, then we'll really be set up: just a day's work in the steppe and you can live like a minister for a whole year! You know, don't you, Lyonka! It's true, isn't it?'

'Yeah, I know,' answered Lyonka, who was turning more and more laconic.

'Only look, lads' – this was a stern warning – 'not a word to anyone, not this neighbour, nor any of the locals, they're kind people, but still . . . Whatever happens, not a word. Especially if anyone turns up and starts asking questions. Say

86

they ask you, Avdiy; all you have to say is, "Listen, I know nothing, see that guy over there? Well, he's the boss, I'm just one of the team, why don't you talk to him?" Got it?'

What could Avdiy answer to that? 'Yes, got it, of course . . .' He was troubled by something else, by the fact that he was forced to keep his counsel, forced to forgo the attempt to influence in some way these lads as they stepped out on to the slippery path, desperate at any price to carry off their criminal profit. His heart was longing to make the attempt, but he could not risk it. Even if Avdiy succeeded in shaking their convictions by the power of word or thought, if he made them think what they were doing to themselves, even if the two of them did heed the voice of reason and decide to break with this way of life, they would not dare to. It would be completely impossible, simply because they were gripped tightly in the vice of a mutual guarantee in which others were involved, others who had the unwritten right to punish them for any breach of trust. How could he break into the vicious circle? Avdiy's only consolation was that he could serve a worthy cause by using his personal exerience of the ways of the *anasha*-runners to raise a storm in the newspapers that would open the eyes of ordinary people to what was going on. On that he pinned his hopes for the first shot in the battle for the soul of that section of the country's youth that had gone astray. Only in this could Avdiy come to terms with the fact that he was now unwittingly a part of their system, a member of Petrukha's group.

On the third day after their arrival in Uchkuduk something insignificant enough took place. Avdiy thought no more about it, but when Petrukha learned what had happened, he became extremely agitated. Petrukha had been absent at the time. The old neighbour, a war veteran, had given him a lift in his invalid-car to the farm shop to buy tins, cigarettes and sugar since they were moving off into the steppe at first light the next day – supposedly to look for work somewhere else.

Lyonka was finishing off the plastering indoors and Avdiy had found a shady part of the yard to make a door for the shed. When he heard the sound of a motorbike from the street, Avdiy looked round, shading his eyes with his hand. A huge bike had stopped by the house and stood there throbbing. The rider vaulted lightly from the saddle and, to Avdiy's astonishment, turned out to be a young woman. How on earth did she manage to control that enormous bike, and on roads like these? The woman pulled off her helmet, the strap hanging by one side, then removed her goggles and shook out her thick fair hair on to her shoulders.

'It's so hot!' she smiled, revealing a row of white teeth. 'And so dusty, my goodness me!' she added joyfully, dusting herself down. 'Hello!'

'Hello,' muttered Avdiy sheepishly, at once mindful of all Petrukha's ridiculous instructions. Who is she? Why's she here? he thought.

'Is the boss at home?' she asked, with the same friendly smile.

'What boss?' asked Avdiy, at a loss to understand. 'You mean the man who owns the house?'

'Yes, of course.'

'He's apparently not here at the moment, he's gone off to the summer pastures.'

'Oh, so you haven't seen him then?'

'That's right. Well, I caught a glimpse of him, he dropped by. But not to speak to.'

'You didn't speak to him? Strange! After all, you are building his house for him, aren't you?'

'Sorry, but there just wasn't time. He was in a hurry, I think. My own boss talked to him. Petrukha. He's not here at the moment, either, but he'll be back soon.'

'No, never mind, I'm sorry to have bothered you. I just wanted to see Orman – he's the herdsman, he knows what I'm after. So I dropped by since I was passing anyway. I thought I'd catch him here. Well, sorry I've been taking you away from your work.'

'No, not at all.'

She put back her helmet, the strap still hanging down, started up the engine, and as she rode off she glanced at Avdiy through her goggles and gave a little nod. Avdiy waved in answer, automatically. For a long time he could not take his mind off the apparently fortuitous and insignificant event. His thoughts were nothing to do with suspicion of her motives for this unannounced visit on the eve of their departure for the happy hunting grounds, or fears that she might have come to sniff around; no, he was thinking of something completely different. Long after she disappeared in a cloud of dust he could still see her, all the visual details, as though he had made a conscious decision to remember her for ever. He now noticed, with pleasure, how pleasing her figure was: not too tall, just slightly taller than average, but as feminine and well proportioned as he could ever hope for. No, really, no kidding, he said to himself, as though arguing with someone. That's how a woman ought to look. That's just how a woman ought to look! Avdiy remembered her unusually fine features, the inner light in her face, and the shining eyes so dark brown that they were almost black, although the hair that framed her face and fell loosely on to her shoulders was very fair. The combination of dark eyes and fair hair was particularly charming. Everything about her pleased him: the tiny, hardly noticeable scar on her left cheek (perhaps she had fallen in childhood?), the suitable way she was dressed (jeans, jacket, worn boots with the calves turned down) and the confidence with which she handled the bike (Avdiy could hardly ride a pedal bike). He had been so much at a loss as to what to say, when she asked about the boss, saying at first that he'd seen him, then that he hadn't, then that he had . . . Just like a little boy! But why had he been so embarrassed?

Avdiy very much enjoyed thinking about her, although there was hardly much to remember – she came, and then she suddenly left again, and that was all. But who was she? Where was she from? She did not look like a local, and what was a woman like that doing out here in the back of beyond?

When Petrukha heard that a strange woman on a motorbike had dropped by he was really worried and went over and over the same ground again and again: What did she say? What was she trying to find out? What had Avdiy said to her? He had to repeat their exchange, word for word, several times over.

'There's more to this than meets the eye,' repeated Petrukha suspiciously. 'What a pity I wasn't there, I'd have sniffed her out at once. Look, Avdiy, you may be clever and all that, but I'd have done better than you in this case; I'd have asked her the questions, if it came to that. I'd have found out who she was and what she wanted, while you, friend, seem to have lost your head, even though I warned you specifically that something of the sort might happen.'

'What's so terrible?' Avdiy tried to reason with him. 'What's happened to put the wind up you in this way?'

'The fact that they might put the sniffer-dogs on to us. The fact that she might have been sent to snoop round a bit and report back!'

'What rubbish!'

'I'd like to hear you say that when you're sitting behind bars or when Sam's asking questions, and Sam's a tougher customer than the sniffer-dogs; he'll have your hide off you, or worse. Do you understand what I mean by worse?'

'Calm down, Petrukha, what will be, will be. We should have thought of all that before. Look at Lyonka – he's still a baby, who got him mixed up in all this? Or look at yourself – how old are you? Twenty yet? And there you are, scared to take a step or say a word for fear of crossing Sam. You'd do better to think of where it's all going to lead to, that's what you should be thinking about.'

But Avdiy's words had no effect, except to get Petrukha's back up.

'You cut that out, Avdiy, and forget about Lyonka. You might have been studying to join the Kiss-the-Cross squad, forget about it now. Forget it. Your fine words don't bring in a kopeck, but with Sam we're all raking it in. Got it? Lyonka's an orphan, nobody cares a fig about what happens to him, but with money he's a somebody. He can pay for anything he wants. You can't fill a belly with your sermons, let alone take out all your friends, sit them down at a restaurant table groaning with food and drink and have the girl with the band sing specially for you, sing so your heart aches with it . . . Look at my brothers, real workers, high earners, but if you saw the way they have to slave for their money! They break their backs all day – while I could wipe my bum with rouble notes, if I wanted to. It's only a fool who's indifferent to money, eh, Lyonka?'

'Right,' nodded Lyonka, smiling a smile of beatific confidence.

For Avdiy this was no more than the lead in to the more serious talk that he wanted to have when the opportunity presented itself, though he realized that he must not go too far or he would lose his credibility as an *anasha*-runner, desperate to make quick money.

The next day they were up with first light brightening the sky at the eastern edge of the world. The scattered houses of the village were still sound asleep and not even a dog barked as the three runners slipped by the back paths out into the open steppe. Petrukha had said that they did not have far to go – he knew what he was looking for and had promised to show Avdiy as soon as he caught sight of the hemp-plants.

Soon it happened. The *anasha*, for the sake of which they had travelled all the way from Europe into the heart of Asia, turned out to be a strong, straight, tall-stemmed grass with thick, velvety clusters of tiny flowers. Well, well, thought Avdiy as he looked at it, it looks so ordinary, just like any other weed growing in the steppe, but so full of sweet intoxication for some that they're ready to trade their lives for a sniff! And here it is, growing like any other weed! Yes, it was the *anasha*, the sun was up and getting hotter every minute, and they were alone in the middle of the empty steppe, not even a single tree for miles around, rubbing the petals between their fingers and releasing the heavy astringent smell of the wild hemp. How many fantastic visions it must have inspired for users, down through the ages! Avdiy tried to picture the old oriental bazaars that he had read about in books – India, Afghanistan, Turkey, somewhere in Istanbul or Jaipur beneath a fortress wall or by the gates of former palaces, places where *anasha* had always been openly traded, where you bought it and smoked it at once to surrender to whatever hallucinations your fantasy was capable of creating, be it plantations and harems, or riding on gilded regal elephants beneath a lustrous canopy while the holiday crowd ebbed and flowed and roared beneath, or the black shadow of loneliness and the attendant bubbling rage at life that breeds the desire to destroy, to bring the world to dust and ashes . . . Was not this one of the fatal flaws of the once magnificent Orient? It seemed incredible that such a delightful misting of the faculties could really be concealed here, in the wild hemp that seemed to grow almost anywhere in these parched steppes.

'There she is, the little darling!' Petrukha murmured, flailing his arms as though to embrace the whole horizon with one sweeping gesture. 'Look! There's more! And more! All *anasha*! But we're not going to pick it here – this is nothing! This is chicken feed! I'll take you to places where your head will be spinning!'

On they went, and an hour later came upon such a thick growth that the smell alone was enough to make them merry, as though they were slightly drunk. There was enough hemp here to keep anyone happy. They started picking leaves and flowers and laid them out to dry. Petrukha assured them that they should dry them for two hours and no longer. They worked hard and effectively. Suddenly they heard the clatter of a helicopter. It was flying low over the steppe and seemed to be coming in their direction.

'Helicopter, helicopter!' shouted Lyonka, jumping for joy like a little boy.

Petrukha's reaction was somewhat different.

'Lie down, idiot!' he shouted with a stream of oaths.

They all lay face down in the grass and the helicopter passed to the side so that the chances of their being spotted by the pilot were very small. Petrukha's wind was up, however, and he nagged at Lyonka for the rest of the day, convinced that the helicopter was out specially to look for the runners.

'After all,' he reasoned, 'you can see everything, every mouse on the steppe, from the air. Jerks like us would stick out a mile, and as soon as they saw us they'd be on the two-way radio in a flash. If the police come after us on wheels, it's curtains: hands up and into the cooler!'

Soon, however, even he got back to work and forgot the interruption. That was the day when the unimaginable happened and Avdiy met the wolf family in the thicket. This was how it happened.

They took a break for a bite to eat, and Petrukha said, 'Hey, Avdiy, you're one of us now, one of the gang, aren't you? There's something I ought to tell you. There's a rule for the new boys, for the likes of you. If you're out in the field for the first time, then you have to bring back a little something for Sam, a little present, like, see what I mean?'

'Present? What present?' Avdiy shrugged in surprise.

'Hey, hang on, don't get all worked up now. You don't think you have to buy him something from a shop, do you? No shops here! No, I didn't mean that at all. You must get some extra "plasticine", at least, say, a matchbox full. You just have to look a little further, I'll show you where and what to do, and then when you meet up with Sam you can hand it over as a friendly little present, like, you're no fool, you know what I mean – he's in charge and you're a new boy, just to seal the bond . . .'

Avdiy's first thought was that it would not be a bad move: by means of a present of 'plasticine', the pollen-paste, the most valuable of the *anasha* products, he would gain access to Sam himself. At last the possibility of setting his eyes on Sam! Just what he needed! He might even be able to have a proper talk with the man who had power over all the runners. Power, power, wherever two people are gathered together, then power always comes into the equation! he thought with a bitter grimace.

'Right,' he said. 'I've got it. I collect the "plasticine" and hand it over to Sam. But when? At the station?'

'I don't know exactly,' admitted Petrukha. 'Perhaps tomorrow, even.'

'Tomorrow?'

'Yes, tomorrow. Time to be off home. We've been here long enough. Tomorrow's the twenty-first of the month. We've got to be there by four in the afternoon at the latest, that's why we've got to move.'

'Where?'

'Never mind where.' Petrukha was enjoying the opportunity to show off his insider's knowledge. 'When we get there, then you'll know. Kilometre 330.'

Avdiy did not need to ask any more questions. He realized that 'Kilometre 330' meant a stretch of the railway on the Chu branch-line. The most important thing was that the meeting with Sam was likely to be tomorrow and likely to be there. Given all that, would it not be best to waste no more time but start collecting the 'plasticine'?

It turned out to be an easy, but tiring task and the technology involved was nothing short of primitive. The secret was to take off all your clothes and run through the grass so that the pollen from the flowers adhered to your skin. This he did, and he had never run as much in a day in his life before! The pollen was hardly visible, almost microscopic, so although it did stick to him, scraping the almost invisible layer from his skin was so difficult that he succeeded in collecting only an infinitesimal amount, but he knew it was essential as his passport to the presence of the leader, of Sam himself, so that once he had enough material he could reveal the secret mechanisms governing the movements of the runners and then use the Word, use the newspapers to send a cry of pain resounding throughout the land. Only that knowledge kept Avdiy running backwards and forwards all day under the baking sun.

As he ran, Avdiy got a fair way away from his friends as he sought out the thickest growth of *anasha* in the steppe. After a while he felt a lightness as though he were almost floating, whether in reality or in his imagination. Avdiy hardly noticed when the feeling came over him. The sun shone brightly overhead, the air was suffused with warmth, larks and other birds sang in the sky, butterflies hovered, insects chirruped . . . It was paradise on earth, and in that paradise Avdiy took off everything except his Panama hat, his glasses, his trunks and his trainers. A skinny, white-skinned northerner, drunk on the pollen, he ran back and forth through the steppe like a clockwork toy, choosing the places where the grass grew thickest and highest. His progress was accompanied by a cloud of disturbed pollen, and inhaling the airborne intoxication had naturally stimulated Avdiy's imagination to various assorted visions. One was particularly satisfying: in it he was travelling fast on a motorbike behind the girl he had seen the day before. It worried him not at all that he was not in front, where a real man ought to be, at the handlebars, but riding pillion where the girl usually sits. So what if he had never ridden a motorbike and was anyway no good with machines? He was perfectly happy to be travelling on the same bike together. Her hair was escaping from the helmet and blowing in the wind, touching his face like the hands of the wind, pressing to his eyes and his lips and tickling his neck, and he was happy. Sometimes she turned and smiled mischievously at him, her eyes shining – how he wished that it would never end . . .

He came to his senses only when he saw the three wolf cubs close beside him. Well! Where were they from? He could hardly believe his eyes! The three cubs wagged their tails and wanted to come closer and play. Although they were shy, they did not run away. Lanky as adolescent children, they had ears which still stuck out to the sides, pointed noses and funny sharp little eyes that were full of trust. Avdiy was so touched that he forgot where he was and called gently to them, hoping to draw them into play. He was melting with delight when he suddenly caught sight of a white flash of lightning, the bared fangs of the advancing she-wolf . . . So sudden was it, so swift, and yet so painfully slow and terrible, that of themselves his knees buckled and he crouched, clutching his head. He was not to know that the gesture saved his life, for the she-wolf was but three paces away and when she jumped she sailed straight over his head, filling the air with her animal smell. Their eyes met and Avdiy saw the flash of blue fire in her harsh and relentlessly blue gaze. He shivered, then the she-wolf jumped back over him like a rush of wind, landing by the cubs and hustling them off by snapping at their heels. She headed off another huge beast that was rising out of the gully, a he-wolf with hackles raised, and the whole group disappeared as though a gust of wind had carried them off . . .

Avdiy took to his heels over the steppe, shouting in terror. His head was spinning, his legs heavy, and the ground was heaving beneath his stumbling feet. All he wanted to do was fall flat on his back and sleep, but instead he started to vomit and felt that his last hour was come. Each time, however, he retained enough sense and will-power to run from the pool of sick and keep going until the nausea overtook him again and he collapsed, clutching in agony at his stomach. Belching out the poison of the pollen, doubled over with cramps, he groaned and swore, 'Oh, Lord, enough! Stop! Never, ever will I collect *anasha* again! I'm through, I never want to see it or smell that smell again, have mercy on me, oh, God . . .'

When at last the retching left him and he started off to find his clothes, Petrukha and Lyonka rejoined him. They were deeply impressed by the story of his meeting with the wolves. Lyonka was particularly affected.

'Come on, be a man! Why are you trembling so?' Petrukha

went into the attack. 'When people went looking for gold, you should hear the dreadful things that happened, but it never stopped them going on looking . . . Scared of wolves, eh? But they'll be miles away by now!'

'Ah, but that was gold,' said Lyonka, after a pause.

'What's the difference?' snapped Petrukha.

Avdiy saw his chance. 'There is a difference, Petrukha,' he said. 'A very big difference. Gold brings a lot of evil too, but it's mined openly, while *anasha* is poison for everyone who has anything to do with it. I've seen that for myself just now – I almost croaked, spewing all over the steppe . . .'

'Oh shut up, you just got a bit too much in your system, not used to it, that's all, no one to blame,' answered Petrukha with a dismissive gesture. 'Anyway, who forced you to come along? You and your God, good, and evil – why spoil it for the rest of us? Why stir things up for other people? It's the money, isn't it! For the sake of the money, you nearly ended up in the jaws of a wolf, eh?'

'I don't want to stir things up, I want to clear them up,' said Avdiy, deciding that he would have to reveal more than he had intended. 'Take you, Petrukha: you're no fool, you must see that you're getting into something against the law . . .'

'Getting into! And what do you think you're getting into?'

'I'm here to save you.'

'To save us?' shouted Petrukha angrily. 'And how d'you imagine you're going to save us, for Christ's sake? Come on, out with it!'

'Well, we could start by repenting before God and our fellow men . . .'

To Avdiy's astonishment, they did not burst out laughing. Petrukha merely spat, as though he had found something foul-tasting in his mouth.

'Repenting! That's a nice one!' he grumbled. 'You can repent, but we're going to make some money. We – need – the – money; got it? It's plain enough. You repent! And if it's a joke, Avdiy, then you should be more careful what you joke about. If Sam gets to hear what you've been up to, trying to get us to give it up, then you'll never see home again, mark my words. I'm warning you, as a friend. Don't you make no mistake, for us it's the money, first and foremost. Hey,

Lyonka, you tell him: what's more important for you – God, or the money?'

'The money!' came the answer.

Avdiy was silent. He decided to prevaricate, to postpone the conversation.

'All right then, that's that, let's get our stuff together,' announced Petrukha, conciliatory now. 'What about your "plasticine", Avdiy? Nothing doing, I suppose?'

'I'm sorry to say, you're right. As soon as that she-wolf flew at me, I dropped everything. I don't even know where my clothes are. I'll go and look for them . . .'

'Your clothes will turn up all right, but there's no time to get more "plasticine" now. It's too late for today. Never mind, we'll tell him what happened, he'll understand. Even if he doesn't, there's always next time . . .'

They walked until midnight towards the railway, their rucksacks stuffed with *anasha*. The going was not rough and their loads were light, just dried grass, but the strong smell of the *anasha*, hardly contained even by the polythene bags, filled their heads and made them sleepy. At midnight they sank down on the ground right where they were in the open steppe, so as to move on at first light. Lyonka wormed his way in between Avdiy and Petrukha, terrified of wolves after what had happened to Avdiy – understandable, since the lad was still a boy. As usually happens, Avdiy was dropping with fatigue while they walked, but once they lay down the desire for sleep abandoned him. He was very touched by the fact that Lyonka asked to sleep in the middle – imagine a big boy like that, afraid of wolves! – but how strong the power of vice must be if it can corrupt the human values in one so young that Lyonka answered without a moment's hesitation that money meant more to him than God. He had meant God in an abstract sense, of course, as a symbol of a righteous life. All these thoughts ran through Avdiy's head.

Summer nights in the steppe have a beauty all their own. The endless silence emanates from the enormity of earth and sky, the warm air is filled with the breath of the many grasses and, most affecting of all, the moon shines above with the twinkling of countless numbers of stars, and not a single particle of dust between the star and the eye of the beholder.

So pure is the air that when men can forget the troubles of the day their thoughts are drawn upwards, into that mysterious kingdom . . . More the pity that it cannot be for long . . .

Avdiy also thought that for the moment everything was going as he had hoped: he had joined the runners and reached the steppes where the *anasha* grew, seen it with his own eyes and experienced it for himself. Now the hardest was to come, catching the train and getting out of here. For the runners the most dangerous part was getting the *anasha* through. Most of the arrests made by the police were at the stations on the Asian side; things were easier once they made it over into Russia proper. If they could make it to Moscow and on to their final destination, then they were home and dry. The greatest of evil could triumph on the shoulders of insignificant successes achieved by insignificant people . . .

Even in his thoughts Avdiy could not accept the fact of his impotence in the face of all this. He might be able to stop some particular crime from being committed in the here and now, but there was no way in which he could persuade the runners to change their whole way of thinking. The man they called 'Sam', 'himself', his opponent, who was somewhere here in these steppes, and who held the invisible reins directing all the runners, controlling even Avdiy himself, was far, far stronger. Sam was the boss – more than the boss, a dictator in microcosm on this expedition for *anasha*; Avdiy had joined up with them like a wandering monk with a band of robbers, and his position was laughable, to say the least . . . However, a monk, zealous in the service of the Lord, must remain a monk, come what may. The test would come later . . .

He also thought of his strange experience that day, of the trusting long-legged cubs who had mistaken a man for a harmless and amusing being whom they could accept as a playmate, and the sudden fury of the blue-eyed she-wolf. What was the anger that boiled up within her? How had he survived? What did it mean that she had jumped clean over him, and twice? She and her mate could have torn him apart in a second, naked and defenceless idiot from the city that he was (except, of course, for the trunks and the Panama hat), the sort of scene you might expect to meet only in some tasteless joke. But no; Fate, in the persons of the two animals, had let him go.

Might that not mean that life still had need of him? How swift and beautiful she had been, the she-wolf in her burst of anger and fear for her children! Of course, she was entirely within her rights and it was his good luck that she did not attack him, that no disaster struck even though he had done no wrong, either. As he thought, Avdiy laughed quietly at the idea of how the girl on the motorbike would have laughed to see him like that! She would have laughed like a child at the circus! Then suddenly his heart froze; what if her motorbike suddenly stalled in the middle of the deserted steppe and she was attacked by wolves? He found himself murmuring a super-stitious prayer to the blue-eyed she-wolf: 'Hear me, beautiful mother wolf! This is your home, and you must live in it as Nature has decreed. My only prayer is that if her motorbike stalls, for God's sake and that of your lupine gods, for the sake of your cubs, leave her be. . . !'

Petrukha woke Avdiy and Lyonka when the light was only just touching the darkness over the steppe. Time to get up and set off for Kilometre 330 – the earlier the better. They were to meet up with two or three other groups of runners, each group bringing the *anasha* that it had gathered and dried in the sun. Then they would stop a passing goods train, climb silently on board and ride all the way to Zhalpak-Saz, from where they could disperse on to other trains. This was the most dangerous part of the journey for the runners. From the sound of it, the whole operation was run by Sam. Petrukha had not explained whether Sam would meet them, or they would seek him out once they reached Kilometre 330. Either he did not know, or else he did not want to say.

They slung their rucksacks back into place and set off after Petrukha. Avdiy was impressed by Petrukha's memory and topographical intuition. He could forecast every gully, each shady stream, all the hollows and ravines. Avdiy could only think what a waste of his memory and his talent he was making! To think how well he knew this place even after only a few visits!

Petrukha explained it by his peasant background. He also told them what he had heard of the Moyun-Kum desert proper, that started two hundred kilometres away, where the saigak antelope roamed free in their thousands and people

99

apparently came, in their official jeeps, from as far away as Orenburg on hunting trips. 'The food was there on the hoof to help yourself, and the drink – any kind you could think of – they brought with them. You could hunt like a tsar!' It was not, however, without its dangers: sometimes the jeeps broke down and the hunters died of thirst as they wandered in the empty steppe. Sometimes in winter they were lost in the snowdrifts, and only their skeletons found, years later. One hunter went out of his mind, and they sent a helicopter to look for him. The helicopter found and followed him, trying to save him, but he ran away and hid. By the time they caught up with him, he had lost the power of speech. His wife had apparently someone else by the time they got him back. 'Bitch! Like all of them! Won't catch me marrying one of 'em! There's one great piece of work back where I come from, just need to give her something to buy a new dress now and then and she's real class – no one to touch her – and, best of all, she gives a guarantee that there won't be any kids or anything like that. The main thing, anyway, is that I've already got a bike, a nice, sporty little Czech number sitting in the shed at home, and next it's a car; a Lada's no problem, but it's a Volga I'm after, that new one that's modelled on the Mercedes, one with a cassette so that you can switch it on, full volume, till it takes off the top of your head. But how do I get one? You need connections, you need to pay over the odds and through the nose as well. Once I've got it, I'll go off to Vorkuta and show those brothers of mine what's what. Ha-ha! Their wives will be green with envy! I'll fill the boot with all kinds of booze, mostly foreign stuff, of course. And vodka, naturally – nothing to touch the old vodka, when it comes down to it. Green with envy they'll be, I was always the one they looked down on, and there I'll be . . . That's why I'm doing the run, and that's why I've brought you along too, friends, to make your pile as well. Live it up while your luck holds out, and pull in your belt when it's up . . .'

As he listened with one ear to the stream of unassuming minutiae with which Petrukha amused himself and his companions, Avdiy was thinking his own thoughts. Man is trapped in the triangular lure of riches, imitation of the lowest common denominator, and vanity; they are the basis for most people's mentality and the pillars upon which the stability of the philistine's world has rested in every age and every place, a safe haven for evils great and small and for the emptiness and impoverishment of people's inner world. What power on earth, including religion, is capable of prevailing against the omnipotent ideology of the philistine world? How many selfless souls have tried, only to be dashed against the walls of this impregnable and indestructible, if amorphous, strong-hold . . . That he was even now making his way to the *anasha*-runners' secret meeting place was yet another proof of the fact that the spirit is weak to act, however strong its staying power . . . So that was to be his role . . . He spent the entire journey preparing for his meeting with Sam, for he must be ready for action . . .

They reached Kilometre 330 a couple of hours early, and were in place soon after two o'clock. As they approached the ditch which ran along beside the railway, Petrukha warned them that they were to hide their rucksacks where he showed them and to lie low, not hang about where they might be seen by passing strangers. They were to wait for full instructions.

They were all pretty tired, after covering so much ground in a day. It was a pleasure to stretch out on the bottom of the ditch, where sage and feather-grass grew side by side. It was a pleasure to listen for the distant rumble of the trains, growing louder as they approached, then the singing and clanking of the rails as the kilometre-long goods trains passed in a whirl of thunder, clattering by in an oily, metallic crescendo and gradually dying away, merging into the ocean of the surround-ing silence . . . Two passenger trains passed, too, one in either direction. Avdiy almost started up, remembering his child-hood love of trains, watching the passengers as they sped away to their destinations, wondering about the people behind the faces and figures he could see at the windows. This time, however, even this fleeting pleasure was not for him, for he had to keep his head down behind a bush and lie low. Worse, he was going to be an accessory, or at least a witness, to the terrorist-style stoppage of a goods train on this section of the track. Not that anyone intended to loot the train, but a temporary stop would allow the runners to vault into the wagons, and the rest of the journey would then run smoothly, as they moved on, hidden among the freight . . .

A few more trains passed, then there was a long silence. Avdiy was half asleep when he heard a loud whistle. Petrukha cocked an ear and whistled back, to be answered by a third whistle.

'Just you wait quietly here,' warned Petrukha, 'I'm being called. Don't move without me, d'you hear, Avdiy, got it, Lyonka? Stopping a goods train's not so easy. Have to use your head.'

With this he disappeared. He returned about half an hour later, in a strange mood. Something in him had changed, his eyes had a sheepish look and he avoided looking Avdiy straight in the eye. Avdiy was not one for letting suspicions get out of hand, and put any such thoughts out of his head. Who knows – perhaps he merely had a stomach-ache . . . So he asked quietly, 'Well, Petrukha? How's things?'

'All right for the moment. We'll soon be going into action.'

'Stopping a goods train, you mean?'

'Of course. That's the best way out of here for us, getting away in a goods train. The very best of all would be to get to the junction at dusk on a train that goes into the sidings.'

'Ah, I see.'

They sat in silence. Petrukha lit a cigarette and muttered casually as he inhaled, 'One of the lads, Grishan, has twisted his ankle. Just seen him. Very unlucky lad, that Grishan. Not much good for collecting in the steppe, hobbling about with a stick. Shame for the poor guy! We thought we might all chip in, there's about ten of us here, give him a share of ours, share and share alike, you know how it is, then we'd cover his losses.'

'Of course,' answered Avdiy, 'I'm happy to. Lyonka's asleep, but I don't think he'd object.'

'Oh, Lyonka – no problems there. You know what, Avdiy, why don't you go and have a chat with Grishan? You could ask him how it happened, you've always got something to say for yourself, you could cheer him up a bit . . .'

'What about Sam? Will he be there?' said Avdiy rashly.

'Sam? Haven't you got anything else to talk about but Sam?' Petrukha was riled. 'How should I know? I'm talking about Grishan, and all you can answer is "Sam". If he needs us, he'll find us, if not, we know we're not the only pebbles on the beach. What's the fuss?'

'Sorry. I wasn't thinking. Calm down. So where's this Grishan? Which way do I go?'

'That way. There he is, sitting in the shade under that bush. Go on!'

Avdiy set off and soon saw Grishan, sitting on a folding chair in the grass and holding his stick. A cap covered his forehead. He seemed quick off the mark, for before Avdiy had even approached he had looked him over and coughed into his fist. Two more men sat a little way off. Three in all. At that moment Avdiy realized that he was coming face to face with Sam himself . . . He slowed his pace, shivered and felt his heart suddenly race . . .

7

'How's the walking wounded, then?' asked Avdiy in the most ordinary voice he could muster, to calm the pounding in his chest.

Grishan, sitting on his tiny folding stool like a fisherman's and playing with a stick, squinted up at him.

'Who's asking?'

Avdiy smiled mechanically. 'Someone who was told to come over and ask how you were feeling.'

'Ah, I see! Well, I'm most grateful for your kind attention at this initial stage of our relationship. Especially out here in the uninhabited wastes in which we seem to find ourselves. A human presence in such a place is such a comforting phenomenon, don't you find?'

Aha, so he's a wordsmith, is he? If it's more than just hot air, then I'll have to make sure I don't drop my guard for a second! Who would have thought it? He obviously wants to make it clear from the start that he knows where the dictionaries are in the library, thought Avdiy to himself. Why? Is it some game of his? At the same time he noted the complete lack of any distinguishing feature in Grishan's appearance. Everything about him was outstandingly ordinary: brown hair, taller than average, thin, dressed with none of the flashiness normally affected by his age group but in jeans and a threadbare zip-up shirt. His cap was the kind you can roll up and shove in your pocket. If it were not for his limp and the consequent thick, gnarled stick, there would be no way of picking him out of the crowd. The only memorable thing about him was his eyes. His sharp brown eyes were full of life, and he was probably himself unaware of the way his expression changed as the conversation developed: at first he frowned, then looked slyly sideways, his pale brows twitching, then backed away like a fierce little animal cornered, bared his teeth, made as if to pounce and finally stiffened into a stance of pure aggression.

The impression of a fierce little predator was probably reinforced by a broken top incisor which gaped as he spoke. With
his money, he could have had a gold crown put on it, thought
Avdiy. I wonder why he doesn't? Perhaps it would make him
too easy to pick out in an identity parade?

'How's the foot, then? Sprained ankle? Miss your footing?'
he asked politely.

Grishan nodded vaguely.

'That's right, a bit of a sprain. Missed my footing, as you say,
Avdiy. That is your name, isn't it?'

'That is indeed my name.'

'What an unusual name, a biblical one, eh?' continued
Grishan, taking pleasure in drawing out the words. 'Avdiy.
Definitely a churchy smell hanging about that name, if I'm not
mistaken,' he added thoughtfully. 'Yes . . . God was once very
much a part of people's lives. Think of the religion in all those
old Russian names, Prechistensky, Bogolepov, Blagovestov
. . . I suppose your surname matches, too, eh, Avdiy?'

'Kallistratov.'

'What did I say? I've got a real no-nonsense name, I'm plain
proletarian Grishan. Anyway, that's not the point. What is the
point is the fact that you're right, Avdiy Kallistratov, I did
indeed miss my footing. The conclusion to be drawn from this
unhappy little episode is that if you've got any brains at all,
look where you're putting your feet. Otherwise you end up an
invalid like me. Stupid, really.'

'And what were the consequences?' asked Avdiy, bearing
Petrukha's hints in mind.

'What do you mean?' countered Grishan warily.

'I mean, the "unhappy little episode" has affected your . . .
er . . . results, if I understand correctly?' explained Avdiy.

'Oh, never mind about that now!' Grishan's tone suddenly
changed and the verbal niceties ceased. 'If you're talking about
what we're here for, you're right. I've got other things on my
mind at the moment, as you can imagine, otherwise I wouldn't
be wasting my time in polite conversation here with you . . .
You must have realized that I'm in charge. I'm a sort of
sergeant-major to this lot, and the most urgent task at the
moment is to break through the front line without any
casualties.'

'Is there any way I can help?' asked Avdiy. 'I think it would be worth while our having a talk together. I've got some ideas of my own about "casualties", albeit of a different sort . . .'

'Well, if we've really got so much in common, then we should make time to have a proper talk,' answered Grishan. 'That was what I was hoping for. For instance, I can't help wondering, strictly, of course, between ourselves . . .' He glanced slyly at Avdiy, then broke off and barked an order at the two runners who sat to one side and took no part in the conversation. 'Hey, you two! Why are you just sitting about? Go on, start getting ready!'

The two loped silently off, presumably to carry out some pre-ordained task. Once he had given the order, Grishan glanced at his watch.

'One hour to embarkation. You can see how it's done,' he promised. 'We're very strict here. The same kind of discipline as the parachute regiments. And the same devotion to duty and the Motherland, with a capital letter. You too will have to do exactly what you're told. No question of "I can" or "I can't". If everyone carries out his orders to the letter, we'll all be in Zhalpak-Saz by evening.'

Grishan let the silence underline the importance of his words. Then, with a crooked smile that revealed his jagged tooth, he turned to Avdiy.

'Now, let's get down to business, to the question of what brought you here. No hurry, we've got all the time in the world. Let me just make it clear that for the so-called criminal underworld in which you've popped up so unexpectedly – we'll come back to that later – this is the way things stand: you are a runner too, you're in this with us and you know too much. You don't look like a fool, but you put your head in the trap yourself. So now, be a good chap: I've shown my trust in you, and now it's your turn to return the compliment.'

'How?'

'I think you can guess . . .'

'Guessing is one thing, talking straight is quite another.'

They both sat wordless, waiting for the thunder of a passing train to die away. Each was preparing in his own way for the single combat that lay inexorably ahead. Avdiy was thinking of

106

the strangeness of human relations and of the fact that even out here in the steppe where all men are equal and all have an equal chance of failure and prison or, if successful, of profit – even here human beings lived according to the laws that run in their blood, so that Grishan enjoyed some unwritten right to give orders, by virtue of being the leader of the group.

'So, it's talking straight that you want, is it?' Grishan suddenly broke the silence. 'All right . . .' he drawled noncommittally, then added slyly as though suddenly reminded of something, 'Hey! Is it true you were attacked by wolves?'

'It most certainly is,' replied Avdiy.

'Then don't you think, Avdiy Kallistratov, that your life was spared in order for you to answer a few questions, here and now?' Again the broken tooth flashed in a smile.

'Maybe.'

'Then let's get straight to the point. You're going to explain to me, right here and right now, why you're trying to stir up my lads.'

'Correction,' interrupted Avdiy.

'Correction? What needs correcting? No corrections needed in this court!'

'I'm trying to return them to the path of righteousness, so "stir up" is hardly an adequate expression in the context.'

'Oh, drop it, Mister Kallistratov. Righteousness or otherwise is something we all decide for ourselves. Forget your clever little jokes, now. This is no place for verbal jousting. I want to know what you came for. Was there something you needed to get to the bottom of? Something the holy father needed for his own satisfaction?'

'You mean, something personally useful to me?'

'Of course! What else?' Grishan shrugged, with a mocking and triumphant smile.

'In that case – nothing. Absolutely nothing,' answered Avdiy flatly.

'Excellent!' There was almost joy in Grishan's voice. 'Perfect! Now it all falls into place. So you are one of that happy race of idiots who . . . Stop! I know what you are going to say! So out you came to the Moyun-Kum, pretending to be an *anasha*-runner, got in with us, one of the family, and not because you've come to love the big money like you used to love Christ, nor because you had nowhere to go once they'd booted you out of the seminary – is that right? If I were one of those old priests, I'd have kicked you out a lot sooner than they did – who needs the likes of you? Not even they do! They're playing an old, old game, while you pop up with your "truth", taking it all for serious . . .'

'That's right! For serious! And I'd thank you to take me for serious, too!' interrupted Avdiy.

'Huh! You'll be lucky! D'you think I haven't seen right through you, through and through? I know what you are! You're mad! You're a fanatic, mad about your own crazy little scheme, and that's what brought you here. That's the only thing that could bring you here. So here you are, all noble aims and messianic missions, to open the eyes of the fallen creatures who make their money out of the *anasha*, buying and selling and making a profit on the forbidden weed. Here you are, with your eternal ideas of salvation, stinking of truisms like a whiff of urine smelled from half a mile away. Here you are, to turn us away from the path of evil, to make us repent and change our ways and take up your standard of comprehensive conscious- ness, whatever that might mean. You can see why the West imagines we're all identical!' Suddenly Grishan jumped up (with surprising alacrity for a man with a sprained ankle) from his canvas stool and took a stride towards Avdiy, till they stood eye to furious eye. 'Hey! You! Saviour! Emissary! Did you stop to think of the power that would be opposing you?'

'I certainly did, and that's why I'm here. I must warn you that I'm going to do it, for your own sakes, whatever the cost to me, so you know what to expect . . .'

'For our own sakes!' screeched Grishan. 'Don't worry, I know what to expect! We've all known what to expect since that other one, the one they crucified, the Saviour of the human race, stretched out his arms, nailed to the cross, hung his head, composed his features in a pained expression . . . and there you are! Weep and wail in admiration, and worship until the end of your days! How do you like that! There's always been someone who thinks he's a cut above the rest and appoints himself the full-time job of saving us from ourselves. Well? Who and what have they managed to save over the course of the ages? Answer me! It's the same now as it ever was, before that business on Golgotha. Man is the same. Nothing in him has changed, even though we sit around waiting for someone to come and save us sinners. A nice little opening, just for you, eh, Kallistratov? So here you are, our own personal little saviour! Squeaky-clean as well!' Grishan made a comic face. 'Let's welcome the new Christ into the fold!'

'You can say what you like about me, but I won't have you take the name of Christ in vain!' cried Avdiy threateningly. 'You're amazed and indignant that I should be here, but there's nothing surprising about it at all. We had to meet, you and I. Just think about it! You must understand! If it wasn't me, it would have been another, but the confrontation would have been the same . . . I've imagined this scene so many times!'

'Oh, really? Perhaps you imagined me, too?'

'Of course! Our meeting was inevitable. So here I am, as you put it.'

'Yes, there's something in that, dammit. We seem to be opposites that had to come to a confrontation in the end. I suppose there's some pig-headed reason why that should be so, but don't start crowing too soon, Saviour Kallistratov, your theory won't get anywhere in practice. Anyway, enough philosophy, although you're interesting enough as a subject for speculation. I've got your measure now. My advice to you, since this is how things have turned out – and I mean this in kindness – is to go, go where you will, and when it comes to saving, think of saving your own neck. Nobody will lay a finger on you if you go now, and as for the stuff you gathered in the steppes, give it to the others, if you like, or burn it, or throw it to the four winds. It's up to you. One thing, though, just you make sure that our paths never cross again!' and Grishan banged his stick emphatically against the stone.

'But I can't take your advice. It's impossible.'

'Are you a complete idiot? What's stopping you?'

'I have to answer for you all, before God and my own conscience . . . Maybe that's something you can't understand . . .'

'Oh yes? And why should I not be able to understand?' shouted Grishan in anger, his face pale. 'My family were all on the stage, I'd have you know, and you can be sure that I understand all right – I know good acting when I see it. The difference is that I think you've got carried away. However

109

good the acting, there's always a curtain at the end, and I'm afraid your one-man audience, Mister Kallistratov, has decided that it's time for you to take your final bow. Cool it! It's over! Don't make me stain my soul with another sin. Go, before it's too late.'

'You talk about sin, and I understand what you're hinting at, but now that I've seen this evil with my own eyes, it would be the gravest of sins for me to pass by on the other side. Don't try and dissuade me. I'm not indifferent to the fate of little Lyonka, or Petrukha, or the rest of your lads. Or your own, if it comes to that.'

'Amazing!' interrupted Grishan. 'What right have you got to interfere in our lives like this? When it comes to the crunch, everyone's free to go his own way. I've never seen you before in my life! Who d'you think you are, to be "not indifferent" to the fate of any of us, as though you had been granted some sort of special powers from above! Get going! And don't tempt fate. If you really are crazy, then go in peace, and we'll get by without you. Got it?'

'But I won't get by! You make jokes about "special powers", but I don't carry anyone's mandate! The knowledge that I'm right and that I know where my duty lies – that's the only brief I carry, and you are quite at liberty to ignore it or not, as you wish – but I can't ignore it. You talk about everyone being free to go his own way, and it sounds wonderful, but none of us lives in isolation. Our lives are all bound together, and the only firm boundaries between them are those drawn by birth and death. Between those two, we are all intertwined, like the threads in one skein of wool. Look, Grishan, when you and those who are in your power leave this steppe with the *anasha* which for you is a way of making money, what you are carrying out of here is misery and unhappiness for others. A moment's illusory pleasure will seduce them into your circle, a circle of desperation and degeneration.'

'Listen to His Honour from the Bench! What right have you to judge how we should live and eat?'

'I'm not judging. I'm one of you, only . . .'

'Only what?'

'Only I realize that above us all stands God, as the highest measure of conscience and mercy.'

110

'Oh, God again! And what are you trying to tell us, then?'

'Just that God's grace is expressed through our will. He is within us, and acts on us by means of our consciousness.'

'So what? What's the point of all these complexities? What's in it for us?'

'What's in it for you? The strength of his reason gives man power over himself, like God. What else is a true realization of our faults, the condemnation of evil within ourselves, a condemnation that puts us on a level with God? Man can redefine a new view of his own essence!'

'So you want to foist some kind of "comprehensive consciousness" upon me? Just what I want to avoid so as not to be just one of the crowd! Don't compare me with yourself, I'm my own master.'

'You're wrong there. Freedom is freedom only when it has no fear of the law, otherwise it is just a fiction. *Your* freedom is under constant pressure from fear of just retribution . . .'

'So what? What is it to you? It's my choice, not yours!'

'It's your choice, but it affects others as well. Remember, though, that there is a way out of the trap. Repent, right here, under the sky of the steppe, promise yourselves once and for all to finish with this business and give up the profits to be made on the black market, give up your vice and seek to make peace both with yourselves and with what they call God, with that which unites us all in the form of human reason . . .'

'And then what?'

'And then you'll be truly human again.'

'Sounds damned impressive, and so simple!' Grishan frowned, playing with his gnarled stick, and waited while another goods train thundered past, out of sight beyond the embankment. When the train was past, he fixed Avdiy with a harsh and mocking glare and said into the ensuing silence, 'Now, listen, my good Avdiy, I have listened patiently to all you had to say, and now I'm sorry to have to disappoint you: you're very much mistaken if, in your righteous complacency, you imagine that you're the only one to enjoy the privilege of speaking to God in your thoughts, and that I don't have any such contact. That's shaken you, eh, the thought that even the likes of me might be in contact with God?'

'Not at all. It's just that the word "contact" seems unusual in the context. On the contrary, I'm delighted to hear such a thing from your lips. Perhaps something is stirring in your soul?'

'Oh, no, nothing like that. How naïve! For your information, Kallistratov, I've got my own way of getting to God: I go in the back way. Your God is not quite as prickly and inaccessible as you imagine . . .'

'And what do you achieve by going in the back way?'

'No less than you, you can be sure of that. I help people to experience happiness, to know God through pleasure. I give them what you could never give them through your sermons and your prayers . . . And I bring people to God far more effectively than anyone else . . .'

'To a god that was bought for money? Through drugs and intoxication? And you call that the happiness of knowing God?'

'No? I suppose you think it's blasphemous? Aha, I can see that I'm shocking you! So you've got a rival, eh? Somebody stealing your thunder! Yes, damn you, yes, for money! Yes, drugs! In case you didn't know, everything turns on money. Did you think there was a different God, where money was concerned? Why, do you do without money in your churches and all those other places?'

'But that's different!'

'Garbage! Leave it out! Everything can be bought and sold, including your God. At least I give people the chance to get high and experience what you can only offer as a promise, and that in the next world. Only the weed can give you that blissful feeling of being at peace with all the world, that freedom from all the constraints of time and space. The bliss may be momentary, it may be illusory, the stuff of hallucinations, but it's happiness, and you have to switch off to achieve it. You righteous fools can't even offer yourselves the pleasure of self-deception.'

'Well, you're right on one score, at least – the self-deception.'

'What do you want? To buy truth with five kopecks, perhaps? There's no such bargain to be had, holy Father! Getting high is our bitter substitute because we don't have any other kind of happiness.'

'But why should you substitute for something that you say

112

doesn't exist in the first place? It's all sophistry, that's what it is!'

'Hang on, hang on, Kallistratov! After all, when all's said and done, I'm your helper!'

'What do you mean?'

'Just this: since the day of creation, it's been nothing but promises for the human race. A humiliated and insulted humankind has been promised miracle after miracle: first it was the Kingdom of God that was just round the corner, then democracy, then equality and fraternity, then happiness through the collective, living in a commune, and those who really tried would get to heaven as the icing on the cake. Those were the promises; but the reality? Words, just words! I'm the one, if you want to know, who can act as a distraction for those whose thirst has not been quenched and whose doubts have not been settled. I'm the lightning-conductor, I lead them off by the back door to an unreal god.'

'So, you're much more dangerous than I expected! I shiver to think where it all might end. There's a little Napoleon lost to the world in you, isn't there.'

'Why "little"? If I only had the scope, I could really set up something worthwhile! If we were in the West, then I could work a network on a decent scale. Then you wouldn't dare to go into all these polemics! Oh, no! You'd have to look at good and evil my way, then!'

'I'm sure I would. But there's nothing too threatening in what you are saying. None of it's new. You're drawing parasitic strength, Grishan, from the fact that people have used up all their power to believe, a fact that is extremely easy to play upon. They're surrounded by mediocrity and false-hood, so they feel they might as well see refuge in what comfort drugs can bring. If you've rejected everything that went before, why don't you try giving people a new view of the world? Faith is not something you can take or smoke to get a high; faith is ground from the sufferings of many gene-rations, it has to be laboured over for thousands of years and every day. You, however, you want to use this despicable money-spinner to overturn the alternation of day and night, the established order of things. Although it starts off fine, remember that after the "high" of which you speak so reverently comes the slump into madness and the final degradation of the individual. Why did you leave that part out? Your "high" is nothing but a sham: it starts by leading you towards some trumped-up substitute for God, but you end up in the arms of Satan. What do you do about that?'

'Nothing. Everything in life has to be paid for. Including that. We pay for our life with death. Have you ever thought of it that way? Well? Say something! I suppose you can't stomach my ideas, eh, holy man?'

'The ideas of Antichrist? Never!'

'Ha-ha! What's the point of your Christianity without an Antichrist? Without that challenge? Who would need you? So you see how essential I am to your scheme of things! Otherwise who would you battle with to sharpen up your ideas, eh?'

'Well, well, you're a slippery customer!' Avdiy could not help laughing. 'Ready to play at contradictions. But don't waste your orations on me. We'll never reach the common ground. We're antipodes, incompatible, and that's why you're so keen to get rid of me. You're afraid of me! However, I still must insist: repent, and free the runners from your web. I'm offering you my help.'

Grishan was suddenly silent. Frowning, he paced the ground, leaning on his stick, and then came to a halt.

'Listen, Mister Kallistratov, if you think I'm afraid of you, then you're very much mistaken. I'd like to do a deal with you. Stay if you like; I'm not trying to get rid of you. It's time for us to get aboard our goods train. Time to organize our transport.'

'Organize? Hijack it, you mean!' Avdiy corrected him.

'Hijack it if you like, but not to rob it: just to hitch a ride. Quite different. Unfortunately your state authorities deny us freedom of movement . . .'

'Leave the state out of this. So, what sort of a deal do you propose?'

'Oh, nothing much. When we "hijack", as you put it, the train' – Grishan nodded in the direction of the line – 'they'll all be there, and all together. Just your chance to have a go at converting them, the young Lyonkas and the sharp old Petrukhas – you can save their souls, Saviour! I won't stand in your way. Not a single word. Just pretend I'm not even there. If you succeed in turning them your way, converting them to your God, then I will fade away, as the loser always fades away after any battle. Do you follow me? Ready to take up the challenge?'

'Ready!' snapped Avdiy.

'Go to it, then! Nobody will ever know what we talked about together here, or if we struck any bargains. If they ask, we'll just be vague . . .'

'Thank you! Though I've nothing to hide,' answered Avdiy.

Grishan shrugged.

'As you wish – but, as it says in the Bible, "Thine own lips have said it." '

It was already after six on one of the last evenings in May, but the sun still shone brightly over the plain. Clouds had been gathering all day, pale at first but thickening gradually towards the evening until they hung in a dark band over the horizon, filling Avdiy with a sense of vague foreboding. A storm was on the way.

Trains were still moving in both directions, north to south and south to north, shaking the earth beneath their heavy wheels. So much land, so much space and light, but still man feels he's missing something, missing freedom, first and foremost, thought Avdiy, looking round at the endless steppe. Man can't live alone, but he finds it hard enough in company, too. What now? What should I say to make all those who have fallen into Grishan's nets follow their reason and shrug off the fear of their comrades and herd instinct, to give them the strength to prevail against the influence of this drug-pusher and his sophistry. What a truly dangerous creature! So, which is the best course to take?

The moment came. Before stopping the goods train the runners, in the shelter of the tall grass and the bushes, settled in groups of two and three all along the line of track where the train would stop. The signal was a whistle. It came as soon as the train appeared, gliding like a snake around a distant bend, and they were all ready. The rucksacks and cases of *anasha* were at hand. Avdiy, Petrukha and Lyonka lay together behind a pile of chippings left over after repairs to the embankment. Not far from them lay Grishan and two others, a gingery man called Kolya and Makhach, an agile lad with aquiline features and a Caucasian accent, whose name probably came from the Makhachkala peninsula. Avdiy knew nothing of the rest, but could see that more runners were hidden along the track and preparing to storm the train. As for the two whom Grishan had sent ahead to do whatever it was that made the driver imagine there was a fire on the track, and leave his cab to walk ahead and check the bridge, they had been sent way up the line, right along to the sign saying 'Kilometre 330'. The bridge in question crossed a deep gully, flushed out by floods each spring, and was the spot chosen for their tricks by the two 'sappers'.

The train was rushing closer, and Avdiy could feel the tension in the air as each man made his own calculations on the time needed to climb aboard and the kind of trucks the train would have. What if the whole train were tank trucks, closed cisterns for carrying liquids? Where would they hide then? It might even be a heavily guarded military consignment, in which case that was the end of them.

Lyonka lit a cigarette, his hands shaking with emotion. Petrukha swooped on him.

'Out! At once! Or I'll kill you, you little idiot!'

Lyonka, however, face pale and lips blue, continued to gulp down the smoke. Petrukha threw himself on the boy like an animal, putting his whole strength behind a blow to the head which knocked Lyonka's cap flying. Lyonka answered blow for blow and twisted round to land Petrukha a kick that made him bellow like a bull. Soon they were engaged in a violent brawl. Avdiy had to intervene.

'Stop it, stop it at once! Petrukha, take your hands off Lyonka. You should be ashamed of yourself!'

Petrukha transferred all his animosity to Avdiy immediately.

'You keep your incense-sniffing nose out of this one, blockhead! Get down, dolt, or you'll be seen for miles around!' and he tugged violently at Avdiy's trouser leg. Still excited from the fight, panting and swearing, they crawled back to their places.

The train was almost upon them. The general tension was taking hold of Avdiy, too. It was, after all, the most dangerous moment of the whole trip.

Avdiy had always been a train-lover and a train-spotter, ever since the steam locomotives of his post-war childhood, those romantic giants belching forth a pillar of smoke and clouds of steam that used to deafen the district with their powerful whistles. Never, however, had he imagined that he would ever tremble in anticipation of an arrival the way he was trembling today, trembling at the illegality of the breaking and entering that they were about to undertake.

The heavy goods train crawled ahead, pulled by two locomotives coupled together, and they measured its progress by the way the skin crawled on the backs of their necks. The massive diesels of today were a far cry from those old steam-engines. Their power was not as manifestly apparent but they pulled along a seemingly endless train of trucks, rolling inexorably on with a rush and thunder of wheels. To Avdiy it seemed impossible that this triumph of perfect engineering could ever actually be brought to a halt.

The trucks were rolling past, open platforms, cisterns, timber trucks, general freight trucks and sealed containers. When more than half of the train was already past, Avdiy decided that the attempt must have failed, the train must have been travelling too fast – but suddenly the speed faltered, the brakes squealed, and the great wheels slowed almost to a stop. Avdiy could hardly believe his eyes. Suddenly a piercing whistle was answered immediately by another.

'Right!' commanded Petrukha. 'We're off!'

Grasping their bags and cases they ran to the dawdling trucks, swift as a battalion breaking out of ambush. They had to grab something, anything, and climb aboard anywhere they could – later they would be able to move about, up and down the roofs, and find somewhere more comfortable. The rest Avdiy remembered only as a vague nightmare, rushing up and down what seemed like a bare wall of trucks, the smell of oil from the wheels searing his nostrils. Somehow he stumbled on board, helping someone, someone helping him, and at last he was in place. The train gave a couple of threatening jolts, the metal clanged and scraped, but nobody fell beneath the rolling wheels. After a final clang, it picked up speed again, and Avdiy looked around to find himself in an empty freight truck with his inseparable companions Petrukha and Lyonka, and Grishan too. God knows how he had managed to climb aboard with his ankle in that condition. Makhach and Kolya were there as well. They were all pale and panting, but their faces shone with relief and satisfaction. Avdiy could not believe that they had pulled it off and the worst was behind them. Now they were headed for Zhalpak-Saz, and from there the road lay back to where they came from, back to the city and the crowds . . .

They had five hours to go. Luckily, there were some abandoned boxes in the truck, which they used as seats. Grishan's orders were to make sure that no one could see them, but it was light enough even with the doors open on one side only and the ventilation hatches in the roof were open too. At the first stop, at some junction, they closed the door tightly and sat waiting silently in the airless heat, but no one came near the train. Petrukha took a cautious look outside and declared that all was well, no one in sight. As soon as a passenger train had rumbled past in the other direction they set off again, and at the next halt Makhach got hold of a whole jerry can of cold water, reviving them all. They had a meal of tinned food and dried bread and discussed the feast of hot food that would be waiting for them in the station diner at Zhalpak-Saz.

The train rumbled over the Chu steppes, towards the mountains . . .

The long May evenings meant that it was still light. They talked of this and that but mostly of food and money. Petrukha remembered his 'first-class' woman who was waiting for him back in Murmansk, which prompted Makhach to respond in his direct Caucasian way.

'Hey, Petrukha, old man, can't you have a woman anywhere but in Murmansk, eh? Couldn't do with a bit of "having" in Moscow on the way? Or aren't there any women to be had in Moscow, then, ha-ha. . . ?'

'Listen, Makhach, what do you understand about that kind of thing?' answered Petrukha, riled. 'You're still wet behind the ears! How old are you, anyway?'

'How old am I? Oh, old enough, if it comes to that! We Caucasians are all fathers, several times over, at my age! Ha-ha!'

The exchange cheered them all up, and even Avdiy could not help a smile; he glanced from time to time at Grishan, who sat condescendingly to one side. He was still sitting on his folding stool and holding the same gnarled stick. The only resemblance between him and the other runners lay in the cheap cigarettes that they all smoked. As they travelled their laughter brought the freight truck to life. Eventually Lyonka curled up in a corner and some of the others too decided to sleep, although the sun had not yet touched the edge of the world and everything was still light. They smoked and chatted, then fell silent. Eventually, after some whispering, they looked over towards Grishan.

'Look, Grishan,' said Makhach. 'What's the point of just sitting here? We've decided by common consent that we ought to have a bit of a smoke, we've got time, and you know what? I've got a bit of stuff, whoosh! Only the Thief of Baghdad himself ever smoked the like!'

Grishan glanced over to Avdiy to gauge his reaction, paused a while, then barked, 'Go ahead!'

They all bustled about Makhach. From his jacket he took his famous *anasha*, the like of which only the Thief of Baghdad himself had ever smoked. He rolled an enormous joint, took the first drag himself and passed it around the circle. Each one puffed reverently and passed it on along the line. When it reached Petrukha, he gulped the smoke in greedily, squinting, then held the joint out to Avdiy.

'Here, Avdiy, you try a bit, too. What's the matter with you? Here, go on! Oh, drop those airs of yours – what are you, a girl or something?'

'No, Petrukha, I'm not going to smoke, so there's no point in trying.' Avdiy refused point-blank.

Petrukha took it personally.

'Priest in skirts you were, and priest in skirts you'll stay. See if I care!'

'Please don't take it personally, Petrukha. I didn't mean it like that!'

'What's the point in talking about it?' Petrukha brushed him aside, took another drag and passed the joint on to Makhach who with Caucasian tact handed it on to Grishan.

119

'Now, leader of the pack, it's your turn! You give the toast for this round!'

Grishan pushed his hand aside in silence.

'Well, your word is law!' said Makhach with a shrug of sympathy, and the joint did the rounds again. Lyonka gulped greedily on it, then ginger Kolya, then Petrukha and back to Makhach again. Soon the smokers' mood started to change, their eyes became clouded and shining in turn, their lips spreading in meaningless, beatific smiles, until only Petrukha remembered the insult he had suffered at the hands of Avdiy, at whom he kept darting discontented glances, muttering something about priests being all the same, weasels and snakes to a man . . .

Sitting on his folding stool, Grishan observed the scene from his corner, calmly watching the smokers with an ironic, condescending smile playing smugly over his lips. The sharp and cutting glances which he darted towards Avdiy, who stood in the open doorway, showed he was pleased with the way things were going and well aware of where it might lead for the righteous Avdiy.

Avdiy realized that Grishan, in allowing the runners to have a smoke in the train, was grinding home a message, showing him how powerful he was and how impotent all Avdiy's calls to combat evil had turned out to be.

Although Avdiy pretended that he did not care what they did, in fact he was inwardly suffering and indignant at his lack of anything with which to counteract the influence of Grishan, of any practical ideas to pluck the runners from the sphere of influence of their leader. At this point his self-possession deserted him. He could no longer control the anger welling up inside him, and the last straw was Petrukha's second offer of a drag from the same joint that had done the round again, getting slimier and slimier from each successive pair of lips until it acquired a sinister yellowish-green tinge.

'Come on, Avdiy, don't squirm away from it, you're not in church now, you know! Really, I mean it, I just want you to have a try. You know, when it's been round a few times, that's when it gives a real kick, turns your brain into jelly with a single drag!' Petrukha warmed to his theme.

'Get off!' snapped Avdiy.

'What d'ya mean, "Get off"? Here I am, in all sincerity, and all you can say is "get off"! What kind of an answer is that?'

'Oh, all right, give it here then,' shouted Avdiy angrily and held out his hand for the glowing stub. When he had it, he held it provocatively aloft and then threw it out of the open door of the truck. It happened so fast that all of them, even Grishan, were rooted to the spot in surprise. In the silence the clattering of the wheels was louder, clearer and more threatening than ever. 'See that?' called Avdiy defiantly. 'See that, all of you?' He glanced angrily round the circle of runners. 'That's the way it's going to be, every time!'

First Petrukha, then the rest, turned questioningly towards Grishan, as though to seek guidance from their mentor on how to react.

Grishan was provocatively silent as he looked with the same little smile from Avdiy to the circle of indignant runners. The first to break the silence was Makhach.

'Hey! Boss! What's up? Lost your voice?'

'Oh no! I haven't lost my voice!' answered Grishan, and added maliciously, 'It's just that I promised my silence to this . . . creature. Sort it out for yourselves. I won't say another word.'

'Is that true?' Makhach turned to Avdiy.

'It is, but that's not all!' cried Avdiy. 'I gave my word that I would unmask this . . .' he nodded towards Grishan '. . . this devil, who's dragged you all into easy perdition! I won't be silent, because the truth is on my side!' No longer aware of what he was doing, he grabbed his own rucksack from the pile. Apart from Grishan, they all jumped up in surprise at what the mousy little priest might do next.

'Look, lads!' shouted Avdiy, shaking the rucksack above his head. 'Look what we're doing, taking this plague, this poison, this ruination back to other people! It's you who are doing it, Petrukha, you, Makhach, you, Lyonka, you, Kolya, drunk, high, the lot of you, on the prospect of easy money! Let alone Grishan! You know as well as I do what Grishan is!'

'Hang on, hang on there, Avdiy boy, come on, there's a good lad, give me the rucksack, pass it over now . . .' Petrukha moved towards him.

'Get back!' Avdiy pushed him away. 'And keep off! I know how to get rid of this poison!'

Before they could react, Avdiy had torn open the rucksack and was throwing handfuls of *anasha* to the four winds out of the door of the truck. The weed (and how much there was of the yellow-green flowers and leaves!) flew out along the track, whirling and spinning like autumn leaves. It was money that flew out of the door, hundreds and thousands of roubles! For an instant the runners were rooted to the spot.

'See that!' shouted Avdiy, throwing the rucksack itself out after the *anasha*. 'Now you do it! I've shown you the way! We will repent together, and God will love and forgive us all! Come on, Lyonka, Petrukha! Chuck it out! Chuck out that accursed *anasha*, out to the four winds!'

'He's flipped! He'll turn us in, once we get to the station! Grab him! Do him over, the snivelling priest!' shouted Petrukha, beside himself.

'Stop! Stop! Listen!' Avdiy thought he could explain, but the smokers were all beside themselves and it was too late. They went for him like mad dogs. Petrukha, Makhach and Kolya laid into him with their fists. Only Lyonka tried in vain to pull them off.

'Stop! Stop it at once!' He ran helplessly round the flailing group. He was one, and they were three. The beating became systematic.

'Get him! Over here! Out of the truck with him!' Petrukha shouted in a fury.

'Get the little incense-sniffer! Chuck him out!' echoed Makhach.

'Stop! Don't kill him! You can't kill him!' sobbed Lyonka, pale and shaking.

'Out of the way, pig, or I'll get you as well!' Kolya tore himself from Lyonka's grasp.

Avdiy defended himself as best he could, trying to get away from the open door into the middle of the swaying truck. Now he saw with his own eyes the savage, ferocious sadism of which the addicts were capable, although a few minutes before they had been smiling beatifically in their euphoria. Avdiy realized that he was fighting for his life, and against lengthening odds. They were three healthy fighting louts, with only

Lyonka, who hardly counted, on his side. Grishan was still sitting on his stool, watching like a spectator at the circus or the theatre, although he did not trouble to conceal his malicious satisfaction.

'Well, well! So that's how it is!' he chuckled. He had set this up, knowing all along that it would come to a fight, and now he was tasting the fruits of victory, watching a man being slowly beaten to death before his very eyes.

Avdiy realized that intervention by Grishan was his only hope. If he shouted, 'Grishan! Save me!' the runners would leave him at once, but nothing would make him turn to Grishan for help. The only other thing to do was roll over to the back of the truck and into a corner, where they could make mincemeat of him if they wanted but could not throw him out to the surest of deaths down on the tracks.

Easier said than done, however. Punches from the shoulder and a hail of kicks were inching him over towards the yawning doorway. It would take only a second for the runners to kick him out of the door. Avdiy rose again and again, trying to get away into the far corner in the hope that the addicts would tire or relent. The first to give up was Lyonka, who received a blow on the head from Kolya to get him out of the way. Nothing was to hinder them from the summary justice being meted out to Avdiy, the stinking righteous enemy of all runners, and the speed at which their fists were flying was in direct proportion to the sums involved.

'Get him! Get him! In the ribs! Get his wind!' shouted the maddened Petrukha, twisting Avdiy's arms behind his back to lay him open to a rain of blows from Makhach who, like a mad bull, was lashing at the pit of his stomach. Avdiy folded and collapsed, coughing blood, on the floor of the truck. The three of them started dragging him towards the door but he still resisted, breaking his nails as he grabbed for the boards of the floor, kicking and struggling, while the sinister Grishan sat imperturbably cross-legged on his folding stool in the corner, whistling as he watched with triumph on his face and played with his gnarled stick. He could still beg for mercy and shout, 'Save me, Grishan!' Grishan might well have relented, shown mercy and stopped their murderous fists, but Avdiy's teeth were clenched and his head left a bloody trail over the floor as

123

they dragged him towards the door for the final skirmish. They were afraid to grasp Avdiy and throw him straight out, since they might be dragged out with him. He succeeded in hanging on in the doorway – or rather, outside it – where he caught hold of the iron fastening of the handle. He was hit by the full force of the wind, pushing him against the side of the truck, but he succeeded in feeling with his left foot for the metal step and hung there, clinging on. Never in his life had he shown such physical strength, never been so greedy to survive as that moment when he strove to evade calamity. Left to his own devices, he would probably have been able to climb back into the truck, but the runners were kicking at his head as though it were a football, shouting and swearing at him, as the blood poured down his face while he clung desperately to the handle. The last few minutes were the worst. Petrukha, Makhach and Kolya were in a complete frenzy. Even Grishan showed his feelings at last and rushed to the doorway to enjoy the spectacle of Avdiy Kallistratov falling to his death on the line below. He stood watching for the inevitable moment when the runners would finish Avdiy off. Grishan knew what he was doing. He was killing Avdiy Kallistratov at the hands of other people. Even if the corpse was found and no one believed that he had fallen or at worst thrown himself from the moving train, Grishan's hands would be clean, since he had not touched the victim. He could always say that the lads had quarrelled and the quarrel turned into a fight, in which Avdiy Kallistratov had missed his footing.

The last thing Avdiy remembered was the smell of blood on the boots that were kicking him and the wind beating like flames in his face. His leaden body dragged him further and further down into the dark, implacable emptiness while the train forged ahead against the wind through a steppe where nobody knew or cared that he was hanging, with his life, by a thread. The sun of that endless day was setting at last, blinding his eyes as they bulged with terror and pain, hurtling down together with Avdiy into a dark abyss of nothingness. Even under the rain of kicks Avdiy's grip stayed firm until Petrukha delivered the final blow with Grishan's stick, conveniently to hand, and convenient for beating fingers and making them let go . . .

Avdiy, a knot of pain, fell headlong. He felt neither the fall, nor the long roll down the embankment, bruising and grazing, nor the tail of the train flashing away, wheels dying to silence as his former companions sped away along the track.

Soon the sun's light was extinguished and darkness came, bringing the lead-grey stormclouds into the western sky . . .

Other trains passed the ill-starred resting-place where the man who would not beg for mercy to prolong his life lay prostrate at the bottom of a railway ditch. All that he had learned in his desperate search for truth, all that he had discovered, was now lost and cast aside. Was it worth it, to pass up the chance of survival? The stake was his life, and all he had needed to say was three little words: 'Save me, Grishan!' Yet he had not said them . . .

In truth, there was no limit to the paradoxes of the Lord . . . Had it not all happened once before? There was once a Galilean, too, who thought so highly of himself that he passed up the chance to say a couple of words that would have saved him from death. Although almost two thousand years have passed since then, the human race is still arguing and grieving over what happened and how it came about. For every generation it is as though it happened only yesterday, so fresh is the impression left by the shock, and every succeeding generation, numberless as they are, steps boldly forward with the declaration that if they had been on Golgotha that day, they would never have allowed the execution of the Galilean. That is how we see it now, but at the time it seemed nothing particularly significant. How could they have known that, whatever would subsequently be forgotten down through the ages, that one day would be remembered in history for ever?

That, too, had been a Friday.

8

It was a hot morning in Jerusalem, promising an even hotter day. On the Arched Terrace of Herod's palace, beneath the marble colonnade where Pontius Pilate had ordered his seat to be placed, a gentle breeze blew from below to cool the sandalled feet. The tops of the triangular poplars in the great garden rustled quietly, their leaves prematurely yellowed in the dryness of this particular year.

From the Arched Terrace perched on this stony mount there was a view of the whole city, shimmering in the heat as the day progressed. The city boundaries, always clearly demarcated, seemed today to merge into the border of the white desert beyond.

That morning a single bird circled high above the great garden, wings spread wide, passing in regular sweeps as though swinging like a pendulum suspended from the heavens. It had to be an eagle or a hawk, since no other bird would have the patience to circle so slowly or so long through the furnace of the sky. When he noticed Jesus of Nazareth, who stood shifting his weight before him, glance upwards at the bird, the Procurator was indignant and even offended at the glance. He spoke irritably and harshly.

'Why look up, King of the Jews? That's your death, circling above!'

'Death circles above us all,' answered Jesus quietly, as though to himself, automatically putting his hand to the dust-stained bruise on his eye. As they led him to the judgment of the Sanhedrin, he had been attacked by a crowd whipped up by the priests and elders. Some of them lashed out at him, others spat in his face, and he understood how much he was hated by Caiaphas's men and how little mercy he could expect from the Jerusalem court – although he could not help his purely human astonishment at the cruelty and fickleness of the crowd, as though none of them realized that he was the wandering preacher to whom they had listened, open-mouthed, in the synagogues and in the streets. Had they forgotten how they shouted as he rode in through the city gates on the grey she-ass with her colt running behind, how they acclaimed him in hope and threw flowers beneath the ass's hooves? 'Hosanna to the Son of David! Hosanna in the highest!'

Now he stood frowning, his clothes torn, before Pontius Pilate, waiting for whatever might happen next.

The Procurator was badly out of sorts and primarily, strangely enough, with himself, with the sluggish way his mind was working and his inability to take a decision. Such a thing had never happened to him before, either during his time as an active soldier in the Roman army, or during his tour of duty as Procurator. Laughable! Instead of giving his immediate approval to the sentence passed by the Sanhedrin and cutting down his work-load, he was dragging out the interrogation in a time- and effort-consuming way. It would have been so simple to summon the Chief Priest and his retinue, who were waiting for his call, and say, 'Here you are, take your prisoner and do with him what you have decided.' And yet something prevented Pontius Pilate from taking this simple step. Was this fool worth taking trouble over?

But just think of the extent of his claims! He was the King of the Jews, the beloved of God, and sent by God to the Jews to lead them directly to the righteous Kingdom of God, a kingdom where there would be no room for Caesar or Caesars and their governors, or subserviently obedient synagogues, but all would be equal and happy for ever and ever till the end of time. All sorts of people had sought supreme power throughout history, but never one as clever, as cunning and perfidious as this one, for if he ever did seize the reins of power, his kingdom would of course have been ruled exactly like the rest, since nothing ever did or would change in life. The plotter himself knew it as well as anyone, but he kept on playing his part, winning over his trusting listeners with promises of the New Kingdom! The Procurator presumed that he was privy to the plans of Jesus the Nazarene, who must be intending to sow discord in the province by promising the people the New Kingdom, and to bring down the established order in the land which he intended to seize for himself at a later date. Him, a wandering prophet! Who would have thought that this pathetic Jew could dare to dream of such a thing? Such were the experienced Procurator's thoughts as he interrogated the wandering tramp, Jesus, in a somewhat unusual way, by putting himself in the subject's place, and he was supremely irritated at the intentions which he assumed to be part of the plan of such an unexpected usurper. Pontius Pilate, incensed as he was, felt at the same time torn by mounting doubts; much as he wanted to finalize at once with his procuratorial signature the death sentence that the elders of the Jerusalem Sanhedrin had pronounced over Jesus the day before, he also wanted to drag out the moment and give himself the pleasure of getting to the bottom of whatever the thoughts and actions of Jesus were threatening for the authority of Rome . . .

The answer which the condemned tramp gave to his remark about the bird in the sky grated upon the Procurator's ears as both honest and irreverent. The man could have remained silent, or said something ingratiating, but no, he decided to comfort himself with the thought that death circles above us all. Look at him! thought Pontius Pilate angrily. He's bringing it upon his own head, as though he really were not afraid of death.

'Well, then, let us go back to what we were talking about before. Do you know, wretched man, what is coming to you?' asked the Procurator huskily, wiping the sweat from his shining brown forehead yet again, then from his bald pate and his short powerful neck. While Jesus thought of his answer the Procurator cracked his sweating fingers, each joint separately, an unpleasant little habit of his. 'I asked you if you knew what was coming to you?'

Jesus sighed deeply, paling from the thought of what lay ahead.

'Yes, Roman Governor, I know: I am to be executed today,' he replied, bringing out the words with difficulty.

'I know, eh?' The Procurator repeated the words mockingly, taking in the luckless prophet with a look of contempt and pity.

The prophet stood before him, hanging his head, gawky with his long neck and long hair dishevelled in the wind, his clothes torn and his feet bare. He must have lost his sandals when he was captured. Beyond him, over the balcony of the palace terrace, the distant hills were covered with houses. The city awaited the man now being interrogated by the Procurator. The vile city was awaiting its victim. Today, in all this heat, it was demanding the shedding of blood. Its darkest instincts were thirsting for a jolt to release the violence pent up in the street crowds so that they could howl and scream in anger like jackals when they see an angry lion tear a zebra limb from limb in the Libyan desert. Pontius Pilate had seen such things among animals and among men, and inwardly he shrank in horror as the thought of the coming crucifixion crossed his mind. Again he reproached the other, not without sympathy.

'You say you "know", but that's not the right word. You'll only really "know" when it's happening to you . . .'

'Yes, Roman Governor, I know and am trembling at the thought.'

'Don't interrupt me, and don't be in a hurry for your death. There's plenty of time,' grumbled the Procurator, put off his stride.

'I beg forgiveness, ruler, if I interrupted by mistake, I did not mean to,' apologized Jesus. 'I'm not in any hurry. I'd like to live longer.'

'But you have no intention of renouncing your blasphemous words?' asked the Procurator, point-blank.

Jesus shrugged, and his eyes were helpless as a child's.

'I have nothing to renounce, Governor; those words were decided for me by my Father and I had to bring them to the people to fulfil His will.'

'You will have it your own way, won't you.' Pontius Pilate raised his voice in irritation. He had a large aquiline nose and a cruel line set in a frame of deep wrinkles for a mouth, whose expression now became coldly contemptuous. 'I can read you like a book, however you twist and turn,' he added expressionlessly. 'What do you really mean by "bringing the words of your Father to the people"? You mean making fools of them, getting the ignorant masses over to your side! Inciting the masses to mutiny and revolt. Perhaps you should be bringing His word to me as well? I'm a person, too, you know!'

'You, Roman Governor, have no need of it as yet, for you do

not suffer or thirst for another kind of life. For you, power is God and conscience, and you possess it in full measure. For you, there is nothing higher.'

'Right. There is nothing higher than the power of Rome. I hope that that is what you meant to say?'

'That is what you think, Governor.'

'That is what clever men have always thought,' the Procurator corrected him condescendingly. 'That is why they say that Caesar is not a god, but God is like Caesar. Convince me that it is not so, if you are so sure of yourself. Well?' He stared mockingly at Jesus. 'In the name of Tiberius, Emperor of Rome, whom I represent here, I can change certain things in time and space. You are attempting to confront this power with some sort of superior force, some other truth, which you claim to represent. Curious, very curious. If it weren't for my curiosity, I would not have kept you here so long. They can't wait in the city to see the Sanhedrin's sentence carried out. So, answer!'

'What should I answer?'

'Are you sure that Caesar is less than God?'

'He is mortal.'

'Obviously. But while he is alive and well, is there God above Caesar for men?'

'There is, Roman Governor, if you choose another dimension of being.'

'I won't say that you're making me laugh,' said Pontius Pilate, frowning in pretended offence and raising his wiry eyebrows. 'But you will not be able to convince me, because what you say is not even funny. I can't think who believes in you, and why.'

'I am believed in by those who are thrust in my direction by oppression, by the eternal thirst for justice; then the seed of my teaching falls in earth that is enriched by suffering and watered by tears,' explained Jesus.

'Enough!' cried the Procurator, with a dismissive gesture. 'We're wasting our time.'

They both fell silent, thinking their own thoughts. Jesus's pale forehead was suddenly bathed in sweat. He did not wipe it away with a hand or the torn sleeve of his garment, too preoccupied with the lump of terror in his throat. The sweat streamed down his face and fell in drops on to the marble paving-stones by his thin, sinewy feet.

'And after that,' went on the gravelly voice of Pontius Pilate, 'you wanted me, the Roman Procurator, to grant you your freedom?'

'Yes, kind ruler, let me go.'

'What will you do?'

'I'll pass through all lands with the word of God.'

'Looking for fools!' shouted the Procurator, and jumped up, beside himself with fury. 'Now I am completely convinced that the place for you is on the cross: only death will cool you down.'

'You are mistaken, great ruler, death is powerless before the Spirit,' said Jesus firmly and clearly.

'What? What did you say?' exclaimed Pontius Pilate in astonishment, not believing his ears and starting towards Jesus. His face, distorted with fury and astonishment, was mottled with dark brown spots.

'Exactly what you heard, ruler.'

Pontius Pilate threw up his hands and breathed in, on the point of speaking, but at that moment the sound of iron-tipped cavalry boots rang out across the marble.

'What is it?' the Procurator asked the armed legionary who approached with a parchment.

'Orders are to give you this, sir,' barked the soldier and withdrew.

It was a note for Pontius Pilate from his wife:

Procurator, spouse, I beg you, do not harm this wanderer whom they say is known as the Christ. Everyone says that he is a harmless and righteous man, a miraculous healer of all kinds of ills. Maybe it is all slander, put about by his enemies, all this about being the son of God, the Messiah and even King of the Jews? I can't tell. You know yourselves what fanatics these Jews are and how they love a fuss. And what if it should be true? They say that the men of the synagogues and the elders of the city took fright because the people followed him, so from envy they slandered him and set the ignorant masses to tear him apart. Those who worshipped him yesterday are stoning him today. As I see it, Pontius, spouse, if you agree to the execution of this holy fool you will be blamed for it for ever more. We won't be in Judea for ever: I want you to return to Rome with full honours. Do not do it, Pontius. When the guard led him past just now, I saw how handsome he was, like a young god. By the way, I had a strange dream last night. I'll tell you about it later. A very significant one. Don't draw curses down upon your own head and upon those of your descendants!

'Ye gods! How have I angered you?' groaned Pontius Pilate and regretted again not having sent him off straight away under guard, with no further ado, this mad, fanatical false prophet, off to the executioners, beyond the allotments of the town, to the place on the hill where they awaited his execution, as demanded by the Jerusalem court. Now his wife was interfering in his procuratorial business, which he viewed if not as the secret workings of the powers protecting Jesus Christ, then at least as heaven's resistance to what he was doing, though he knew that the denizens of heaven had little interest in what went on on earth. Anyway, what did his wife understand of the world of politics? Why should he court the enmity of Caiaphas, the Chief Priest, and the men who ran Jerusalem, committed and faithful as they were to Rome, for the sake of this suspicious tramp Jesus, reviler of the Caesars? Whatever made her find him 'like a young god'? Well, young, but that was as far as it went. Nothing 'handsome' about him at all. There he stood, beaten in the scuffle like a dog. Whatever could she see in him? The Procurator paced thoughtfully as he mulled over the contents of the note, then sighed as he settled back into his chair. At the same time a thought that had crossed his mind before came back to him again: in spite of men being such a paltry race, excreting, mating, being born, dying, bearing others who die in their turn, in spite of their worthless insignificance and the evil that they bore within them, in spite of all this loathsome morass in which they lived – somehow, surprisingly, they could produce prophets, seers and spiritual impulses. Before him stood an example, who believed so strongly in his mission that he seemed to live in a dream and not in the realm of real life. However, enough was enough: time to bring him back to his senses! Time to wake up!

'Anyway, this is what I want to know,' said the Procurator to Jesus who still stood silently in his place. 'Just supposing you are a righteous man and not a plotter spreading dissension amongst the simple-minded; just supposing when you speak of the Kingdom of Justice you are questioning the right of Caesar to rule the world, and just supposing that I believe you; tell me this: what is it that makes you willing to go to your death? Share the secret with me! What is the force that moves you? If this is the way you have chosen to seize kingly power over the people of Israel, then I do not approve, but I do understand. But why cut the branch on which you are intending to sit? How can you be a Caesar if you deny the power of Caesar? You understand that it is in my power to leave you with your life or to send you to your death. Why don't you answer, then? Or are you frozen with terror?'

'Yes, Roman Governor, I am afraid of a savage death. And I have no intention of becoming a Caesar.'

'Then repent in all the squares of the city, admit the error of your ways. Admit that you are a false seer, a false prophet, stop claiming to be the King of the Jews, send away the common people and cease to tempt them with vain and criminal expectations. There can never be a Kingdom of Justice. That which is, is just – always. We have the Emperor Tiberius, and he is the firm, unshakeable pillar of the world. But the Kingdom of Justice, with tales of which you incite the simple-minded to murmur against Rome, is an empty dream. Just think! And stop bothering yourself and everyone else with it. Anyway, who are you, for the Roman Emperor to need to guard against you? An unknown wanderer, a questionable prophet, a market-place crackpot the like of which you can find all over the land of Judea. But you were spreading temptation with your teaching, much to the consternation of your High Priest, and that is why you must admit your falsehood. Afterwards you can take yourself off to Syria or somewhere else, and I, as Roman Procurator, will try to help you. Agree, before it's too late! What? Silent again?'

'I'm thinking, Roman Governor. We're so different that I don't think we'll ever understand one another. Why should I be a hypocrite and deny the teaching of God in a way that is good for Caesar and for you, but which will trample on the truth?'

'No riddles. What is good for Rome is the highest good.'

'The highest good is truth, and there is only one truth. You can't have two truths.'

'Riddles again, tramp?'

'No riddles, either then or now. My answer is this: first – I must not deny that which was said in the name of truth, for the truth was what you demanded. And second – I must not take upon myself the blame for what I have not done and beat my breast, merely to be rid of slander. Since the slander is lies, it will die of itself.'

'But you will die first, King of the Jews! And so, you are determined on death, even though I am showing you a path to salvation?'

'For me, this is the only path to salvation that remains.'

'To what salvation?' The Procurator was puzzled.

'To the salvation of the world.'

'That's enough of playing the holy fool!' erupted Pilate. 'So, you are going voluntarily to your death?'

'I must be, since there is no other way for me to go.'

'Ye gods, ye gods!' murmured the Procurator tiredly, running a hand over the deep lines that furrowed his brow. How hot it is! Perhaps it means a change in the weather? He muttered to himself, and then, taking the plunge, What's all this to me? Why should I try to save a man who sees no point in my efforts? I must be crazy myself! Out loud he said, 'In that case I wash my hands of it!'

'Your will be done, Governor,' replied Jesus, and hung his head.

They were silent again, and must both have been aware, beyond the palace fence, beyond the splendid garden, out there where the streets breathed the midday heat in the valleys and on the hills of Jerusalem, how a vast and sinister silence was swelling gradually towards bursting point. For the moment, all that reached them were confused sounds, the hum of the great bazaars where since early morning there had been an eddying stream of people, goods, draught-oxen and other beasts of burden. Between lay that which divided them and protected the upper world from the lower one; the

134

legionaries moving back and forth beyond the fence, and lower down, in the trees, the cordon of cavalry. They could see the horses brushing away the flies with their tails.

Once he had declared that he was washing his hands the Procurator felt a certain amount of relief, since now he could say to himself: I did all that I could. As the gods are my witness, I did not provoke him into insisting on doing it his own way, into choosing his teaching in preference to life itself. Since he refuses to recant, so be it. From our point of view it's more satisfactory, if anything. He's signed his own death-warrant . . . As he pondered these thoughts, Pontius Pilate was preparing his answer for his wife. He glanced again at Jesus the Nazarene, silently awaiting his pre-determined fate with a vague smile on his lips, and wondered: What's he thinking, now? He must be bitterly regretting that oh-so-wise 'teaching' of his, aware of what it will cost him if he refuses to thrust it aside. He's caught in his own trap. No escape! One God for all, for all lands, for the whole human race, for all times. One faith. One Kingdom of Justice for all. Of course, that's what everyone would like to see, that's what he's decided to play on! But life has a way of putting us straight, of cutting us down to size if we get too clever. This is what happens to those who grab for a throne not predestined to them by birth. What was he after? He decided to whip up the common people, to make them rise up against the Caesars, and then infect the whole world, one crowd passing it on to the next. He wanted to turn on its head the established order. He was aiming high, you had to grant him that! No, a man like that could not be left alive. He looks so beaten and humbled, too, but there must be a lot more to him than meets the eye, for him to set out with a plan of those proportions. Who would have thought it?

And in such thoughts Procurator Pontius Pilate found peace with himself. He was also glad to have avoided an unpleasant exchange with Caiaphas, the Chief Priest, who was openly demanding in the name of the Sanhedrin that he countersign the sentence pronounced on Jesus the Nazarene by the court.

'Fear not, wise ruler, you will find peace with yourself and be justified in every respect,' announced Jesus, as though he had guessed the Procurator's thoughts.

135

Pontius Pilate was indignant.

'Don't you worry about me,' he answered brusquely. 'For me it's respect for Rome that comes first. Think of yourself, wretch!'

'Forgive me, great ruler, I was wrong to say those words aloud.'

'You were indeed. Now, so that you should not have cause to be sorry when it's too late, I will leave you alone a while to think. If by my return you have not changed your mind, then I will pronounce the final word upon the matter. Don't make out that you're King of the Jews, pillar of the world, and that the earth will never survive without you. Everything's gone against you. Your time is long since up. You might still save yourself, but only by renouncing all. Have you got my meaning?'

'I have, ruler . . .'

Pontius Pilate rose and retreated into his apartments, adjusting the swirling toga on his shoulder as he went, an angular, large-headed, bald man, secure in his dignity and omnipotence. As he passed along the Arched Terrace his glance fell again upon the bird planing regally high in the sky. He still could not make out if it was an eagle or one of the other birds of prey; what disturbed him, however, was the fact that the bird was inaccessible, beyond his power, not to be chased away any more than it could be summoned or dismissed. Frowning, the Procurator darted an angry glance towards the sky where the bird circled and circled, indifferent to all that passed on the terrace below. The thought crossed his mind that the bird was like an emperor in the sky. No coincidence that the eagle was the symbol of imperial grandeur, with its powerful beak, its predatory eye and wings as strong as steel! The stuff of which emperors were made! High above all the Emperor was visible but unapproachable, and from the heights he ruled the world, no equals on this earth, with even his own private gods, different from those of other men, indifferent to his subjects and scorning their concerns. That was the foundation of power, that it was which made men fear authority, that was the bastion of the established order in the world. And to think that the Nazarene, so stubborn in his teaching, who wanted to make all men equal, from emperor to slave (for God he imagined on a throne, with all men equal in his eyes), the Nazarene was claiming that the Kingdom of Justice was coming for all. He had sown dissension, stirred up the people and tilted at rebuilding the world his own way. And what had become of his efforts? Those same people had beaten him and spat in his face, the false seer, false prophet, deceiver and scoundrel . . . What sort of man was he? In spite of the hopelessness of his situation he behaved as though it were not he who suffered defeat, but those who judged him . . .

These were the thoughts of Procurator Pontius Pilate, Governor for the Roman Emperor, half an emperor himself, at least in this part of the Mediterranean, as he left Jesus the Nazarene alone for a few minutes to let him glance for a moment into the yawning pit over which his life was hanging. He should have broken the man's spirit, made him crawl in humiliation and disavow his 'one God for all', his universal equality, so that then he could be driven from the land of Israel like a reptile with a broken back, to wander and perish unknown. He would not have lasted long! His own disciples would have finished him off, once they lost their faith in him . . .

Such were his thoughts as Pontius Pilate, the experienced Governor, struggled with his doubts and sought the surest, most profitable and instructive way to eradicate this new-found form of sedition. As he left the Arched Terrace he presumed that the prisoner, once he was left alone, would realize what fate awaited him, and when the Procurator returned would fall at his feet. If only he knew! In fact the strange man was thinking of something completely different, or rather, in a completely different way. He had retreated into his memories, for memories are also one of the attributes of life and one of the last blessings to which we cling when we stand on the threshold of death.

As soon as the Procurator left, four guards appeared from side niches and took up their places at the corners of the Arched Terrace, as though the prisoner could escape. He made so bold as to address the nearest legionary.

'May I sit down, kind guard?'

'Sit!' answered the guard, striking the floor with his spear.

Jesus sat hunched on a marble step by the wall, his pale, sharp features framed in long, flowing waves of dark hair. He covered his eyes with his hand and retreated into himself. A drink . . . he thought, or a long swim in some river! He could vividly see water rushing past a river bank, kissing the earth and the riverside plants, and imagined the sound of the water lapping and oars, bringing a boat to the place where he sat, as though he could be put in a boat to sail away from here. It was his mother, rowing towards him in anxiety and fear. Mother! he whispered, silently. Mother, if only you knew how hard it is! Last night in Gethsemane, on the Mount of Olives, I lost heart, trembling in the face of a despair which cloaked me like the darkest night. I could not take comfort, and later, as I sat awake with my disciples, the feeling still haunted me and in that terrible foreboding I sweated blood. I turned to the Lord, to my heavenly Father, and prayed: 'Father! If only You would give Your blessing for this cup to pass me by! But be it done according to Thy will, and not to mine.' And so here it is, this cup, full to the brim, and it will not pass me by: it comes inexorably closer, and all will be fulfilled as no doubt you can foresee. You must have known – oh God! How did you live all these years, dear Mother, you who gave me breath and bore me? What can your thoughts and hopes have been as I grew up, destined by God's plan for this great and terrible day? There is no greater grief for a man than his own death, but for a mother, when the fruit of her own womb, her own seed, is killed before her eyes, the grief is doubled. Forgive me, Mother, but I have determined your fate, as did my Heavenly Father, so let us turn our eyes to Him without a murmur, and His will be done!

I am taking my leave of you, now, Mother. Don't take it hard if I can't or don't have time to speak with you before I die. I am afraid of death, and my feet are cold, in spite of the heat today. Forgive me, Mother, and do not murmur against your fate in this my hour of darkness. Take heart! I have no other path to truth amongst men, who are the heaviest burden borne by the Creator, than to affirm the truth through my own death. There is no other way to the hearts of men, where I am going. Forgive me, Mother! I can hear footsteps, it's my unwilling executioner, Pontius Pilate. Farewell, Mother, farewell in advance.

Pontius Pilate returned to the Arched Terrace with the same firm tread with which he had left it. The guards drew back immediately, and the two men were alone again. With an expressive glance at Jesus, who had risen to his feet at the other man's approach, the Procurator assumed that everything was going his way, and the victim was moving steadfastly towards the limit of his endurance. This time, since things were going in the right direction as it was, he decided to take it a little more gently.

'Well, your time is up,' said Pontius Pilate at once. 'Changed your mind?'

'No.'

'Very foolish. Think again.'

'No!' Jesus shook his head. 'Let it be as it must be.'

'Very foolish!' repeated Pontius Pilate, although less convincingly. His heart sank, shocked by the decisive answer from Jesus the Nazarene, even though something else in him did not want to see Jesus recant and seek salvation by begging for mercy. Jesus understood at once.

'Don't grieve.' He smiled mildly. 'I believe that your words are sincere. And I understand you. I want to live, too, I want it very much. It is only on the threshold of nothingness that a man realizes how dear life is to him. I am sorry for my mother, too. I've loved her so much, from my childhood, though I never talked about it. Anyway, whatever happens, Roman Governor, you remember this: you could have saved one man, and you would have been thanked by many for doing so, but I must save many, even the souls of those who will be born after we are dead.'

'Save them? When you are no longer here?'

'Yes, when I am no longer living amongst men.'

'You have only yourself to blame for your fate. We won't come back to the subject,' Pilate suddenly announced decisively, unwilling to take any more risks. 'But answer my last question,' he added, standing by his chair, and fell silent, thinking, twitching his bushy brows. 'Are you in a fit state to talk?' he suddenly asked gently. 'If you don't feel up to it, then don't bother, I don't want to keep you. They're waiting for you on the hill.'

'As you will, ruler, I am at your disposal,' answered his

interlocutor and raised his translucent blue eyes to the Procurator's face. They showed the power and concentration of his thoughts, as though there was nothing inevitable waiting for him on the hill.

'Thank you,' said Pontius Pilate unexpectedly. 'In that case, answer me one last question, for the sake of my curiosity. Let us walk like free men. I am in no way dependent on you, and you, as you understand, are on the threshold of complete freedom, so let's be frank,' he proposed, settling back into his seat. 'Tell me, did you tell your disciples, your followers – and you well understand that I do not follow your teaching – did you assure them that if you were crucified, you would rise again on the third day, and once arisen would come back to earth for a Last Judgment of those who are alive today, and those who are yet to be born, of all generations since the creation of the world? Your second coming? Did you?'

Jesus gave a strange laugh, as though saying to himself, Oh, so that's it! He moved over the marble on his bare feet, silently, as though deciding whether it was worth answering or not.

'Is that what Judas Iscariot was saying?' he asked mockingly. 'And it's got you worried, eh, Roman Governor?'

'I don't know who Judas might be, but that's what I was told by the elders, by trustworthy men. So, what? Empty words?'

'Think what you like, ruler,' answered Jesus coldly. 'Nobody's forcing alien ideas upon you.'

'No, I'm serious, I'm not joking,' said the Procurator hurriedly. 'It's just that I was thinking we wouldn't have another chance to talk like this. As soon as they lead you away from here, there's no turning back. I just wanted to find out for myself how a man could come back to earth after he was dead, without being born again, and sit in judgment over all. And where will the judgment take place? In heaven, or somewhere else? How long will those who believed you have to wait for the day when eternal peace will be theirs? Allow me to start by giving you my own view of all this. Your reckoning is simple: you're counting on the fact that everyone seeks to be comforted in the next world. That's what mortals are, ever wanting, ever longing for something! It is so easy to tempt them with promises – even in the next world, they'll follow you like dogs! Still, even if it is the way you teach, prophet, your life has almost run its course, and your only way to prolong it lies in conversation . . .'

'I don't need to prolong it at all.'

'But you won't go to the hill leaving my question unanswered. In my understanding, to leave like that would be worse than death.'

'Carry on.'

'Right then, just supposing that your teaching is correct, then tell me this: when will it be, the day of your second coming? And if the expectation is to last an unimaginably long time, what good is it to mankind? There is little to recommend an event that will not come about in the individual's own lifetime, and to be quite frank, I can't imagine anyone waiting for such an unlikely event at all. Or do you think they should wait, believing blindly? And what is the point? What good does it do?'

'Your doubts are to be expected, Roman ruler: your thinking is coarse and earthly like that of your teachers, the Greeks. Don't take offence. While I stand before you as a mortal man, you have every right to argue. We're so different, too, like fire and water. Our ideas are bound to be different, since we approach all things from a different direction. So, to get back to the thing that's worrying you, ruler . . . It is indeed true that the Second Coming will be awaited for a long, long time. You're right in that. No one can predict when the day will come, for it is all laid down in the plan of Him who made the world. What lasts thousands of years for us is perhaps the twinkling of an eye for Him. But that is not the point. The Creator gave us the greatest gift of all the world, the gift of reason, and he gave us the will to live according to our understanding. The story of human history will be the story of how we use this gift from heaven. You will not deny, Roman Governor, that the point of man's existence is his spiritual journey towards improvement and perfection: there is no higher aim in life. That is the beauty of intelligent life, the daily trudge up the endless staircase towards shining perfection of spirit. It's harder to be human from day to day, which is why the length of wait for that day in which you do not believe, ruler, depends on men themselves.'

'So that's it!' Pontius Pilate jumped up excitedly, grasping

141

the back of his chair. 'Stop! Stop! It's unimaginable that such an outcome should depend on men themselves! For one who does not believe in your teaching it is impossible to understand. If men could, by an act of will, bring closer or put off such an event, why then, they would be like gods!'

'In a way you're right, Roman ruler, but I'd like to start by separating the half-truth from the truth. A half-truth about a truth is a great misfortune. Half-truths are like mud in water, that in time can transform a deep lake into a shallow puddle. It's always like that in life: any great idea, born to bring good to men, achieved in visions and suffering, will be distorted as it passes from mouth to mouth, transforming the truth to evil and itself to truth. That's what I'm getting at, Governor: the fables you believe are half-truths, while the truth lies elsewhere.'

'Won't you reveal that truth?'

'I'll try. I won't evade opportunity for conversation, especially as this is the last time I shall talk about these things. So, Roman ruler, remember this: God's plan is not to surprise us one day, like summer thunder out of the blue, with the Son of Man, resurrected, descending from heaven to sit in judgment over the nations; it will all be quite different, though the final objective remains the same. It is not I, who have only the distance across the city to Golgotha left to live, who will return, resurrected; it is you, the human race, who will come again to live in Christ, a righteous life, in countless future generations. That will be my Second Coming. In other words, I will return to myself in men, through my suffering. That is what I teach. I will be your future, left thousands of years behind in the chronological past: this is the Almighty's plan, to raise man in this way on to the throne of his true calling, his calling to goodness and beauty. That is what I have preached and therein lies the truth, not in the half-truths or fairy-tales that eventually vulgarize all great conceptions. My path will be the hardest of all for the human race, and infinitely long, and you are right, Roman Governor, to fear it. The path will stretch forward from this fateful day, from the killing of the Son of God, and succeeding generations will be ever repenting, trembling at the price to be paid by me today in expiation for human sinfulness, to open their eyes and awaken within them

142

a spark of the divine. That is why I was born on earth, to serve as an undimmed example to men, so that they should hope in my name and come to me through suffering, through the struggle with evil within themselves, day after day, through disgust with vice, with violence and bloodlust that all attack the soul if it be not filled with love for God and therefore for our fellows too, for men!'

'What, Jesus of Nazareth, you equate God and men?'

'In some sense I do. And more than that: all men, when taken together, are the image of God on earth. The name of this manifestation of God is the God of Tomorrow, the God of Eternity, given to the world from the time of its creation. I am sure that you, Roman ruler, have noticed how often your desires are directed towards the future. For today you accept life the way it is, but you always wish for tomorrow to be different; even if you're happy today you still want tomorrow to be even happier. That is why our hopes live on in us, inextinguishable as God's own daylight. The God of Tomorrow is the spirit of eternity, the essence and sum of all human action and striving, and that is why it depends on men whether the God of Tomorrow is fine or ugly, mild or punitive. It is permissible – imperative even – to reason in this way, as God the Creator has ordained His thinking creation to reason, and that is why men themselves must think to the tomorrow on their earth, for each one of them is a particle of the God of Tomorrow. Man himself is the creator and judge of every one of our days.'

'Then what of the Last Judgment, of which you preached so threateningly?'

'The Last Judgment . . . Has it not struck you, Roman ruler, that it has long since commenced for us?'

'Are you trying to say that the whole of our life is one Last Judgment?'

'You're not far from the truth, Roman ruler. To follow the path that began in pain and suffering with the curse of Adam, through the evil that men have imposed on one another throughout the ages, ill breeding ill and lies breeding lies – to follow that path must mean something for those who have lived and are living on this earth of ours. Since our first parents were driven from the Garden of Eden, what a pit of evil has yawned beneath us, what wars, cruelty, murders, persecutions, injustice and humiliation the human race has known! And all the terrible sins against goodness, against nature, committed on this earth since the world began – what are they, if not a punishment far greater than the Last Judgment? Is not the purpose of history to draw thinking creation closer to the divine heights of love and sympathy? Instead of drawing closer, however, many lives have been broken in the course of human history, with no end in sight to the evil that surges up on every side like waves in the ocean. Is not life in this hell worse than any Last Judgment?'

'And do you intend, Jesus of Nazareth, to put a stop to history in order to conquer evil?'

'History? No one can put a stop to history. I intend to eradicate evil from the minds and works of men; that is my concern.'

'Then there will be no history left.'

'Ah, but which history? The history that is of concern to you, Roman Governor? Unfortunately there is no way to wipe that history off the slate, but if it had never been, we would all be much closer to God. I understand your thinking, Governor. The real history, however, the history of the flowering of humanity, that has not even started yet.'

'Wait, Jesus of Nazareth, leave me aside for the moment. How do you aim to bring individuals and people to reach such a goal?'

'By proclaiming the Kingdom of Justice without rule by the Caesars, that's how!'

'Is that enough?'

'Yes, if all of us wanted it . . .'

'Very interesting. Well, Jesus of Nazareth, I have listened most carefully to all you had to say. You are clear-sighted, but are you not over-confident? Do you not have too much hope in human faith, forgetting how fickle and venal they are out there in the streets and the squares? You'll soon see what I mean once you pass beyond the city wall, but you won't be able to deflect the tide of history: that is a river that no one can turn from its course. One thing puzzles me: why are you lighting a fire in which you yourself will be the first to perish? Without the Caesars, and Caesars in general, human society could not exist: it needs the power and majesty of the few and the subjugation of the many, and all your efforts to introduce another state of things, invented by yourself, as a new kind of history, will be in vain. The Caesars have their own gods; they do not worship your abstract "God of Tomorrow", a vague and amorphous infinity of tomorrows that belongs equally to all men, like the air we breathe. Anything that can be given equally to all men is worthless and empty: that is why the Caesars can rule over each and every one of their subjects, and of all the Caesars who have ruled, Tiberius has been singled out by the gods, for his authority, the Roman Empire, covers half the world. That is why, in the name of Tiberius, I rule over the Jews. This is my role in life, and my conscience is at peace. There is no greater honour than to serve all-conquering Rome!'

'You are no exception, Roman Governor: almost every man thirsts for power over at least one fellow creature. That is man's misfortune. You say that such is the way of our world. Vice is always easy to justify. Few, however, are those who stop to think that this is the curse of the human race, that the evil of hunger for power with which we are all infected, from the chief sweeper in the bazaar to the mighty emperors themselves, is the blackest of all evils, an evil for which the human race will one day have to pay in full. Nations will perish in the struggle for power and land; they will tear each other up by the roots and eradicate each other in the struggle.'

Pontius Pilate gestured impatiently, interrupting his interlocutor.

'Stop! I am not one of your pupils, to sit and listen piously to all of this! Stop! You can use words to destroy anything you fancy, but whatever you prophesy, Jesus of Nazareth, you're wasting your breath. A world ruled by the powers that be will never change. The foundation remains the same: he who is strongest seizes power, and the strongest will always rule the world. This rule is as firm as the stars in the sky. No one can move them. It's useless to care for the human race, and useless for you to want to save it at the price of your own life. Man will never learn, neither from teaching in the temple, nor from voices in the sky! They will always follow the Caesars as the sheep follow their shepherds and, bowing to strength and privilege, will respect the one who proves himself most merciless and most powerful. They will glorify their commanders and the battles they win, where blood is shed in rivers for the sake of triumph for some and abject humiliation for others. This is the valour that is sung and lauded from generation to generation, banners waving and trumpets sounding, stirring the blood of the masses as they swear not to give an inch of ground to the enemy. In the name of those same masses, fighting will be elevated into something essential, and hatred for the enemies of the fatherland will be taught to the young: let our ruler prosper, but crush the other, drive him to his knees, enslave him along with the whole of his people, and take their land . . . There's the spice of their life, point and meaning since time immemorial, and you, Nazarene, want to reject and put it all away; you praise the poor and meek, you want only good, forgetting of course that man is an animal, he can't live without war, just as our flesh cannot live without salt. Reflect on your illusions and mistakes at least now, when the hour has come for you to go under guard to the Place of the Skull, to Golgotha. My final words to you in parting: you see the root of all evil in men's love of power, in subjugating lands and people by force, but by doing so you are only compounding your guilt in the eyes of the authorities, for he who is against power is also, *de facto*, against those who exercise that power. You must be tilting at our Roman Empire when you proclaim your Kingdom of Justice. You wish to hinder the growing power of Rome, to prevent its taking control of all the world; just to want such a thing is enough to condemn you three times over!'

'No need to be so open-handed, kind ruler, I think one execution is perfectly adequate! But let us carry on with what we were saying, although I do appreciate that the executioners waiting for me on Golgotha must be getting restless in this heat. Let us carry on the conversation, this time as the last wish of a condemned man. So, Roman Governor, you are convinced that the thing which you consider power really is power? But there is another power – the power of good, much harder to achieve than your kind. Virtue demands no less courage than going to war. Listen to me, Governor; as it has turned out, you are the last person to whom I will have the opportunity to talk before I go to the Place of the Skull. I want to be open with you, but fear not: I won't ask you for a pardon . . .'

'That would be simply laughable.'

'That's why I mentioned it, so that you should not worry, Governor. Now you are the only person who will know what I am about to say. Last night my spirit was in torment, for no reason at all, as I thought at first. Gethsemane was cool and pleasant, for a small breeze blew on the hills of the city. I could not settle, however; fear and despair weighed me down, and groans seemed to rise from my heart up to the very sky. My followers, my disciples, tried to watch with me, but they brought no comfort. I knew that the hour was coming, that inexorable death was upon me. I was gripped with terror . . . After all, the death of every man means the end of the world for him.'

'Why should that be?' gloated Pontius Pilate. 'What about eternal life, Nazarene? You said yourself that life does not end with death.'

'You're judging by the half-truths again, ruler! In life after death the spirit floats soundlessly, like a shadow on water, the reflection of an elusive thought in the outer darkness, but it is no place for the flesh. It is another sphere, another kind of being, one which we can never know on earth. Time flows there in a different way, under unmeasurable laws different from our earthly ones. I'm talking about life here, on our measurable earth. I was labouring under a strange premonition of total abandonment on earth; I wandered in Gethsemane that night like a shade myself, could find no peace, feeling as though I were the only sentient being left in the whole universe, flying over the earth and never seeing another living soul. Everything was dead, everything was covered with the black ash of some long-since-raging fire; the earth lay in ruins, no forests, no fields, no ships on the sea. Only a strange ringing sound filled the air, like a sad groaning in the wind, like a sobbing of metal deep within the earth, like a funeral bell, while I flew like a single speck of dust beneath the stars, burdened with fear and the foreboding of ill, and the thought, "This is the end of the world." A great anguish seared my soul. Where had all the people gone? Where was I to lay my head? And I murmured in my heart, "There, Lord, there's the fatal outcome all generations

147

have been waiting for, there's the Apocalypse, there's the end of history for thinking beings . . ." But what had caused it? How could everything die like that, wither away, its progeny die within it? And suddenly I guessed a terrible answer: this was the retribution for my loving the human race and sacrificing myself for its sake. Had the harsh world of men killed itself in its cruelty, as a scorpion stings itself with its own poison? Had man's incompatibility with man, the incompatibility of boundaries between empires, the incompatibility of ideas, of pride and hunger for power, the incompatibility of great Caesars, sated with absolute power, and of the peoples who follow them in blind obedience and hypocritical praise, armed to the teeth, boasting of victories in countless internecine struggles – had all this brought the world to such a terrible end? Would this be the end, would men carry off with them to the nothingness beyond the grave the divine gift of reason? "O Lord," I murmured, "why did you give mind and speech, and hands free to create, to a race which killed all that was human in humanity and turned its earth to a wasteland of shame?" I sobbed and moaned alone in a silent world, cursing my fate, and said to God, "That which even Thou wouldst hesitate to touch, man has befouled . . ." So understand this, Roman ruler: not I, nor natural calamities, but the enmity of men will bring about the end of the world: that enmity and those victories which you so praise in the thrill of power . . .'

Jesus paused for breath and continued.

'That was my vision last night, and I thought about it all night. I did not sleep, but was wakeful in prayer and, summoning up my courage, was intending to tell my disciples of this vision vouchsafed me by the Father, when suddenly a great crowd appeared in Gethsemane, with Judas among them. Judas swiftly embraced me, kissing me with his cold lips. "Hail, Master!" he cried to me, but before that, he had said to those he came with, "He whom I shall kiss, He is the one. Take Him." And they seized me. And so here I stand before you, as you see, Roman Governor. I know that now my path lies to Golgotha; but you were merciful to me, ruler, and I am glad to tell someone before I die what I lived through yesterday in Gethsemane.'

'Are you sure that I have been convinced by all I heard?'

'It is for you, Governor, to believe or not to. You're far more likely not to believe, since you and I are two different elements. But you heard me out. Now you can never say that you didn't hear, and you can never stop yourself thinking about what you've heard. And I need not reproach myself with taking to the grave my vision in Gethsemane. My conscience is now at peace.'

'Say, Nazarene, you didn't by any chance tell fortunes in bazaars?'

'No, ruler, why do you ask?'

'I can't decide: either you're play-acting, or else you're fearless and unafraid of an excruciating death. Will you really care, once you're gone, what you had time to say and what you had to leave unsaid, who heard you and who did not? Who cares, then? Is it not all vanity, vanity of vanities?'

'Far from it, ruler, nothing vain at all! Before death, thoughts fly straight up to God; God cares what a man thinks before his death, and that is how God judges the human race which He once created as the highest of all forms of life, for the last thoughts of men are always clear, perfectly honest, the purest truth without any admixture of mere cunning. No, ruler, I'm sorry, but you're wrong to think that I am play-acting. Playing is something I finished with when I put away my toys, and I've never taken it up again. There's no point in trying to hide my fear of suffering, I've already spoken about it before. I am afraid! Very much afraid! And I pray to my Lord, the Father of All Good, to give me the strength to bear with dignity the fate being prepared for me, not to let me sink to bleating like an animal or disgace myself in another way . . . I'm ready, Roman Governor, don't keep me here any longer . . . There's no point. It's time to go.'

'Yes, to the Place of the Skull. How old are you, Jesus of Nazareth?'

'Thirty-three, ruler.'

'How young you are! Twenty years younger than I am,' noted Pontius Pilate with pity. He shook his head, paused and said, 'As far as I know, you are not married, so you don't have any children, I presume. That's what we'll put in the record.' He fell silent, seemed on the point of saying something else, changed his mind and lapsed into silence again – just as well, since he had almost said something to embarrass them both. He was about to ask, Have you ever known a woman? He blushed. What a meddling, female question! How could a self-respecting man in his position even think of asking such a question?

At that moment he glanced up at Jesus the Nazarene and caught his eye. He could tell that the other had guessed the question he was wanting to ask, and that he would not have answered. Jesus's translucent blue eyes darkened, and he withdrew into himself. Looks so mild, but what strength! thought Pontius Pilate, feeling with his foot for a sandal which had slipped off. 'Right then.' He would turn the question in another direction, as though to compensate for the lost question about women. 'They say that you grew up in a cuckoo's nest. Did you?'

Jesus smiled an open and friendly smile, revealing even, white teeth.

'In a way, I suppose you could say I did.'

'Well, did you, or didn't you?'

'Yes, I did, kind ruler,' answered Jesus, feeling Pilate's rising irritation. This question, too, was hardly commensurate with the dignity of a Procurator. 'I was made incarnate by my heavenly Father, through the power of the Holy Spirit.'

'I'm glad you're not going to be able to play the fool any longer,' grunted the Procurator tiredly. 'But who was the mother who bore you?'

'She's in Galilee. Her name is Mary. I can sense that she'll be here in time today. She travelled all night. I know.'

'I don't suppose she'll be delighted at what's to become of her son,' said Pontius Pilate darkly. At last this endless talk with the holy fool from Nazareth was coming to an end.

The Procurator pulled himself up to his full height beneath the arches of the terrace and stood there, tall and broad-browed, with big features and a firm stare, in his snow-white toga.

'Just one more time, for the record,' he said and repeated, 'Father: what d'you say his name was? Joseph? Mother: Mary. From Nazareth. Thirty-three years old. Unmarried. No children. Incited the people to revolt. Threatened to destroy the great Temple at Jerusalem and to rebuild it within three days.

150

Made himself out to be a prophet, the King of the Jews. There's the story of your life in a nutshell.'

'Never mind the story of my life. One thing I will tell you, though, Pontius Pilate, is that yours will find a place in history,' said Jesus the Nazarene quietly, with a direct, serious look into the Procurator's eyes. 'For ever.'

'Ha-ha!' Pontius Pilate brushed the suggestion aside, flattered, however, by the suggestion. Suddenly he changed his tone and announced triumphantly, 'It's our glorious Emperor Tiberius who will live for ever in history. Glory to his name! We are merely his faithful outriders, nothing more.'

'You know, you really will find a place in history, Pontius Pilate,' he repeated stubbornly, the man who was setting off for the Place of the Skull, beyond the city walls . . .

The bird (kite or eagle?), which had been circling above Herod's palace all morning as though in wait for something, left its place at last and flew slowly across the city to where a man, tied up like a dangerous criminal, was being led by a multitude of armed guards, the same man who had talked so long with Pontius Pilate himself, Procurator of all Judea.

The Procurator stood on the Arched Terrace, watching the strange bird with surprise and consternation as it flew off in pursuit of the man they were leading to Golgotha . . .

'What can it mean?' he whispered in puzzlement and alarm . . .

9

It came at last, far into the night, the long-awaited summer steppe rain that had piled up the evening before on the horizon in silent bursts of lightning and moving clouds. As Avdiy regained consciousness he felt the heavy drops on his face. At first they drummed on the dry ground, then poured down in a cascade. They were Avdiy's first gift from life.

He was still lying in the ditch by the railway embankment down which he had rolled when they threw him out of the train. His first thought was: Where am I? Feels like rain! He groaned and tried to move, but the searing pain in his side and the leaden heaviness in his head knocked him out again. Only later did he fully recover consciousness. The saving rain brought him back to life. It rained generously and long and the water running down off the embankment gathered in the ditch where Avdiy lay. It inched towards him, bubbling up towards his throat, forcing Avdiy into a superhuman effort to crawl out of his now dangerous place of refuge. The first minutes were the worst, while his body adjusted to the movement. Avdiy could hardly believe that he was still alive. He had been harshly beaten in the train and cruelly slung out at full speed, but what was that compared with the fact that he was alive, alive, in spite of it all! He was alive and moving, if only at a crawl, he could see and hear and rejoice in this blessed rain that poured down and washed his broken body, cooling his hands, legs and burning head. He would crawl for as long as he could: it would soon be light, morning, and life would begin again . . . Then he would decide what to do. Just get himself back on his feet . . .

Meanwhile several successive night trains sliced clattering through the rain and the darkness . . . They brought him joy, too, like everything else that spoke of life . . .

Avdiy would not have sheltered from the downpour even if

he could, for he realized what this life-giving rain was doing for him. As long as his arms and legs were still there, he could bear without a murmur the splinters, grazes, bruises and even the stabbing pain in his right side . . . He managed to crawl out of the sheltering ditch on to a little mound where he lay in the rain, gathering his forces to survive . . .

He had risen from the dark void, and once resurrected, he rebuilt the whole essence of his life and marvelled at the clarity and wholeness of the thoughts which immediately assailed him . . .

He cried out to the One who had been led away to Golgotha from the palace of Pontius Pilate: 'Master, I'm here! What can I do to help You, Master? How afraid I am for You now that I have come back to life!'

The man for whom events in the past are as real as what is happening at this moment, who experiences the past as though it belonged to him personally, as though it were his own life, is bound to suffer. Knowing in advance the outcome, he cannot change the course of events.

Avdiy found himself in despair on the eve of the Passover, seeking throughout the lower town on that airless vigil evening the house where the Last Supper had been celebrated the day before, where He had broken bread, saying, 'This is my body,' and poured out wine, saying, 'This is my blood.' Even then he could have warned of the approaching danger, of Judas Iscariot's treachery, of the need to leave this terrible city at once and get out on to the open road. In his search for the house he ran through the narrow, twisted streets, looking into the faces of passers-by (as though he might recognize anyone here!), but amongst all the citizens hurrying home to their evening meal or doing some last-minute shopping he found no one to confide in. Many of the passers-by did not even have any idea of who Jesus Christ was. There were lots of wandering tramps in the city; what was so special about this one? One kind man invited him home for the Passover, but Avdiy thanked him and refused. He was still hoping to warn the Master. His head was aching from all the sights and smells, so he fled from the narrow streets to Gethsemane, hoping to catch the Master praying there with his disciples in the garden. In vain! Here, too, he was too late. The garden was empty and the huge fig tree under which they had seized the Master was deserted, too . . . The disciples had scattered, as the Master had foretold . . .

The moon was sailing over land and sea. The time was after midnight, bringing near the fateful day whose echoes would resound down the ages and make its mark in so many different ways on the annals of human history. In Gethsemane and the other gardens on the hills it was quiet, and the plantations and vineyards were empty save for the night birds singing in the bushes, and the frogs. Unsleeping Kedron bubbled and burbled over its bed of stones on the way down from the cedar-clad mountains of its source, dividing and uniting its streams as it flowed. Everything was quietly in its place, and only Avdiy could find no peace because all was being fulfilled as it must be fulfilled, and he could do nothing to stop it, to prevent it, although he knew the outcome only too well. In vain did he cry and call upon the God of Tomorrow. He could not come to terms with what had happened although one thousand nine hundred and fifty years had passed by since that time, and in his thoughts he returned again and again to that time so long ago when the knot which bound his own being had first been tied. He sought the answer, ranging over the years in between, and permitted himself a certain degree of leeway, putting, for instance, the idea of a Last Judgment, which arose much later, into the mouths of men who had lived many centuries before. Avdiy was keen to air the subject before Pilate himself, since the ghost of the powerful Roman governor still haunted him to this day. Was the world not full of potential Pilates? Avdiy's anachronistic approach was based on a conviction that the basic laws of life are always valid, even if they have yet to be discovered. It was the same with the Last Judgment and the eternal human fear of retribution for all the injustice rampant in the world.

But who was this Jesus, who set the clock ticking by which we count off the years in the tragic history of man's spiritual self-awareness? What was it all for? Just to give us something to repent, year in, year out? Why was the human race so enthralled by the image of a man on a cross? Many others had claimed to be immortal and were now dust and ashes. No one should forget that life was constantly advancing, and what was new today would be old by tomorrow, what was good would fade before something even better; so why did Jesus's words not age and lose their power? And was His life, everything that happened to Him between birth and execution on the cross, really so essential for the human race? What was the meaning of His life, in the context of human history? What had been achieved? And if the fundamental, final objective of the life of men was love of man, the idea of humanism, as many wise men have said, man's journey to find himself, a journey to perfect the spirit within a thinking creature, then why did it all have to start from such a cruel and incomprehensible event? Could not men have lived without it, each with his own interpretation of humanism, from Christian to universal, from social, egoistic or class humanism to the principles of abstract humanism. . . ? And what did the twentieth century want with religion, already well worn and threadbare from its journey down the ages? What did the twentieth century want with religion? Every schoolboy knew the score. Had not materialist science driven a stake into the grave of the Christian faith and teachings, to fling them decisively out of the path of progress and culture, the only true path? One would imagine that in today's world, men could get by without the comforts of some worn-out old religion; it was enough simply to know a little about its dead teaching, merely in order to be an educated person. It had all outlived its usefulness. But where did we stand now? What did we have to replace that merciful, self-sacrificing ideal, long since cast out on the side of the road and laughed out of existence by the exigencies of a 'realistic' world view? What did we have to equal it, or, rather, to surpass it, since an innovation should always be better than what it replaces? Did we have something new? The cult of military superiority, the god Goliath, was hardly a worthy substitute . . .

Such thoughts passed through the mind of Avdiy Kallistratov from time to time. Now that he was experiencing the past as vividly as the present, like new water flowing in an old channel, he returned to the primary source of all sources, to that pre-Passover Friday, to carry on his search for the Master to explain what would happen centuries later. The Master would be horrified at the thought of humanity rushing it knew not where in an evil race to rule the world with mighty weapons.

Unhappily he did not find Him. Judas had already done his work and they had seized Him and led Him away, and Avdiy cried in the empty garden for what was come to pass, and what lay in the future, alone in all the world. To reach Gethsemane he had to travel back in time, past the origins of his own ancestors, still living in clearings in the northern forests and worshipping wooden idols, unaware of any biblical names like Avdiy. Only later would the Bible become a part of the Russian language, and he would have to wait as long again to be born in the distant future of the twentieth century. Long did he weep beneath the fig tree where the Master was seized, bound and carried off, as though his tears could change a single fact . . .

Then he rose and wandered sadly back to the city whose people slept soundly, secure behind their walls, while he alone walked and wondered: Where is the Master? What has become of Him? Suddenly it seemed that there was still time to save Him, and he started to beat upon all the windows he could reach. 'Get up! Get up! Disaster has struck! Let us save the Master, before it is too late! I will take him back to Russia, there's a little island in the river, in the Oka . . .'

Avdiy's idea was that the Master could live in safety on the island in prayer and meditation, perhaps have some new revelation and show men a new path in life, perhaps grant them divine perfection, for the Messianic mission which he took upon Himself need not then lie through spilled blood; need not be paid for in the sufferings and humiliation which He blindly took upon Himself, for the sake of men, for the sake of the truth which every persecutor fears, and therefore strives so mercilessly to eradicate. It was for the sake of future generations that He took His death upon Himself, as a duty, a necessity on His chosen path of liberation for man from the curse of his own participation in eternal injustice (for in the world of Nature there is no such thing as injustice: it exists only of and between men). But can the goal be reached by such 'unhistoric' methods? And can we be sure that the Master's lesson will not be forgotten every time it is convenient to forget the Master, to quench our conscience and find a million justifications for what we wish to do, like the need to answer blow for blow, to fight evil with evil? How can man, the crown of creation, be turned aside from the deadly passions that dog him in sickness and in health, for richer, for poorer, when he has power and when he does not. How can man, the crown of creation, be turned aside from his crude thirst for power over others and from his constant downhill slide into the nihilistic emptiness of 'anything goes'? Pride and complacency lead us to bully our fellows when we have power, and to crawl and be hypocritical, using our cunning to achieve the same goals, when we have not. So what is the meaning of life? What is its aim? And who can answer the question in such a way that none could doubt the truth and clarity of the reply?

And You, Master, are going to the cruellest death, to teach men kindness and compassion, to start by distinguishing what is worthy of our reason from what is not, for our life on earth is hard and the seeds of evil are planted deep within us. Can this path ever lead us to the ideal of a mind on wings of free thought, and a heart that has banished the anachronism of evil for evermore? If only it were possible! Lord, why did You take upon Yourself the burden of trying to correct an incorrigible world? Saviour, stop! Those for whose sake You are going to death and suffering on the cross will soon be laughing at You! It's true! You will be written off with mocking laughter as useless and irrelevant when in future years materialist science, leaving no stone unturned in its wholesale demolition of both God and faith, announces that everything You achieved was a child's fairy-tale: 'Fool! Idiot! Who asked him to do us favours? Why bother to go through that show with the crucifixion? Who's he trying to impress? Has he changed anything, one iota, for humanity?' That is how future generations will think, generations to whom Your life and work will seem worse than ridiculous, generations which penetrate the secrets of matter and overcome the force of gravity to fly beyond the confines of the earth and squabble over space in a nightmare of greed, striving for mastery of the galaxies. Although the universe is infinite, it will not be enough for them, for they must compensate for failures on earth by feeding their ambitions in space, even if they destroy in the process the planet on which You tried to establish the cult of mercy. What can God mean to them, when to themselves they are greater than God? What is a fool hanging on a cross to them, when at the touch of a button they can destroy us all, and erase even the memory of You from the face of the earth? My poor, trusting Master, let us fly together to the Oka, to the Volga, to some lonely island in the river, and there You shall live as on a star in the sky, seeing all, but out of reach of Your enemies. Think about it; it's not too late, we've still got all night and the morning – perhaps You can escape Your cruel fate? Is the path You have chosen really the only one?

Burdened by these thoughts, Avdiy wandered the dark streets and squares of the close Jerusalem night, trying to change the mind of Him whom the Lord sent to earth for a terrible and tragic fate as an example and reproach to men . . . Such a creature is man that none ever takes the reproach as referring directly to himself, and everyone finds his own justifications, claiming that he cannot do anything to change things, and anyway, why should he? How ironic that He should have over-estimated human nature to such an extent . . .

In the morning the city awoke anew, all cares and bustle, the bazaars and markets filling with camels loaded with saddle-bags, brought in from the desert by the Bedouin, donkeys and mules with smaller burdens, loaded pack-horses, porters with their special baskets, everything sprang to life, passions, goods, sounds, and was sucked into the whirlwind of buying and selling. Many of the citizens gathered at the white-walled city temple, then moved off in an agitated crowd to the residence of the Roman Procurator, Pontius Pilate. Avdiy Kallistratov joined them, too, for he understood that it was something to do with the fate of the Master. He followed them to Herod's palace, but the armed guard did not let the crowd in to see the Governor. They stopped by the palace and waited. More and more kept arriving, although the heat had been rising since early morning. All sorts of rumours were flying: some said that the Procurator would pardon Jesus of Nazareth by authority vested in him from Rome and let him go on condition he left Jerusalem, went as far away as possible and never came back to the city; others said that because a prisoner was always freed to celebrate the Passover, this year it would be Jesus; others again simply believed that Yahweh would swoop down and rescue him before the whole crowd – but all of them waited without knowing what was taking place inside the walls and palisades of the palace. Many were laughing at the poor man paying the price for proclaiming himself 'King of the Jews', mocking the poor fool and indignant that the Procurator should take so long to do what he had to, with the sun so hot and a long climb ahead up to Golgotha . . . Pilate must be talking to him. That Jesus of Nazareth could out-talk anyone who took him on! Suppose he even got round the Governor? He might let him go, and that would be a wasted morning . . . All right for that Jesus, promising the sky, but where was his New Kingdom now? They'd string him up, like a dog . . . That's the way it was . . .

As he listened, Avdiy plucked up courage. 'How dare you talk like that? You fickle, ungrateful creatures! How dare you belittle the great struggle of the human spirit to conquer its lower self? You should be proud of Him! He should be your yardstick and measure!' he shouted in despair, choking back his tears in the Jerusalem crowd. But nobody heard him; no one noticed his presence. After all, he wouldn't be born for another twenty centuries . . .

Gradually the night's rain died away. It left as it had come, to go and fall elsewhere. At last there was just the odd droplet. It was nearly time for a clean and star-studded sunrise. The sky was still agate-dark at the crown, but fading at the edges after the rain. There was a cool smell from the damp earth and the grasses that had grown up overnight.

None of the creatures of the steppe took as much delight in that morning as Avdiy Kallistratov, although no sense of well-being accompanied his joy.

Avdiy had been lucky; yesterday's heat had not completely dissipated from the air, so he did not freeze. Although he was soaking wet, and black and blue all over, he was engrossed in the trance-like state which let him feel that he was in two places at once, past and present. He felt he had been given his life back as a gift, and so was doubly grateful for the opportunity to live and think. When the rain stopped, Avdiy was sitting beneath a railway bridge to which he had hobbled with his last strength in the dark.

It was relatively dry under the bridge. He installed himself beneath it like a tramp, delighted to find a place where he could shelter from the rain and dream. Under the bridge the brickwork echoed like the vaulting in a medieval cathedral. When a train passed overhead, it sounded like a hail of mortar-fire, coming from afar and gradually fading away again to nothing. Avdiy's thoughts flew free that night, developing for themselves and entraining his spirit with them. He thought first about Christ and Pontius Pilate, imagining himself a part of those times, and the sound of trains thundering overhead did not intrude upon his experience of ancient Judea, standing in the crowd on Golgotha and seeing with his own eyes all that happened there. Then he remembered Moscow, and his recent visit to the Pushkin Museum where the Bulgarian choir gave its concert. He remembered his double, the Bulgarian singer who looked so surprisingly like him, and immediately the singer stood before him, in full voice. What beautiful sounds those Bulgarians had made, and how they had elevated his heart and thoughts! His father, Deacon Kallistratov, had had a great love for liturgical music and could never hear it without tears coming to his eyes. Once his father had been given the text of an astonishing prayer by a contemporary nun. She was still a young woman at the time. She had grown up in an orphanage, then worked in one, and taken the veil during the war after the man she lived with for only six weeks was killed on a warship, sunk by a German U-boat. Every time Deacon Kallistratov read her 'document of the soul', which combined a lament with a prayer, he would weep. He loved Avdiy, who was still only a little boy, to stand in the best corner and recite the prayer about the shipwrecked warship in his thin, childish voice. Avdiy still knew it by heart, the prayer by the nun who had grown up in an orphanage:

First light has broken in the sky, and while the world still sleeps . . . O Merciful, Blessed and Righteous Father, forgive me that I importune You with my incessant appeals. There is no self-interest in my prayer – it is not worldly benefits I seek, nor do I pray for the prolongation of my days. It is but for the salvation of souls that I call upon You untiringly.

All-forgiving Father, do not leave us in ignorance. Do not

let us seek to justify our actions by the fact that good and evil are inextricably entangled on this earth. Vouchsafe enlightenment unto the human race.

For myself, I seek nothing. I do not fear my end, whatever it may be: to burn in the fires of hell, or enter the Kingdom to which there shall be no end. Our fate is in Your Hands, O Invisible and Unbounded Creator.

I ask but one thing, one miracle . . . As long as night follows day and day follows night in the way ordained by You for our earth as it spins through the empty wastes of space, as long as the spray beats salty into the air and the seagulls cry, may the ship hold its course for the radiant city on the distant shore, though none may cast anchor there in all the aeons of time . . .

Lord, that is all. I ask for nothing else in my daily, nightly prayer. Forgive me, All-Good and Merciful, that I pester You with such strange requests, a prayer for a shipwrecked warship, but You are the steadfast ground of all our hopes, be they lofty, earthly or unearthly. You were and remain the Ubiquitous, Omnipotent and Loving essence of all essences, so we come to You with our prayers as we always have, do now and always will. And because, once I am gone, there will be no one left to pray in the end, let the ship sail over past the ocean and out into eternity. Amen.

Avdiy did not himself understand why he remembered the nun's prayer again that night. When he found himself thinking that if he met the girl who came to Uchkuduk on the motorbike again he would recite the prayer to her, he could not suppress a laugh. How would she like to see him squatting beneath the bridge so pathetically, like a wandering thief or highwayman down on his luck? Things would look bad enough without reciting the ship prayer on top of it! She would think he was mad, and she would of course be right. But even like this, when he risked making her despise him, he would still have liked to see her . . .

So Avdiy sat under the bridge until the very break of day, the trains thundering over his head as they travelled across the steppe. Uppermost in his mind was the question: Where were the runners now, his one-time travelling companions, what had become of them? Perhaps they had already got through Zhalpak-Saz and were pressing ahead. Where were Petrukha, Lyonka and the others? Where was the mysterious and elusive Grishan? Avdiy regretted his blunder, his stupid mistake, regretted that Grishan had prevailed and his dark genius triumphed. Everything had ended so badly. And yet Avdiy was convinced of the inevitability of the ordeals which had fallen to his lot over the last few days. Perhaps he had failed to reform the runners, but he had gathered some interesting material for the article, for the paper, and he had gathered it by his own endeavour.

Thinking along these lines brought Avdiy a certain measure of calm, but he was sore inside, and mainly for Lyonka's sake. Now there was someone who could have been shown the true path, but it was not to be.

Avdiy recalled all he had seen and discovered in the Moyun-Kum steppes, including the time he had come across the wolves, and the way the grey she-wolf sprang over his head, instead of sinking her fangs into him. It was odd the way she had done that, very odd – and he would never forget the savagery and wisdom in her blue eyes.

Now the sun came up again over the railway line and the cycle of life was starting anew. It was marvellous in the steppe after the night rain. The heat had not yet set in and the expanse of steppe, as far as the eye could see, emanated purity, while the air was filled with the singing of larks. The steppe birds darted and cascaded between land and sky. All the while the trains rolled across the steppe, from horizon to horizon, bringing reminders of the life teeming in distant parts.

Harmony and tranquillity reigned that morning over the steppe which overnight had soaked up its fill of the life-giving moisture of the skies.

As soon as he could feel the warmth of the sun Avdiy decided to dry out his clothes, but when he started to remove them he was shocked to find them so tattered that he would be ashamed to be seen in them. As for his body, it was covered in grazes and enormous bruises. It was just as well he had no mirror with him: if he had seen his reflection he would have been appalled, though he did not need a mirror to show him what was wrong, for he could not even touch his face.

In spite of everything he had sufficient good sense to persuade himself that everything could have turned out much worse, and it was a great blessing to be alive at all.

When he undressed beneath the bridge another unpleasant fact came to light: his internal passport and the little money he had in his pockets had been rendered unusable. The passport, first ripped in his fall and then soaked by the rain, had become a ball of sodden paper, while all that could really be salvaged of his money was two notes: a twenty-five and a ten. He had to get himself back to Moscow and then on to Prioksk on this money.

Avdiy fell to thinking sombre thoughts. After his expulsion from the seminary he had been forced to live in fairly straitened circumstances. With the consent of his sister Varvara he had sold the old piano on which she had learnt to play as a child. The second-hand shop only gave them half-price for it, explaining that there was now no shortage of musical instruments – on the contrary, they were inundated with them. Even old tape-recorders were impossible to get rid of, so what hope was there for pianos? They had to accept the price, there was no other alternative, so now he was left with nothing. The situation was dire!

A new day was beginning, life must go on, and the necessity of making his way back into the material world now seized the idealist Kallistratov by the throat.

He had spent the entire night under the bridge deep in thought and now had to decide how he was to get away, besides where his daily bread was going to come from.

For once, it seemed, fortune smiled on Avdiy. When it grew light he discovered that a country road passed beneath the bridge under which he had taken shelter. Admittedly, the signs were that not many vehicles passed this way. There was no knowing how long he would have to wait for a lift, so he decided to go on foot to the nearest halt, and from there find his way somehow or other to Zhalpak-Saz. Once he had decided to make a start Avdiy cast about for something to use as a crutch. His badly swollen right knee, which he had injured falling from the train, was giving him great pain. As he searched Avdiy chuckled to himself: Maybe Grishan's thrown out the stick Petrukha used on me! Grishan won't have any more use for it now! He did not find the stick, of course, yet he did observe a vehicle driving across the steppe in the direction of the bridge.

It was a truck with a home-made plywood canopy built on to the chassis. In the cab next to the driver sat a woman with a child in her arms. The truck braked sharply and the driver, a sturdy, swarthy-faced Kazakh, peered out of the window at Avdiy with a certain measure of surprise.

'What's this, lad, gypsies beat you up, hey?' he asked for some reason.

'No, not gypsies. I fell out of a train.'

'You drunk?'

'I never touch the stuff.'

The driver and his woman passenger clucked sympathetically and spoke in Kazakh, peppering their phrases with the word *'bichara'* – 'poor thing'.

'Come on, climb in, we're going to Zhalpak-Saz. You'll die on your own in the steppe, *bichara*. There's not much traffic passing this way.'

Blinking back the tears welling treacherously up in his eyes, Avdiy was as overjoyed as a small child.

'Thank you, brother,' he said, placing his hand on his chest. 'I was just about to ask if you could give me a lift, if it was on your way. I can't walk properly, my leg's bad. Thank you.'

The driver jumped down and helped Avdiy into the back of the lorry.

'You hop in here. I'll help you up, *bichara*. Climb in, don't be afraid: there's wool in there. I'm delivering it to the depot from the farm. It'll be nice and soft for you. Only you mustn't smoke.'

'I don't smoke anyway. Don't worry,' Avdiy reassured him earnestly. 'I spent the whole night in the rain and got soaked through, so I'll just warm up here, then I'll be on my way . . .'

'All right, all right, I was only warning you just in case. You take it easy, *bichara*.'

The woman glanced out of the cab and said something to the driver.

'The wife wants to know if you're hungry,' explained the driver with a grin.

'I'm starving,' confessed Avdiy. 'Thank you. If you've got any food you could let me have I'd be really grateful.'

To Avdiy the bottle of soured ewe's milk and flat loaf of freshly baked bread, white and fragrant, were manna from heaven in compensation for the torments of the night.

After eating, Avdiy fell fast asleep on the bales of wool, which gave off a sharp odour of fat and sweat. All the while the truck rolled across the steppe, still fresh after the downpour of the night before. The journey did Avdiy the world of good, like a spell of recuperation after an illness.

He woke when the truck came to a stop.

'We're here. Where do you want to go?' The driver was standing by the tailboard, peering over. 'Hey, lad! You still alive?'

'Very much so, thank you,' replied Avdiy. 'So we're already in Zhalpak-Saz, are we?'

'Yes, at the station. Now we have to go to the wool depot – what about you?'

'I must go into the main station building. Thanks again for helping me out. And a big thank you to your wife . . . I really am grateful to you.'

As he climbed out of the truck with the driver's help, Avdiy gave a groan of pain.

'Hey, *bichara*, you're in a very bad way. You'd better get yourself to hospital,' advised the driver. 'You'll need a stick to help you walk.'

It took Avdiy a good half-hour to hobble into the station building, and that thanks to a broken plank he had found along the way, which served him as an improvised crutch.

Above the din of the trains on the bridges, the floodlights and loading cranes, the shunting locomotives and the station square – in other words, above all the cacophony of a little railway town in the steppe – rang out the commands barked by the shunting foreman; the air was rent by the whistle of locomotives, while the public address system announced the arrival and departure of every passenger train. After his time in the wilderness, Avdiy was all the more keenly aware of this seething life. All around people scurried to and fro – not for nothing was Zhalpak-Saz one of the major junctions in Turkestan.

Now Avdiy had to decide how to get away, which train to

take and what to do next, bearing in mind that he had only thirty-five roubles. The ticket to Moscow alone – third class, and assuming there was room on the train – cost thirty roubles. How would he eat? What was he to do about his leg, his cuts and injuries? Should he go to the local hospital or try to get away as soon as he could? Lost in these reflections, Avdiy propelled himself laboriously through the crowded and stifling station. With his tattered clothing and his bruises, and wielding that ridiculous broken plank for a crutch, he inevitably attracted attention, people constantly turning round to stare at him. On the platform, on the way towards the departure board, he noticed that a policeman was following him.

'Just a moment, lad!' called the policeman, stepping up to Avdiy. The irritation in his voice and stern look on his face boded no good. 'What are you doing here? Who are you?'

'Me?'

'Yes, you.'

'Well. I want to catch a train. I'm looking at the timetable.'

'Got your documents?'

'What documents?'

'The usual ones: passport, ID, a note from your work.'

'Yes, I have, only . . .'

'Well, let's see them, then.'

Avdiy stammered: 'Uh, you see, I, uh, c-comrade . . .'

'We'll hear your explanation later. Let's see your documents.'

Reluctantly, Avdiy extracted from his pocket the ball of sodden paper that had once been his passport.

'Here,' he said, handing it to the policeman. 'This is my passport.'

'Passport?' The policeman looked contemptuously at Avdiy. 'You trying to pull a fast one? Call that a passport! Take it back and let's step along to the police station. Then we'll find out who you are.'

'Uh, comrade lieutenant . . .' ventured Avdiy uncertainly, embarrassed at his appearance, his plank crutch and the crowd of gapers that had quickly gathered around them, 'I, er, I'm a journalist.'

'You – a journalist!' exclaimed the policeman with indig-

166

nation, convinced that the suspect was lying through his teeth. 'Very well; let's go, journalist!'

The crowd of onlookers roared with malicious laughter.

'That's a good one – a journalist no less!'

'Sure you're not the Minister of Foreign Affairs, while you're about it?'

He had to hobble through the waiting room behind the irritable lieutenant. All those they encountered on their way turned to stare at Avdiy, whispering and giggling to one another. As they walked past one family disposed with their chattels on a long wooden bench, Avdiy caught the following snatches of dialogue:

Small girl: 'Mama, Mama, look: who's that?'

Woman's voice: 'Lord, child, that's a bandit. Look, that nice policeman has caught him.'

Man's voice: 'Ha! That's no bandit. He's just a petty thief, a pickpocket, nothing more.'

Woman's voice: 'Oh, I wouldn't say so, Misha. He only looks pathetic. You cross his path in a dark alley and he'll cut your throat . . .'

For Avdiy the worst shock was still to come. Following the lieutenant through the doors of one of the numerous railway offices he found himself in a spacious charge room with a window overlooking the square. A junior-ranking police officer manning the telephone at the desk half rose on the entrance of the lieutenant.

'Everything's in order, comrade lieutenant,' he reported.

'Sit down, Bekbulat. Here's another surprise visitor for us,' said the lieutenant, with a nod in Avdiy's direction. 'We've got ourselves a fine specimen here! What's more, he's a journalist!'

Looking round the room as he came in the door, Avdiy almost cried out, so startled was he by what he saw. In the left-hand corner, near the entrance, was a crude cage, fashioned from roughly welded lengths of reinforced steel bars reaching from floor to ceiling, behind which sat the *anasha*-runners, caged like animals in the zoo: Petrukha, Lyonka, Makhach, Kolya, the two 'sappers' and a few others – in all about a dozen of them, practically the entire team with the exception of Grishan. 'Sam' was not among them.

'Hey, guys, what's all this? How did it happen?' Avdiy

involuntarily exclaimed. Not one of them responded, or even moved a muscle. They sat on the floor of their cage, huddled close together, quite changed, hostile and sullen.

'So you're one of them?' asked the irritable lieutenant with a peculiar smirk.

'Of course!' said Avdiy. 'I'm one of them.'

'Are you indeed!' The lieutenant was surprised, and studied Avdiy with interest. 'Is he, then?' he asked the runners.

No one answered. They all sat in silence, their eyes on the floor.

'Hey, you, I'm talking to you!' shouted the lieutenant angrily. 'Why don't you answer me? All right, we can wait. I'll have you dancing yet, like sprats in a frying pan, oh yes, when they put you away under article 317, then you'll sing all right! And if you've got any "mitigating circumstances" in mind, like being under age, or having no previous convictions, forget it. It won't help, no, nothing will help you now. You were caught in the act,' he sneered, with a nod towards the *anasha*-stuffed rucksacks and suitcases – so familiar to Avdiy – which were scattered about the room. Some of them were open, others ripped apart, *anasha* spilling out of them, and the room was filled with the heavy odour of wild hemp. Over the desk next to the telephone were matchboxes and jam-jars filled with 'plasticine'.

'So, you don't want to talk! Sulking, are we? We got you red-handed!' repeated the lieutenant, with mounting severity, his voice trembling with anger. 'There's the evidence! There's the material proof! There's your dope!' He started to prod the rucksacks with his foot. 'Only one scoundrel from your gang escaped the round-up, but we'll nail him too, like the rest of you bastards. Get up! You can hear me: on your feet! Look at you, sitting there. On your feet and look at me. Don't look away! That's an order: don't look away! You scumbags, you were shooting at me from underneath the railway trucks, so don't think you'll get any mercy from me! Hardly dry behind the ears, the little bastards, and it's guns they're toting now! What next? I'll give you guns! I'm the sworn enemy of the likes of you, and you'll see what that means once I get to work! I'll be after you everywhere, on every train, on every road, I'll round you up like rabid dogs, you won't get away from me, none of you!' He was yelling now, in fury. 'Right, the question is, who is this tramp who calls himself a journalist? Who is this joker?' And seizing Avdiy by the arm he dragged him up to the bars. 'Answer me, while I'm still asking nicely. Is he one of you?'

For a moment they were all silent. As he stared into the sullen faces of the runners Avdiy simply could not believe that those young toughs who only the day before had stopped a train in the steppe, got high on *anasha* and thrown him from the moving carriage, were now cooped up in a cage – beltless, shoeless, bare-footed (probably to prevent them running away when they were led out to the lavatory), wretched and sheepish.

'This is the last time you get asked!' roared the lieutenant, almost choking with exasperation. 'Is this character that I've detained one of you or not?'

'No, not one of us,' sneered Petrukha, speaking for them all, and reluctantly lifting his head to look at Avdiy.

'What do you mean, not one of you, Petrukha?' retorted Avdiy in amazement, lurching right up to the cage on his crutch. 'Have you forgotten me or something?' he reproached them, through the bars. 'I really feel for you,' he added. 'But how did it happen?'

'This is neither the time nor the place for condolences,' interrupted the lieutenant. 'I'm now going to interrogate each one of you separately,' he threatened the runners. 'If any of you lie – and we'll soon know if he does – he'll have another charge to answer. We'll start with you,' he said to Makhach.

'Not one of us,' answered Makhach, baring his teeth.

'Now you,' the lieutenant ordered Lyonka.

'Not one of us,' answered Lyonka and sighed heavily.

'Not one of us,' muttered the red-head Kolya.

To the last man they denied any knowledge of Avdiy.

For some reason their attitude cut Avdiy to the quick. Their mass denial, so curt, so abrupt, in words of one syllable, both offended and humiliated him. Avdiy felt himself reddening as his head throbbed.

'But how can you, how can you say you don't know me?' he cried in bewilderment. 'I'm, er . . .'

'So there you are, Mr New York Times,' interrupted the lieutenant mockingly. 'That's enough of your "I er" and "you

169

er". Just don't you mess me around any more. We've enough work without you on our backs as well. Just get the hell out of here. And steer clear of this lot. There's a law against louts like that, and no mercy – the processing and distribution of narcotics, and dealing in them, all mean instant conviction. There's short shrift for the likes of them. As for you, my journalist friend, beat it, and don't ever let me see you again.'

His words were met by silence. Avdiy shifted from one foot to the other, but did not depart.

'Didn't you hear what the comrade lieutenant said to you?' piped up the policeman, who had been filling in forms all this time. 'Get lost before it's too late. Say thank you and go.'

'Have you got a key to this door?' Avdiy pointed to the padlock hanging from the iron bars.

'Sure, but what's it to you?' answered the lieutenant, puzzled.

'Then open it,' said Avdiy.

'Right away, sir! Just who do you think you are?' stormed the lieutenant indignantly. 'I've had enough!'

'I want to join them in the cage! My place is there!'

Avdiy's face burned, and he felt the madness surging within him again, as it had in the train, when he flung the priceless *anasha* into the wind. 'I demand that you arrest and convict me,' he shouted, 'just like these unfortunate wretches, who have lost their way in a world full of contradictions and evil! I bear the same responsibility as they. After all, I did the same things. Open the door and put me in there with them! At the trial they'll confirm that I'm just as guilty! We will repent of our sins and this will serve as our purgatory!'

At this the policeman pushed his forms aside and leapt to his feet.

'But he's out of his mind, comrade lieutenant. Just look at him. You can see right away that he's got a screw or two loose.'

'I'm perfectly sane,' objected Avdiy. 'And I should be sharing their punishment. What's so crazy about that?'

'Hang on . . .' hesitated the lieutenant. Evidently, in all his hard years of service in the railway police, he had never come across as strange a case as this. Who would believe it?

There was silence again, then a sudden sob, choked with tears. It was Lyonka, weeping, his face turned towards the wall. Petrukha clapped a hand over his mouth and whispered something menacingly in his ear.

'Well now, comrade,' said the lieutenant to Avdiy, in a voice that was suddenly softer. 'Let's go and talk. I promise I'll hear you out, only not here. Let's go outside. Let's go, come on, do as I say.'

Once again they went into the waiting room, which was crammed with every type of traveller. The lieutenant led Avdiy to a vacant bench, invited him to sit and sat down beside him.

'I earnestly request you, comrade,' he said in an unexpectedly confiding tone, 'don't interfere with our work. If anything is wrong, don't be angry. You know how tough it is, the job we have to do. I mean, you've seen for yourself. Please just get on your train and go. You're quite free. Only don't come near us again. Have you got that?'

While Avdiy gathered his thoughts, wondering how to explain his conduct to the lieutenant and to express what he really felt about the runners' arrest, his interlocutor stood up and pushed through the crowd to disappear.

Once again the passengers indulged their idle curiosity in sideways glances at Avdiy: even among this motley crowd he stood out like a sore thumb. His battered face covered in bruises, his clothes in tatters, a rough plank beneath his armpit in place of a crutch, Avdiy excited a mixture of curiosity and contempt. Furthermore, he had just been escorted to where he sat by a policeman. He started to feel worse and worse . . . His temperature was rising and his head ached intolerably. The events of the previous day, the downpour that night, his swollen and useless leg and, finally, this latest unexpected encounter with the runners, now faced with the prospect of a terrible retribution for their crime – all this had shocked him to the core.

As the fever began to take hold he started first to shiver, then to burn. He writhed uncomfortably on his seat, shoulders hunched, physically incapable of rising to his feet. The ill-starred crutch lay where it had fallen at his feet.

Everything started to swim before his eyes, as though a mist had descended. As the shapes swam together, losing their clear outline, people's faces and figures were elongated or shrank in size, and superimposed one image upon another. Avdiy felt nauseous, his thoughts confused, fighting for breath in this fetid, crowded room surrounded by total strangers. I feel dreadful, he thought, strange, the way people are. Everybody's so isolated. How empty it all is, how alienating. Avdiy thought he would soon be over it and able to return to his attempts to help the detainees, threatened as they were with imprisonment. The fact that only the day before they had hurled him from a moving train, in the hope that he would be killed by the fall, now seemed of minor significance. Criminals, thugs, half-witted murderers that they were, they should have kindled his hatred and desire for revenge, but not compassion.

Avdiy, however, was an idealist and refused to learn from experience, remaining deaf to the promptings of reason. Subconsciously he realized that the downfall of the *anasha*-runners was also a downfall for him and for the altruistic notion of trying to influence them for the good. He had been unable to do so or to save them from this terrible fate. He could not fail, however, to understand how vulnerable this all-forgiving attitude made him, and how fateful its consequences might be . . .

The world is not devoid of kind souls, even in that crowd of strangers on the station. A middle-aged woman, grey-haired and wrapped in a shawl, sitting with her belongings on the bench opposite Avdiy, must have realized that the man was in a poor way and needed help.

'Citizen,' she was about to say, but instead it was her motherly concern which carried the day. 'What is it, son, aren't you well? Are you sick or something?'

'I think I'm sick, but don't you worry about it.' Avdiy tried to smile.

'What do you mean, not worry? Lord God Almighty, what's all this, you must have had a bad fall. And you're running a high fever,' she continued, feeling Avdiy's brow. 'I can tell from your eyes how sick you are. Listen, son, you stay where you are and I'll go and find out, maybe there's a doctor here somewhere, or maybe they can take you to a hospital. We can't just leave you here like this.'

'Please don't bother, it's not necessary,' protested Avdiy feebly.

'No, no, it's no trouble. You sit nice and tight. I'll be back in a jiffy . . .'

Asking her neighbour, a woman with small children, to keep an eye on her things, the soft-hearted Samaritan set off on her quest.

Avdiy did not remember how long she was away. He started to feel even worse. Now he realized what the trouble was: his throat hurt intensely. He could not even swallow. 'Must be tonsillitis,' he thought. He felt so weak that he wanted to lie down, to stretch out right there on the floor – he did not care if people stepped on him – and to sink away, forgetting everything . . .

He was dropping into unconsciousness when the crowd in the waiting room suddenly stirred, and the hubbub of voices increased. As he opened his eyes he saw that the runners were being led out of the police office. A detachment of police had them surrounded on all sides. The irritable lieutenant went in front – people stepped aside to let him through – and the handcuffed runners followed. They walked under escort in single file – Petrukha, Makhach, Lyonka, Kolya, the two 'sappers' and the rest, about ten in all. They were being taken out of the station.

Summoning all his flagging strength, Avdiy reached laboriously for his crutch and hobbled in pursuit. It felt as though he was moving fast, but for some reason he was quite unable to catch up with the escort. The crowd of gapers was also in his way. As the runners were led out of the station he could see a closed van parked near the doors, with a grille on the back door. Two policemen seized each of the runners under the armpits and bundled them one by one into the van.

Then the escort climbed in and the door was slammed shut. The lieutenant took his seat next to the driver and the van drove off from the station square. The crowd of onlookers now put forward their various theories.

'They caught some bandits. Whole gang of them.'

'Those are the ones who've been going around murdering people in their homes.'

'Lord, what horrors!'

'You call those bandits? They're just a bunch of kids.'

'Kids, you say? Kids these days are murdering people without batting an eyelid.'

'No, no, good people, those are *anasha*-runners. Those are the ones who transport the hashish. You should see how many they catch on the goods trains . . .'

'However many they catch, there's always more to come . . .'

'What are things coming to. . . ?'

Thus ended the sorry history of the runners. Avdiy felt an inexplicable emptiness within him . . .

Barely able to remember where he had been sitting, Avdiy dragged himself back into the waiting room. He was crawling painfully back, when suddenly he came up against the same grey-haired woman.

'That's him, there!' she declared to a white-coated nurse.

'Where did you go, son, we've been searching for you all over? Look, the nurse is here. You must have a fever, and they're afraid you might have something infectious.'

'I doubt it,' answered Avdiy weakly.

The nurse felt his forehead.

'You've got a high temperature,' she said. 'Your stomach upset? Diarrhoea with a bad, rotten smell?' She went through the symptoms.

'No.'

'Well, all the same, we must go to the first-aid post. There we can get a doctor to look at you.'

'All right.'

'Where are your things?'

'I haven't got any things . . .'

10

In the Zhalpak-Saz hospital to which they had sent Avdiy, Dr Aliya Ismailovna, a dour Kazakh woman, examined the patient and grimly announced, 'You're not in good shape. We'll have to get a specialist to have a look at the injury to your leg. For the time being we'll treat you with antibiotics, to prevent infection spreading, but you, as the patient, will have to tell me exactly what happened. I'm not asking out of curiosity, but as your doctor . . .'

Among the many encounters and partings in life there is always at least one meeting which we feel can only be seen as a gift from God, though only later do we realize how easily this meeting might have led to nothing. We shudder for a moment at the thought, though after all, the consequences of any meeting depend not on God but on ourselves.

Something similar occurred with Avdiy Kallistratov. In the evening of the third day he had a visit which more than fulfilled his wildest dreams – dreams, because his visitor was the last person he expected to see, and only our dreams are not confined to what we know and expect to happen.

By the afternoon after his injections and tablets his temperature had dropped somewhat and by evening it no longer rose above 37.3 degrees. The swelling on his leg had not yet subsided, and one rib on the right side appeared to be broken – a crack showed up on the X-ray. On the whole he was on the mend, though. He was feeling much better. Dr Aliya Ismailovna was a true healer, it transpired, using not only her knowledge but also her personality to speed his recovery. All her instructions, even the way she spoke, inspired her patients with calm and confidence and helped them fight their way back to health. Her psychotherapy was restrained and sensible, and after all his unpleasant experiences Avdiy was keenly aware that occasionally what we most need is a dose of tender loving care. To be honest, he was even glad to be taken ill and to fall into the hands of such a good doctor – so splendidly peaceful was it in that modest provincial hospital, surrounded by a small park.

The white-curtained window, looking out on to an avenue, was slightly open. His fever still had not completely abated. His two ward-mates had stepped outside for some fresh air and for a smoke while Avdiy lay in solitary splendour, periodically checking his temperature. He was very anxious that it stay down. He heard the click of high heels outside the window and a woman's voice asking the duty sister about him. Who could it be? The voice seemed very familiar. The sister opened the door into the ward.

'He's in here.'

'Hello, how are you?' said his visitor. 'Are you Kallistratov?'

'I am,' answered Avdiy, unable to believe his eyes.

It was the very same girl who had so struck him when she arrived on her motorcycle in Uchkuduk. Avdiy was so taken aback that he hardly heard what she said and was able to divine the meaning of her words only by intuition. The girl's name, it turned out, was Inga; Inga Fyodorovna. She had come to the hospital because Dr Aliya Ismailovna, with whom she had been friendly for the past two years, in fact, ever since she had arrived in the district to do her research work, had told her about him and she was intrigued: after all, they – that is he, Avdiy, and she, Inga Fyodorovna – were dealing with similar problems, both connected with *anasha*, in so far as she was studying the Moyun-Kum distribution of the plant (she gave the complicated Latin name of that same genus of steppe cannabis), and so she decided to come and make his acquaintance and ask whether he needed any more information . . . As far as she could see, a journalist could use the scientific information she had to offer.

But, God, how could he take in 'scientific information' when he was so completely dazzled by her sudden appearance that he could hope to gain only the vaguest idea of what she was talking about, and remained oblivious of everything but her eyes. No one else in the world had eyes like hers . . . he was like an astronomer who discovers a new star amidst a million similar stars, all of which look absolutely identical to the uninitiated star-gazer. Every time she looked at him he was floating.

All this came back to him later, when he was alone again and had recovered some of his composure, but for the first few minutes he made a complete fool of himself. Fortunately, Inga Fyodorovna was able to put this down to his high temperature – who but a complete idiot could have blurted out immediately, 'How did you know I've been thinking about you all this time?' By way of reply she raised her eyebrows in surprise, which served only to increase her charm, and smiled mysteriously. He hoped that she would not take this stupidly primitive question as a sign of familiarity or, worse, vulgarity: thoughts like this made Avdiy squirm and curse himself later. But God is merciful: Inga had sufficient tact not to lend any significance to his words. They spoke happily of her arrival in Uchkuduk and their first meeting, and laughed at that coincidence, fleeting perhaps, yet something they both remembered. Inga was even more amused to hear how the following day Avdiy and the two experienced runners, Petrukha and Lyonka, had taken cover in the grass when a helicopter flew over the steppe – amused because she had been on board that very helicopter, flying with a small research team from Tashkent: one of the Tashkent research institutes was investigating chemical and biological methods for the eradication of cannabis in the areas where it proliferated.

Avdiy now realized that the campaign against this evil was being waged on two fronts: to counteract the dependence on the drug and to destroy the plants containing it. As is usual with such things, the problem was not easily to be resolved. In particular, it emerged from Inga's explanation that while it was perfectly feasible to find chemicals which would destroy cannabis not only by stripping the leaves but by attacking it in its reproductive phase, to stamp it out as a species, this method involved an even greater evil: it affected the soil and rendered the land useless for at least two hundred years. The weapon was double-edged: fighting the drug, on the one hand, while ruining the soil on the other. Inga's own assignment was to find an optimal solution to this tricky ecological problem. Lord, thought Avdiy, if Nature could think and feel,

177

how burdened she would be by this monstrous interdepen-
dence between a wild plant and the moral degradation of man.

Although he dubbed his new relationship with Inga a 'new era
in my destiny', Avdiy Kallistratov was careful not to admit any
romantic flights of fancy. Immediately after his return to
Prioksk he wrote her a long letter, and this after sending her a
postcard from every railway station at which the train had
stopped for more than five minutes. There was something
irrepressible, something outside the usual concept of love, in
the tautened cord of feelings, in the passion which had
gripped Avdiy ever since his path had crossed hers.
    He wrote to her:

It's incredible what's happened to me! I used to think I was
a fairly restrained person, that my reason and my emotions
were pretty well balanced, yet now I am quite unable to
analyse myself. In fact, to my astonishment, I have lost all
desire to do so! I am totally in thrall to some unimaginable
joy, which has engulfed me like a mountain avalanche; I
once saw a film where an avalanche swept everything away
before it – well, I'm happy that that avalanche has swept me
away as well. There is not, and never was, a happier man
on this earth. I'm unique in my good fortune: I feel like a
frenzied savage, swirling with my drum, and thanking the
goddess of Fate for all the ordeals to which she has
subjected me this summer: after all, she let me live, and
taught me the things that can only be learnt in the
maelstrom of life. I would go so far as to say that, within an
individual, love is the true revolution of the soul. If I am
right, then long live the revolution of the soul: a revolution
that destroys and gives new life at the same time.
    Inga, please forgive all this drivel. But I do love you, I
can't find either the strength or the words to express
everything that you mean to me . . .
    Now let me change the tone a little. I've already called at
the newspaper. They're hurrying me, they want my story.
It's possible that I'll do a whole series of articles on this
subject, as it's so topical. I'm even pinning my hopes on a

178

full-time job with the paper, though it's still early days for that. The main thing is that from tomorrow I must get cracking on my story. You know, I deliberately kept no notes. I'll have to reconstruct everything from memory.

Whether I like it or not, the fate of those runners, who – quite rightly – will get a very stiff sentence for distributing narcotics, still really bothers me. You know, for me they're still living people with their wretched, broken lives. I'm especially sorry for Lyonka. That poor guy will never survive. And this is where we see the moral problem which you and I discussed at such length, Inga. You're quite right, Inga, that any malicious deed, any crime committed by any person in any place on earth affects us all, even if we're far away, have no knowledge of it and deliberately maintain our ignorance. Let's face it, sometimes we even laugh when we see to what depths they can sink in those countries that we tend to think of as our 'enemies'. There's even some logic in the fact that the newspapers like to concentrate on crime which takes place abroad – after all, there's a sort of universal equilibrium in the world of all human hardships; we are the only creatures in the entire universe capable of thought, and this one property, whether we like it or not, unites us in spite of all the political differences between us. In the end we will come to understand this, despite all our various differences, and ultimately it will be the salvation of reason on earth.

It's so gratifying, Inga, to write and tell you all the things that most concern me, knowing that they'll find a sympathetic response in you – I'm convinced of that. I'm afraid you might get tired of me with my interminable letters – I could write them one after the other, without stopping, I just have to do it! I must be with you the whole time, even if only in my thoughts. How I wish I could be back in the Moyun-Kum steppe and seeing you again for the first time, riding your motorbike into Uchkuduk and enslaving me at first sight, me, the zealous reformer of Christianity! I'm also ashamed to admit it, but I was so stunned by your sudden reappearance that I'm still overcome by a mixture of timidity and rapture. You descended from heaven, like a goddess in modern dress . . .

And now, as I recall all this, I can't forgive myself for failing, when I came into contact with the runners, to ensure that the scales of human suffering were tipped – even just the slightest fraction – away from bad and towards good. I reckoned they would come to fear God, but it was money which had the real power for them. Now I'm agonizing over whether there isn't some way to help at least those runners that fate threw me into the company of, whom I had learned to talk to at least. It's repentance I'm thinking of mainly. That's what I wanted to lead them to. Repentance – one of the great attainments in the history of the human soul – has been discredited in our time. You might even say that it has been totally excluded from the moral horizons of modern-day man. But how can you be human without the grace of repentance, without the shock of self-revelation and the vision that comes with acknowledging one's own guilt – whether in thought or in deed – when we are moved to self-castigation or self-condemnation. . . ? The path to the truth is a constant, daily journey towards perfection . . .

There I am, on my hobby-horse again! Forgive me, Inga. It's only because I'm so full of conflicting emotions, because I'm always thinking of you. It always feels as if I haven't expressed a thousandth part of what I want to say to you . . .

I can hardly believe it's been a whole week since we were together: oh, how I long to see you again as soon as possible . . .

My longing for you and the fact that you are not here beside me is the only cloud on my horizon. Everything else, problems, anxieties, has vanished into thin air or paled into insignificance . . .

It had been the end of June when Avdiy stepped out of the newspaper offices, feeling depressed. He was very disheartened to find the editor's attitude to the steppe articles suddenly changed. Even his colleagues on the paper, who had urged him to go in search of a scoop, were behaving strangely too, as if there was something for them to feel guilty about. It was all very upsetting. The sense of making someone feel guilty bothered him. He did not want anyone feeling guilty when they saw him coming, for then he in his turn felt guilty for causing their guilt . . .

When he left the newspaper he swore that he would stop turning up and hanging about – if they ever needed him again, they could call him. If they didn't – well, too bad. He would know that nothing had come of it and there was nothing to hope for.

He walked along the boulevard. Summer was at its most beautiful, and he found no pleasure in it. He had put such effort into writing the steppe stories, trying to impart to them all the pain he felt as a citizen – had written them as a self-revelation, a confession – but now he was up against some argument about the prestige of the nation (it really made him wonder why on earth we created secrets to keep from ourselves) which now threatened to bury his hard-begotten stories. He was upset beyond words. Strangest of all was how the editor could bring himself to say, 'By the way, perhaps you should think about bringing this to the attention of the appropriate authorities so they can take the necessary measures.'

Those were his exact words.

Avdiy could not contain himself, and retorted, 'Will we ever give up the notion that even our disasters are somehow superior to everyone else's?'

'What's this got to do with disasters?' frowned the editor.

'I'll tell you what: drug addiction is a social disaster.'

On that note, he took his leave. The only thing which brightened his existence was Inga's letters, which he read and reread whenever he felt his heart tighten at the memory of her. No doubt about it, telepathy does exist – how else could he explain the way her letters anticipated his innermost thoughts, the agonies of his soul, his most gnawing anxieties? More and more her letters fed his hopes and gave him confidence, for he knew that fate had not decided to make a fool of him. After all, he was not the sort to appeal to a modern miss – a failure, an ex-seminary student, with his archaic religious views about moral values! What a nonentity he was in comparison to all those muscle-flexing macho types. And yet in Inga's letters he found so much trust, so much – he was not ashamed to say it – respect and, most of all, such an unmistakable echo of his own feelings that it gave him stature in his own eyes. What good fortune that he had happened to meet her, his Inga! Was this not evidence of the magic of love, drawing two people ever closer together?

For the time being they were not weighed down by any worldly problems, though he even found joy in the fact that such problems existed and had to be faced. He had to find some sort of permanent employment, some regular source of income. For the moment he was living on the proceeds of the sale of his father's antiquarian books, and this depressed him. He thought of going to join Inga in Asia, to set up home there, to find a job and live near her. He was even prepared to join her team as a menial and do anything he could to ensure the success of her research, for by now this research had become inextricably linked with his own efforts: he was trying to eradicate drug abuse through moral endeavour; she was tackling the same problem from another angle – through science. He was very much infected by her enthusiasm. Her work was not in a particularly fashionable or prestigious field, nor would it lead to any rapid promotion. Strictly speaking, Inga was practically the only person to tackle the question of the eradication of the wild cannabis seriously, as a scientific project. The direction of her work was strongly influenced by the fact that she was from the area, from Djambul, and had studied nearby too, in Tashkent, all of which taken together was naturally bound to influence the nature of her interests.

Inga had her own problems in life. She had been separated from her husband, an airforce pilot, for almost three years, since their son was born. Now, it seemed, the pilot was planning to remarry. For that reason they had to meet for one last time, to dot the 'i's and cross the 't's regarding their son. Little Igor was with his grandparents in Djambul, a doctor's family, but Inga was very anxious that the child should live permanently with her. When she wrote and told Avdiy that she was hoping in the autumn to take the boy with her to Zhalpak-Saz – she had been promised a place for him in the railway workers' kindergarten – he was delighted for her and replied that she could depend on him totally.

Then she wrote that during her leave that autumn she really wanted to take him with her to Djambul to visit the boy and her parents. He was thrilled by this plan of hers, to travel together. He replied that he was ready to drop everything and place himself at her instant disposal, that he wanted his entire life to be governed by their shared interests, above all by what she wanted, and that his happiness lay in being useful and indispensable to her.

All the signs were the autumn would decide their fate. How he lived for that moment! He worried ceaselessly about the trip to meet Igor and Inga's parents. So much depended on that, but it required a certain financial outlay. The flight alone cost enough. He had been counting on his series of Moyun-Kum stories to pay for it, but his plans collapsed, and not through any fault of his own. So he took a temporary job as a night sub in the local printshop, and this brought in a little money.

Finally the day came when a letter from Inga asked whether he could be in Zhalpak-Saz towards the end of October, to go to Djambul for the November holidays . . .

He dashed madly to the post office and sent a telegram . . . Now he had to sell his books as quickly as possible and use the money for his ticket.

11

Kandalov, the 'Ober', discovered Avdiy Kallistratov at the station while recruiting manpower to carry out the cull in the Moyun-Kum steppe. Whoever selected Kandalov for the job had known what he was doing: Kandalov, a worldly-wise character, had seen service as a commander in the railway fire brigade and had been a regular soldier in the notorious 'disciplinary battalion' where they put all the delinquents; in fact he was the ideal candidate for the special job to be done in the steppe. Actually, Kandalov had his own subtle views on this. He reckoned that, having once helped the local authorities reach their meat production target for the region, he would (as a side-effect) be rehabilitating himself, and with the mediation of the necessary people high up in the hierarchy he would be readmitted to the Party. After all, they hadn't thrown him out for embezzlement or any serious abuses but for an isolated incident which did absolutely no harm to the state: committing sodomy in the barracks, and misusing his official position to coerce his partners. Well, perhaps there was some truth in it, perhaps he did coerce them, but he was a sergeant who'd already exceeded his statutory period of service, and they were ideologically unsound individuals, assorted religious cranks and drug-addicts, so why waste pity on them? And how much punishment should a man be given? Wasn't it enough that his wife had left him, once he started seriously to hit the bottle, although he had never been particularly abstemious anyway. Anyone could see how much men like him were needed. For once he had been given a serious assignment, and in no time at all he had cobbled together a team. He had done it by haunting the railway station late at night, carefully studying people who hung out there, picking out with his practised eye only the most desperate cases, the ones likely to go along with him to the

Moyun-Kum, to earn a fast rouble. Now this instinct led him to Avdiy Kallistratov.

Avdiy accepted Kandalov's proposal, not simply out of financial need, but because of the unforeseen and alarming circumstance that he had failed to find Inga Fyodorovna in Zhalpak-Saz, although he had come as soon as he received her letter. Now he was in a state of despair, even though there was still no reason to assume anything had gone wrong. He had come by plane, and this had meant going first to Moscow; it had taken him an entire day in Moscow to get a ticket, and he had anyway had to travel the last section by train from Alma-Ata. He had rushed to her side, you might say, but it still took him two whole days. When he finally arrived at the little house in the yard of the laboratory near the hospital, it was only to find it locked with a note from Inga pushed into the keyhole. In the note she asked him to collect a letter from her at poste restante at the railway station post office. Naturally, Avdiy raced to the station. He was given the letter at once. With a sinking heart he sat on a park bench and read:

Avdiy, my dear, forgive me. If I had known what a mess things were going to get into I'd have let you know, so that you could have postponed your departure. I'm afraid my telegram may not have reached you and that you've already set off. The point is, my ex-husband has suddenly turned up in Djambul to start court proceedings about our little Igor. I've had to dash off to Djambul. Maybe this is all my fault. I wrote to him quite openly that I was planning to start a new life with a man whom I care for. I had to put him in the picture for the sake of our son.

Avdiy, my darling, please forgive me for things turning out like this. Maybe it's for the better: sooner or later we would have had to resolve this issue anyway. Better that we get it out of the way right at the beginning.

When you arrive you'll find the door locked. I'll leave the key with our lab assistant, Saula Alimbayeva. She's a wonderful person. You know where our laboratory is, don't you? So please get the key from her and stay in my flat. Make yourself at home and wait for me there. It's such a pity Aliya Ismailovna is on leave at the minute, you would

185

have found it really interesting to spend some time with her. You know how much respect she has for you. I hope to be back in a week. I'll do all I can to ensure that nothing comes between us after this. I really want you to meet Igor; I'm sure you'll be good friends, and I really want us all to live together, but before that, as we had planned, I want us to visit my parents and you to meet them. My father's name is Fyodor Kuzmich, my mother's is Veronika Andreyevna. Don't be cross with me, Avdiy, sweetheart, and don't be sad. I'll do the best I can.

Your Inga

PS If the lab is closed when you arrive, Alimbayeva's address is 41 Aba Street. Her husband's called Daurbek Iksanovich.

The letter, which Avdiy read straight through, left him quite bewildered. He was shaken to the core: this was a totally unexpected development. He did not go for the key, remaining instead in the waiting room, determined that he would first think everything through. Then he left his suitcase in left luggage, returned to the park, sat there for a while, wandered around near the hospital, so familiar to him, and then, finding a quiet path between the station and the town, started to pace up and down . . .

The steppe was now arrayed in its late autumn colours. The weather was growing cool. Wispy streaks of cloud, like sheep against an expanse of ocean, showed white in the October sky, now faded after a summer of brightness; the trees had lost half their foliage and dried brown and purple leaves lay underfoot. The fruit and vegetable plots were now harvested and bare. The streets of Zhalpak-Saz were deserted and cheerless. The air bore occasional strands of gleaming cobwebs, which would suddenly touch your face. All this filled Avdiy with melancholy. Meanwhile the station, whose vast industrial power managed somehow to overwhelm the boundless expanse of the steppe, resounded with tumult and clatter, seething with a life which never ceased for an instant, pounding on like an arterial pulse. The trains continued their shunting on the countless tracks, crowds jostled and the controller's loudspeakers crackled out for all the district to hear.

Once again Avdiy recalled those summer days, recalled what finally became of the runners. Yet again, the thought of them led him back to his ideas of repentance. The more he thought about it, the more convinced he was that repentance is something we can achieve only as our experience of life increases, and that conscience is something which must be trained, nourished and cultivated by the faculty of reason. No creature apart from man has the ability to repent. Repentance is the eternal and inescapable concern of the human soul with itself. It follows that any punishment, whether for a misdemeanour or a major crime, must be such as to evoke in the soul of the recipient a sense of repentance, or else you might as well be punishing an animal.

Lost in thoughts like these, Avdiy returned to the station. Here he was reminded of the irritable police lieutenant and had a sudden urge to discover whether the lieutenant remembered him, to find out what had happened to the runners, to Petrukha, Lyonka and the others. Something else was driving Avdiy, the desire to rid himself of the tormenting thoughts hanging over him, like stormclouds over the horizon – thoughts of Inga. His whole life, even his future, was now being determined by whatever happened in distant Djambul. No, even if there was nothing else he could do, at least he could run, he must get away from his thoughts. Unfortunately, Avdiy failed to find the irritable lieutenant. When he knocked on the door of the police office a policeman stepped up to him.

'What do you want?'

'I, er – wanted to see a lieutenant here,' Avdiy started to explain, sensing at once that his quest was futile.

'What's his name? We've got lots of lieutenants.'

'Unfortunately I don't know his name, but I'd know him if I saw him.'

'Why do you need him then?'

'Er, it's a bit hard to explain – I, er, just wanted to talk, to have a little chat . . .'

The policeman surveyed him with interest.

'Well, who knows, maybe you'll find your lieutenant after all.'

On this occasion, however, the officer sitting talking on the

187

telephone was a stranger. Avdiy apologized and took his leave. As he left he glanced in passing at the iron cage in which the apprehended runners had huddled. On this occasion it was empty.

Once again, despite all his resistance, Avdiy's mind returned inexorably to the thoughts which continued to torment it. How was Inga managing? He still hadn't fetched the key she left him: he knew that once he entered Inga's flat with all its heart-rending associations he would feel even more lonely and depressed. He could even wait at the station, if only he knew how Inga was getting on and when she would return. Avdiy tried to imagine just what was going on at that moment in Djambul. What sort of an ordeal was she going through, with him powerless to help her? And what if her parents, anxious not to separate the child from its father, put pressure on her to patch things up with her husband? Things could easily take such a turn, and then he would have no option but to take himself home. Avdiy could picture the dashing airforce pilot, handsome in his uniform with its officer's pips, a major's at least, and he realized that with competition like that he stood no chance. Although Avdiy knew in his own mind that Inga had no time for rank or outward affectations, who knows, it may well be a matter of some importance to her parents whether they had as son-in-law an airforce pilot, who was also Igor's father, or some strange character with no fixed occupation . . .

Evening was falling. As the darkness grew Avdiy became increasingly morose. A murky semi-darkness settled over the station, still thronged with people; it was stuffy and smoky, and Avdiy's spirits sank to their lowest ebb. He felt as though he were in a dark and gloomy forest, quite alone. An autumn wind whistled through the tree-tops and snow was imminent, threatening to engulf the entire forest and Avdiy himself, burying everything in oblivion . . . He felt he would welcome death, and if at that moment he had been told that Inga would not return, or would not return alone, but would come back with the sole purpose of collecting her books and things and then depart again with her pilot, he would without a moment's thought have stepped out and thrown himself under the first passing train. It was then, in the depths of his

188

despair, and late in the evening, that Avdiy was spotted on Zhalpak-Saz railway station by Kandalov, recruiting a suitable team for the Moyun-Kum 'safari'. Kandalov, clearly not lacking in perspicacity, sensed intuitively that Avdiy was in a state of emotional turmoil, not knowing where to turn. Indeed, when Kandalov offered Avdiy the chance to get away for a few days into the Moyun-Kum savannah in order to make some fast money on a profitable little job, the latter agreed with alacrity. He was ready for anything, as long as he did not have to sit in solitude waiting for something to happen. Anyway, it occurred to him that by the time he returned from Moyun-Kum with his earnings Inga might return and everything would be settled: either (oh joy!) he would be united with his beloved for ever, or he would have to leave and somehow find the strength to continue living . . . But he dared not even contemplate that possibility . . .

That same evening, 'Ober' Kandalov took Avdiy off in a convoy of vehicles to mount the cull in the Moyun-Kum savannah. The team was in high spirits.

Now the same team was putting Avdiy Kallistratov on trial. Five hardened alcoholics – Kandalov, Mishash, Kepa, Hamlet-Halkin and Uzyuk-Bay, 'The Aborigine'. In fact Hamlet-Halkin and the Aborigine were present only as witnesses and they did try, albeit somewhat half-heartedly, to mitigate the ferocity of the triumvirate of judges.

The fact was that Avdiy had provoked their wrath by another bout of the madness that had overtaken him that time on the train. The hunting raid on the Moyun-Kum saigak had so appalled him that he insisted this slaughter must cease. He called on these brutal hunters to repent and turn to God, and he begged Halkin and Uzyuk-Bay to join him: then the three of them could leave Kandalov and his stooges, raise the alarm, and – each of them filled with the knowledge of God the All-merciful Creator – they would place their trust in His infinite mercy, and pray to be forgiven for the evil which they, as humans, had inflicted on the wildlife of the savannah. Only true repentance could bring them any relief.

Avdiy shouted, gestured towards Heaven and begged them to join him in seeking to repent and be cleansed of evil.

In his frenzy he cut a ludicrous figure, wailing and thrashing about, as if, in some premonition of the end of the world, he could see all creation plunging into the fiery maw of hell.

He wanted to bring to God all those men who had come here in search of easy money . . . He wanted to halt the terrible juggernaut of destruction which was raging across the wide open plains of the Moyun-Kum savannah, to stop this mechanical monster from crushing all that lay in its path.

He wanted to surmount the insurmountable.

Then, on Mishash's advice, they bound him and bundled him into the back of a truck, right on top of the carcasses of the saigak they had killed.

'Lie there, you bastard, and croak if you like. Fill your lungs with saigak!' shouted Mishash, hoarse with the exertion. 'Now call up your God! Maybe he'll hear you now, you effing nuisance, and come down from heaven to join you . . .'

It was night and the moon was rising over the Moyun-Kum savannah where they carried out their act of carnage. All its living creatures, even the wolves, were forced to witness the collapse of their world . . .

Those responsible, meanwhile, with the exception of Avdiy Kallistratov, who was there that day only by a wicked stroke of fate, caroused as one . . .

For his refusal to participate, they now prepared to pass judgment on him . . .

After dragging him from the truck, Mishash and Kepa hauled Avdiy over to Ober and forced him to his knees. Kandalov was seated on an empty crate, his crumpled raincoat open and his feet planted wide in their imitation leather boots. Illuminated by the radiance of the truck's lights, he seemed larger than life, his huge brow furrowed, his expression ominous in the extreme. To one side, beside the small camp fire still redolent of charred kebabs prepared from fresh saigak meat, stood Hamlet and the Aborigine, shifting uneasily. They were still well under the influence and for that reason grinned awkwardly as they awaited Ober's verdict, whispering, exchanging winks and nudging each other from time to time.

'Well then?' pronounced Ober at last, with a contemptuous look at Avdiy kneeling before him. 'Have you considered?'

'Untie my hands,' said Avdiy.

'Your hands? And why are they tied – have you thought about that? It's only rebels, plotters, mutineers, the unruly and disorderly who have their hands tied, isn't it? Mutineers, do you hear, mutineers!'

Avdiy remained silent.

'Very well, let's try and untie your hands and see how you behave,' conceded Ober, with apparent kindness. 'All right, untie his hands,' he ordered, 'he's going to need them now.'

'Untie him, my ass,' grumbled Mishash automatically, undoing the rope. 'Puppies like this should be drowned at birth. Squash him like a cockroach we should, and put him straight in the cold earth.'

Only after he was untied did Avdiy realize that his shoulders and hands were numb.

'All right, we've granted your request,' said Ober. 'You've got one more chance. For a start, drink this!' And he thrust a glass of vodka at Avdiy.

'No, I won't drink,' refused Avdiy flatly.

'Have it your own way, then, you scum!' Ober suddenly tossed the contents of the glass into Avdiy's face. He almost choked in his surprise and leapt to his feet, but Mishash and Kepa pounced and pressed him back to his knees.

'No, you lying bastard, I'll make you drink!' roared Mishash. 'Like I said, drowning's too good for the likes of him! Hey, Ober, pour us some more vodka. I'll pour it down his throat, and if he doesn't swallow it I'll swat him like a fly.'

The sharp edges of the glass, which cracked in Mishash's paw, cut Avdiy's face. Choking on the vodka and his own blood, Avdiy extricated himself and started flailing out at Mishash and Kepa with his arms and legs.

'Hey, lads, pack it in, leave him be. He doesn't have to drink it, we can drink it for him!' whined Hamlet plaintively, scurrying around the fighting men. Aborigine darted behind one of the trucks and peered fearfully out, not knowing whether to stay where he was – there was still plenty of vodka left – or run as far away as he could from the scene of mayhem . . . Only Ober Kandalov, enthroned on his crate, remained where he was, as if entranced by the capering of the clowns in the circus. Hamlet-Halkin ran up to Ober.

191

'Stop them, Ober, please, they'll kill him – and then we'll all be in the dock!'

'In the dock!' snorted the chief haughtily. 'What other dock is there in the Moyun-Kum, eh? I'm the judge and jury here! You try and prove anything afterwards. Who's to say, maybe the wolves got him. Show me the witnesses!'

Avdiy lost consciousness, and fell beneath their feet as they laid into him with their boots. His last thought was for Inga, for what would become of her, since no one would ever be able to love her as he did.

The world of sound was dead and a grey mist covered his vision when suddenly he fancied he saw the grey she-wolf, the very one which had leapt across him that hot summer in the hemp fields . . .

'Save me, she-wolf,' Avdiy suddenly blurted out.

Some instinct must have told him that Akbara and Tash-Chainar were even now approaching their lair, which was still occupied by these humans. The beasts were drawn to their customary sleeping place: that was why they returned, hoping, no doubt, that the humans would have abandoned the hollow by now and be heading further afield.

No. The menacing black shape of the truck still loomed up before them in the same spot, and they heard the noise of shouting, of heavy blows . . .

Yet again the wolves were forced back into the steppe. Exhausted, rootless, they stumbled off blindly, not caring where they went. Night or day, there was no place for them with these humans about . . . They wandered slowly off, their tails between their legs, and the moon picked out the shape of their dark silhouettes.

Meanwhile the 'trial' continued. The drunken judge and jury no longer noticed that the defendant, Avdiy Kallistratov, now made almost no effort to rise each time they knocked him down with their fists.

'Come on, on your feet, son-of-a-bishop,' urged Mishash and Kepa in turn, with hefty kicks and foul oaths, but Avdiy merely groaned softly. At this Ober grabbed him savagely, lifting him off the ground like a sack and holding him by his collar, and started to lay into him, temper rising with every word.

'So, you bastard, thought you'd frighten us with your God, did you, wanted to ram your God down our throats, you slime! You won't frighten us with God, you chose the wrong congregation this time, you filth. So who do you think you are, anyway? We're carrying out an official government assignment, fulfilling the plan, and you're trying to implement economic sabotages undermining the economy of the region; you're a bastard, an enemy of the people, an enemy of the people and the state. There's no room for enemies, wreckers and saboteurs like you! It was Stalin who said, "He who is not with us is against us." Enemies of the people should be rooted out and destroyed! In the army they put you up against the wall for subversion like that – bang! To keep our good earth clean of all sorts of vermin. And you, you church rat, what have you been doing? Sowing subversion! You had a secret mission! You wanted to take us for a ride – all the way to the front door of the church, perhaps, eh? I could strangle you, you runt, as an enemy of the people, and I would be thanked for it, seeing as you're an imperialist agent, you snake! You think that because Stalin's dead no one can do anything against you? You dirty priest, get on your knees. I'm your higher authority now, so you renounce your God or it'll be curtains for you, you pig!'

Avdiy could not stay up on his knees, and fell to the ground. They lifted him up.

'Answer me, snake!' roared Ober Kandalov. 'Renounce your God! Say there's no God!'

'There is a God,' groaned Avdiy weakly.

'So that's the way it is!' screeched Mishash. 'Like I said: you tell the bastard one thing and he answers just the opposite!'

Breathless with anger, Kandalov shook Avdiy again by the scruff of his neck.

'Let me tell you something, God-lover, we're going to put on a little show for you that you'll remember all the rest of your days! Haul him over to that tree there, hang him up, hang the bastard up!' shouted the chief. 'And we'll light a little fire under his feet. Just to warm him up a bit!'

Together they hauled Avdiy over to a gnarled *saxaul* tree spreading its branches at the edge of the hollow.

'Bring the rope!' shouted Ober to Kepa.

Kepa dashed across to the cab of the truck.

'Hey, you there! Uzyuk-Bay, you old Ali Baba, get your effing ass over here – you too, what's-your-name, Marlon Brando, skulking in the corner, eh?'

'Get over here, on the double! Otherwise no vodka for you two!' shouted Ober threateningly to the two wretched drunks, who scurried across to hoist the hapless Avdiy into his tree.

Their thuggish prank was taking an ominous turn. A stupid practical joke now threatened to turn into a real lynching. 'There's only one problem, dammit – no cross and nails in this stinking steppe! A real bloody pity,' grumbled Mishash, noisily cracking the twigs of *saxaul*. 'That would have been the thing! To crucify the bastard!'

'What the hell! We'll tie him on with ropes! It'll be as good as any nails!' proposed Ober as a way out of the dilemma. 'We'll stretch him out by the arms and legs like a frog and lash him so tight he can't even twitch! Let him hang there till morning and then he'll see whether there's a God or not! I'll teach him a lesson he'll remember to his dying day, scummy priest, he'll learn what's what! I taught worse than him to dance to my tune in the army! Snap to it, lads, grab him! Hang him up on that branch over there, the high one! Twist his arm over the top branch and his leg under the bottom one!'

The deed was soon done, since Avdiy was incapable of any resistance. Lashed to the gnarled *saxaul* tree, bound hand and foot with ropes, he dangled like a cured skin, hung out to dry. Avdiy could still hear his tormentors cursing, but as if from a distance. His sufferings had sapped all his strength. There was a shooting pain in his abdomen, on the liver side, and his back felt as if some ligament had been snapped or torn, so agonizingly did it hurt. Strength gradually ebbed away from Avdiy. The fact that his drunken tormentors were unsuccessful in their attempts to kindle a fire beneath his feet was no longer of any consolation. Nothing mattered to him any more. The fire came to nothing: the grass and twigs, sodden from the snow which had fallen the previous day, refused to burn . . . None of them thought to splash petrol over the kindling. They were content to see Avdiy hanging like a scarecrow in an orchard. The look of him, something between a scarecrow and a gibbet, amused them all no end. Ober was particularly inspired. He had visions of far more impressive and extensive spectacles – why stop at one rat hanging there in the middle of the steppe?

'That's what I'd do with the lot of them, like it or lump it, and don't you forget it!' he threatened, staring up at Avdiy in the *saxaul*. 'I'd string them all up, everyone who's against us, not like this but so's they'd croak right away. Hang the lot of them, all those who aren't with us, and leave them hanging in a long line all around the world, circling it like a hoop, then no one would ever dare oppose a single word we said, and they'd all dance to our tune . . . Come on now, commissars, let's have another! What the hell, we only live once!'

Eagerly nodding their assent, they made their noisy way to the truck and, sending round a couple more half-litre bottles, polished them off without further ado.

A little later the truck roared, headlights blazing as it turned and slowly bumped off through the steppe. Avdiy remained alone in all the world, lashed to his tree. There was a burning pain in his chest, his battered insides were racked by an unbearable, stupefying pain . . . He gradually slipped into unconsciousness, like a small island disappearing slowly through the waters of a flood.

My little island on the Oka . . . But who will save you, Master? His last thought flashed for a moment, like a spark, and was gone . . .

The final flood of human life was moving in . . . Before his fading eyes there was a vision of water, an infinite, uninterrupted expanse without beginning and without end. The water seethed soundlessly, and silent white waves rolled across its surface, like a snowstorm over a field, their source and their direction unknown. On the very edge of that soundless sea he could just make out the figure of a man, and Avdiy recognized him: it was his father, Deacon Kallistratov. Then Avdiy heard his own voice, speaking as a boy, repeating to his father his favourite prayer about a sunken ship, just as he had repeated it so often at home in his childhood, standing beside the old piano; only now the distance between them was immense and he heard his father's voice ringing with inspiration, reverberating across the surface of the earth:

First light has broken in the sky, and while the world still sleeps . . . O Merciful, Blessed and Righteous Father, forgive me that I importune You with my incessant appeals. There is no self-interest in my prayer – it is not worldly benefits I seek, nor do I pray for the prolongation of my days. It is but for the salvation of souls that I call upon You untiringly.

All-forgiving Father, do not leave us in ignorance. Do not let us seek to justify our actions by the fact that good and evil are inextricably entangled on this earth. Vouchsafe enlightenment unto the human race.

For myself, I seek nothing. I do not fear my end, whatever it may be: to burn in the fires of hell, or enter the Kingdom to which there shall be no end. Our fate is in Your hands, O Invisible and Unbounded Creator.

I ask but one thing, one miracle . . . As long as night follows day and day follows night in the way ordained by You for our earth as it spins through the empty wastes of space, as long as the spray beats salty into the air and the seagulls cry, may the ship hold its course for the radiant city on the distant ocean shore, though none may cast anchor there in all the aeons of time . . . Amen.

His voice gradually faded, growing ever more distant . . . And Avdiy heard himself weep over the ocean . . .

All night long the silence of the boundless Moyun-Kum savannah was flooded with bright, blinding moonlight, illuminating the stiffened figure of a man crucified on a *saxaul* tree. The figure was like a large bird with outspread wings, struck down as it soared heavenwards, and blown into the branches.

The truck had stopped in the steppe, a mere mile from there. In the back, their hideous deed successfully completed, Ober and his accomplices slept sprawled over the saigak carcasses, lying in pools of raw vodka vomit. The air reverberated with a thick and laboured snoring. They had driven off to leave Avdiy alone for the night and teach him a lesson: let him see how he got on without them, then he would surely renounce his god and worship power instead . . .

The punishment was devised for Avdiy by the ex-actor Halkin, alias Hamlet, after seeking inspiration countless times from the bottle, swallowing back the vodka like tasteless, stagnant water. Hamlet hoped in this way to worm his way into favour with Ober. 'Let's give the God-lover the fright of his life,' he had said. 'Let him panic and think we've tied him hand and foot, strung him up and pushed off for good. Even if he wanted to catch us up, he wouldn't have a hope in hell!'

In the morning at first light the wolves sidled tentatively towards the site of their former lair. First came Akbara, her flanks sunken after the night's exertions, and behind her big-jowled Tash-Chainar, sullenly limping along. Their old haunt was now empty, the humans having disappeared during the night. Still the animals took every step as gingerly, if the simile is tolerable, as though they were walking through a minefield. With every step they stumbled on something alien and hostile: burnt-out fire, empty tins, broken glass, the acrid smell of rubber and iron still lingering in the wheel tracks left by the lorry, and everywhere the foul miasma that lingered round the empty bottles. Resolving to abandon this defiled place for ever, the wolves walked around the edge of the hollow, when suddenly Akbara recoiled and froze to the spot. A man! Two steps from where she stood, a man hung from a *saxaul* tree, his arms spread out and his head lolling to one side. Akbara rushed headlong for the bushes, followed by Tash-Chainar. The man in the tree did not stir. A slight breeze whistled softly through the boughs, disturbing the hair falling across his white brow. Akbara flattened herself to the ground, her body tautened like a spring, preparing to leap. Before her was a man, the most loathsome of creatures, the perpetrator of all the wolves' misfortunes, their sworn enemy. A monstrous rage welled up within her, and Akbara edged back slightly in her fury, the better to hurl herself up at the man, and sink her fangs in his throat. At that very moment, however, the she-wolf suddenly recognized her foe. Where was it she had seen him? Yes, it was the madman who had crossed her path before in the summer, when she travelled across the steppe with her litter to breathe the smell of the fragrant grass. Akbara recalled that summer day and her cubs frolicking with this man; she remembered sparing him and jumping over him, when he cowered in fear on the ground, covering his head with his arms. She remembered the shock in his terrified eyes and how he had fled, defenceless, naked . . .

Now this man hung awkwardly in a stunted *saxaul*, like a bird caught in a cage, and the world could not tell whether he was alive or dead. The man did not move, he uttered no sound, his head hung to the side and a thin trickle of blood ran from the corner of his mouth. Tash-Chainar was on the point of attacking the hanging man, but Akbara headed him off. Instead she stepped up closer and, gazing intently into the face of the crucified man, started to keen softly for all her summer brood, her wolf cubs who had perished. Her life in the Moyun-Kum had turned to dust and ashes. She had no one to grieve with . . . This man could give her no help, his own end was close, but still she sensed in him the warmth of life. The man, with a supreme effort, raised his eyelids slightly and whispered to the keening she-wolf, 'You've come . . .' And his head sagged again.

Those were his last words.

Suddenly they heard the noise of an engine and an army truck appeared over a hillock. The truck drove towards them, growing larger as it approached, the slanting windows of the cab gleaming dully in the light. It was the Kandalov gang returning to the scene of their crime . . .

The wolves slunk away in fright, increasing speed as they went. They gave no backward glance. The Moyun-Kum wolves were leaving the Moyun-Kum, that great savannah, never to return . . .

Akbara and Tash-Chainar spent a year of their lives in the Aldash reedlands. Here they brought forth their biggest litter – five cubs, a fine brood! The cubs were already growing when the beasts were overtaken by new disaster – the reeds were burnt down. Approach roads to an open-cast mine were being built in the area, and the reeds had to go. The ancient reedlands covering hundreds and thousands of hectares around the Lake Aldash suddenly were put to the torch. After the war, large deposits of some rare ore had been found in this region, giving birth to yet another vast and nameless secret industrial enterprise. Why balk at a few reeds, when they could countenance the destruction of the whole lake? So long as a rare ore was to be found, no one would dare object. For the sake of minerals men are willing to disembowel the whole earth, like gutting a pumpkin.

It started with planes that flew slowly across the edges of the lake, spraying a special combustible mixture from the air so that the reeds would ignite instantly when the time was ripe.

The fire was started in the dead of night. The reeds, doused with inflammable chemicals, flared up like gunpowder, the fire far fiercer and more powerful than if even the densest forest were burning. Flames leapt into the sky and a pall of smoke covered the steppe like a dense winter mist. No sooner had they caught the smell of burning and seen the flames all around than the wolves were thrown into a frenzy of activity in their reedbeds, fighting to save their cubs. They carried them in their teeth from one place to another, seeking sanctuary. Chaos broke out in the thickets around the lake. Birds flew above the water in dense clouds, their shrill cries deafening the steppe for miles around. All the creatures which had made these shores their habitat for centuries, from the wild boars to the snakes, were thrown into a panic – the reeds were caught up in a frenzy of activity. The wolves found themselves surrounded by fire on all sides, and could save themselve only by plunging into the water. Abandoning three cubs to the flames and holding the two others in their mouths, they endeavoured to save them by swimming across the bay. When at last the wolves climbed out on the opposite shore it was only to find that both cubs, despite their efforts to hold them high above the water, had drowned.

Yet again were Akbara and Tash-Chainar forced to seek a new home. This time their quest took them to the mountains, which instinct told the wolves were now the only place on earth where they could hope to survive.

They trotted on for a long time, leaving behind them the man-made fires whose dense smoke still obscured the horizon. Their path took them through the Kurdai plateau, where on several occasions at night they had to cross major roads along which vehicles roared with their dazzling headlights, and these hurtling blazing lights terrified them more than anything else on their entire trek. After Kurdai the wolves crossed into the Ak-Tyuz mountains, but here too they sensed danger, and resolved to press on. Traversing the Ak-Tyuz pass they entered the Issyk-Kul basin. They could go no further. Before them lay the inland sea . . .

Yet again Akbara and Tash-Chainar began their lives afresh . . . Yet again they produced a litter of cubs – this time four wolflings, their last desperate attempt to perpetuate their line.

And there, by Issyk-Kul, the story of these wolves came to its terrible, tragic conclusion . . .

WOLF

1

Men seek their fate, but fate seeks its man, as well . . . Round
and round life follows the pattern, fate always contriving to
find its target, just as this time it darted straight and sure to the
inexorable conclusion of a tale begun in another place, at
another time.

Trust Bazarbai Noigutov to get the job of guide to a team of
geologists. Bazarbai was not to know that geologists even
needed guides, but they sought him out and made him an
offer he couldn't refuse. They had made their way as far as
Taman by following a tractor-track used to bring fodder up for
the sheep, but from there on the route was only a vague line on
the map, so they decided it would be better if some local man
could guide them through the mountains. Well, why not?
There was good money in it. Money for old rope: taking four
townies with their packs up into the Achy-Tash gorge, where
they would drill for geological samples (gold, of course: the
usual story, it was always gold they prospected for). Big bonus
money in gold. Well, good luck to them, that was their affair,
but Bazarbai had to make his way back by nightfall to the
Taman Roshara – the camp where he wintered with his flock.
That was all there was to it.

This lot were pretty clueless about money, not the usual city
types at all. Bazarbai went into the usual routine: 'I can't be
wasting time guiding folk around, any moment the farm
authorities might put in an appearance and start asking what's
going on. "Where's senior shepherd Bazarbai Noigutov?"
they'll say. "What does he mean by taking off without leave,
with the lambing season on us and all?" After all, who's
supposed to be in charge? Me, of course!' As soon as they
heard this the geologists did a spot of mental arithmetic and
offered him twenty-five roubles. Idiots! Still, who cares, it's the
government's money, and what's twenty-five roubles to the
state treasury? No doubt they're not backward in coming

forward, either, when it's a question of finding uses for the petty cash! So let them cough up. What a piece of cake for Bazarbai, to guide the geologists to a site less than a day's ride away. He rode out that far at least once a day or so, attending to his own important and less important duties, particularly when there was a wedding or funeral in the offing and the smell of vodka in the air. His whole team would be worried sick when the end of the month came round and he visited the farm office to collect everybody's pay packets. A team consisted of the shepherd, the two herdsboys, the night-watchman and especially the wife (she was also classified as one of the workers), and at lambing time it also included seasonal workers.

Bazarbai would arrive home after dark, drunk as a lord, barely able to sit on his horse, oblivious of the responsibility entailed in delivering people their pay. Eventually his hag of a wife went and complained to the director of the state farm, so for the past three months the book-keeper Boronbai had been bringing the wages up to the winter camp himself, saying that legally everyone should sign for them on the pay list in person. Well, let him do the journey each time, if that was what he wanted . . .

And now twenty-five roubles, fallen straight into his lap from heaven! True, the track up Achy-Tash was stony and in places sheer enough to make the blood run cold; the slightest slip meant a broken neck, but what the hell, that's mountains for you, not like the track these townies run round and round on television, to get medals round their necks and hear the national anthem played in their honour. There never had been any justice in the world, and there never would be. Here you were, summer and winter in the mountains, no nice tarred roads or plumbing or electric light, just get by somehow, even if it means following your sheep around the whole year, treading in their stinking droppings, while out there somewhere some smart young fellow in nice white running-shoes does a couple of turns round the stadium or kicks a ball into some stupid goal – fun for him, and a roar of satisfaction from the crowd. Then it's fame and glory all the way and his face splashed all over the sports page, while the poor sod who's grafting away from morning to night, with no days off and no summer holiday, hardly makes enough to feed his family. So you have a few drinks because you're fed up, and then the wife gets on your back and makes things even worse. Then the other side's on to you to increase the yield, so that every ewe will lamb every year and the sheep be fatter, with better quality wool. They keep on threatening to discover something synthetic as good as fleece, but they haven't yet. Then when shearing-time comes round you've got a hundred inspectors breathing down your neck and they sweep the place out as clean as a whistle, you won't be left with a single strand of wool to put away for yourself. They say we need this fine-fleeced wool for foreign exchange . . . Foreign exchange! Huh, that's a fine one! All we produce just disappears into some bottomless pit. To hell with it all! To hell with sheep and people and all this stinking rotten life . . .

Such mirthless thoughts occupied Bazarbai's mind as they rode along. It meant he was silent all the way, only occasionally turning round to the geologists riding behind him, to warn them of an approaching danger . . . He felt crushed by misery. And all because of that hag of a woman . . . What a bitch! Trust her to go and stick her nose where it didn't belong – she had to go and raise hell, shouting her mouth off this time for everyone to hear. Enough to make you sick. His life was a mess. There was truth in the old saw: a wife is a kitten by night and a snake by day. Trust her to start shouting as soon as she heard! 'That's all you need,' she said, 'somewhere to skive off to. Where did he pick them up, these geologists? There's more work than what we can manage as it is, the sheep have started lambing and the children on our hands as well, the older ones turning into proper hooligans at boarding school, and when they come for the holidays it's only to eat till they're fit to burst, it's all give, give, give, and no help from them, smoking like chimneys and knocking back the vodka, no discipline at school, after all – the headmaster's an old soak, and what sort of example do they get at home? You're off whenever you can, so long as there's the smell of vodka in the air. It's just as well the horse knows its own way home or else you'd have pegged it on a bender somewhere by the road . . .'

What a stupid old hag! He'd tried to tame her by beating the hell out of her, every week she was covered in bruises so that now they called her Kok Tursun, black-and-blue Tursun, though she still hadn't learned how to hold her filthy tongue.

This time she'd gone too far, letting rip in front of the geologists. And to think how often he'd had her by the throat and pressed so hard her eyes almost popped out! Afterwards she would give her word not to cross him, but would that stop her? He had to find a way to stop her mouth this time, and fast. He called her into the house as if to talk it over, and the moment she was inside grabbed her and pressed her in silence up against the wall, squeezing all the breath out of her lungs. As they struggled he could see his wife's face at point-blank range, already like that of a corpse, the skin bluish and wrinkled, the eyes dull with fear and brimming with all the misery and joylessness of their years together. In her deadened gaze he could read all the failure and resentment that made up the sum of her life. Her toothless mouth suddenly twisted to one side, and he felt a spasm of shame for what he was doing as he whispered menacingly, 'Now, bitch, one more peep from you and I'll squash you like a cockroach.' Then he flung her aside.

Without a word she picked up her buckets and went out, slamming the door. He got his breath back, followed her, mounted his horse and set off with the geologists.

At least his horse was a decent one, his only joy, rejected from a stud farm because some maniac didn't like the colour of its coat, something intermediate between a bay and a brown. What difference did the colour make, anyway? The animal was frisky, it knew how to pick its way along the mountain paths without guidance and, most important, it was hardy, tough as a wolf. He rode it all day long, but not even a single rib was showing. No, no denying it, he had a fine horse, probably none of the other shepherds in the region had such a nice beast, except maybe Boston, the local *peredovik*, the model worker, an odd character and a real skinflint. There had never been much love lost between the two of them. Boston had a fine horse and a good colour, too, a chestnut-golden Don stallion that he called Donkulyuk. Boston had been lucky to get him. He looked after that horse – as well he might: he had to cut a dash on his horse, now he had a young wife, Ernazar's widow. Ernazar had fallen about three years before into a crevasse on the Ala-Mongyu pass. They'd never retrieved the body . . .

They rode single file for most of the way, and therefore in silence, although Bazarbai's mood after his row with his wife was anyway hardly conducive to conversation. Winter was already on its way out. On the south-facing slopes, which had trustingly discarded their protective mantle of snow, the fragrance of spring was already making itself felt. It was bright and still on earth at that hour. On the opposite shore of the great mountain lake, over the deep, opaque blue waters, the midday sun was already riding high in the sky.

Bazarbai brought the geologists to the mouth of the ravine where they caught their last glimpse of the pure, mirror-like surface of Issyk-Kul before the lake was hidden by a flank of the mountains. The sheer cliffs hung morosely above. They were surrounded by rock and by barren wilderness. What could they hope to find there? wondered Bazarbai, gazing around him. He decided that the moment the geologists reached their destination, he would head back. The Achy-Tash gorge was not as long as the gorge parallel to it, which reached right down to the lake shore. For his own part he decided to return through the Bashat gorge, a shorter route for him. When he took leave of the geologists he put the coveted twenty-five rouble note into his pocket, then tried an old trick. 'Well, friends, we're all grown men here,' he grinned, arrogantly stroking his moustache. 'And I'm no farmboy, either. You wouldn't send me off without wetting my whistle now, would you?'

Bazarbai was reckoning on a glassful, but they generously donated him a half-litre bottle – one of the greenish bottles from the local distillery. Here, they said, drink it at home! This unexpected stroke of fortune had an immediate effect on Bazarbai. He bustled about, showing them the best place to pitch their tents, where to get thorn bushes for their fire, and spent ages shaking their hands, saying goodbye to each in turn and even forgetting to feed his horse the oats he had brought in the *kurjun*, a double saddlebag. Well, he'd make it back, it wouldn't be the first time. He hastened back into his saddle and set off on his return journey. As he had planned, he quickly found the track and, following the ridge half concealed by snow, rode down into the Bashat gorge. Here in the gorge the slopes were sparsely forested and it was a little brighter – not as gloomy as in Achy-Tash, but – more important – there were a great number of the little streams and springs that gave the gorge its name: Bashat – a spring.

The bottle constantly bumping about in the pocket of the raincoat which he wore over his sheepskin bothered him. He periodically stroked it and pondered which brook to stop beside. He knew his limit – he could take half a bottle, wash it down with water and ride on. The main thing for Bazarbai at times like this was the problem of hauling himself back into the saddle; once that was accomplished, his horse was reliable, and could be trusted to get him home. The long-suffering Kok-Tursun was right to say that Bazarbai was propped upright by the devil himself – he had never once fallen out of the saddle.

At last he spotted a stream in his path, slightly frozen, bubbling happily over the pebbles beneath its fragile, translucent ice-crust. It seemed a good spot to Bazarbai. All around were thickets of reeds and barberries, there was not too much snow and he could water the horse and give it some oats. He unbridled it, untied the saddlebag of oats, undid the drawstring and thrust the open side under the horse's nose. The horse munched the oats, snorting with pleasure, eyelids drooping as it shivered to shake the fatigue from its body. Meanwhile, Bazarbai disposed himself comfortably on a dead branch beside the stream, took out the bottle, admired it, and held it up to the light, at which point he noticed that day was drawing to a close and the shadows in the mountains were lengthening with barely an hour to go before sunset. So what? Bazarbai had no reason to hurry home. Savouring in advance the familiar numbing sensation from the vodka, and taking his time, he prised off the top with a thick thumbnail, sniffed, shook his head, and put the bottle to his lips. Feverishly, he downed several large, burning mouthfuls. Then he scooped up a handful of water from the stream and gulped it down together with the fragments of ice. He crunched the ice between his teeth, the crunching reverberating in his head. Bazarbai's face suddenly distorted into a monstrous grimace, he coughed, wheezed and closed his eyes, waiting for the rush of alcohol to his head. Soon would come that moment when the entire surrounding world – the mountains, the cliffs – started to totter and swim before his eyes, exploded and filled his head with a confused babble of noise. Then he would go quite still, and squinting happily surrender himself to the intoxication. At that moment of surrender he heard an indistinct whining somewhere near by, like the whimpering of a child – what could it be? There it was again, somewhere behind the barberry scrub, behind some loose rocks, another whine, just like a puppy's. Bazarbai pricked up his ears, took a further gulp from the bottle, then put it down against a rock, wiped his mouth decisively and stood up. He listened again, straining his attention. There it was again. Some young animal was giving voice near by.

It was the wolves' lair, and the whimpering came from Akbara and Tash-Chainar's cubs, who were crying for their parents. After the massive trek from the Moyun-Kum savannah, after a cubless year following the fire in the Aldash reedlands, they had had an unseasonably early litter; Akbara bore four cubs before the spring was in.

Bazarbai made for the lair, following the tracks. Had he been sober, he would probably have first considered the wisdom of proceeding any further. It took him some time to find the lair, in a crevice in the rock. Here experience came to his assistance: carefully scrutinizing the ice-crush that had formed over the snow he found a distinct chain of prints. It was the usual story: caution dictated that the wolves always stepped in their old tracks. Further on in the bushes Bazarbai found among the piles of rock a whole cemetery of gnawed and half-eaten bones, from which he learned that the animals tended to drag part of their prey here where they could eat at their leisure. To judge by the quantity of big bones and joints remaining from their feasts, the beasts had been living here for some time. There was now no difficulty in finding the lair. It is hard to conjecture why Bazarbai crawled so boldly into the crevice, in which there might have been adult wolves. The cubs, desperately hungry, ignorant of their danger, continued to whimper, giving themselves away and as good as inviting their foe to come in and find them.

The cubs did not know what drove Akbara and Tash-Chainar to set off on this hunting raid together. Hard times were beginning for the wolves as spring approached, when all animal life grew thin. All the weaker wild goats and mountain antelope in the region had been killed, and the horned herds retreated into the more inaccessible mountain areas where they would bear their young. Domestic herds, for the same reason, were now confined to sheds and closed pastures, and in these conditions it was not easy to produce enough milk for a permanently hungry litter. Akbara had grown lean and almost unrecognizable, big-headed and skinny-legged, with dangling teats. Generally speaking, wolves are hardy creatures – they can go several days on end without food; but this does not hold true of a she-wolf with cubs to feed. Akbara had no choice but to take the risk of going out on a hunting expedition, though if she happened to be killed her cubs would also perish.

Tash-Chainar, as always, trotted along behind her. They had to be out and back as soon as possible, find their prey swiftly, kill it and eat their fill of meat, gulping down the food in large chunks, before running quickly back to the lair to digest it. For a she-wolf, the most important thing is to produce milk for her cubs.

That day their path was slippery where it had caught the sun's rays and hard as steel in the shady parts, where it was still frozen. The wolves kept up their speed, however, and bounded swiftly across the mountain terrain. At this time of year, when the small mammals were concealed below ground and the wild and domestic herds were beyond reach, there was the further complexity of the fact that to bring down the large beasts – horses, cattle or camels – a hunting partner is required. However powerful Tash-Chainar might be, he could not drag such a large animal back to the lair unaided. The last time he had killed an ass which had strayed into the foothills. Under cover of night Akbara ventured out of the lair and stocked up with donkey meat, but not many donkeys were so careless as to stray off towards the mountains. They usually had people with them. This was why Akbara now sallied forth herself – to satisfy her hunger at the site of the kill.

Initially Akbara felt uncertain and perturbed. Once or twice she almost headed back, anxious for her cubs and aware that they needed her warmth and milk, but she forced herself to forget the lair for a while. Once they were down near the lake they came on a scent and her hunter's instincts prevailed over all else.

The wolves were fortunate: a fresh trail led them into a broad hollow on the edge of which three yaks were grazing in isolation from their herd. The wolves had already had dealings with these animals a year ago, and then too in a time of extreme need. Then, as new arrivals, they had had no alternative but to take whatever was at hand. Now it was time that was short. There were no humans around and the wolves, after glancing to right and left, went into the attack. Once they spotted the racing wolves the yaks scattered, kicking out and bellowing as best they could, but the wolves caught up and the yaks stopped, their flanks heaving, turned and charged the wolves with their horns. They had no other option. For a moment the primordial balance of nature reigned: the sun in the sky, empty mountains, complete silence, the total absence of humans – ruminants and predators were equals in an empty world. The yaks were anxious to avoid a confrontation, but their hunters could not turn on their heels and retreat; they could not ignore the hunger that tormented them. They had to do battle and bring down at least one of the yaks, if they were to survive themselves and preserve the lives of their offspring. The yaks were not particularly large, but neither were they small; they were reasonably well fed and still covered with their shaggy winter coats. These strange creatures – bulls with horses' tails – saw that a fight was inevitable. In their fear and anger they lowered their heads, lowing deeply and pawing the ground with their hooves. The sun still shone down and the mountains, on which the snow had already started to melt, stood silent witness to this confrontation between herbivore and carnivore. The wolves circled the yaks, moving in leaps and bounds, waiting for the right moment to pounce. For Akbara time was running out: her cubs were awaiting her return. She leapt first, risking her own life, choosing the yak which looked weakest to her. The yak's eyes were bloodshot with anger but Akbara sensed a hesitation in his look, although she might have been mistaken. It was too late to change her mind now. She sprang at the yak's neck. The matter was over in seconds. While the enraged yak thrashed his head, trying to throw off the she-wolf and pin her with his horns to the ground, Tash-Chainar prepared to pounce from the other side, sink his fangs into the beast's throat, and in one motion to sever its jugular artery and stop the supply of blood to the brain.

First, however, the yak succeeded in throwing Akbara off and pinning her to the ground, bellowing and prodding her with his horns. Another moment and he would finally have trampled her to death, but she slipped out from beneath the horns, lithe as a snake, and sprang back on to the beast's head, biting into his thick mane with its coarse sedge-like wool that cut her jaw. In this attack she displayed her ruthless lupine nature, following the merciless destiny of her kind: kill to live. On this occasion her prey was hardly a defenceless victim – no saigak or hare, meekly succumbing to violent attack. The ferocious yak could put up a long and vicious fight, despite the blood streaming from its neck, and even emerge victorious. In the end Akbara's star prevailed: at that moment Tash-Chainar pounced from the side and sank his teeth into the yak's throat as Akbara held its attention. Tash-Chainar had the leap and the jaws of a true killer, and put every ounce of his strength into his jump. The yak tottered, wheezing as it choked on its own blood, then crashed to the ground, its throat fatally wounded, lowing and shuddering. Its eyes glazed over. While the fight raged the two other yaks took to their heels, putting a good distance between themselves and the wolves before they dropped to a walk and strolled casually on through the upland hollow as if nothing had ever happened.

The wolves now tore at the flesh of the bull, still gasping for breath. They had no time to wait until their quarry finally gave up the ghost, or to pick and choose the daintiest morsels. Akbara tore into the yak's groin, using her paws and claws, and was soon gulping back chunks of still warm, pulsating meat. She knew she had to swallow as many such pieces as possible and go straight back to the lair where her little cubs were waiting anxiously for her. Nor did Tash-Chainar lag far behind. Growling fiercely he crushed the animals's joints in his powerful jaws and like some barbarous butcher ripped its flesh into shapeless lumps. Everything had gone according to plan. The wolves would first eat their fill of meat, then hurry back to the lair and, under cover of night, return to eat their fill again and drag the remaining meat somewhere to store it. For the moment the beasts gulped the meat frantically down, as fast as they could.

Meanwhile, back in the crevice beneath the overhanging rock where they had their lair, the starving cubs whined and whimpered, huddling together for warmth. When they heard a rustle outside (it was actually Bazarbai crawling into the lair) they set up an even louder wailing and tottered forward on their shaky little legs towards the opening, thereby greatly assisting the intruder in his self-appointed task.

Bazarbai was sweating with tension. He groped his way into the tight crack in the rock, abandoning his sheepskin and wearing only his jacket, grabbed the cubs, popping three of them into the front of his jacket and, holding the fourth by the scruff of its neck, crawled out into the light again. When he emerged he screwed up his eyes against the brightness of the mountains. He took a deep draught of air. The silence was all-pervading, empty save for the sound of his own breathing. The cubs inside his jacket started moving and the one in his hand tried to free itself. Bazarbai hastened on his way. Still panting, he picked up his sheepskin and rushed back to the stream, and from there everything went smoothly. The four cubs, which he had decided to steal and sell, would fit nicely into his saddlebag. He was more than convinced that he would get a good price for them: only the year before a shepherd had sold an entire litter to a zoo, raking in for each of the cubs fifty roubles.

Bazarbai grabbed the bag from beneath the champing muzzle of his horse, quickly emptied the oats on to the ground, popped in the cubs, two in each side of the bag, threw it back over the saddle, tying it to the girths to keep it in place, to stop it shaking about, put the bridle back on the horse and put his foot in the stirrup without further ado. He had to get back before it was too late. What a real stroke of luck! He had to make himself scarce before the wolves appeared – Bazarbai knew that only too well. Once in the saddle he remembered the unfinished bottle of vodka, propped up against a stone. To hell with the vodka! He would get enough for the cubs to buy dozens more bottles like that one. He spurred on his horse, for

213

he had to get as far as possible from the gorge before the sun went down.

Afterwards Bazarbai himself would wonder why he didn't take any precautions. Before crawling into the lair, he didn't even have a gun with him! What if the mother – or, worse, the male wolf – had been in the area . . . To protect its young, even the meekest of deer will attack an enemy . . .

Only much later, however, did he think of all this. Later, he would recall with queasy horror the terrible price he might have had to pay for what he did. But for the moment he thought only of urging his brown-bay on, along the stony bottom of the Bashat gorge, to cover as much ground as possible before the approach of dusk. He had to head for the foothills and then the open ground around the lake – there he had a sporting chance of escape, unlike here, stuck in this narrow ravine . . .

As Bazarbai neared the lake and the familiar country around it, his confidence grew (and his self-esteem with it). He looked forward to bragging about his lucky find and even wondered whether he might call in on one of his fellow shepherds and drinking mates, to show off his prize and celebrate with a drink or two – at least one big tot for each cub – it would be no problem to return the favour once he sold the cubs. Now he regretted that in his haste he had left the rest – almost two thirds! – of his half-litre bottle at the stream: it would be good to have a swig as he trotted along . . . He deserved a little reward tonight. Good sense prevailed, however, and persuaded him that there was always time for his reward: for the moment he had to think about getting the cubs safely home and feeding them. They might be hardy little creatures, but they were still tiny, their eyes only just open, and still taking in nothing of the world they saw about them. He only hoped they hadn't suffocated in the saddlebag.

Unknown to Bazarbai, he was not alone on the trail down from Bashat that night. Behind him padded a dangerous adversary, the wolves, and if they should catch up with him his chances were slim . . .

Once they had eaten their fill of yak flesh the wolves followed the track back to their lair, Akbara ahead and Tash-Chainar following behind. Their one aim was to be back with their cubs in the lair under the rocks, lie down with them in a tight circle, get back their breath and then return to the unfinished yak carcass where they had left it in the hollow.

Such was their life; a wolf is always on the move . . . This too was something to worry about, for other wolves might smell their carcass, just as they themselves would willingly feed off another wolf's kill, and confrontation would inevitably lead to a fight, a serious and bloody fight. Every wolf knew its rights and was willing to defend them with all its strength.

Akbara sensed that something was wrong while still some way off, on the approach to the lair. As sharply as if it had been a bird flying beside her, like a shadow, she sensed something tangible and terrible in the light of the setting sun. The disturbing, deep red reflection on the snowy peaks suddenly took on a darker, sombre tone. As they drew closer to the lair she increased her pace, without even looking back at Tash-Chainar, and finally broke into a run, seized by an inexplicable premonition. Her alarm intensified as she caught an alien scent in the air, the strong smell of horse and something else, something revolting and befuddling. What was it? Where did it come from? The she-wolf sprang across the stream, through the gaps in the bushes, making for the crevice beneath the cliff. She plunged into the lair, froze and then sniffed feverishly about, like a hunting dog, searching in all the corners of her deserted, cubless nest, then shot out again, colliding with Tash-Chainar in the entrance. She lunged furiously at him as if he were guilty, as if he were her enemy and not her mate and the sire of her missing cubs. Tash-Chainar also dashed into the lair before catching up with her on the banks of the stream. Akbara ran frantically from side to side, following the scent and reading from the tracks what had happened. Someone had been here, the fresh tracks informed her of the recent visit of a human. She found a heap of spilled oats, smelling of horse saliva, a pile of horse droppings and something in a bottle, with a strong and penetrating smell that made her shudder. There were also human tracks in the snow, synthetic leather boots, the kind that the shepherds wore. Their most terrible enemy had been here on his horse with some foul liquid in a bottle, had raided their nest and taken their cubs! What if he had devoured them! Once again Akbara attacked the

215

completely innocent Tash-Chainar, biting him in a fury; then, with a low growl, she set off in pursuit, following the scent. Tash-Chainar followed.

The wolves followed the trail unerringly, pressing further and further ahead, leaving the ravine behind them and heading towards human habitation, following the tracks towards the lake . . .

Meanwhile Bazarbai left the ravine and trotted through open country, down gentle slopes, past extensive summer pastures, until at last in the distance he could see the dark waters of the lake. Another hour and he'd be home. By this time the sun was poised on the horizon; then it settled between the mountain peaks and passed from view, its rays gradually fading. An icy wind rose from the direction of Issyk-Kul. I only hope the little beasts don't freeze, thought Bazarbai, but he had nothing to wrap them in, so he decided to peep into the *kurjun* and check that they were still alive. He didn't want to arrive with dead cubs – what point to that? He dismounted and started to untie the saddle girth to remove the bag and look inside, but at that moment the horse started to make water, spreading its legs wide. Then suddenly, abruptly cutting off the copious stream, it shied to one side and almost wrenched the reins out of Bazarbai's hand.

'Whoa!' shouted Bazarbai. 'You cut that out!'

The horse bounded to one side in fright as if scalded. At once Bazarbai guessed what was happening, without even looking round. Behind him he could sense the approaching wolves and his blood ran cold. He jumped to the stirrup and was barely able to seize hold of its mane when the beast, snorting and bucking, raced off at a headlong gallop. Bending down out of the wind, Bazarbai looked behind him. A pair of wolves was running there not far away. The horse must have shied when they leapt on to a mound. Now they were aiming to cut them off. Bazarbai started to pray to gods in whom he had not believed in years. He cursed the geologists for landing on him out of the blue: 'I hope you choke on your gold!' He repented and swore to seek forgiveness from his wife: 'I give you my word! If I survive this day I'll never lay a finger on you again!' He regretted his resolve to steal the cubs: 'Why did I have to touch them, why did I crawl into that hole? I should have smashed their heads in with a rock, one after the other, and that would've been an end of it, but now – I'm stuck with them!' The bag was firmly tied down to the saddle girth, so he could not reach in and throw the cubs out as he galloped. On top of all this it was getting darker and darker, the shadows running together to fill the desolate spaces. No one would know, no one would care about his terrible fate! Only his faithful horse raced on at full speed, demented with fear.

Bazarbai's greatest regret was that he had no gun with him – he would have flattened them with a bullet each, and no way would he have missed. Every shepherd or herdsman had a gun at home, but no one carried it around with him the whole time! If he could have known! Bazarbai yelled with all his might, hoping to scare off the beasts. All his hope was now pinned on the horse – good thing it was a thoroughbred . . .

It was a race now to the death . . .

On they sped through the dusk – the rider on his mount with his booty in the saddlebag and behind him Akbara and Tash-Chainar. Catching the scent of their cubs, the wolves sent up their own prayer, their own cry of despair. If only the horse would stumble, if only for a moment! If only they hadn't stuffed themselves with yak meat they would not have moved so sluggishly; they would have caught the predator by now and torn him limb from limb, with bloody retribution reaffirming justice in the harsh, eternal struggle for the perpetuation of their kind. When they hunted the saigak in the Moyun-Kum steppe the wolves were capable of running at top speed and then giving an even greater spurt, to head off their quarry in the right direction; but in the Moyun-Kum the wolves had hunted on empty stomachs, well prepared to strike, when they had to, like lightning.

For Akbara the running was particularly hard, since she had taken on extra food in reserve, for the benefit of her young; she still held her pace, racing for all she was worth, and if she had caught up with the rider she would have pounced without a moment's hesitation, regardless of the possible consequences for herself. Of couse, she had Tash-Chainar, but if death comes then you are alone. She was ready to accept any death, if only she could first reach this man on his swift horse . . . If only . . .

Although Bazarbai's horse was swift he was appalled to see the wolves gaining slowly but steadily, approaching on the right-hand side, aiming to cut off his retreat towards the plain of Issyk-Kul. The cunning beasts planned to turn the rider and chase him back into the mountains, where sooner or later he would have to face them man to beasts. Beside itself with fear, the horse tried constantly to get away from the wolves on its right by heading for the mountains. The human rider, however, was in charge and Bazarbai guessed what the attackers were planning, a factor which the wolves failed to take into account.

One other circumstance came to Bazarbai's rescue. Suddenly, the lights of a nearby camp showed ahead of them and he realized – what a stroke of luck! – this was Boston Urkunchiev's winter pasture – that same Boston, *kulak* and model worker, whom he so despised! No time like the present to bury the hatchet! Any living soul was an equally welcome sight. A human habitation in his path – what joy, he was saved! He whooped with delight, pounded his horse's flanks with his heels and the horse hurtled forward to where there were people and sheep. It seemed like an eternity to Bazarbai before he dared to believe that he would save his skin, but at last he heard the machine-gun rattle of Boston's generator, and the excited barkings of the sheepdogs racing out to meet him. Still the wolves did not retreat – they even closed the gap, as the horse was rapidly fading, and Bazarbai could now feel the hot breath of his pursuers. 'Oh Baubedin,' prayed Bazarbai, invoking a pagan god, 'if you only save me I'll sacrifice seven head of cattle to you!'

'I'm safe! I'm safe!' he rejoiced.

Hardly an hour would pass, of course, before he forgot all the promises he had made, for such is man . . .

When the shepherds came running up to him, he literally collapsed into their arms, repeating, 'Wolves, wolves chased me! Water, give me water!'

The wolves, meanwhile, hovered around in the vicinity, preparing stubbornly for a long vigil. Boston's winter camp was suddenly thrown into great turmoil – shepherds ran out, to slam shut the doors to the sheep-pens, shouting to one another in the gathering darkness. One of them crawled on to the roof and fired a few rounds from a rifle. The dogs raised a deafening barking, but refused to venture from the yard, preferring to huddle close to the light. The shepherds were indignant at the dogs' cowardice.

'Go on, geddim! Stupid mutts, you're no wolf-hounds!' shouted someone in a hoarse voice, trying to set the dogs on the wolves. 'Off with you! Aktash, Zhulbars, Zhaisan, Barpalan! Geddim! Sikkim! Look at you, tails between your legs, afraid of a few hungry wolves!'

'A dog's a dog,' interjected another voice. 'You're wasting your breath. They can drag a grown man off a horse by his boot but they're no match for a wolf! Waste of breath, I tell you! Not a single dog will go against a wolf. Leave them alone, let them bark away!'

It was some time before Bazarbai remembered why the wolves had been chasing him. It was only when the youngster who had been told to unsaddle his horse suddenly asked, 'Bazarbai, what have you got in your saddlebag? There's something wriggling about inside,' that he suddenly came to his senses.

'In my saddlebags? Hey, that's my cubs! There are four of the little blighters, four sucklings. I took them straight out of the lair in Bashat. That's why the wolves chased me.'

'That was smart! I like that. Straight out of the lair? You're lucky you've still got a nose on your face . . .'

'They haven't croaked in the bag, have they? I hope they didn't get smothered, or squashed, while we were galloping along.'

'Squashed, he says! What did you think they were, apricots? Don't you worry, they're alive and kicking.'

'Let's have a look! What do they look like?'

The saddlebag was finally untied and brought into Boston's house. An important ceremony like this had to be performed in his house, as Boston was the most important person here, boss of the camp. Boston himself was not at home: a meeting was being held in the regional centre, and as usual model worker Boston Urkunchiev had to sit on the committee.

Bazarbai was given a hero's welcome into Boston's house and he was quite happy to submit to the treatment. So, at last he had set foot in this house, by accident perhaps, but still as a guest.

Bazarbai had had occasion to cross the threshold of this house before. Over the many years that he had been herding his flock near Boston's, a mere seven kilometres distant, Bazarbai had called here on three occasions: the first time during the wake for the herdsman Ernazar, who had plunged into a crevasse on the Ala-Mongyu pass; the second time for more obsequies – six months after Ernazar's death Boston's first wife died (a good wife the late Arzygul was said to be), and along came Bazarbai for the funeral, together with all the local shepherds and villagers. There were hordes of people and countless horses, tractors and trucks. His third visit had not been made voluntarily: he came because the local authorities decided to organize a production seminar for Boston Urkunchiev to pass on his experience to the other shepherds. He had not wanted to go, but he could not get out of it, they insisted, so he had to sit almost half a day listening to a lecture on what to do, when, and how so as not to lose the lambs and to get better yields of wool and meat. In other words, how to fulfil your production plan. As if things like that needed teaching! He knew it all anyway: give them their feed in good time in winter, get up at the crack of dawn at the summer pastures in the mountains and go to bed well after midnight, in general work your ass off and don't let the animals out of your sight. You have to be a fanatic, like Boston, and he's not the only one. Still, some manage, others don't. Some are lucky, others aren't. See the way Boston had a generator at his camp, lights on all night, electricity in the houses and the barns and all round the yard. Why? He was able to wangle two machines – when one was not working or gone for servicing he switched over to the other. All the other shepherds – including Bazarbai – only had one generator, year in, year out. Having one was hopeless: half the time it would be broken or you'd run out of fuel, and if it needed attention you could be sure the mechanic had buggered off to town – let's face it, who's going to hang around in a backwater like this if he's got the choice? That's how it was: on paper all the shepherding teams had electricity, but in fact it was candles and oil-lamps all the way . . .

So, who were the good guys? Boston was a good guy, of

course, what with not drinking and all that. And the bad guys? The Bazarbais of this world, the ones that like to share a bottle now and then. If they weren't satisfied with your work, why not just sack you? Oh no – if you didn't like it and asked for a transfer, they treated it as practically a criminal offence, taking away your passport, refusing to issue any documents, come on now, get back to work, my good fellow, and stay put, nowadays no one wants to go herding, they've got more sense today, they all want to live in the towns. In town, when you'd done your day's work, you could go out and enjoy yourself, as long as you didn't go over the top, or if you preferred you could stop home, and never need to lift a finger, everything laid on for you, no need even to make up your stove, the lights working all round the clock, all day and all night if you wanted, piped water where you needed it, toilet right there, just across in the hallway . . . What sort of a life was it, stuck out here with the sheep? During lambing time you were dealing with close on fifteen hundred head of sheep, all bleating their lungs out, dung everywhere, it was all a man could do to keep going and keep his hands off the kids working under him, and of course the bottle . . . and then they had the cheek to criticize Bazarbai and all the other Bazarbais on the farm . . .

If anything went wrong, they started making comparisons: look at Boston Urkunchiev, now there's a model worker for you, there's an example to us all . . . I'd like to punch that model worker right in his exemplary face. Boston was lucky, he got good workers, they didn't quit, but worked together like one family. Bazarbai and plenty of other shepherds had long ago given up their hopeless generators, and lived the old way, with paraffin-lamps and torches, while Boston's fancy generator, an MI-115, ticked away behind the hut just like a clock, you could hear it half a mile away and see the light from the next hilltop. It was this that scared off the wolves – another moment and they would have caught their quarry, but as soon as they saw the light and heard the noise of the generator they stopped instantly.

The dogs kept up their barking. No doubt the wolves were lurking in the shadows, but they were afraid to come any closer . . .

Yes, Boston was a lucky one all right – look at his camp, all spick and span, lights shining brightly, nice and clean, you'd hardly think they lived on a sheep station like the rest. They made you take off your boots and foot bindings in the hallway and walk in your stockinged feet on the felt rugs indoors.

The man was lucky, there were no two ways about it. Bazarbai hadn't even noticed before that Ernazar's widow – Ernazar, who died in the crevasse – was such a handsome girl, and not too old, either. Gulyumkan – that was her name – was now Boston's wife, and for all the grief she must have suffered seemed happy enough. She was approaching forty, maybe even less, her two daughters by Ernazar were at boarding school and no sooner was she settled with Boston than he struck lucky again – a boy this time, while Boston's own two daughters by his first wife were already snaring themselves husbands. As for that charming Gulyumkan, there was a woman who knew what she was up to, for sure – she knew he and Boston couldn't stand each other, but she didn't show it, she received him cordially and was full of sympathy. Come in, she said, neighbour of our neighbours, come in and sit down on the carpet, dear, dear, what a thing to happen, what a fright, wolves snapping at your heels like that, thanks be to God and all the *arbaks* – the ancestral spirits – for saving you from a terrible fate, but the husband's not at home, some meeting in the regional centre, he should be back soon, they promised to run him back in the director's jeep, do sit down, you must have some tea after your ordeal, and if you wait a little longer we'll give you something nice and hot to eat.

Seeing as he had got himself into this mess, Bazarbai decided to put his hostess to the test, to see whether she was really being sincere with her uninvited guest – and anyway he was dying for a drink to recover after his experience, so he mustered all his nerve.

'Tea's a drink for women,' he said, coming straight to the point. 'Pardon me for asking, but isn't there anything a bit stronger in the house of a man of means like Boston? A local celebrity?'

That was typical of Bazarbai's vile character. Even if it did not get him a drink, it was enough of a pleasure to see Boston's wife's sudden change of expression. Bazarbai's plain language went right against the grain with her. But what was the point of standing on ceremony – they weren't beys or khans but simple farmers.

'I am sorry,' she answered, with a frown. 'You know Boston doesn't, er, go in for that much . . .'

'I know, I know your Boston doesn't drink!' interjected Bazarbai dismissively. 'I was only hoping. Thanks for the tea. I thought that maybe, for his guests . . .'

'Well, yes, of course,' protested Gulyumkan, embarrassed, and then she looked at Ryskul who sat next to Bazarbai with the cursed saddlebag and the cubs lying at his feet.

Ryskul was about to go and look for some vodka when Boston's second assistant appeared in the doorway, the student Marat, who never finished his teacher's training, a smart young fellow who had sown his wild oats around the district and now settled down working for Boston.

'Listen, Marat,' said Ryskul. 'You've got half a litre stashed away somewhere. I know: don't worry, if anything happens I'll take the rap with Boston. Run and get your bottle, we must celebrate Bazarbai's find.'

'A celebration! I'll be back directly!' agreed Marat with a loud laugh.

After only the first half-tumbler, which helped alleviate his ill humour, Bazarbai stretched out on the carpet feeling quite at home, fear now giving way to his customary self-assurance and familiarity. He started to tell his story and showed off the cubs. He untied both sides of the *kurjun*, pulled out the little creatures and had his first good look at them. Initially the cubs were listless, hardly reacting and continually trying to hide, but then they perked up as they got warm, crawling around on the carpet, whimpering, pushing their little noses into the hands of the people around them, staring with bewildered, uncomprehending eyes and looking for their mother and her teats. Gulyumkan shook her head in pity.

'Ah, the poor little things are hungry! A baby is a baby, even if it's a wolf. You're going to let them die of hunger! You mustn't!'

'Who says they're going to die?' objected Bazarbai, taking offence. 'They're tough creatures. I'll feed them up for a couple of days, then I'll sell them in the town. They know how to look after them at the animal centre. The people in charge can do everything – they can tame a wolf and make it perform in a circus, and circuses make money. Maybe these guys will end up in the circus.'

At this everyone smiled, although they had initially shared their hostess's compassion. The women who had come running to look at the live cubs started whispering together.

'Bazarbai,' said Gulyumkan, 'we get orphaned lambs which aren't weaned, and we feed them milk, so what if we feed these cubs from a lamb's bottle?'

'I like it!' Bazarbai laughed heartily. 'Sheep feeding wolves. That's terrific! Let's try it!'

What happened next would later be remembered by all of them with horror. They watched with enjoyment as the cubs drank ewes' milk, laughed at the little creatures' funny antics and noticed how trusting they were. They also remarked that one of them – a female – had blue eyes – no one had ever heard of a blue-eyed wolf before, you didn't even find such animals in folklore. They were amused to see Boston's youngest, little Kenjesh, playing with the cubs. It was great fun for Kenjesh – four little animals in the house at the same time. The adults were charmed to hear the chubby little fellow, only eighteen months old, babbling away in his own private language, to see his little eyes light up and to watch him so absorbed in his game with the cubs. The four little wolves seemed to feel an affinity with the child, as if they could sense that he was the creature closest to them. The adults remarked on it – Look, they said, one child recognizes another – and asked Gulyumkan to translate what the little boy was saying to the wolves.

Gulyumkan smiled happily and squeezed her son, saying caressingly, 'Kuchuk, Kuchugom, my little puppy! Look how the little cubs come running to you. Aren't they sweet and grey and cuddly? Are you going to be friends with them?'

Bazarbai's next words none of them would ever forget.

'First there was one little wolf in the house and now there are five. Do you want to be a little wolf? Come, let me stick you in the wolves' lair and Boston's baby can grow up with the cubs . . .'

They all laughed uproariously at these jokes and drank their tea. Bazarbai and Marat, flushed with drink, disposed of the half-litre bottle, chasing it down with chunks of salted lard and roast meat, and grew increasingly merry. Outside, however, silence had set in – the dogs had stopped barking and the largest of them, Zhaisan – a shaggy, red-haired giant – suddenly appeared through the half-open door. He hesitated on the threshold, wagging his tail, afraid to proceed. Someone threw him a piece of bread, which he caught in flight with a loud snapping of teeth. Then Marat, slightly the worse for wear, grabbed one of the cubs for a joke and took it over to the dog.

'Here, Zhaisan, take him! Go on, take him!' and he put the trembling, puny little creature in front of the dog.

To the astonishment of those present, Zhaisan growled viciously and took to his heels, his tail between his legs. Only when he was back in the yard, outside the window, did he give a timorous and pathetic bark. Everyone roared with laughter, Bazarbai louder than the rest.

'Your wasting your time, Marat! You won't find a dog that doesn't shit itself at the mere smell of a wolf! D'you think your Zhaisan's a lion or something? Forget it!'

They all stopped laughing when little Kenjesh suddenly burst into tears – he was sorry for the cub and toddled over to it, anxious to protect it from the extraordinary pranks of these grown-ups.

Bazarbai now stuffed the four hapless wolf clubs back into his saddlebag and prepared to leave. His horse was well rested by this time, so it was re-saddled and he departed from Boston's winter camp at a brisk trot. Alongside Bazarbai trotted Marat and Ryskul, with rifles across their backs. They were both pretty tight, but Marat more so, and this made him exceptionally garrulous. The pair of them had volunteered to see Bazarbai home, hoping to some extent to smooth over an unfortunate little incident just before the departure of the uninvited guest from Boston's house.

While he was preparing to leave, Bazarbai, delighted to be the centre of attention in Boston's house, handed the saddle-bag with the cubs to Marat, for him to attach it to the saddle, and then took a rifle from the wall, where it hung next to an enormous wolf-skin. He studied the weapon closely: it was a very fine one – a well-made, high-calibre repeater for big game, with a rifled bore and a pleasing, elegant line. The pelt hanging as a trophy on the wall had been won by Boston with an accurate shot from this rifle. Everyone knew the story.

'Listen, Gulyumkan,' said Bazarbai, taking his time and shifting his drunken gaze from the gun to his hostess. If he could get his hands on this Gulyumkan, said the look in his eye, in some cosy spot . . . He was used to taking his women without ceremony, occasionally in an open field or on the side of the road; sometimes he got away with it and sometimes not, but either way he had no regrets. He surreptitiously compared Gulyumkan with his own bruised and battered Kok-Tursun and pictured vividly to himself the pleasure it would give him at this moment to strike Tursun across the face with the back of his hand simply because it was her, and not Gulyumkan, that he was stuck with, because she had grown so loathsome to him. Summoning up his courage he said, 'This is a good house, and you're a good hostess. But what I was going to say. . . ? You see, Gulyumkan, I'm scared the wolves will start chasing me again. So what if I take this gun with me and then I can send it back with one of my men tomorrow. . . ?'

'I beg you, put it back in its place,' said Gulyumkan firmly. 'Boston doesn't let anyone touch that gun.'

'So you haven't got any say over his gun when he's not here,' snorted Bazarbai morosely, imagining how he would like to give this wench a good squeeze, given half a chance.

'Are you crazy? If Boston came home and found his gun was gone . . . It's more than . . . Anyway, I don't know where he keeps his ammunition. He's got it hidden away somewhere, never gives anyone a single round.'

Inwardly, Bazarbai heaped abuse on Boston and on himself as well: he should have known what a miserable old skinflint Boston was, and his wife, so it seemed, was no better. He felt like telling her where she could put her gun, but at this point Ryskul came to the rescue and defused the situation.

'No need to worry, Bazarbai. Me and Marat will see you home, if you want, with our guns,' he assured him, laughing. 'We've got plenty of time, the whole night ahead of us. It's true, you better not touch that gun, hang it up again. You wouldn't know it, but Boston's like that, he likes things in their place!'

226

They were about to set off but Ryskul had to hold back for a few minutes, to placate Boston's little boy: Kenjesh set up a terrible howling because they had stuffed the cubs back in the bag and taken them away. The boy squirmed and wriggled free of his mother's arms, begging them to give back the little creatures with which he had fallen in love . . .

They rode together out of the yard. At that hour the night with its pall of stars lay silent over the whole world, sky and distant lake glittering vaguely in the darkness. The three horsemen rode on, telling jokes, towards Taman, none of them suspecting that as they rode fate was tying a terrible knot never to be undone . . . Their voices faded fainter and fainter, and with them the click of hooves on stone road. All that remained was the familiar ticking of Boston's generator, the light of which wrested from the darkness a small circle of dwellings and outhouses.

Somewhere close by lurked the wolves . . .

2

Gulyumkan finally managed to get her little boy to sleep, but only after many caresses and entreaties. She waited up for her husband, who was expected back at any moment. When the dogs outside started barking in concert she threw a shawl over her shoulders and pressed her face against the window. With its bright headlights scything through the darkness, the director's jeep was turning round by the big shed where they kept the breeding ewes. Gulyumkan saw Boston jump from the cab, say goodbye and slam the door, whereupon the jeep turned swiftly around and drove away. She knew her husband would not come straight back to the house. He would first inspect the sheep-pens and sheds, check the outhouses and have a word with Kudurmat, the nightwatchman, to ask how things had been that day, had any sheep fallen sick, or miscarried, and were there any new lambs.

Stoking the stove with the firewood that lay in readiness so that she could greet her husband with the piping hot food and fine fresh tea of which he was so fond, Gulyumkan listened for his footsteps and contentedly imagined how little Kenjesh would wriggle in the warm bed and purse his lips after kissing his daddy's moustache, still icy cold from the frosty night air. Boston usually put the boy to bed after playing together for a long time and sometimes even giving him his bath, always ensuring that the house was nice and warm and all the doors and windows shut. The neighbours reckoned that in his old age Boston was getting too fond of the child – in the old days he had not been like that, he always preferred his work to his other children, those children who were now themselves parents with their own lives, paying only the occasional flying visit to their father's home. The last-born is always the favourite who gets the most love and attention. All this was fair enough, but Gulyumkan knew only too well the bitter truth behind Boston's particular attachment to little Kenjesh. Neither had ever imagined that one day they could be husband and wife and have a son of their own; if her first husband Ernazar had not been killed and Boston's wife Arzygul not died soon after, none of this would have come to pass. They tried not to remember what was gone before, but they knew perfectly well: left on their own each of them would return in thought to the past . . . The boy was their shared joy, one which united them, and they had paid dearly with tragedy in their lives for this happiness. It had been Boston who wanted to open up the trail across the pass and his assistant Ernazar had died before his very eyes, he had left him lying there at the bottom of the deep crevasse . . . Only the child could heal the terrible emptiness in his soul, for, as they say, only a birth can compensate for a death.

Finally Gulyumkan heard footsteps and rushed out to meet her husband, helping him pull off his boots and bringing him water, soap and towel. In silence she poured the water on to her husband's hands, leaving conversation until later, over tea, when Boston would begin with his favourite opening words: 'You wouldn't believe the things that go on in this world,' then tell her in detail what he had seen, what news he had heard, and at such moments, especially if they were alone, they would both be happy. They chatted together in the comfort of their intimacy, secure in the knowledge of each other's shallows and deep water, their talk a landing-stage in the storms. She remembered how, after the memorial cere- mony a year after Arzygul's death, when they finally decided to wed, Boston had come down from the mountains to visit her in her widow's house on the edge of the lakeside village, and how they left Boston's horse tethered to a post, boarded the local bus, feeling awkward on this, their first public outing together, and rode into town, to the registry office, trying to get through all the red tape as quickly as possible. Afterwards they had not wanted to go back on the bus nor to meet anyone they knew in the street, so they had walked to the lake and followed the shoreline back to her house. On that dry, windless autumn day the limpid, deep blue waters of Issyk- Kul were as pure and serene as ever. As they followed the path through the larch trees by the water's edge Boston saw two boats moored to a jetty and stopped. The boats rocked in the gentle swell, and beneath they could see the sandy bottom.

'Look all around – water, mountains, land – that is life. And these two boats are you and me. Where the waves will take us remains to be seen. The things that have happened to us and the things we have lived through will always be with us. Let us always be together. I am an old man now, this winter I'll be forty-nine, but you still have small children, they must be brought up and given their place in life . . . Come, we must pack our things. Once again you're going into the mountains, fisherman's daughter, but this time with me . . . I can't live alone any more . . .'

Gulyumkan, without knowing why, burst into tears, and it took him a long time to calm her . . . In later years, when they were alone and talking about their life together, Gulyumkan often remembered those two boats on the lake. That was why she thought of their conversation as a familiar landing-stage. On this occasion, however, she could not help sensing that her husband was more troubled than usual. By the flickering light in the hallway Boston, who towered head and shoulders over her, crumpled up the towel as he wiped his large, coarsened hands with deliberation. There was a sombre look in his narrow green eyes, and his tanned, weather-beaten face with its heavy, fleshy chin flushed a deep red, the colour of well-worn bronze. What could all this mean? Putting down the towel, Boston went straight to the child, knelt down by the wooden cot he had made himself, kissed his son with his chapped lips, whispering little endearments, and smiled as Kenjesh squirmed in his sleep.

'Kudurmat says that Bazarbai was here when I was out,' he remarked casually, as he sat down to eat. 'I don't like it . . .'

Gulyumkan, putting her own construction on his words, blushed and flared up, 'So what was I supposed to do? He crashed in like a whirlwind. Said he wanted to show us some cubs. And you know what Kenjesh is like – it was such fun for him . . . So I gave him some tea . . .'

'I don't mean that. To hell with him, let him come and go. There's just something I don't like about it, that's all . . .'

'What's wrong?' said Gulyumkan, failing to grasp what he

was driving at. 'You've shot wolves too. There's a skin hanging there, from last year, and it's been beautifully cured . . .' She nodded towards the wolf-pelt on the wall.

'A pelt is a pelt,' answered Boston, holding out his empty cup for a refill. 'You're right, I've shot wolves in my time, that's the way things are in the world, there's wolves and there's people. But I've never burgled a wolf's lair. That Bazarbai, the swine, has stolen the cubs and left the wolves to run free. That's a really dirty trick he's done us. The wolves live here – there's nowhere else for them to go, and now, don't you see, they will be in a frenzy . . .'

His words stunned Gulyumkan. The woman in her sighed deeply and she pinned up the braid which had fallen on to her shoulder. 'What a terrible thing! Why on earth did he have to come sniffing round here, that good-for-nothing? Why did he have to tamper with the lair? I feel so sorry for them – any creature loves its babies, everybody knows that. I must have been blind not to have seen it like that.'

'What I'm wondering now,' continued Boston anxiously, 'is this: which wolves are they? Perhaps the same ones?' Boston was silent a moment, then added, 'According to Kudurmat the wolves chased Bazarbai from the direction of the Bashat ravine.'

'Well?'

'I only hope it's not those same migrant wolves – Tash-Chainar and Akbara, the two we know about.'

'You're joking, of course!' Gulyumkan laughed gaily. 'You don't mean to say that wolves have names like people? What an idea!'

'Joking? I'm in no mood for joking, woman. We know these wolves. They don't look like our local ones. Some of our men have seen them. They're a fierce, powerful pair; you won't catch them in any trap and you won't get close enough to shoot them. Trust that drunk, that scumbag Bazarbai, to stumble on their lair and wipe out their entire family. You're surprised that they've got their own names! The male, Tash-Chainar, is powerful enough to bring down a horse. The she-wolf Akbara is a real *anabasha* – a matriarch of wolves and a damn clever beast! That makes her especially dangerous.'

'Come on now, father of my son, stop your teasing! Do you

think I'm a foolish child?' laughed Gulyumkan in disbelief. 'You talk about them as if you've lived with them all your life . . . How do you know all this?'

'Forget it,' he said, after a moment's silence. 'Put it out of your head. I only wanted to give you a laugh. Go and get the bed ready. It's very late. We'll have to get up really early tomorrow, as you know it's only a few days now to the lambing season. Some of the ewes might drop in the night or early morning, especially those with twins and triplets!'

Only when they were finally in bed, with the light out, did Boston, before he went to sleep – and he fell asleep quickly – tell her about the meeting in town, at which they deliberated for the umpteenth time why youngsters these days did not want to be sheep-farmers and what they could do about it. Suddenly they heard the clatter of horses' hooves outside. Gulyumkan sprang from the bed, ran to the window in her underclothes, quickly throwing a shawl over her shoulders, and saw two horsemen with rifles galloping past the big shed.

'It's our men coming back, Ryskul and Marat,' she said. 'They went to see Bazarbai home.'

'Fools!' muttered Boston, and fell asleep.

Gulyumkan did not go to sleep right away. She covered her little son up snugly in his home-made cot – he would always kick off his bedclothes in his sleep. He was such a rascal, always keeping her awake, especially when she was really exhausted. But tonight sleep eluded her. It had been such a chaotic day, and unpleasant, somehow. It was all that Bazarbai's fault. The way he had landed on them like that, out of the blue. For Boston he was a red rag to a bull. Boston was that sort of man – didn't like fuss and bother, and he couldn't stand louts like Bazarbai, even if they had never done him any personal wrong. Of course, Bazarbai had no great love for Boston either, he envied him his prosperity . . . Bazarbai never stopped to think how hard Boston had to work for what he had. Tomorrow he would be up at the crack of dawn, slaving away until late at night, always on the move, trying to keep an eye on everything at once . . .

Gulyumkan went to the window and peered into the dark night. The moon shone brightly just above the swelling mountains and a myriad stars twinkled sharply in the clear air. By morning the moon would have risen high in the sky and the stars would fade, but at that late hour the night seemed eternal, all-embracing. In the deep silence guarded by the surrounding mountains, the only sound to be heard was the familiar rhythmic thud of the generator on the edge of the camp . . .

Gulyumkan did not know how long she slept. Perhaps she had only dozed off, but suddenly her sleep was invaded by the barking of dogs and, above that, a protracted howling. She woke at once, fighting back sleep, and could now clearly hear the painful, full-throated keening of wolves, directed into the sky. The howling made her flesh creep. Gulyumkan pressed closely up against her husband in fear. Now the howling turned into a pitiful wail, the persistent pain and grieving of a bereaved animal.

'That's her, Akbara!' announced Boston in a voice still thick with sleep, lifting his head from the pillow.

'What Akbara?' Gulyumkan failed to grasp what he was talking about.

'The she-wolf!' said Boston, and, listening carefully to the howling, added, 'And there's Tash-Chainar, adding his voice. Listen, he's bellowing like a bull in a slaughterhouse.'

They lay very still, holding their breath.

'Woo-oo-oo-ooa-aa-ah!' followed by wild sobs, full of anguish, which reverberated into the infinite night.

'What's she saying? Why's she howling?' whispered Gulyumkan in fright.

'Why's she howling? The beast is mourning!'

They were silent for a while.

'What a disaster!' Boston cursed in vexation. 'You lie here and make sure the boy is asleep. But don't be scared, you're not a child! All right, so there's a wolf howling somewhere near by, lamenting its cubs, but there's nothing we can do about it. I'm going to check the sheep!'

Saying this, he quickly dressed, left the light on and went out to put on his boots, then returned to the room, switched off the light and went out, shutting the hall door firmly behind him. She heard him walk past outside the window, cursing to himself and calling the dog: 'Jaisan, Jaisan! Come here!' and the sound of his footsteps gradually died away. Once again the

233

lingering howl of the she-wolf rent the air, while her mate accompanied her with a deep, visceral wail. The note of seething rage and menace in their howling gave way to pitiful lamentation, rising again in a crescendo of despair and anger to subside once more to entreaty and supplication . . .

It was more than she could bear, to listen to this howling. Gulyumkan closed her ears, then went and bolted shut the door, as if the wolves might enter her house, and, shivering and wrapping herself tight in her wool shawl, returned to the bed, not knowing what to do and afraid the wolves would strike up again. Her main fear was that Kenjesh would awake and take fright.

The wolves continued their howling, and it sounded as if they were roaming about somewhere close, shifting from place to place. In answer the dogs barked and yelped in anger, but did not dare leave the confines of the yard. Suddenly the deafening sound of a shot rang out, and then another. Gulyumkan guessed that Boston and Kudurmat, the night-watchman, were firing shots as a warning.

After this all was silent. The dogs quietened down, and so did the wolves. 'Thank God for that, it was too awful!' sighed Gulyumkan in relief. But there was still a heavy weight on her soul. She gathered up the sleeping Kenjesh, carried him across to their big bed and placed him in the middle, so that he would be between his parents. Meanwhile Boston returned.

'So much for my night's sleep, curse the lot of them,' he muttered angrily, presumably referring to the wolves, the dogs and everything else. 'What a swine that Bazarbai is, what a swine!' he grumbled, climbing back into bed. Gulyumkan spared her husband further questions. He had to be up early the next morning, for he was not the sort of shepherd to allow himself a lie in.

Gulyumkan felt more at ease when she saw her husband calmer, delighted to have his son snuggle up to him, and whispering endearments. Boston loved his little Kenjesh, whose full name – Kenjebek – meant 'little master' or 'youngest prince in line'. Every shepherd longs to be a prince, but fate has ordained that every shepherd should live and die a shepherd whatever age he lives in. In this sense Boston was no exception.

They fell asleep, this time with the boy between them, but soon they were woken again by the doleful wailing of the wolves. Once again the dogs set up their frantic barking in the yard.

'What on earth! We can't live like this!' cried Gulyumkan angrily, but regretted her words at once. Boston got up without speaking and started to dress in the darkness. 'Don't go out,' she begged. 'Let them howl. I'm afraid. Please don't go!'

Boston decided to follow his wife's bidding, so they lay in their darkened house on that black night in the mountains, forced to listen to the howling of the wolves. Midnight had long passed, dawn was approaching, but the wolves continued to give voice, maddening their human listeners with their sorrowful and malevolent wailing.

'I can't stand any more, what more do they want?' exclaimed Gulyumkan, unable to contain her anger.

'What more do they want? It's quite simple: they want their cubs back,' answered Boston.

'But they're not here, the cubs. They were taken away long ago.'

'How are they supposed to know that?' answered Boston. 'They're animals, they know one thing only: they've followed a trail here and this is where the trail ends as far as they're concerned; this is the end of their road. You go and explain to them. It's such a pity I wasn't at home. I would have wrung that swine Bazarbai's neck for him. What a dirty trick: he takes the booty, but we have to pay for it . . .'

As if in affirmation of his words the howling resounded through the house – first baleful and distressing, then frenzied and menacing – the wolves, blinded by their grief, continued to roam the darkness. Akbara's wailing was particularly heart-rending. She keened like an old woman at a burial, and Gulyumkan was reminded how she herself had wailed and beaten her head against the wall when Ernazar was killed on the pass. She was seized by an unbearable anguish, and it was all she could do not to blurt out her thoughts and fears to Boston. There they lay, eyes wide open, while only little Kenjesh slept the innocent sleep of a child. As she listened to Akbara's untiring lamentation for her stolen cubs, the mother grew increasingly more anxious for his safety, even though he was in no danger.

The first light of dawn showed over the mountains. The darkness retreated, melting in the air, its nightly duty done, and with it the stars faded, showing more distinctly the outline of the mountains, near and far. The land stirred back into life . . .

At last Akbara and Tash-Chainar retreated into the mountains, heading for the Bashat ravine. Their silhouettes stood out against high ground before disappearing again in the gloom. The wolves padded along downcast – the loss of their cubs and then a whole night's unrelieved howling had taken their toll. Their route took them past the hollow where they had killed the yak the previous day and where they would still find most of the carcass. Usually they would not have passed over an opportunity to stock up on fresh meat, but on this occasion Akbara had no heart to return to her lawful spoils, and Tash-Chainar dared not do so without her.

As the sun rose and they approached the lair, Akbara hustled forward, as if her cubs were waiting to suckle. Her self-deception communicated itself to Tash-Chainar, and now they both raced along the ravine, spurred on by the vain hope of seeing their brood.

Everything lay as before – plunging through the gaps in the thicket Akbara dashed into the crevice beneath the hanging rock, again sniffed in all the empty corners, sniffed the cold stone and realized again that her cubs, her sucklings, were gone. Refusing to accept the truth, she sprang out of the hole and in her blind grief lunged again at Tash-Chainar, colliding clumsily with him in the entrance, and dashed to the stream, following the scent of Bazarbai's visit the day before. Everything here was repellent and hostile – particularly the unfinished bottle of vodka leaning against the rock. Its sharp and acrid smell threw the wolf into a frenzy; she snarled, bit herself, chewed the ground and then started a lingering whine, craning her neck in the air, wailing as if she had been mortally wounded. Tears flowed copiously from her extraordinary blue eyes. But there was no one to console her in her grief, no echo of lamentation joined with her own. The great mountains were cold and impassive . . .

3

The next morning, at about eight o'clock, Bazarbai Noigutov was about to saddle up his horse to ride into town when he noticed another horseman riding towards him. Who could have any business here, in the Taman winter camp? The rider, wearing an unbuttoned fawn sheepskin coat and foxfur cap, approached at an easy trot from the west following the base of the foothills. He had a good seat, the picture of elegance as he sat firm and upright in his saddle. Bazarbai recognized him immediately and to make quite sure took another look at the golden Don stallion – yes, it was Boston Urkunchiev riding Donkulyuk. Boston's unexpected arrival was an unpleasant surprise for Bazarbai, so unpleasant in fact that, lest Boston think that he had come out to greet him, he put his saddle aside and set about rubbing his horse down with a handful of straw, resolving to wait for his hated neighbour to reach the compound. He pretended to be absorbed in what he was doing, but he had the strange sensation that Boston had caught him doing something he shouldn't. He looked quickly around the yard, at the sheds and the shepherds busy with their morning chores, to check that everything was in order. Naturally, Boston's camp was more orderly than his: when it came to discipline Boston was quite ruthless, but then he was a model worker (idle tongues used to say that in a different age he would have been sent as a *kulak* to Siberia), while Bazarbai was nothing more than an average typical Central Asian shepherd. There were countless more like him in the mountains and across the steppes, herding the millions and millions of sheep whose hooves kept the grass from showing above the ground, stamping it out at the root. After all, each man to his own. Boston and he were very, very different men. As Boston approached, he racked his brains: To what do we owe the honour of this early morning visit from our model *kulak*? We've never had this before! What's going on? What does he want? He was about to invite Boston into his house, since the man was here, but then he thought of how broken down it all was, and, worse, his wife, the unfortunate, bad-tempered Kok-Tursun (just compare her with Gulyumkan!), and he abandoned the idea.

As he approached the Taman camp Boston reined in his horse at the edge of the yard, looked all round and, spotting the master behind the shed, headed for him. They greeted one another with considerable restraint – Boston remained mounted, and Bazarbai continued to rub his horse. That way both felt that their dignity was intact.

'A good thing I found you home,' said Boston, stroking his moustache with the palm of his hand.

'Yes, I am at home, as you can see. So what's the problem, if it's no secret?'

'No secret at all, something I want to talk about.'

'A man like you always does things for a good reason,' remarked Bazarbai haughtily. 'Am I not right to say so?'

'Indeed you are.'

'In that case come down off your horse, if there is something to discuss.'

Boston dismounted in silence, tethered his horse and – as always – loosened the saddle girth, to allow the horse to rest and to give it freedom of movement. All this without a word. Then he looked around, as if evaluating the work of the farm.

'Why are you standing there staring? What's so interesting?' called Bazarbai, with barely disguised irritation. 'Take a seat here on this stump,' he suggested, seating himself on a tractor tarpaulin which lay on the ground. They studied each other with silent disapproval. Everything about Boston was odious to Bazarbai: the fact that he had such a fine sheepskin coat, edged with black lambswool, the way it was thrown open to reveal his broad chest, his robust physique, his bright eyes and his bronzed complexion – and to think that Boston was a good five years older than Bazarbai! Nor did he like the idea of Boston lying in bed at night with Gulyumkan, although it might be asked what business this was of his.

'All right, fire away, I'm listening,' said Bazarbai.

'This is why I've come,' began Boston. 'As you see, I've tied a bag to my saddle. Give me those wolf cubs, Bazarbai. They must be put back again.'

'Put back where?'

'Back in the lair.'

'So that's what it is!' snorted Bazarbai venomously. 'And there was I wondering what business could have brought our model worker out at this early hour! Abandoning his own work and galloping over to our humble abode! You must be forgetting that I'm not one of your shepherds, Boston. I'm a senior *chaban*, same as you. And I don't take any orders from you.'

'Who's talking about orders? Can't you hear me out without losing your temper? If you think the wolves will forget what happened yesterday, you're sadly mistaken, Bazarbai.'

'What's that to me? So what if they don't forget, what do I care? Come to that, what do you care?'

'What I care is that last night we didn't sleep a wink all night, the wolves set up such a din howling and wailing. The animals won't calm down until they get their cubs back. I know what wolves are like.'

Boston had come to ask him a favour. Bazarbai was tempted to swagger and mock a bit, to put on a show. Never in his wildest dreams would he have expected Boston to come to him to seek a favour. Bazarbai decided that since fate had thrown him this bone, he would grab it. In addition, the thought that they had no peace at night, and Boston would not be interested in Gulyumkan's favours, filled him with malicious delight. If only it could always be that way! So, with a sideways look at Boston, he said, 'Don't try and pull a fast one, Boston! What sort of an idiot do you think I am? I didn't take those cubs just so that I could hand them over to you with a bow. Who do you think you are? You've got your problems, I've got mine. And I don't care a donkey's grunt whether you and your woman had a good night's sleep or not, it doesn't make a blind bit of difference to me.'

'Just consider it, Bazarbai, don't refuse without thinking it over.'

'What's there to think about?'

'You're wrong to say that,' said Boston, barely able to contain his anger. He realized that he had made a big mistake.

239

He now played his last card. 'In that case,' he said, still struggling to maintain his composure, 'let's agree on a price like honest men. You want to sell them and I'm willing to buy. What difference is it to you who buys them? Name your price and we'll shake on it!'

'I won't sell!' Bazarbai leapt to his feet. 'I won't sell to you for any price! You think I'll sell them, just like that! Because you've got money and I haven't! I don't give a toss for your money! I'll swap the cubs for vodka, sooner than sell them to you, d'you hear? I don't give a stink who you are and what you are! So why don't you just get back on your horse and get the hell out of here!'

'Don't be stupid, Bazarbai. Let's talk like reasonable men. What difference is it to you, who you sell the cubs to?'

'What difference? Don't you try and teach me. I know what's what without you – you wait till I sort you out at your next Party meeting, when you're up on your hind legs, telling them all what a model worker you are, telling them all how to do their jobs. I'll teach you a lesson you'll never forget till your dying day!'

'Well – ' started Boston, in genuine surprise, involuntarily flinching from Bazarbai's raised fist. 'Stop trying to scare me and explain what's eating you.'

'What's eating me? I'll tell you what! You're going against the authorities, that's what! Think you're so smart! The authorities tell us we've got to destroy predators everywhere, and you want to spare some wolves, set up your own little breeding programme – isn't that so? You just get that into your thick *kulak* head! I captured an entire litter, and that means I've brought great benefit to the state, and you want to stick them back in their lair. Let them grow, let them multiply – isn't that so? And you even tried to bribe me!'

'I didn't want to bribe you, I swear, I wanted to buy the cubs. You're making a mistake, trying to threaten me like that. Think about it first, try and see what you're doing and what this makes you! If you want to be such a hero, why don't you take grown wolves? Take the she-wolf first, seeing as you've discovered her lair. And if you're too feeble to do it, find someone else who's man enough, and let him get on with it.'

'So who did you have in mind – yourself, I suppose?'

'Even me, if you want! But no point trying to find wolves now – you might as well look for a wind in a field. Now that you've violated their lair you'll never track down or kill the she-wolf and her mate. Now they'll kill all the animals in the area, all the sheep and cattle, and be ready to spring on humans as well, to get their revenge. There'll be no stopping them now. Have you thought of that?'

'Well, well, so the wolves have got a spokesman now, eh? Go on, let's have the summing up for the defence: think anyone will believe you? You're talking about wolves as if they're people. I know you're used to leading us all up the garden path, but I see right through you! Let me tell you something else. If you came here just to put the screws on me . . .' Without finishing his sentence Bazarbai sprang up to Boston – just like a bull about to charge – and the two stood eye to eye, seething with suppressed hatred.

'So what else have you got to tell me?' said Boston, in a voice hoarse with tension. 'Don't waste my time!'

'I always knew what a miserly bastard you really are, hands on the purse strings, keeping it in the family – that's why you're always hanging about at these meetings; no meeting's complete without our esteemed colleague Boston. Only what no one knows is that you spit blood if someone else has a stroke of luck for once. It wasn't you, you see, that bagged the cubs, you didn't find the lair, so you've missed out on that one, and now you can't sleep nights because Lady Luck smiled on someone else for once!'

'To hell with you!' exclaimed Boston, losing his temper. 'To think that I wanted to talk to a reptile like you! What a fool I was! If I'd known, I wouldn't have bothered coming! Now even if you wanted to give me the cubs I wouldn't take them. Do what you want with them!'

Boston, by now in a white-hot rage, walked over to his horse, seized the reins, tightened the girth so violently that the horse staggered, and leapt into the saddle. He was so angry that he did not hear Bazarbai's wife calling to him. The poor woman was only a moment late. Coming out of the house she saw her husband shouting and gesturing. Who is that? she wondered. Surely Boston hasn't come visiting, what reason would he have to come here? Thereupon she realized that the

241

men were arguing and hastened across to them. But she was too late – Boston had already ridden off on his stallion, his face set in implacable fury. Clamping his foxfur cap on to his head he whipped his horse and galloped away, the skirts of his coat fanning out like wings.

'Boston! Boston! Stop! Listen to me!' shouted Kok-Tursun, but Boston did not turn round – either he did not hear, or did not wish to respond.

'What did you have to offend the man for? What was that argument about?' said Kok-Tursun, striding up to Bazarbai.

'None of your business! What are you yelling for? What did you call out to him for? What do you want with him?'

'The only time the man ever called on you, and what do you do? How did you ever come to be born? You're a monster, not a man!'

His wife's words only further enraged Bazarbai, who leapt up on to the stump and shouted after Boston, 'I spit on your mother's grave! You chose the wrong man to attack! Think everyone bows their head to you! Son of a . . .'

'Belt up! Pack it in!' Kok-Tursun fearlessly seized her husband and dragged him off the stump. 'Why not beat me up instead, why do you want to insult the man? What for?'

'Get away from me, you old pest!' shouted Bazarbai. 'Mind your own business! He imagined that Bazarbai would grovel before him. Yes, sir, no, sir, here you are, sir, please take the cubs, if you want, just as you please! Well, he chose the wrong man!'

'So it's all because of the cubs?' said Kok-Tursun in amazement. 'And I thought it was something important! Anyone would have thought it was the end of the world!'

4

That day the wolves moved off. They left the lair, did not return at night and set off to roam at large – sometimes dejectedly resting up wherever they found themselves, then roving again through the district, taking little care to conceal themselves, acting brazenly as if they no longer had any fear of men. During the ensuing days many local shepherds spotted them in the most unlikely places. The she-wolf always went in front, her head hung low in dejection, while her mate invariably followed behind. It seemed as if the wolf pair was courting destruction, so openly did they disregard all danger. On several occasions they walked close to human dwellings and sheep-sheds, rousing the dogs to a frenzy of barking. The dogs would rush wildly back and forth, as if about to throw themselves into the attack, but the wolves ignored them stubbornly and did not even quicken their pace when shots were fired behind them, but would continue on their way, oblivious. The affliction of these wolves became a legend among the local people. Their notoriety increased even further when Akbara and Tash-Chainar broke the wolves' unwritten taboo and started attacking people. On one occasion they pounced on a tractor-driver in broad daylight. He was pulling a load of hay on a trailer. The steering wheel had jammed and the driver, a young fellow, crawled under the vehicle to see what was wrong. He poked around there with his spanners for some time and suddenly observed two wolves approaching across the thawing snow. He was most struck by their eyes. They came towards him with a wild and, as he later described it, fixed stare, the she-wolf a little shorter at the shoulder and blue-eyed. Her eyes were moist and staring. Fortunately the youngster did not lose his head, but hopped quickly into his cab and slammed the door. Fortunately, too, the engine fired from the starter or else he would have had to start it with the crank handle. Most fortunate of all: the tractor coughed into life, and the wolves recoiled, but without withdrawing completely. They kept trying to approach from one side or the other.

On another occasion a young herdboy survived only by a miracle. Once again it was broad daylight. He had set off on his donkey in search of firewood and ridden a short distance from home. While cutting down some dead brushwood with his sickle he saw two wolves spring out of nowhere. The donkey did not even have time to bray; the attack was over in an instant, silent and bloody. The boy ran, keeping hold of his sickle, and as soon as he reached the home camp fell to the ground and started screaming. When people ran out from the camp with guns to the bushes the wolves casually loped off over the hill. Even the shots ringing out did not cause them to quicken their pace . . .

Then, a little later, the wolves carried out a terrible massacre of ewes in lamb which had been driven out a little way from the shed to graze. Nobody saw how it happened. They realized only when the animals that survived rushed in panic into the yard. About fifteen ewes lay ripped apart in the pasture. They had all been brutally butchered, their throats torn, killed senselessly, not for food but for the sake of killing.

The score of Akbara's and Tash-Chainar's crimes mounted steadily. With it grew their fearful renown. But people saw only the outer aspect of things and knew nothing of the true reason underlying them, the unending anguish of the wolf-mother for the theft of her cubs from their lair . . .

Bazarbai made merry and showed off. He drank his way through the money he had earned so easily, and caroused in the lakeside restaurants, bleak and deserted in the off-season, but still stocked with plentiful supplies of vodka. Everywhere Bazarbai, so sozzled that even his bald pate flushed red, told one and the same story – how cleverly he had put that skinflint Boston in his place, that high-minded stuck-up swine, that secret *kulak*, who in the good old days would have been put up against a wall as a class enemy, and quite right too. What a pity that those times were no more. A character like that should be got rid of, the sooner the better. In the twenties and thirties any policeman could have shot him as a *kulak* or hoarder right there in his back yard. There's books written about that and he

244

heard a programme on the radio once about a *kulak* who put the screws on everyone, cheated his farmhands out of their pay, and for this they put him up against the wall in full view of everyone, to teach him not to take advantage of the poor. Most of all he loved telling the story, growing more and more excited as he did so, of how he gave Boston the bum's rush, how he sent him packing with a flea in his ear when he turned up at Bazarbai's place in Taman. Bazarbai's drinking partners, for the most part seasonal workers from the tourist centres now laid off and loafing through the winter, guffawed so uproariously that the window panes rattled in the musty drink shops, rank with cigarette smoke, and they egged the drunken Bazarbai on, flattering him on to further flights of fantasy. All this reached Boston's ears and led in turn to the row at the state farm council meeting.

The night before, Boston had been unable to sleep, his mind plagued by worrisome thoughts. It all began with the wolves returning to haunt their winter camp and setting up again their unbearable, soul-rending plaint; once again Gulyumkan had shuddered with fear and pressed up close to her husband, then brought Kenjesh into their bed, petting him and tucking him up, just as if she felt the threat was to him. All this deeply disturbed Boston, although he knew it was understandable for a woman to be affected by darkness and strange noises.

On several occasions Boston was about to go outside and fire a few rounds from his gun, but his wife would not let him, loath to remain alone for a single minute. In the end she dropped off into a light, disturbed sleep, but Boston was quite unable to fight off his insomnia. All sorts of thoughts kept crowding into his head. It somehow seemed that the longer he lived on this good earth the harder and more difficult life became, and not only harder to live, but harder even to understand why he lived and what it was all about. Things he had never thought of before, or had only thought of very vaguely, somewhere deep inside him, now came sharply into vision, crying out for clear answers.

Ever since childhood he had always lived by his own labour. He had had a tough life: his father died in the war, when he was in his second year of school, then his mother died, his older brothers and sisters had already left home, he had no

245

other living relatives, and he had only himself to fall back on, himself and his own abilities. As he now realized, he had set himself a goal and pursued it relentlessly, bringing himself a little closer every day, working tirelessly and believing firmly that this and this alone was the true meaning of life. He expected just the same fierce commitment from those who worked for him. He helped set many of those who passed through his 'school' on their own feet, he taught them how to work and through their own work to value life itself. Boston had no time for anyone who did not share his aspirations, he could not understand such people. He regarded them as useless, and treated them in an off-hand and unfriendly way. He knew that for this many people abused him behind his back, called him a skinflint and a *kulak*, regretting that Boston had been born a bit too late to be sent to rot in Siberia. As a rule Boston paid no attention to insults, for he never doubted for a moment that truth was on his side. Anything else was unthinkable. Only once in his life had the ups and downs of fate forced him to his knees and made him seek painful repentance, ever since which he had known the bitter taste of doubt . . .

5

He and Ernazar, Gulyumkan's late husband, had worked
together for three years before Ernazar's tragic accident. He
was a good colleague, without any doubt, and a reliable man –
just the type that Boston needed for his team. Ernazar had
turned up one day asking for a job. One autumn he came up to
Boston in Beshkingei, where the herd was grazing before the
first snows. He said he had come to talk. He was fed up,
complained Ernazar, with working under just anyone: however hard you tried, if your boss-*chaban* didn't know his job
you were wasting your time and effort. The years were
passing, his two daughters were growing up, it would soon be
time to give them away in marriage, time was flying and
however much he worked he couldn't shake off his debts; he'd
built a house, and everyone knows how much that costs, and
he knew that with Boston a man could work hard and earn
well. With Boston there were always bonuses, and big ones,
for wool, for lambs, for fatstock. That's why he had decided to
come and ask him, if he had no objections, to have a word with
the director and get him to transfer Ernazar to Boston's team,
to work under Boston. He swore he wouldn't let him down,
otherwise why make the request in the first place. . . ?

Boston already knew Ernazar; they all worked on the same
state farm after all, and Gulyumkan was a distant relative of his
own wife Arzygul. In a sense they were family. The main
thing, however, was that Boston immediately trusted Ernazar
and he never had cause to regret this faith.

And so they began to work, soon adapting to each other's
ways because Ernazar, like Boston, had a strong proprietory
instinct, treating the farm's animals as if they belonged to him
personally, a very sound attitude which underlay his approach
to the rest of his work. He toiled away as if the profit were going
into his own pocket, caring for the farm as if it had been in
his family for generations. Ernazar was naturally industrious.

All his life he had been developing the natural capacity for hard work with which he had been born, a gift which all receive as their birthright, yet few take the trouble to nurture. Most let it shrivel away. You only have to look around and see the hordes of idlers and slackers everywhere – adults and youngsters, men and women. Some people obviously do not realize what unhappiness and misery have been caused throughout the ages by laziness. But Boston and Ernazar were gluttons for work and this was the secret of their kinship. It enabled them to work in tune together and to understand each other so well, even without words. And yet . . . it may have been this very trait which played such a fateful role in their lives . . .

Whether or not that was so, the point was that long before the official emergence of any system of awarding sub-contracts to teams or family production units, Boston Urkunchiev insisted, prompted no doubt by some intuitive belief, that he, or rather his team, should be granted the permanent use of their land. This simple objective expressed in an entirely ingenuous way was seen in certain orthodox circles as an act of defiance, and interpreted as a demand for his own winter quarters and summer pastures – i.e. let me have my own land, and I will be responsible for it myself rather than some farm manager, who doesn't get his head wet if the roof leaks. Let me have full charge of everything and then I'll work a hundred times harder and get yields far in excess of the target, far more than on some communal or state land, where I would work like a common tenant farmer, a *batrak-jaldama*, who transfers God knows where the following autumn.

No, Boston's ideas would not wash. Initially everyone agreed that in principle his ideas were right, of course, quite sensible, everyone should have plots reserved for them, let people feel like owner farmers and let their children and families know this and work together on their own land, but it took just one alert political economist at the local level to express his doubts – might this not be a violation of the sacred tenets of socialism? – and everyone did an about-face and started contradicting their previous opinions. No one wished to be suspected of heresy. Only Boston Urkunchiev, an ignorant shepherd, stubbornly continued to plead his case at practically every farm or regional meeting. He was listened to, admired and made fun of: what's it to him, they said, to Boston? He can say what he thinks, he's got nothing to lose, he can't lose his job, no one's going to ruin his career. Lucky man! Every time he would be given a sermon on the theoretical doctrine – a particular zealot in this was the farm's 'Partorg' – the Party Organizer Kochkorbayev, a typical village egg-head, with a diploma from the regional Party school. Boston could never treat this Kochkorbayev as anything but a joke. Kochkorbayev had been the farm's Party Organizer for ever and a day but Boston could never decide whether he was just pretending to have swallowed a dictionary (a stance which probably gave him certain advantages) or whether he really believed the speeches he spouted. In appearance he was a classic, red-cheeked eunuch: his face as smooth as a hard-boiled egg, he always wore a tie and carried files with a permanently preoccupied look – so much to do, rushing hither and thither and holding forth as if he were reading speeches from a newspaper. Sometimes Boston would wonder whether he talked in his sleep as if reading from a book.

'Comrade Urkunchiev,' scolded Party Organizer Kochkorbayev from the rostrum, 'it's about time you understood that the land is our national, communal property. That's enshrined in the Constitution. The land in our country belongs to the people, only to the people and to no one else. Yet you are demanding winter and summer pastures, sheds, feed and other items practically as your private property. This we cannot allow – we have no right to distort the principles of socialism. Do you realize what you're driving at and where it would all lead?'

'I don't want anything to lead anywhere,' insisted Boston. 'If I'm not in charge and the "people" are, then let them, whoever they are, go and work in my farm and I'll stand back and see what happens. If I'm not master of my own business surely someone else must be master then?'

'The people, comrade Urkunchiev, may I remind you – the Soviet people, the state.'

'The people? So who am I, in your opinion? There's something here I can't quite figure out. Why am I not the state? Look at you, Party Organizer, you're young and educated but I can't

249

help wondering what they taught you in your Party school if you can't understand what I'm saying.'

'Don't come at me with your *kulak* speeches, comrade Urkunchiev! Remember – your time is past, we don't allow anyone to tamper with the fundamental principles of socialism now.'

'Well, have it your own way, you bosses know better,' snarled Boston. 'But mark my words – I'll work for me and no one else. Every time I open my mouth you shut me up again with your talk of the people! The people! The people is the master! Fine, so let the people give some thought to this: every year there's more and more animals, the farm now has forty thousand head of sheep and goats alone – no one ever dreamed it would grow that big, there's less and less free land, and production figures we're expected to produce for the plans keep getting bigger. Look at it for yourself: I'm now shearing three point seven kilos of wool per head of sheep, and twenty years ago when I started out – as you all know – it was only two kilos per head, which means that in twenty years I just about managed to increase my yield by one point seven kilos. Now they're increasing the production target by half a kilo. Where am I supposed to get that from? By witchcraft? If I don't fulfil the target the team gets no bonus. And they have families to feed. How can you expect people to work, to herd sheep year in, year out, for nothing? And how can you fulfil a target like that when every other shepherd is hovering like a hyena, waiting to grab the best grazing ground and getting away with it because the ground's held in common, no one's master over it. Look how many fights there've been between shepherds over grazing grounds, and you, the Party Organizer, do sweet all about it yourself and prevent the director taking any action either. You think I'm blind, or stupid, or something?'

'What I do or do not do is for the regional committee to decide. But don't expect the regional committee to go along with your dangerous proposal, comrade Urkunchiev!'

Their discussions always ended at loggerheads . . .

Now fate had brought Ernazar into his team, and Boston had gained a close ally and confederate. Their wives, Arzygul and Gulyumkan, used to laugh at them: what a pair they made, going without rest and sleep, just work, work, work. Then

Ernazar had the idea of driving their herd for the summer over the Ala-Mongyu pass. Why, he said, do we spend the whole summer traipsing round the foothills, battling with the neighbours for every blade of grass? Why not cross the pass for the summer, into the Kichibel pastureland? The old-timers say that in their day the bey-farmers used to go there with their herds of sheep and horses. They knew that although the Kichibel *jailyau* – the pastures – were not very extensive, the grass in them was superb. In five days a beast would put on more weight than after a whole month in a feeding pen.

Boston wondered about Kichibel, feeling that there were many unanswered questions about the place. Before the war the collective farmers used to cross to Kichibel over the only available pass – the icy Ala-Mongyu. During the war, when there were only old men and children left in the mountain villages, no one dared to make the journey any more. It was then that the collective farms, which were struggling to survive, came together into a big state farm with a ridiculous name made of the six initial letters of some anniversary or other, and which the local people renamed Berik after the stream Berik-suu, and in all that bustle of unification and transformation gradually forgot that in summer for two entire months, and sometimes even longer, the herds could be put out to pasture beyond the snow-covered pass across the mighty Ala-Mongyu. Perhaps it was that no one wanted to scale those great heights: after all, to drive one's flock across such an arduous mountain pass required enthusiasm, the single-minded obsession of an owner-farmer, anxious to fatten up his animals as best he could. Hence the origin of the old Kirghiz greeting: 'Mal jan amanby?' – 'How are the beasts and your soul?' It was the animals they asked after first. Well, that's life . . .

Filled with enthusiasm for this idea from the past, Boston and Ernazar took up their pencils and worked out all the possibilities: even taking the very lowest estimates, assuming that by crossing the pass both ways the animals would lose some of the weight gained, the game was well worth the candle. The venture promised great profits – after all, there was practically no direct outlay, barring the provision of saltlicks. Admittedly, at this stage it was all speculation – tempting, perhaps, but only theoretical.

Boston decided that in the first instance they should apply to their divisional manager, and then to the state farm director, but not to bother approaching the Party Organizer who was not only a windbag but also a stickler for the rules: no this, no that, all he was interested in were the meetings at which he could regurgitate the rubbish written in the papers and look smart in his tie. Boston did tell the director, the overall head of the state farm, about their plan: it's like this, Ibraim Chotbae-vich, he said, Ernazar and me are planning to resurrect the old pastures on the other side of the Ala-Mongyu pass. First, he said, we'll go together to check out the route, we'll find good pastures in Kichibel, and see what the grass is like, and then we'll come back and take the whole flock over for the rest of the summer. If everything worked out as they hoped, then the Kichibel pasturelands would be theirs again, and if any other shepherds decided to cross the pass after him, no problem, there was plenty of room, the main thing was that he, Boston, would know which grazing grounds to allot to them and which he could count on for himself for the season. 'That's why,' he said, 'I've come to you. Ernazar and me, we've decided to head off for the Ala-Mongyu pass the day after tomorrow – just giving all the last-minute instructions so that our wives and assistants know what to do in our absence.'

'By the way, Boske, what do your wives think of this idea of yours?' asked the director. 'It's a big step, after all.'

'They seem to understand. Let's face it, we've got no reason to complain. My Arzygul is a smart woman, and Gulyumkan, too, Ernazar's wife, for all that she's a bit younger, is no fool. The two of them get on well together. I'm glad of that, I can tell you. There's nothing worse than when the women start squabbling. You get no peace then . . . I've seen it happen before . . .'

He and the director went on to other matters. It seemed that an official trip to the exhibition centre in Moscow was being organized in the autumn for all the best workers and that Boston was on the list, perhaps even at the top of it.

'Tell me, Ibraim Chotbaevich, what would you say to my

taking my wife? My Arzygul's dying to visit Moscow,' confessed Boston.

'I understand, Boston,' smiled the director, 'we'll see what we can do. Why not, indeed? All we need is the consent of the Partorg. I'll mention it to him.'

'The Partorg?' Boston was pensive.

'Don't worry, Boske. You don't think he'd refuse your wife because of some grudge he has against you? That wouldn't be decent.'

'Well, it's not the end of the world if she doesn't get to Moscow. There's something else I wanted to discuss with you, though, director. Tell me, this Party Organizer – do you really need him in your business? Is there no way you could get rid of him?'

'Why do you ask?'

'I need to know. Take a cart, for instance, with four wheels all working nicely together. You stick on a fifth wheel which doesn't turn, and stops the others from turning. Tell me: do I need that fifth wheel or not?'

'You see . . .' The director, a tall, well-built man with narrow eyes slit in his broad, coarse-featured face, suddenly grew serious, shuffled the paper on his desk, and lowered his weary eyelids. You can see he doesn't get enough sleep, too much going on, thought Boston. 'To be honest,' said the director, 'we need a Partorg who knows his job,' he said after a pause.

'And this one?'

The director looked him briefly in the eye.

'What's that got to do with you and me? Seeing as the regional committee sent him here, there's precious little we can do about it.'

'Regional committee. See what I mean!' expostulated Boston. 'Sometimes I wonder if he's doing it deliberately, if perhaps there's some reason behind the way he carries on. Why does he have to waste so much time running round setting off alarm bells, making out that I'm trying to undermine socialism? I mean, it's just not true. If I ask for something I do so for a good reason. I'm not going to sell this land, I won't give it away to anyone, it always has belonged to the farm and it always will. But as long as I live and work, I'll do it my way, thank you very much.'

'What are you trying to prove to me, Boske? You know you can't do what you're suggesting.'

'Why not?'

'Because you can't.'

'What sort of an answer is that?'

'What else can I say?'

'I know what you're getting at, Ibraim Chotbaevich. You had big ideas once, you wanted to make things work, and all the thanks you got was a demotion – transferral from the regional committee to the state farm.'

'That's right, and I'm not going to stick my neck out again: I've learnt my lesson.'

'That's just it, every man thinks of himself first and foremost. I've no quarrel with that: you have to think of yourself, but you must do it in a reasonable way. It's not the man who does something new you should punish, but the man who could have done something and didn't. With us it's the other way round.'

'You can talk,' laughed the director grimly.

'Everyone answers, "You can talk." But I'm sick of living like a guest on someone else's land. What sort of a guest is going to break his back on someone else's land? You know it yourself. He'll work hard for the first couple of days, then he gets tired of it . . . That's the way it feels: you work your guts out and Kochkorbayev keeps prodding you to remind you that you're a guest, you're not your own master.'

'I'll tell you what, Boske, let's do it this way: keep it quiet, don't quote me, do whatever you think is necessary.'

With that they parted.

Three days later, at first light, he and Ernazar set off for Kichibel. Everyone was still asleep when they mounted their horses. Boston rode the light chestnut gelding, his Donkulyuk – only a two-year-old at that time, still only a colt, although it's better to take a more staid horse into the mountains, since there's no place upon the pass to gallop anyway. Ernazar also rode a good horse. By that time of the year the horses were in fine condition, and moved quickly. Each of them carried a saddlebag of oats for the night stop above the snowline. They also took sheepskin coats with them to keep the cold out at night.

A ride is often a pleasure in itself, particularly if you have a travelling companion you like and the conversation flows evenly along. The day was fine and bright – the mountains towered up before them, sparkling crests succeeding each other into the distance, each one more massive and snow-laden than the one before, and behind them in the far distance the great lake, stretching as far as the eye could see. They felt an inner compulsion to look back and stare at the deep blue surface of Issyk-Kul, frozen like a tinted mirror.

'If only you could carve out a piece of that blue and stick it in your bag to take home,' joked Ernazar.

'So what would you feed your horses with, instead of oats: Issyk-Kul blue?' replied Boston, quite reasonably.

They both laughed. It was rare for them to get away from the arduous daily grind of a shepherd's duties. Although they were riding to check out the route across the pass, and when it came to moving the flocks they faced an even more arduous and back-breaking task, at that moment they were both in the best of spirits, and so far the route had been easy going. Ernazar was in an excellent mood – after all, it was his idea they were putting into practice. In all the forty years since the war no one had dared to ride across this pass, and now he and Boston had plucked up the courage to do so.

Ernazar had an enquiring, and a questioning, mind. In build he was a fine figure of a man, and turned out to have served in the last cavalry units after the war. He still had a cavalryman's bearing, even though so many years had passed. Gulyumkan loved to tell people how Ernazar had once almost become a film star. Some film director had come and tried to persuade him to act in a film. If your Ernazar lived in America, so he said, he would play cowboys in all the films. But Gulyumkan answered him, 'I know all about your films, I heard how they took a horse-breeder off to act in a film, and he went right to the dogs – some starlet got her claws in him. You're not going to get my Ernazar.' They had all had a good laugh.

Boston was thinking that when they returned in the autumn from Kichibel, he would help Ernazar get his own team. The man should have a permanent job, it was high time they made

255

him a shepherd in his own right, it wasn't fair to keep him a herdsman so long; if he, Boston, was farm director or Partorg he would know who to put in which job and when, but unfortunately as the villagers used to say: *'Biri kem dunie'* – 'Things are never quite the way they should be.'

This high in the mountains they no longer encountered any tractors or riders, and the winter camps and animal sheds were fewer and further between. The landscape was changing: Nature here was cold, alien, and harsher. By evening, before sunset, Boston and Ernazar had made their way along the stony ravine to the foothills of the Ala-Mongyu pass. While there was still light they could have pressed on further, but they reckoned that if they were driving their flocks before them, even if they had started at very first light, with the stars still showing, this would be the place to make camp the first night, here, in the ravine, at the opening of the pass. The herdsmen used to call this sort of camp a *'shykama'* – 'the night before storming the pass'. Furthermore, this was a very convenient spot for a *shykama* – a stream flowed past from the glacier above, they could find a good spot beneath the overhang, sheltered from the bitter wind that blew off the ice. The shepherds knew only too well that the piercing and dangerous wind off the glaciers always rose at midnight and blew until sunrise. The idea of a good *shykama* was to find proper shelter for the herds from this icy wind and be ready to storm the pass, refreshed and invigorated, the following morning.

Dismounting and unsaddling their tired mounts the travellers made their preparations for the night. They chose themselves a good spot under a small overhang and gathered up some firewood, Ernazar climbing energetically quite far into the ravine to reach some stunted trees. Then they sat by the fire and dined off the provisions they had brought with them from home, even brewing up some tea in a tin teapot, and contentedly settled down to sleep after their long trek.

The high ground below the pass grew dark quickly, and at once the cold set in – just as if winter had returned. The distance between summer and winter could be measured in a single day's ride. Frosty air blew down from the Ala-Mongyu's glaciers – they were not far, after all, a mere stone's throw, from the great, eternal ice fields. Boston had read some article about how this ice had covered the upper slopes for millions of years and was the cause of the fertility of their valleys – the ice was constantly thawing to form trickling streams, which carried their waters down into the warm valleys and fields. How wisely Nature ordered her affairs.

'Ernazar,' said Boston, before dropping off to sleep, 'feel that cold – brrrrr! It's a good thing we brought our coats.'

'What use are coats!' retorted Ernazar. 'In the old days people used to say a special prayer – the crossing prayer, it was called. Do you remember it?'

'No, I don't remember it.'

'I can remember my grandfather saying it.'

'Well, tell us then.'

'Very well. I'll say it, and you repeat after me. Do you hear, Boston? You repeat: "O lord of the frozen heavens, blue Tengri, do not make more arduous our path across the icy pass. If you wish that beasts should perish in a snowstorm, take instead a raven from the sky. If you wish that our children should die in the cold, take instead a cuckoo from the sky. We shall tighten the girth belts of our horses, lash the loads on the backs of our oxen and turn our faces to you; only we ask that you, Tengri, should not stand in our way, let us pass through to the green grasses beyond, to the icy streams, and accept the gift of these our words . . ." Something like that, but I don't remember how it goes on . . .'

'Pity . . .'

'Why's it a pity? Nobody needs prayers like that nowadays, now they teach you at school that that's all backwardness and ignorance. We're in the space age now.'

'What's space got to do with it? Just because people are flying into space does that mean we have to forget our old incantations? Only a handful of people fly into space, but look how many millions of us there are here on earth. Our fathers and our grandfathers lived off the land, so what's space got to do with us? Let them fly round and round if they want – they've got their job to do, and we've got ours.'

'That's easily said, Boske, but the Kochkorbayevs of this world get up at their meetings and rain abuse on all the old

257

ways. They say our weddings are all wrong now, why don't you kiss at the wedding, why shouldn't the bride and her father-in-law hold each other in a clinch and dance? You're even giving your children the wrong names, he says – there's an approved list of new names, and it's time to replace all that old junk. He sticks his oar in everywhere – our funerals are wrong as well, he says, that's no way to mourn the deceased in modern society. He'll even show people how to weep: you mustn't weep in the old way, he says, you must do it the new way.'

'Yes, I know, Ernazar, don't think I don't know all that. You wait till I get to Moscow – they're supposed to be sending me there to an exhibition in the autumn – if I get there, I swear I'll go to the Central Committee, and ask: does the country need creatures like Kochkorbayev? Or did we just pull a short straw? You hardly have to open your mouth – say the least little thing and he's at your throat: "You," he says, "are going against the Party." He's the whole Party, you see, rolled up in one man. And nobody can go against him. That's how things are. Even the director tries to avoid him. Ah, to hell with him. The worst of it is that there are Kochkorbayevs all over the place . . . Let's sleep, Ernazar. We've got a tough day ahead of us . . .'

And talking like this about one thing and another the two shepherds finally dropped off to sleep, in the ravine below the great glacial pass of Ala-Mongyu. The stars already twinkled high above the mountains in the translucent darkness, scattered in their multitude across the firmament, and Boston lay and wondered how it was that such massive heavy stars, some as big as his fist, could hang there twinkling in the sky and not fall to earth, and all the while the cold wind raged fiercely through the crags . . . He was always on the move, Shamalu the wind god . . . Always howling his displeasure, nurturing some secret grudge . . .

The same gusty, cold wind whistled through the narrow chink in their window deep in that dark night, as Boston relived in his memory the journey with Ernazar while listening to the howling of the wolves outside. Once again he chewed over the whole series of events, sifting through the sands of the past, and his heart ached with the hurt inflicted by those worthless people who exploit even the tragedies that befall their enemies if they offer an opportunity to mock and slander them. What power they wield in their ancient and odious trade! They can punish an enemy at will and rob him of his sleep, be he emperor or humble shepherd. Boston grew so disturbed from the interminable thoughts jostling for space within his head that at moments the howling of the wolves seemed to him the lament of his own tormented spirit. He imagined his ailing soul roaming the darkness beyond the sheds, blind with grief, weeping and wailing together with the she-wolf Akbara. He could no longer bear the terrible lament and longed to silence the animal! Will it never give up?! What the hell can we do about it? What do you want from me? cried Boston in his mind, in exasperation. I cannot help you in any way. I tried but I failed. Akbara, believe me, it didn't work. Don't howl any more! They're not here, your cubs are not here, you can run a hundred versts and you still won't find them, they've been sold and the money gone for drink. You'll never find them now! So pack it in! How much longer are you going to punish us? Go away, go away, Akbara! Forget it, once and for all. I know it's tough for you, but go away, disappear, and God forbid that I ever clap eyes on you, I'll shoot you, you miserable animal, I don't care, I'll shoot you because you're making our life impossible. Don't push me any further, things are bad enough without you, at least I can kill you, but what am I going to do to those who make a mockery of my own misfortune? You'd better make yourself scarce, never let me hear your howling again! There are some others I would kill, as God's my witness, and my hand won't even tremble. We have a common enemy, you and me, Akbara, he took your cubs, and now this drunken swine is vilifying my name with his foul mouth. When I think how I ripped my hands climbing into that icy crevasse, and how I called and called to Ernazar and then wept all alone in those merciless mountains, I wish I could die, honest to God. And die I would, to hell with everything, if it weren't for the boy. Here he is next to me, rolled into a little ball, sleeping soundly where his mother put him in the bed beside me. A woman is afraid of the howling of wolves, but the child sleeps, because he is pure, because he is innocent, because he has been sent me for my torments, for all that I have had to go through, he is flesh of my flesh and blood of my blood, he is the last image cast in my mould. I did not seek out the fate that befell us; it came to me unbidden, just as surely as day comes after night and night after day. It is true what they say, you can never escape your own fate, and that reptile Bazarbai is dragging my name in the mud. I'd like to throttle him, just like a dog, because there's no way to get satisfaction from a lying toad like that. Just see who's singing to his tune, none other than our fine Party Organizer, you'd think he has nothing better to do! He latches on to any yarn that drunkard spins and now he wants to take my little boy away from me . . . How well I understand your suffering, Akbara! Such were Boston's thoughts as he tossed and turned through that sleepless night, but even he with all his wisdom and sensitivity could not imagine the full measure of Akbara's suffering. Even though she had no words, she still suffered all the torment but without the means to express it. She could no more cast off this sorrow which so totally consumed her, than leap out of her own skin. Had she not tried to wander aimlessly and endlessly over the mountains and floodlands together with Tash-Chainar, who followed her always and everywhere, in the hope of running herself at last into the ground, of collapsing and expiring with sheer fatigue? Had she not tried to assuage, to suppress the persistent pain of the loss, savagely and despairingly hurling herself together with Tash-Chainar at everything and everyone they encountered in their path? Had she not tried to return to her lair beneath the cliff, in order once again to make sure that it was really empty, in order finally to destroy all hope within her and be deceived no more by her dreams. . . ?

What a heavy lot had fallen to her . . . That evening, as they roamed aimlessly about the vicinity, Akbara suddenly turned abruptly towards the Bashat ravine and set off at a run, constantly quickening her pace, just as if something demanded her urgent attention. As always Tash-Chainar followed, never falling more than a step behind. Akbara continued to build up speed until eventually she hurtled like a demon over the rocks, through snowdrifts and forests . . . And then along that familiar path, through the old chink in the

260

rock, through the thickets of berberis and into the lair, convincing herself for the umpteenth time that it was empty, and once again she started to howl, whimpering in a pitiful voice, scratching and sniffing at anything that might still retain the scent of her little cubs: where were they, what had happened to her puppies, her four little balls of fluff? When would they grow strong and tall, when would their fangs harden, when would they run along behind her and learn how tough their mother was, and how tireless her legs? Akbara dashed to the stream, where her nostrils were still assailed by the foul smell from the neck of the bottle. The oats that still remained after the scavenging of birds lay frozen in the ground . . .

Then she returned again to the lair, lay down, and pressed her nose into her belly. Tash-Chainar lay beside her, warming her with his thick shaggy coat.

It was already night. Akbara dreamt that her cubs lay beside her, here in the lair. They blundered clumsily around, hunting for her teats. How she had longed to give them her milk, all the milk stored up inside her till it hurt, every last drop . . . And how eagerly the little cubs sucked, smacking their lips and choking from the abundance of milk, and how deliciously wearying the sensation of maternal languour that rippled through her body; only for some reason in the dream the milk was not growing any less . . . The mother-wolf grew alarmed: why was it, why was there no relief in her teats, why were the cubs not satisfied? Yet there they were beside her, all her four pups, the brightest little one, with the white tip on his tail, and the one who always fed the longest and fell asleep with the teat in his mouth, and the third one, quarrelsome and whimpery, and the only female among them, a tiny little she-wolf with deep blue eyes. This was her – a new, a future Akbara . . . Then the she-wolf dreamt that she was not running but flying, her feet not touching the ground – once again in the Moyun-Kum steppe, in the great savannah, with her four cubs beside her, and they were also flying, and with them was Tash-Chainar, their father, bounding along with immense leaps. The sun shone brightly over the earth and the cold air flowed past, streamed past like life itself . . .

At this, Akbara awoke and lay for a long time without

moving, weighed down by the harsh reality . . . Then she rose cautiously to her feet, so cautiously that even Tash-Chainar did not hear, and stepping gingerly she left the lair. The first thing she saw as she stepped outside was the moon above the snow-covered peaks. In that clear night air the moon seemed so near and stood out so sharply against the starry sky that she could almost spring up and touch it. The wolf walked over to the bubbling stream, prowled dejectedly along its bank, hanging her head, and then sat on her haunches, her tail pressed beneath her, and stared long and hard at the round moon above. On that night Akbara saw more clearly and distinctly than ever before the goddess of wolves Byuri-Ana, who lives in the moon. Her crooked outline on the moon's surface was very similar to that of Akbara herself – the goddess Byuri-Ana hung in the sky just like a real wolf, with her tail stuck out behind her and her jaws open. Akbara could sense that the moon-wolf saw and heard her. Craning high in the air she called to the goddess, weeping and complaining, and clouds of steam rose from her nostrils in the cold air: Look down on me, goddess of wolves, Byuri-Ana, it is I, Akbara, here in the cold mountains, wretched and lonely. Do you hear how I weep? Do you hear how I howl and sob, my bowels aching with pain and my teats swollen with milk? There is no one for me to feed, no one to give suck to, for I am bereft of my wolflings. Oh, where are they, what has become of them? Come down, Byuri-Ana, come down to me and let us stand here together, side by side, and howl together. Come down, goddess of wolves, and I shall take you into those lands where I was born, into the steppe, where there is now no place for wolves. Come down here, into these rocky mountains, where also there is no place for us now, for as you see, the wolves must leave their every home . . . But if you will not come down, Byuri-Ana, take me, your cubless wolf-mother Akbara, to you. I shall live on the moon, I shall live with you and I shall grieve for the earth. Oh, Byuri-Ana, do you, do you hear me? Hear me, oh, hear me, Byuri-Ana, hear my lament!

So Akbara lamented and howled at the moon on that cold night among the frozen mountains . . .

Ernazar was the first to rise after the first night in their *shykama*

262

on the pass. Wrapping himself in his coat he went to look at the hobbled horses.

'Cold?' asked Boston, warily peering out from under his coat, when Ernazar returned.

'It's always like that here,' answered Ernazar. 'It's cold now, but the moment the sun rises it warms up instantly.' He lay down for a while on his horsecloth.

It was still very early, and it is gloomy at that hour in the mountains.

'How are our horses?'

'Fine.'

'You know what I'm thinking – when we drive the flocks across it would do no harm to put up a tent for the night. It would be much warmer.'

'No reason why we shouldn't,' agreed Ernazar. 'We could put it up in a jiffy. The main thing is to mark out the trail, the rest we can play by ear.'

Once the sun rose it did indeed feel much warmer. The air warmed quickly and as soon as it was barely light they saddled up their horses.

Before mounting, Boston had a good look round again, surveying all the surrounding slopes and cliffs. They were sheer and savage, and Boston was aware how paltry and insignificant the two human figures must seem – yet here they were, challenging the might of these mountains. We are not afraid of this pass, thought Boston. Our lives are at stake. And when lives are at stake you feel not fear but the exhilaration of a world that is yours, the sea, the bowels of the earth and the sky. We'll make it!

First they looked for the old scar of the track and tried to figure out the route it would have taken along the pass. The path followed a snow-covered saddle between two peaks. Beyond it they expected to find the descent down the other side of the Ala-Mongyu crest, and the Kichibel *jailyau* where, as the old-timers used to say, there were birch woods and swift-flowing mountain streams. How often Nature's most magnificent treasures are also her most inaccessible! When his daily bread is at stake man is forced to fight for what he wants; he has to secure his survival on earth . . .

The path grew gradually steeper. As they climbed higher a

263

crust of ice appeared on the snow, which made the going heavier for the horses, and the snow was deeper and deeper. The sun shone down, the wind had subsided, and in the deep silence they could hear the accelerated breathing of the horses as clearly as their own.

'Well now?' Boston asked Ernazar, turning round in his saddle. 'If the snow comes up higher than the sheep's bellies we'll have problems. What do you reckon?'

'You'll get nowhere without problems, Boske! The main thing is that they don't last too long. If the worst comes to the worst we'll have to dig out a trail for the sheep, and in other places we can trample it down.'

'That's what I was thinking too. We'll have to bring shovels with us. Remember that for the future, Ernazar, we'll have to bring shovels.'

When the snow was above the horses' knees the shepherds dismounted and led their horses by the reins. By now they were feeling the lack of oxygen, and had to breathe through their mouths. The white blanket of snow dazzled their eyes – they needed dark glasses. The horses' breathing became laboured, they perspired and their flanks trembled with exertion. Happily there was not too far to go to that critical saddle . . .

By now the sun had reached its zenith above the jumble of age-old peaks and impassive, snow-laden ranges. Nothing gave warning of the sudden change in the weather, except perhaps the few little clouds that lay in their path. They were able to pass through them, or, more accurately, over them, as if walking on cotton wool. It was hard to believe as they shivered that at the foot of the mountains, round Lake Issyk-Kul, holiday-makers were sun-bathing on the lake's beaches.

They had a mere five hundred metres to go and were hoping that things would not be any worse on the other side of the pass.

At last they were through the pass, and Boston and Ernazar paused to rest. They were both exhausted, and quite out of breath. The horses too were tired from their exertions. Full of contentment and satisfaction they gazed down at the route they had covered.

'Well, here we are, Boske,' said Ernazar with a smile. His

eyes shone with joy. 'We can cross with our flocks here. That is, of course, if the weather permits.'

'We certainly can. If the weather's right, of course.'

'So you and I have been going for two and a half hours,' said Ernazar, looking at his watch. 'Not too bad, was it.'

'With the sheep it would take about three hours,' remarked Boston, 'if not more. The main thing is that we've proved we can cross by the pass. Now let's press on. See over there, that looks like where the descent starts, and maybe we can even see Kichibel. It should be lovely and green there now . . .'

They walked on. All around lay virgin snow, in places laid out in smooth sheets, in others whipped up by the winds into sparkling snowdrifts. They could sense that somewhere ahead the snow blanket ended and another world began. They longed to reach it as soon as they could, and to see Kichibel, the goal of their journey, with their own eyes. They continued their way over the saddle between mountain peaks like a dromedary's humps and their destination, which they had so longed to see, now seemed near at hand. Boston was walking ahead, ploughing through the snow, leading his horse by the reins, when suddenly he felt something judder beneath his feet. He heard a shout behind him.

He turned swiftly and froze in his tracks: Ernazar was suddenly not there, he had vanished – neither he nor his horse were anywhere to be seen. Where he had been walking there was only a puff of snow.

'Ernazar!' shouted Boston in horror and was shocked at the terrible sound of his own voice echoing in the deathly silence.

Boston rushed back to the spot where the snow was disturbed and by a sheer miracle stopped just in time – before him yawned an abyss. From the gaping crack there wafted only a terrible blackness and the icy cold air. Boston lay on his stomach and crept up to the very edge, still not grasping, or, rather, refusing to grasp, what had transpired. He was now, with all his thoughts and sensations, possessed by a terrible fear. It stiffened his limbs but he steeled himself to crawl closer and closer, some unknown force propelling him forwards and forcing him to breathe. He crawled on his elbows, wiping away the snow that stuck to his face. He now realized that there was an ice-crust beneath him and recalled all the stories of cracks and fissures in the ice, concealed beneath the snow, through which entire herds sometimes plunged into the bottomless chasms below. Why should this terrible curse now fall on Ernazar, and not only on Ernazar, but on him as well?

He was cursed because he was insatiable, never satisfied, never prepared to take it easy and relax . . . If only he had foreseen that such an accident could happen . . .

Boston crawled up to the edge of the hole. Before him there yawned a black and ragged precipice, descending into the darkness of a craggy wall. He shuddered with horror.

'Ernazar,' whispered Boston quietly – his throat had dried up – and then he roared wildly, suddenly regaining his voice, 'Ernazar, where are you? Ernazar! Ernazar! Ernazar!'

When he fell silent he heard, or fancied he heard, a groan from below and the barely audible words, 'Get back!'

Then Boston yelled, 'Ernazar! My brother! I'm coming, I'm coming! Just hold on! I'll pull you out!'

He leapt up, at the risk of plunging down the chasm himself, ran over to his horse and started to pull off the animal's harness: the coil of rope and the axe, which they had brought along just in case, were strapped to Ernazar's saddle and had disappeared into the crevasse with him. Boston wrenched his knife from its sheath and cut off all the leather straps – crupper, martingale, stirrup leathers, reins, bridle and lead-ing-rein – he then spliced them and knotted them into one long strap. He even cut himself in the process, his hands were shaking so badly. Once again he dashed across to the chasm, crawled up to the very edge, pulling himself blindly forward, wheezing as if in agony, as if afraid that he might suddenly be killed before he had managed to save Ernazar.

'Ernazar! Ernazar!' he called. 'Here's a rope, catch the rope! Do you hear, a rope! Do you hear me? Ernazar! My brother, answer!'

Winding one end round his fist he lowered the makeshift rope into the chasm. But no one took hold of the other end, no one responded to his call. He did not even know how far the rope stretched or how deep the chasm was.

'Answer me, Ernazar! Answer me! Just one word, Ernazar! My brother!' called Boston repeatedly, but all that came in reply was the echo of his own voice, which filled him with horror. 'Where are you, Ernazar?' called Boston. 'Can you hear me, Ernazar? What should I do?' Finally he lost control of himself and wept, shouting incoherent words. He called upon his father, who had died at the Front, his mother, also long dead, his children, brothers and sisters, and his most poignant cry was the name of his wife Arzygul. His mind simply could not take in the tragedy . . . Ernazar was gone, Ernazar – dead! And there was no one to console him in his grief . . . Henceforward it would remain with him for all the days of his life . . . Then Boston cried out, 'Why didn't you heed our prayers! What have you done? What sort of a god are you, after this?' not really understanding whom he was addressing.

He stood up, swaying, and realized that evening was drawing in. He sensed that the weather on the pass was about to turn. Stormclouds had suddenly appeared, and a gusty ground wind blew over the snow. What was he to do? Where should he go? The horse which he had left on the track was already heading back – he could see it making its way down the pass, he could not catch it now. Anyway the horse would be of little use to him, without its bridle and stirrup leathers. In his anger Boston kicked the useless saddle. There he stood, breathless and half demented, his cap blown into the ravine, gazing helplessly around, quite, quite alone between the cliffs and the frozen ground on the Ala-Mongyu pass. The piercing wind blowing through the pass filled his already tormented soul with unbearable anguish. Where could he go? What could he do? How smoothly everything had been going! Why did they have to come across this accursed, terrible ravine? Studying the pattern of their tracks in the snow, he realized that Ernazar had plunged into the ravine by sheer bad luck – he himself had passed literally a yard and a half from the edge of the precipice, while Ernazar, tragically, had ridden a little further to the right and had plummeted with his horse into the icy abyss concealed beneath the snow.

He could not reconcile himself to the fact that there was effectively no way he could help his friend. Suddenly he thought: What if Ernazar was still alive? What if he had merely lost consciousness? In that case he must be helped out of the crevasse somehow or other, and urgently, before he froze to death in there. In that event it might be possible to save him.

Throwing his coat on the snow he set off down the slope at a run, although it was hard to run over that surface. He had to get word to the farm as quickly as possible, then they could send men to help, with ropes, spades and torches, and then he would be able to lower himself on a rope into the chasm, to find Ernazar and save him.

Several times he fell, and thought with horror: God forbid I break a leg! He stumbled to his feet, and ran on faster than ever.

He ran, still hoping to catch up with his horse. The weather grew worse with every passing minute. The air was already full of powdery snow, although this did not worry Boston – he knew there would be no snow further down, even if there was a blizzard on the pass. He was afraid of what would happen to Ernazar. Would he live long enough to be rescued, even if he was still alive? Faster, faster, the blood pounded in his head. He was afraid the darkness would settle in around him, and he would not be able to move fast in the dark.

Boston never did manage to catch his horse. Once it sensed its freedom the light chestnut galloped back to its home.

Boston headed straight across the lower slopes which he knew so well, considerably shortening his route. He was exhausted not so much by the physical exertion of walking and running across countless gullies and ploughed fields as by the thought of the accident, which plagued his mind unceasingly. His head buzzed with an endless succession of plans for Ernazar's rescue. First he decided he should not have left the pass and left Ernazar alone, but should have stayed and, if necessary, been swept away by the snowstorm. Or he imagined that he heard the dying Ernazar groan in the impenetrable darkness of his icy dungeon, while above the mountains raged a fierce blizzard. When he tried to imagine what he would say to Ernazar's family, to his children and his wife Gulyumkan, he couldn't bear to think of it and felt he would go quite mad.

After all this misfortune, there was one small piece of luck. That day one of the shepherds was celebrating a wedding in his house in the foothills, marrying off his student son who had come home for the holidays. The guests had departed late, the last to go finally leaving in a truck well after midnight. The moon shone brightly, and a cold wind rose from the lake. Far below, the shimmering mirror-like surface of Issyk-Kul still gleamed vaguely in the darkness. The departing guests were in a mood of celebration and one song after the other rang out from their truck.

When he heard the singing Boston dashed out on to the road and signalled desperately. The truck eventually brought him to the Berik state farm, well after midnight. The truck stopped next to the farm director's house. His dog barked and tried to bite Boston's boot. Boston paid no attention to the animal and pounded with his fist on the window.

'Who is it?' asked an alarmed voice.

'It's me, Boston Urkunchiev.'

'What's happened, Boske?'

'Something terrible.'

By midday the next day the rescue team was already climbing in single file towards the Ala-Mongyu pass. There were six of them, including Boston. They had been taken as far as possible by jeep, and now they pushed on up hill on foot with their ropes and climbing gear, walking behind Boston in silence, saving their breath. At any moment they expected the arrival of a helicopter from the city, which would bring them three mountain rescue experts to join the team.

Boston thought of how the evening before he and Ernazar had walked along this very same track, unaware of the terrible fate that awaited them . . .

He realized that even if Ernazar had survived the fall he would hardly have survived a whole day and night at the bottom of an icy crevasse. Even so, he still wanted to believe in a miracle.

After the blizzard which had raged the previous night the pass was quiet under its blanket of painfully brilliant fresh snow. Unfortunately the snowfall had completely obliterated their tracks and now Boston could not tell for certain where the cleft in the ice had been, but one of the rescuers found Boston's fur coat where he had thrown it down the previous day, and a few paces from the coat the abandoned saddle. Taking their bearings from these objects they were able to identify the area of the chasm, which had been concealed by the snowfall of the previous night. By this time the mountaineers had arrived. They lowered themselves into the crevasse, which, they said, was six storeys deep.

When they came back to the surface the mountaineers declared that they were unable to recover Ernazar's body. It had frozen hard to the ice, as had the body of his horse. They explained that any sharp blows might cause the ice to shift, leading to a massive cave-in, and to the rescuers themselves becoming victims, crushed to death by collapsing snow and ice . . . The mountaineers said that all Boston could do was to lower himself into the chasm and take his leave of Ernazar. There was no other solution . . .

For a long time after this, for years and years, Boston was haunted by a terrible nightmare, seared firmly into his memory. He dreamed of being lowered on ropes into the chasm, illuminating its icy walls with a small torch. He had a spare torch with him, in case he dropped the first one. Suddenly he saw that the spare torch had vanished, and the realization filled him with anxiety. He wanted to cry out, but continued his descent deeper and deeper into the monstrous icy abyss, until finally the beam from his torch picked out the frozen corpse of Ernazar: Ernazar (this is how he really was) on his knees, his coat rucked up around his head, his face covered with blood, his lips firmly pressed together, his eyes closed. 'Ernazar!' called Boston in his dream. 'It's me! Listen, I wanted to leave you my spare torch, it's so dark and eerie in here, but I've lost it. Do you understand, Ernazar, I've lost it. Never mind, I'll give you mine. Here, take my torch. Take it, Ernazar, I beg you!' But Ernazar neither took his torch nor gave any response at all. Boston would then weep, his body convulsing as he sobbed, and, waking, he would find himself in tears.

For the rest of the day after dreaming that dream he would be sullen and bad-tempered. He never told a soul about the dream, especially not Gulyumkan, even after she had become his wife. Neither did he tell anyone in his family about his descent into the chasm to take his leave of Ernazar.

By the time he returned home from the pass everyone in the team knew about the tragedy. The very worst thing for Boston was to see the weeping Gulyumkan, devastated by her grief. It made him wish it had been he who had perished on the pass. He would rather descend a thousand times into the chasm to relive all that horror than see her in such a state. Gulyumkan took the death of her husband very badly, and they even feared for her reason. She kept trying to break free, shouting, 'I don't believe it! I don't believe that he's dead! Let me go! I'll find him! I'll go to him!'

One night she did in fact run away. Exhausted after a harrowing day, Boston was about to go to bed. For several days in succession he had not been able to undress and have a proper night's sleep because of the constant flood of sympathizers: people came from all over the district, many of them following the traditional custom and calling out their lament as they approached: 'Ernazar, my brother, flesh of my flesh, where shall I see you now?' Boston would help them dismount and console them . . . On that day the evening had been relatively quiet and Boston, bare to the waist, was washing himself in the yard, pouring water over himself with a ladle. Arzygul was keeping Gulyumkan company: these days she spent nearly all her time with her neighbour.

'Boston, Boston, where are you?' Arzygul could suddenly be heard shouting.

'What's happened?'

'Run quickly, you must catch Gulyumkan! She's run off somewhere. Her girls are crying, but I couldn't stop her.'

Boston quickly pulled on his vest and dressed as he was, with the towel still round his neck, ran off in pursuit of the crazed Gulyumkan.

He did not catch her at once.

She was striding along ahead of him, up a gently sloping gulley, heading for the mountains.

'Gulyumkan, stop, where are you going?' Boston called to her.

She walked on without looking round. Boston quickened his pace, expecting Gulyumkan to hurl accusations at him, something he feared more than anything else – the reproach that he, Boston, was responsible for Ernazar's death. The thought of this was like a scalding splash of boiling water, for as it was he was tormenting himself with the very same thought. What could he answer?

He could not try to tell her that the guilt lay not on him. Would she believe him, anyway, if he did? How could he prove that if fatal circumstances conspire, then man is power-less against them? Such words would not console her. No words could reconcile her grieving soul to what had happened. Nor could words explain to Gulyumkan why he himself had been spared by the tragic event.

'Gulyumkan, where are you going?' Breathless from the exertion Boston finally caught up with her. 'Stop, listen to me, let's go home . . .'

It was still quite light at that evening hour. The mountains could still be seen in the quiet dusk of the declining day, and when Gulyumkan turned round it seemed to Boston that her grief emanated from her, as though in transparent rays, and the features of her face were disfigured as if she was looking at him from deep under the water. He found it unbearably painful to see her suffering, her look of wretched misery – when only days before she had been a vivacious woman, in the prime of her life. It hurt him to see her running in that demented way, to see the crumpled silk shift which the other women had dressed her in coming undone at the breast. Her braids too, loosened as a sign of mourning.

'Where are you going, Gulyumkan?' asked Boston, automa-tically taking her by the hand.

'I'm going to him, to the pass, I must,' she said in a strangely decisive tone.

Instead of asking: Are you out of your mind? How do you think you'll get there? You'll freeze to death up there in that thin dress! he started to beg her, 'No, please don't go now. It'll be night soon, Gulyumkan. You can go another time, I'll show you the place myself. But you mustn't go now. Let's go home. Your little girls are crying. Arzygul is worried. It'll be night soon. Come, let's go, I beg you, Gulyumkan.'

Gulyumkan paused in silence, stooped beneath her burden of grief.

'But how am I to live without him?' she whispered disconso-lately, shaking her hands. 'How can he be left like that, all alone, not even buried in the ground, unmourned – with no grave?'

Boston did not know how to comfort her. He stood before

her, downcast, guilty, in the baggy vest which hung shape-lessly from his thin shoulders, the towel round his neck, in the leather boots which every shepherd wears winter and summer. He was miserable, guilty and dejected. He knew that there was no way he could make up for this woman's loss. If he could bring her husband back to life by taking his place, he would have done so without a moment's hesitation.

They remained silent, each thinking their own thoughts.

'Let's go.' Boston took Gulyumkan's hand. 'We must be there for the people when they come to pay their last respects to Ernazar. We must be at home.'

Gulyumkan let her head fall on his shoulder and, as if pouring out her sorrows to her own father, she mumbled something incoherently, choking with sobs and trembling all over. He supported her by the arm and thus they returned home, grieving together and weeping. The quiet summer evening was on the wane, and the air was full of the sharp smells of flowering mountain herbs. Arzygul came out to meet them, leading Ernazar's girls by the hand. When they saw each other the two women embraced and burst into tears again, as if reunited after a long separation.

Some six months later, when Arzygul was in the regional hospital and Gulyumkan had long since moved to the fishing village on the lake shore, Boston would recall that evening, and with it the turmoil of emotions the memories excited within him.

Boston sat in the hospital ward, beside his wife's bed, and gazed with pain in his heart at her drained and emaciated face. It was a warm autumn day, her wardmates were mostly in the yard, and thus it was that Arzygul was able to have the following serious conversation.

'I have something to say to you.' Uttering the words slowly and laboriously, Arzygul looked up with difficulty at her husband, and Boston noticed that during the night her face had grown even yellower and more haggard.

'I'm listening. What do you want to say, Arzygul?' asked Boston tenderly.

'Did you see the doctor?'

'I saw him. He said . . .'

'Wait. It's not important what he said, we can come to that

273

later. You do understand, Boston, that we must have a serious talk.'

Boston's heart sank at these words. He took his handkerchief from his pocket and mopped his brow.

'Maybe we shouldn't bother, you'll get better and then we can talk.' Boston attempted to head off the conversation, but realized from his wife's look that he was wasting his efforts.

'There is a time for everything,' the sick woman insisted, barely moving her pale lips. 'I have been thinking a lot in here – what else is there to do in hospital, but think? I thought how you and I have had a good life together, and I am content with my lot. I have no reason to be angry with God – the children have grown up and are standing on their own two feet: now they can lead independent lives. We shall have a separate talk about the children. But it's you I'm sorry for, Boston, more than anyone else. You have no tact, you don't know how to approach people, you won't grovel before any man. And you're no longer young, either. After I'm gone don't avoid people, Boston. What I mean is: when I go you mustn't turn into a hermit. Organize the wake, then think what you're going to do next. I don't want you to live alone. The children have their own life now.'

'Why are you saying all this?' protested Boston feebly. 'Must we talk like this?'

'We must, Boston, we must! What else is there to talk about? These things have to be said sooner or later. You can't say them when you're dead. So I've been lying here thinking about you and about me. I often think of Gulyumkan. As you know, she's hardly an outsider. Life has left her a widow with small children. A fine woman. My advice to you is: marry Gulyumkan. You can work out how you should go about it. Each person must decide such things for himself. When I'm gone tell her what I said . . . Who knows, it may turn out as I wish. And Ernazar's children will have a father . . .'

Tourists visiting Issyk-Kul often make fun of the local people: they live by the lake, but they never see it – they're always too busy. Boston spent his life longing for the time to visit the lake, yet all he could do was admire the enticing blue expanse of Issyk-Kul from a distance, while busy with other chores.

274

On this occasion, however, he stepped out of the hospital towards evening and walked straight to the lake – he felt an urge to be alone by its piercing blue beauty high among the mountains. He watched the wind whip up white horses over its surface and then drive them into long, straight rows, like furrows laid by an invisible plough. He wanted to weep, to be subsumed into Issyk-Kul – he wanted to live and he wanted to die . . . Just like those white horses – the waves would surge up, vanish and then re-form themselves again . . .

In the end Boston could stand no more – the wolves howled so long and loud around the camp that they forced him out of his bed. First they wakened Kenjesh. The little boy woke up crying. Boston moved him closer, hugging him and squeezing him to comfort him.

'Kenjesh, hey, Kenjesh! I'm here. What's all this, you silly boy? And Mama's here – look, there she is! Do you want your milk? Do you want me to turn on the light? Don't be afraid. That's only the pussy cats yowling. That's the noise they make.'

Gulyumkan awoke and also tried to calm the boy, but he would not settle down. They had to turn on the light.

'Gulyum,' Boston addressed his wife from the door, where he had gone to turn on the light, 'I'm going to go and deal with these creatures. It can't carry on like this.'

'What's the time now?'

Boston looked at his watch.

'Twenty to three.'

'Look at that,' protested Gulyumkan. 'You've got to be up at six. How can you do it? That cursed Akbara is driving us mad. What have we done to deserve this punishment?'

'Calm down. What else can I do? I'll be back in a trice. Don't you worry about a thing. I'll bolt the door from outside. Don't worry. Go back to sleep.'

He walked past by the windows, clomping loudly along in the boots which he had pulled on over his bare feet. Boston was at last ready for the confrontation, and so he deliberately called together all the dogs and heaped abuse on them. He was ready for desperate measures, driven to the end of his tether by the grief-maddened wolves.

There was nothing he could do to help them. His only hope was to shoot the beasts if he saw them; luckily he had a semi-automatic rifle.

He did not meet the wolves, however. Cursing indiscriminately he returned home, but was unable to get to sleep. For a long time he lay in the darkness, his head spinning with painful and uneasy thoughts.

He thought of various things. Most of all he thought how from each year to the next it was getting harder to do an honest day's work and that people nowadays, particularly the youngsters, had no shame. Nobody took you at your word any more. Above all, everyone was interested only in his own profit. And to think how before the war, when they were building the famous Chu canal, people had gathered from all over the nation, working voluntarily and without pay. Nobody would believe it now, they'd say such things couldn't happen. Nowadays you couldn't get anyone to work as a shepherd even if you tried to lasso them and carry them off! Everyone knew it, but they made it out to be just a temporary problem. If you dared mention it you were accused of slander, of some deliberately orchestrated anti-government campaign. Nobody wanted to think seriously about the future. The only thing that gave him comfort and joy was that Gulyumkan did not hold against him the fact that he had to spend the entire year herding his flocks with no days off and no holidays. You couldn't leave your flocks, you couldn't just turn off, flip a switch; animals need to be watched day and night. That's the way it was, and now wherever you looked there was a shortage of hands. Not because of a lack of manpower but because people didn't want to work. Why should that be? You couldn't live without work, after all. That meant certain ruin. Maybe it was because people had to live and work in a different way now? The worst problem of all was how to get part-timers during the lambing season, to look after the new-born lambs. Once again, you wouldn't find young people doing this work. It meant staying on your feet for twenty-four hours at a time. Those lambs had to be watched carefully, conscientiously, and wild horses wouldn't drag today's young people on to the land and into the farms. Anyway, the pay was a pittance, a young lad or girl could earn far more for an eight-hour day in a factory or on a construction site in town. 'How was it,' complain the old-timers, 'that we slaved away all our lives where they needed hands, and not where they paid well? But now, when the time comes for youngsters to go out to work, they have no shame, no sense of duty.' Conflict was building up between the generations. A particular conversation suddenly surfaced in Boston's memory, and not for the first time, one where he had not been able to bite his tongue. That was a mistake. Once again he had been putting forth his idea that people must be given the chance to work their own flocks and their own land. He believed there was no other way, and for this it was essential that the worker had a personal stake in the fruits of his labour. As always, the rebuke was administered by Partorg Kochkorbayev. The *'gazet-kisi'* – 'half-man, half-newspaper' as they dubbed Kochkorbayev on the farm – sat on the right hand of the director's desk, facing away from Boston, his brow furrowed – obviously not feeling himself – and periodically adjusting his tie, to affirm his importance. Kochkorbayev gave Boston an unfriendly, side-long glance. The farm director, Chotbaevich, could easily imagine what Kochkorbayev was thinking. Over the many years they had worked together he had come to know only too well the indestructible, immutable and thoroughly ingrained logic of the demagogue; once again he was confronted by Boston Urkunchiev, whom he regarded as the new type of *kulak* and counter-revolutionary. No one worked harder than Boston, but the Partorg kept harping on his old tune: *kulaks* should be sent to Siberia, like in the old days . . .

The workers' committee meeting that day was also attended by a new official from the regional committee, a modest-looking young man and unfamiliar to the people on Berik farm. He listened attentively to all the speakers and noted everything in his notebook. Chotbaevich guessed that Kochkorbayev would not miss the opportunity to show his paces before the new official. He was not mistaken: after Boston's contribution Kochkorbayev asked for the floor, apparently to answer the previous speaker. He spoke exactly as if he were reading off his words: it was his great forte that he could address any subject exactly as if he were reading a newspaper article.

'If I might ask, comrade Urkunchiev,' he said to Boston, addressing him in his customary official manner, 'how much longer are you going to try and confuse people with your dubious proposals? The nature of production relations within a socialist collective has long since been determined by history itself. And now you want the shepherd to decide, as though he owned the farm, who he will and won't work with, who he's going to pay and how much. I ask you, what is this but an affront to history, to our revolutionary achievements? You attempt to subjugate politics to economics. You are arguing merely from the narrow interests of your own work unit. For you this is the first and only priority. But remember: behind your work unit stand the district, the region, the nation! What are you aiming at – the distortion of the socialist principles of management?'

Seething with rage Boston leapt to his feet.

'I'm not aiming at anything! I'm sick of talking about all this. It's none of my business as a shepherd what's going on somewhere in the province, or the nation, or the world come to that. There are enough smart-asses around without me. My business is my flock, my work unit as you call it. If the Partorg doesn't want to know what I think about my flock why do you summon me to these meetings, and not leave me to get on with my job? All this hot air isn't for me. Perhaps some people see the point of all this, but I certainly don't! Comrade director, don't summon me again! Leave me to get on with my work. I need these meetings like a hole in the head!'

'Come on, Boston, what's all this?' Chotbaevich felt distinctly uneasy. 'You're a model worker, best shepherd on the farm, a man of experience, we need your opinion about things. That's why we call you.'

'You surprise me, director.' Boston was really losing his temper now. 'If I am a model worker, then you of all people, director, must know what it's cost me. So why don't you say so? I only have to open my mouth and Kochkorbayev butts in, afraid that I might get a word in edgeways, picking and poking away, just like a lawyer, and all you can do, director, is sit there with your mouth shut as if it's all no business of yours.'

'Stop, stop,' interrupted Chotbaevich.

The director was clearly alarmed; he found himself in a very awkward situation – this time he had failed to keep the peace between Boston and Kochkorbayev. In the presence of the higher official he was forced, as director, to take sides. But he was very loath to tussle with Kochkorbayev, the man-cum-newspaper, who had formidable forces at his demagogic beck and call, for Kochkorbayev was by no means the last link in that pedantic chain of command. On this occasion Kochkorbayev had deliberately stirred up the discussion, casually accusing a shepherd of, no more nor less, 'an affront to our revolutionary achievements' – and who would dare raise his voice against him after that? Some way had to be found out of the impasse.

'Just wait, Boske, don't get so heated,' said the director, rising from his chair. 'Let's try and work this out, comrades,' he continued, feverishly wondering how to reconcile the two sides. Of course Boston was right, but Kochkorbayev was not a man to trifle with. What could he do? 'Now, where exactly is the problem?' reasoned the director. 'The shepherd, as I see it, wants to be the master of his own flock and land, and not a hireling, and he's speaking not only for himself but for his whole team and the other shepherds and their families. As I see it there's some sense in what he says. The shepherd's team is our smallest economic unit. This is where we have to begin. If I understand right, Urkunchiev wants to take everything into his own hands, the animals, the pastures, the feed and the buildings – in other words everything which is necessary for production. He's arguing that the team should be accountable, that everybody in it should know how much he'll earn if he works for his own profit and not for someone else's. That's how I see Urkunchiev's argument, and we would do well to listen to it, Djantai Ishanovich,' said Chotbaevich, addressing the Partorg.

'Whereas I, as Partorg of the state farm under your and my management, comrade Chotbaevich, take the view that encouraging the idea of private enterprise ill becomes anyone, and most especially the manager of a farm,' came Kochkorbayev's rebuke, with a note of triumph in his voice.

'But you must realize that it's being proposed for the good of our cause,' the director tried to justify himself. 'After all, young people these days won't join the shepherds' teams . . .'

'That means you're not carrying out an extensive mass popularization programme. You must remind young people about the Komsomol hero Pavlik Morozov and his Kirghiz counterpart Kychan Kjakypov, who were prepared to inform on their parents rather than compromise their ideals.'

'Now that's your department, comrade Kochkorbayev,' interjected the director. 'You hold all the cards. You do the reminding, you go and popularize. Nobody's stopping you.'

'Don't worry, I will,' said the Partorg defiantly. 'We've mapped out a whole series of popularization measures. But it's vital to nip any ideas of private enterprise in the bud, however cleverly they may be disguised. We will not allow the foundations of socialism to be undermined.'

Deeply despondent, Boston listened to this polemic, conducted in full seriousness. Despite himself he felt a cold rush of fear, yet he had only said that for once in his life he wanted to work the land according to his own beliefs and not under instructions from someone else.

'We make no exceptions or concessions for anyone,' continued Kochkorbayev. 'The socialist forms of production are compulsory for all. My words are intended primarily for comrade Urkunchiev. He seems to think that he's special, and wants special conditions.'

'I don't want to be made an exception,' protested Boston. 'Everyone needs what you call "special conditions"! Then we'll really start to work efficiently.'

'I doubt it! Anyway, what gives you the right to start dictating conditions? Do this, do that. As if it isn't enough that you, comrade Urkunchiev, in your rush to get private grazing lands for your flocks, caused the death of a man on the Ala-Mongyu pass. Doesn't that suffice?'

'That's all I needed!' retorted Boston with an angry flourish. He felt deeply hurt and offended that anyone could speak of the tragedy in this impersonal, off-hand way.

'What do you mean, "That's all I needed"? Am I not speaking the truth?' asked Kochkorbayev maliciously.

'No, you're not.'

'How can you say it's not true when Ernazar's corpse is lying in ice on the pass to this very day, and may lie there for another thousand years.'

Boston held his tongue. It was most unpalatable that they should be discussing this subject in their meeting. But Kochkorbayev would not leave it alone.

'Why don't you speak, comrade Urkunchiev?' he asked, pouring fat on to the fire. 'Is it not true that you were going to open up some new, private grazing just for yourself?'

'Yes, I was going for myself,' answered Boston curtly. 'But not only for myself, for everyone, including you, Kochkorbayev. Because I provided for your food and drink, you don't provide for mine. And now you're spitting in the well from which you drink!'

'What are you insinuating?' objected Kochkorbayev indignantly, his face flushing red. 'I owe my gratitude only to the Party!'

'So where do you think the Party gets the food from to feed you?' snapped Boston. 'From heaven?'

'What are you talking about? How dare you speak like that!' shouted Kochkorbayev, leaping to his feet, feverishly adjusting his tie.

Now a real row had developed. Kochkorbayev and Boston were both on their feet – the one by the table, the other by the wall – like condemned men. It looked as if at any moment one of them might crumple on the floor. The situation was slightly defused by the young official.

'Calm yourself, comrades,' he said, unexpectedly speaking up from the corner where he sat writing in his notebook. 'It seems to me that shepherd Urkunchiev is right in principle. The worker, as we are so fond of saying, the creator of our material welfare, has the right to voice his own opinion. Only was it necessary for him to take his ideas so far?'

'But you don't know him, comrade Mambetov,' Kochkorbayev chipped in swiftly. 'Urkunchiev has really gone over the top. Like the Noigutov business, for example. Recently another shepherd – yes, Bazarbai Noigutov – discovered a wolves' lair in the mountains. So he pulled out the entire litter, expropriated them, so to speak, that is to say he made a clean sweep of all four cubs, in order to liquidate the whole pack in the bud, so to speak. He acted in a right and proper manner. And what do you know? This Urkunchiev starts literally persecuting Noigutov. First he tries to bribe him, and when that trick doesn't work because Noigutov is a man of principle, Urkunchiev starts to threaten him, demanding that Noigutov puts the cubs back where he found them. Why? Presumably he wants the predators to breed and multiply! What do you make of that? Could it be, comrade Urkunchiev, that on top of all your other activities you also wanted to breed your own private wolves? Your own personal, exclusive wolves, so to speak? Perhaps you would like the state farm to provide you with wolves? First your own land, and your own sheep, then your own wolves! Is that it? Let's have lots of wolves, after all, when they kill our sheep it's only public property.'

By this stage Boston had regained control of himself and he calmly replied, 'What you say about the wolves is quite true, only the problem for the wolves is that they don't know it's public property they're attacking.'

Despite themselves his listeners all laughed and Boston made use of the interruption to continue.

'It's not wolves we should be talking about here, but seeing as we've started this conversation, I'd better have my say. In any event, let's be reasonable about it, that's what we were given brains for. It seems that some of us are lacking in reason, though they make up for it in hot air. Take the business with the wolves, for instance. As you've already been told, Bazarbai grabbed those cubs, or, to put it bluntly, he stole them from their lair, and there was such a fuss made of him – anyone would think he'd done something heroic. Unfortunately, our hero didn't think that first he should have tracked down the parents of those cubs, and shot them, the adult wolves, first. Then he could start thinking about what to do with the cubs. He was in too much of a hurry to sell the cubs and spend the money on drink. Why I asked Bazarbai to give me the cubs or sell them to me was so that I could use them to lure the she-wolf and her mate into a trap, because you don't want crazed wolves running around loose after their lair has been robbed. You must remember that a crazed wolf is worse than a dozen ordinary wolves. It'll never calm down until it gets its revenge. All the shepherds know what those wolves are like now, the ones whose cubs were taken, Akbara and Tash-Chainar we call them, a vicious pair. They won't be pacified now, they'll even attack humans, they're quite capable of it. People who do things like that are called "provocateurs" – I've read the word in the papers and in books. That's just what Bazarbai is: he's a provocateur, he provoked the wolves like a coward and a provocateur. And let me say it to you, Partorg, let me say it to your face: I can't figure out what sort of a man you are. You've been all these years on our farm and still all you know is reading your newspapers and threatening the shepherds like me, telling us we're going against the revolution and against the Soviet government, and meanwhile you don't understand the first thing about farming or else you wouldn't start accusing me of wanting wolves to breed and multiply. To hell with the wolves – your accusation is enough to make a chicken laugh. But you made another accusation, comrade Kochkorbayev, and I won't let you get away with that one. Yes, Ernazar was killed on the pass. But why did he and I make that trip? Not for fun, let me tell you! Do you think, Partorg, we would have set off across the pass, risking our necks, if we didn't have such a desperate shortage of grazing land? A shortage that's getting more acute with every day that passes? The director's sitting right there: let him tell you what it was like when he took over the farm, what the grass was like then, and the grazing, and the land! Look at it now! Nothing but dust and dry earth, the blades of grass so sparse you could count them, and all because they run ten times more head of sheep on the land than it can sustain, and the animals rip it up with their hooves. That's why Ernazar and I headed off to Kichibel. We had the best of intentions, but luck was not on our side. Our expedition ended in tragedy. With that, I scrapped the whole idea and shut my mouth about it. The tragedy forced me to hold my peace. My heart wasn't in it any more. But if things had turned out differently I would have travelled to Moscow the same year, to the Exhibition. I would have gone to see our leaders and I would have told them all about you, Kochkorbayev. You strut about bragging that you think only of the Party, but does the Party really need characters like you, who only get off your butt to tie other people's hands and stop them from working?'

'Now you've gone too far!' exploded Kochkorbayev. 'That's slander! You will be made to answer for those words, Urkun-chiev, through the Party's disciplinary procedures.'

'I'll be very pleased to answer for my views at a Party meeting. And if I really am doing something wrong or not thinking on the right lines, then you can turn me out of the Party and you need not think twice about it. But look out for yourself, too, Kochkorbayev.'

'I've nothing to look out for, comrade Urkunchiev. My conscience is clear. I am always with the Party.'

Boston took a deep breath, as if he were about to run up hill, and said, addressing the new official, 'And I sincerely hope that our new comrade will report all this to his committee. Let them call us to a Party meeting and sort it all out. I'm not prepared to carry on like this.'

Soon Boston Urkunchiev discovered to his cost that his squabble with Kochkorbayev had been inflated out of all proportion. Later that same day he travelled to the lake to attend to some business. The fruit trees around Issyk-Kul were all in bud. Spring was drawing to a close and Boston still had not had a chance to spray the apple trees in their orchard by Ernazar's old house. Boston and Gulyumkan now had two houses and two plots, and they both suffered from neglect. This was because a shepherd spends his life in the mountains and never has the time to do all the chores round the house and garden. He keeps putting things off, and before he realizes – it's too late, and the seasons have moved on. Be that as it may, he still had to do the spraying, or else the pests would multiply at an astonishing rate, infesting all the buds and ruining his crop. On this occasion Gulyumkan had finally blown her top at Boston: he was always behind, why didn't he go in good time to one of the neighbours, and arrange for them to do it, as he never had any time himself? Let the neighbours do it for them – and be paid for it.

'What use are you around the house?' scolded Gulyumkan. 'Day and night you're traipsing about with your flocks or sitting at meetings. If you can't look after your own orchard, sit here with Kenjesh for the day – you can't let that little rascal out of your sight for an instant – and I'll go down to the lake and do everything the master of the house and home is supposed to do.'

Gulyumkan was quite right, and there was nothing he could say, he had to sit and listen to her in silence. And so early that morning Boston set off to the lake, to get to work in his orchard. He rode Donkulyuk. As old people will tell you, in spring the grass gains new strength and with it so do the horses. In addition Donkulyuk was in his very prime: his eyes blazed with a fiery gleam as he tossed his mane, eager to break into a headlong gallop. Boston was in no mood for galloping. He reined in his frisky horse, for he wanted to ride along quietly, thinking things over. The previous night he had slept badly, tossing and turning, unable to forget how the Partorg had accused him of causing Ernazar's death. When he returned home from the meeting he briefly put his wife in the picture, but he kept the accusation to himself. He did not wish to dredge up unnecessarily Gulyumkan's memories of her late husband, for all that many years had passed since his death, since inevitably the talk would be distressing to both of them, reminding them how Ernazar lay unburied in the Ala-Mongyu pass, frozen for ever into the ice at the bottom of that terrible, benighted abyss. Better say nothing about the accusation. No sooner had Boston dropped off than the wolves were there again. Once again they took up their position on the rise behind the camp and Akbara gave voice, lamenting her stolen cubs. Tash-Chainar accompanied her in his visceral bass. If before Boston had been filled with pity for the wolves as he listened to their howling, and had sympathized with them in their distress, now he brimmed with anger, and wanted to go out and kill these importunate pests, to put an end once and for all to their wailing and to the terrible curse which had been visited upon his innocent head. As he listened to them he firmly resolved to destroy the wolves at any cost, and even devised a plan of how to do it. To make matters worse, while he was at the meeting arguing with Kochkorbayev, Akbara and Tash-Chainar killed three sheep from his flock. The herdboy told him afterwards how the wolves had come right up to the flock and no amount of shouting or waving his stick had frightened them away; then they had attacked and killed three sheep and disappeared. This news threw Boston into a terrible rage. If it carried on like that, he thought, they would have no option but to pack up and go, to admit shameful defeat to the wolves. Akbara and Tash-Chainar did not realize that with their interminable howling that night they were signing their own death warrants. Now Boston knew exactly what he had to do, and he would have been prepared to set his plan into action without any delay, if it were not for the trip he had to make down to the lake the following morning. He decided to stick to his promise: first he would sort out the orchard and pacify Gulyumkan, then he would deal with the wolves.

In a single day he organized the spraying and dug over the soil, packed hard after the long winter. He managed to find a hard-working youngster in the village whom he hired to get through the work as quickly as possible. Boston promised him one of the lambs from his black sheep.

When they finished Boston decided to go and buy Kenjesh a new toy. He wanted to give the boy a surprise. Kenjesh was such a fine little chap now, running round the house, and he would be turning two in a few weeks. With old age approaching Boston was constantly delighted by the antics of his bright little son. Each new word uttered by the boy entranced his old father. It was his birth that gave Boston's life a profound and sacred meaning, as revealed in his attachment to the child and to its mother. Now he knew why he had been born on earth. He wanted to love his wife and child, and beyond that he asked for nothing from life, for was this not the greatest joy that a man can wish for? He never spoke of it, but within himself he knew it to be so. He believed that his wife shared his feelings.

Boston dismounted beside the local general dealer's, the Madaniyat, went inside and bought a clockwork frog, a funny little thing with bulging eyes – that was sure to make the boy laugh! As he came out he was about to remount when suddenly he felt a pang of hunger and realized that he had not eaten since morning. There was a canteen right next to the shop, and to his eternal misfortune, Boston decided to drop in. No sooner had he entered the dimly lit room, rancid with the smell of the cheap food which was served here to truck drivers, and sat down at a table near the entrance, than he heard behind him Bazarbai's voice. Boston did not look round – he knew without looking that Noigutov was carousing with his cronies. Here he sits in the middle of the day drinking with all these hangers-on, and doesn't give a damn! The man has no conscience, thought Boston contemptuously. He wanted to get up and away from the man, but then he thought again: Why should he? Why the hell should he leave without eating first? He ordered borscht and meatballs, expecting that by now Bazarbai would have been informed that Boston was sitting in the corner. Suddenly there was a hostile silence behind him, and then the din started up again. Soon one of Bazarbai's cronies was sent across to Boston, a local barfly and scandal-monger known as Kor-Samat, or 'Crooked Samat', who had had an eye punched out in a fight when still a boy. 'Salaam, Boston, salaam!' Samat held out his hand to Boston with a telling leer. There was nothing to be done – he had to shake it. 'What are you doing sitting here on your own?' he said. 'Bazarbai and me are sitting over there. We haven't seen each other for ages, having a little get-together. Come and join us. Bazarbai sent me to ask you.'

'Tell him I'm in a hurry,' said Boston, trying to keep his cool. 'I'll just eat up and then I'll be off back to the mountains.'

'What's the hurry – your mountains will still be there a bit later!'

'No thanks, I'm busy.'

'You're making a mistake, you'll see,' warned Kor-Samat and walked away.

Next Bazarbai himself came over, visibly the worse for wear, his other hangers-on following behind.

'Turning his nose up, hey? We invite you over like a decent citizen, and what do you do? Aren't we good enough for you then?' sniped Bazarbai without further ado.

'I said I'm busy,' retorted Boston calmly, and started demon-stratively to slurp his borscht, a swill he would have aban-doned after one spoonful on any other occasion.

'I've a bone to pick with you,' said Bazarbai and brazenly sat down opposite Boston.

The others stood around waiting for the fun to start.

'What business could you have with me?' asked Boston.

Bazarbai frowned and shook his head. 'We should at least have a little talk about those wolf cubs, Boston.'

'We've already talked about them, is there anything left to say?'

'There is indeed.'

'Not in my opinion there isn't. Now don't disturb me. I'll finish my meal and be on my way.'

'What's the hurry, you dog?' Bazarbai stood up abruptly and bent over, thrusting his face, twisted with hatred, into Boston's. 'What's your hurry, bastard? We still have to talk about the wolves. Who was it who called me a "provocateur" at a public meeting, in the director's office? Who said that I caused the wolves to go mad? You think I don't know who the real provocateur is? You think I'm a dirty fascist and you're the only honest man among us?'

Boston had also risen to his feet. They now stood eyeball to eyeball.

'Stop talking nonsense,' said Boston, not mincing his words. 'I never called you a fascist – I should have, but I didn't. As for you being a provocateur and a witless scab – that's quite true. I've said it before, and I'll say it now. But I'd be happier if you went back to your table and got off my back.'

'Don't you be telling me where to go and what to do!' snapped Bazarbai in real anger now. 'You've got no authority over me. I spit on you. All right, so you reckon I'm a provocateur, but who do you think you are? You reckon you got away with killing Ernazar, doing it on the sly? You swine, you'd already sniffed out his wife, while Ernazar was still alive, and your old woman was about to peg. So you decided to heave Ernazar into the crevasse on the pass, and to marry his bitch Gulyumkan. You try and prove it wasn't like that. Why was it Ernazar and not you who fell into the crevasse? You were following the same track. You think nobody's rumbled you! But he's the one who died, and you're still alive. So what does that make you, you and your bitch Gulyumkan? Ernazar's lying under the pass, frozen into the ice, without even a decent grave, and you've got your dirty hands on his shameless wife, you filthy swine. You're sitting pretty, got her just where you want her! And a member of the Party too! They should strip you of your membership. Some model worker we have here, a real Stakhanovite! You should be inside!'

It was all Boston could do not to throw himself at Bazarbai and pound his ugly mug to pulp. Bazarbai was obviously goading him into a fight, hoping for a real show-down, a fight to the death. But he held himself in check, clenching his jaw, and said to Bazarbai, now breathless with fury, 'I have nothing to discuss with you. Your words mean nothing to me. And I shan't sink to your level. You can think and say just what you like about me. But now get out of my way. Hey, lad,' he called the waiter, 'take this.' He handed him a five rouble note and walked off without another word.

Bazarbai grabbed his sleeve.

'Just you wait! No need to hurry back to your bitch! Maybe she's humping another shepherd while the boss is out, you don't want to disturb them!'

Boston snatched up an empty wine bottle from the next table.

'Take your hands off me!' he hissed quietly, fixing his eye on Bazarbai, who suddenly blanched. 'I won't say it again, take your hands off me! You hear?' he warned, brandishing the heavy, dark green bottle.

With the bottle clenched firmly in his hand, Boston walked out into the road. It was only after he had leapt into the saddle that he came to his senses, tossed the bottle into the ditch and gave Donkulyuk his lead. It was ages since he had really let rip like this, and the wild gallop helped him recover his composure. When he calmed down he realized with a shock how very close he had come to committing murder. By the grace of God he had stopped short just in time, or else he would have split open that odious Bazarbai's ugly skull. Some workers travelling in the opposite direction on a tractor-drawn trailer watched him pass in amazement: Boston, such a sober, respectable man, and galloping like a harebrained youth! It was some time before Boston worked off his fury, and he finally regained his full composure after taking a deep draught of icy water from a brook. He rode on at a sedate walk, still relieved that he had avoided committing a murder.

However, as he rode and relived the whole scene he grew morose again. Then he remembered that he had left Kenjesh's present, the toy frog – and such a funny toy with its bulgy eyes and big mouth – on the windowsill in the canteen, and he felt thoroughly aggrieved. Of course, it was not particularly expensive and he could easily buy the boy a toy on some other occasion, in the same shop if need be, but for some reason this oversight struck him as a bad omen. He should not on any account have forgotten a present specially bought for his boy. But he had forgotten it . . .

He was annoyed at himself for being superstitious, but wondered how he could counter this undesirable course of events. Then he set to planning how he would set a trap for the wolves and shoot the cursed beasts, so that he would never hear or smell them near him again. He felt choked with rage. What an evil curse, he thought, even his row with Bazarbai in the canteen, which almost ended in an act of murder, had started with an argument about these same wolves . . .

Boston decided to carry out his plan the very next day. During the night he thought out all the details of the operation, and for perhaps the first time in their life together he concealed a project of this importance from his wife. Boston was loath to talk at all about the wolves and the cubs, who had in their turn caused his row with Bazarbai; nor did he want to discuss anything which could bring reminders of Ernazar's death on the pass. For this reason he was uncommunicative at home that evening, playing with his little son and giving monosyllabic answers to Gulyumkan's questions. He knew that his silence would disturb his wife, and make her puzzled, but it was the only thing he could do. He realized only too well that his altercation with Bazarbai and the ugly row that had erupted around them would sooner or later come to her ears. But for the time being he preferred to keep silent – he had no wish to repeat to her the words of that pig Bazarbai, it was all too vile and revolting.

He also considered how many hardships Gulyumkan and he had had to face together. Ever since they had become man and wife they had encountered so much concealed ill-will and open hostility in other people, and so much slander had circulated about them. Yet Boston never regretted having tied up his fate with that of Ernazar's widow. He even found it hard to imagine now how he had ever lived without her, he needed to feel her presence constantly beside him . . . No, life without her would have been nothing in comparison. His life could only be together with her, and even if on occasion she could be cross with him, even unjustly so, she was still quite devoted to him, and this was what mattered. This was something they never discussed, and it went without saying. If anyone had asked Boston what his little son meant to him, that fidgety little scamp who could only speak a few words, that smiling, bright-eyed busy bee on his chubby little legs, his last-born, Boston would have been at a loss for an answer. He would not have been able to find the right words. His feeling was greater than any words could contain, for in the boy he saw a divinely ordained, innocent, infant version of all that was best in himself . . .

In his heart of hearts he understood all this, and as he lay down that night beside his wife and child he grew quite calm, his anger subsided, and he felt kindly disposed towards the world again. He even thought that if the wolves did not appear that night he might put off his project, or perhaps abandon it altogether. All Boston wanted was peace and quiet . . .

But as if to spite him, the wolves appeared again around midnight. Once more Akbara took up her stance on the little rise behind the camp and set up her howling and moaning, and Tash-Chainar accompanied her in his low, wheezing bass. Once again Kenjesh awoke in terror and started to cry, while Gulyumkan muttered in her half-sleep, cursing their life which gave them no peace from these crazed wolves. Boston's anger rose again; he felt like charging out of the house and chasing those damned wolves to the end of the earth if he had to, and then he remembered again how he had been abused, insulted and humiliated at the hands of that vile and worthless Bazarbai, and he regretted not having cracked him over the head with the bottle. One swipe of that heavy bottle against Bazarbai's loathsome skull and that would have been the end of him. He wouldn't have regretted it for an instant, mused Boston; on the contrary, he would have rejoiced at finally squashing that odious insect disguised as a human being . . . And all the while the wolves continued to howl . . .

He had to take up his rifle again and go out at least to frighten them away. Instead of letting off only one or two shots, Boston fired five rounds one after the other, aiming into the murky night. Then he returned to the house, but could not get to sleep, so set about cleaning his rifle. He sat himself down in the corner of his other room and, leaning over his hunting rifle, cleaned it with close attention and a strange sense of urgency. As he busied himself with this task he considered again how best to deal with the wolves and decided to take immediate action the moment it started to get light.

All this time Akbara and Tash-Chainar, taking fright at the rifle shots, retreated into the ravine for the rest of the night. The rootless pair no longer had a permanent lair, and they spent the nights wherever they found themselves. As always, Akbara went ahead. Her coat was shaggy and untidy as they were due to moult soon, and she looked hideous in the darkness. Her eyes glowed with their phosphorescent gleam, her tongue dangled like that of a rabid dog. Never had her grief abated, the grief of a she-wolf bereft of her cubs. Some instinct continued to tell her that the cubs were somewhere in Boston's Koshara – there was nowhere else they could be, for their kidnapper had taken refuge there when they pursued him on that ill-fated day. Her animal mind could reason no further than this. And so the wolves rampaged and massacred sheep all through the district, to satisfy not only their hunger but also their irrepressible and implacable urge to deaden and stifle that nagging feeling of rancour against the world with a terrible surfeit of meat and blood. Once they had eaten their fill of their victims the wolves would drift back to the spot where they had first lost the trail of their cubs. Akbara suffered most acutely – she was quite unable to contain her grief and simply could not accept her loss. Never a day passed without her returning to that place, never a day without her and Tash-Chainar pacing up and down near Boston's camp. Boston was counting on this pattern in his plan to destroy the wolves at any cost.

The following day Boston issued instructions for the flocks not to be driven out to pasture, but to be kept in the two sheds and given grain and watered from the drinking troughs in the yard. Meanwhile he selected from the flock some twenty ewes with spindly-legged lambs, choosing those with twins as far as possible, for the maximum of din and bleating, and he drove this small flock before him into a deserted area without any roads.

He took no one with him but walked alone, driving the flock forward with a long stick. Across his back he carried his gleaming and newly polished rifle, with a full clip of bullets. He walked along, taking his time, but careful to put as much space as possible between himself and his home.

It was a warm day, real spring weather. The mountains soaked in the warmth of the sun, transforming it into the lush green grass that grew on the mounds and in the hollows. An occasional wisp of pure white cloud floated serenely across the brilliant azure sky. Larks sang and he heard the mating call of the mountain grouse from behind the rocks. It was paradise on earth, and only the mighty snow-covered peaks, looming up along the horizon, ominous with the menace of sudden blizzards, and the dark stormclouds chased across the sky by fierce winds which threatened at any moment to eclipse the sun, served as a reminder that this paradise was transient. For the moment there was no reason to suspect that the weather would turn. The small flock of ewes and lambs, emitting a constant chorus of bleating, headed obediently before their shepherd. The lambs frisked together, nosing up to their mothers to suck while they walked. Since the previous night Boston had been in sombre spirits. The more he thought about it the more he resented the wolves and Bazarbai, the culprit responsible for this entire awful business. He wanted nothing more to do with Bazarbai, calling to mind the proverb, Don't touch, and your hands will stay clean, but the wolves had to be destroyed, shot, eliminated – there was no other option. His plan was simple: the bleating of the ewes and lambs would be bound to attract the wolves and he would lie in wait for them. The wolves would attack the ewes with lambs and with a bit of luck he ought to be able to shoot them both. But, as they say, man proposes and God disposes . . . And that is how it turned out this time, too . . .

Until nearly noon the beasts showed no sign of themselves. Boston herded his sheep into a secluded and easily observable hollow, then lay down to wait on the edge, concealing himself with his rifle in among the rocks and sparse bushes. He was a good marksman, and had been a keen hunter since child-hood, with a good few Issyk-Kul wolves already to his credit, so had no reason to doubt his ability to shoot the wolves once he had lured them into his trap. The noisy ewes and lamb twins kept up their strident racket, bleating to one another,

293

but time was marching on and the beasts still had not put in an appearance. On other days they made their raids swiftly, venting their rage on the local flocks and always, as a rule, in broad daylight.

The heat of the sun beat down. Lying there on his jacket beneath the bushes Boston might, in different circumstances, have dozed off, but now he could not permit himself this luxury. In any case there was a weight pressing on his heart: it was hard for him to accept that anyone could accuse him of causing Ernazar's death. His enemies, Kochkorbayev and Bazarbai, had joined forces, and each in his own way was slandering and defaming him, feeling they had him cornered. He could not understand how life could be thus ordered: why should he be hated by two such totally different people? Added to which he had the problem of the wolves gnawing away at his heart. He no longer had any peace at home with them. God knows what would happen when his wife got to hear about his encounter with Bazarbai. The canteen had been full of people when Bazarbai had heaped vile abuse on his wife and him, and many of those onlookers had been ill-wishers . . .

Still the wolves did not come, and Boston's patience was starting to wear thin. Nevertheless, he sharpened his eyes and ears as he lay in wait on the alert. It was vital that he spot the beasts as early as possible, so he could get a shot at them before they had a chance to attack the sheep. To catch the moment when the wolves first appeared was no easy matter: domestic sheep have no sense of smell and their vision is fairly poor – in other words there's no more stupid and defenceless creature on God's earth. Sheep are the easiest possible prey for wolves, and only human beings are capable of protecting them from this terrible foe. For that reason wolves have only humans to fear, as now when Boston waited . . .

Even now the helpless sheep did not sense any danger. They grazed contentedly, breaking off only to attend to their bleating lambs, resignedly offering their teats, and showed no other concern. It was only Boston who was aware of any danger . . .

A pair of white-cheeked mountain magpies which had been busy nearby suddenly started chattering in alarm and darting from place to place. Boston pricked up his ears, cocked the trigger, but did not show himself; on the contrary, he hid even more carefully. When he moved he had to be certain of his quarry. He was prepared to sacrifice one or two sheep, if only to lure the animals into an open space. But the wolves appeared to have sensed the danger, scared off, perhaps, by the movements of the magpies. Be that as it may, the wolves did not pounce at once – afterwards it transpired that they had parted: Akbara crawled between the boulders and was creeping up from the far end, while Tash-Chainar approached from the opposite side (in fact he was creeping very close to the spot where Boston lay concealed with his rifle).

All this, however, did not come to light until later.

As he waited for the wolves to attack Boston gazed carefully all around him, but could not tell from which side the animals would strike. All around reigned complete silence: the sheep peacefully grazed, the lambs frolicked, the magpies had stopped their racket – all that could be heard was the babble of the mountain stream and the song of the birds in the bushes. Boston was tiring of this interminable waiting when suddenly a grey shadow flitted among the rocks and the sheep shied to one side, standing there frozen in terrified expectation. Boston was as taut as a guitar string: he knew that the wolves had deliberately frightened the herd in order to flush out the human who guarded them; in such an event any shepherd would raise havoc and rush over to his sheep. But Boston's scheme was somewhat different, and thus he remained where he was. Then the grey shadow flitted past the boulders again and with two powerful leaps Akbara had reached the panicking sheep. Boston raised his rifle, took aim and was on the point of squeezing the trigger when a faint rustle behind him caused him to wheel round. He fired point-blank at an enormous beast which was almost upon him. The bullet hit Tash-Chainar as he leapt, but did not fell him immediately. Fangs bared in a savage grimace, and talons spread before him, he was carried some distance, eyes glittering fiercely, by the momentum of his leap, until he collapsed dead in a heap less than half a yard away from Boston. It was all over in an instant. At once the shepherd swung back with his rifle, but he had missed his moment – Akbara had cut down one of the sheep and disappeared behind the rocks. Slinging the rifle across his shoulder Boston raced off in pursuit, hoping still to get a good shot at her, but as he emerged from the hollow Akbara was bounding away across the stream. He fired and missed . . .

Boston recovered his breath and looked dejectedly about him. In his agitation he was pale and breathing heavily. He had failed to achieve his main objective – Akbara had escaped. Now the she-wolf would be very hard to catch. Still, thought Boston, if he hadn't turned round in time to catch Tash-Chainar with his first bullet things might have been a good deal worse. As he mulled over the incident he realized that the animals had sensed danger as they approached the herd and deliberately separated. When Tash-Chainar saw their human foe threatening his mate, who was oblivious of the trap, he had hurled himself into the attack, mindless of the possible consequences . . .

Rounding up the panic-stricken sheep, Boston walked over to inspect the dead wolf. Tash-Chainar lay where he had landed, on his side, his huge yellow fangs bared and his eyes already glazed over. Boston reached out and touched his head – Tash-Chainar's massive head, fit for a horse – it was hard to imagine the animal could have carried such a weight – and his paws – Boston lifted them in his hand, feeling their weight and marvelling at the force that they had wielded. To think of the distance these paws had carried him, of the beasts they had pulled down!

After some hesitation Boston decided not to skin Tash-Chainar. To hell with the pelt, that was not what he'd been after. Especially since the she-wolf had escaped unharmed – he had no reason to celebrate.

Boston stood in reflection for a while longer, then threw the sheep slaughtered by Akbara over his shoulder and drove his flock home.

Later he returned to the spot with a spade and pick-axe, and spent the rest of the day digging a grave for Tash-Chainar. It took him a long time as the ground was hard and stony. At times he paused and listened in silence, looking carefully around, in case the she-wolf had decided to show herself. His trusty rifle lay beside him, within easy reach . . .

But Akbara returned only late at night . . . She lay beside the fresh mound of earth and remained there until daybreak, only to disappear with the first rays of the sun . . .

6

Spring was well under way, with even a hint of summer in the air. It was time for the shepherds to move with their flocks to the summer grazing grounds. Those who had wintered in the foothills now moved to the higher valleys and gorges, to the new mountain pastures, moving gradually nearer the passes. Those who had wintered in the lowlands, keeping their animals stalled, now released them into their reserve spring pastures. It was a busy time of year: the flocks had to be driven, domestic chattels transported and, toughest of all, the sheep had to be sheared; all these chores together meant a buzz of frenzied activity, compounded by the race to secure the best summer grazing for the flocks. Only Akbara was idle, unaffected by the activity seething around her. In a sense she had been forgotten: after Tash-Chainar's death she gave no sign of herself, and even stopped howling outside Boston's house at night.

Akbara now subsisted in a state of unrelieved anguish. She had become listless and apathetic – feeding on any small creatures who crossed her path and for most of the time moping wretchedly in some secluded spot. She ignored even the mass migration of flocks, with thousands of head of sheep being driven across the mountains, when it would have been an easy matter in all the confusion to slip in and carry off an unsuspecting lamb, or even a grown sheep.

Akbara was now indifferent to the world, was now confined to memories of the past. Resting her head on her paws she would lie for days on end, recalling her joyless and unhappy days in the Moyun-Kum savannah, in the Aldash steppes, and here, in the mountains round Lake Issyk-Kul. Time and again she remembered her past life, her daily routine with Tash-Chainar, and invariably – unable to endure the anguish of her memories – she would rise, prowl around dejectedly for a while and then resume her position, placing her now grizzled

head on her paws. Then she remembered her wolflings – the litter stolen from her not so long ago, the victims of the Moyun-Kum cull, and the cubs which had been burnt to death in the reedlands – but most of all she remembered her he-wolf, the faithful and mighty Tash-Chainar. At times she would remember too that strange man whom she had met in the fields of *anasha* – defenceless in his bare skin, he had wanted to play with her cubs, and when she hurled herself at him, ready to rip out his throat, he had crouched down in fright, shielding his head with his hands, and then run away from her without looking round . . . And then she had seen him again one dawn in the Moyun-Kum savannah, this time in early winter, crucified to a twisted *saxaul* tree. She remembered gazing into his familiar features, and how he had half opened his eyes, whispered something, and then fallen silent . . . Now all that past life seemed a dream, gone for ever, although the spark of hope never entirely died in Akbara's breast – there were moments when she believed that one day she would find again the lost cubs from her final litter. Then at night Akbara would creep up to Boston's winter camp, no longer to howl in her old heart-rending and menacing way, but listening carefully from afar, hoping the wind would carry back to her the yelps of her cubs, or their familiar, sweet smell. They would be half grown by now . . . If only such miracles were possible! How Akbara would have rushed to her adored cubs – fearing neither people nor dogs, she would have extricated her babies, freed them from captivity, and fled with them to untried lands where they could start anew in the wild and savage freedom that befits the life of a wolf.

For Boston it was a time of tedious chores. As it was he had enough to do with moving camp, added to which there was a lot of stupid bureaucratic nonsense to attend to. Kochkorbayev did after all submit a complaint, as he had threatened, to the higher authorities, and a commission was dispatched to ascertain the rights and wrongs of the case. The members of the commission could not agree among themselves. One group believed that the shepherd should be expelled from the Party forthwith, for personally insulting the Partorg and thereby injuring the prestige of the Party itself, while another maintained that this was quite unjustified as shepherd Boston

Urkunchiev had been acting in the interests of his job and his criticism was aimed at increasing productivity. Bazarbai Noigutov was also summoned before the commission. They received a written explanation from him about the wolf cubs, which Boston Urkunchiev had supposedly insisted he replace in the lair . . . In other words, they conducted the disciplinary enquiry strictly according to the rules . . .

Boston did not answer the following two summonses. He sent word that since he had yet to drive his flocks into the hills and decamp there with his entire family for the summer, time was getting short and they would therefore have to sort it out without him. He added that he was prepared to accept any punishment the commission might decide to impose, a concession which greatly delighted Kochkorbayev, as Boston's attitude suited his purpose perfectly.

Boston had no alternative. The migration to the summer pastures was already under way and Boston was not the sort of man to be late in making the move. He usually drove the sheep up the mountain on the first day, returning for his portable cabin and household chattels once the livestock was safely installed. On the second trip he drove the truck as far as it would go, proceeding from there in the way of his ancestors, hauling everything with pack animals. This was the easiest way to manage the move, and meant that the sheep spent less time on the road. He left assistants to watch over the flocks while he himself rode back to load up the truck and take the family into the mountains for the whole summer.

At last the fateful day arrived . . .

The night before, Akbara had returned to her old lair for the first time since Tash-Chainar's death. The lonely she-wolf had been avoiding the old lair beneath the overhang, but the day came when in her unbearable longing she suddenly felt the urge to follow that familiar track again and dart through the crack into the lair, just in case . . . The temptation was irresistible and she succumbed to self-deception.

Akbara ran like a demented creature, skimming the track, through water, over rocks, past the fires burning in the summer camps, past dogs barking frantically, and as she ran shots rang out behind her . . .

Alone and crazed with longing she ran through the moun-

tains beneath a moon high in the night sky . . . When finally she reached the lair, she found the entrance so choked with new growths of grass and berberis that she hardly recognized where she was. Suddenly her courage failed her. She lacked the strength to fight, to force herself on . . . So once again Akbara turned to Byuri-Ana, the goddess of wolves, and long did she wail and whimper, lamenting her ill-starred fate, and implore the goddess to take her to herself in the moon, where there are no humans . . .

That night Boston was returning to the winter camp after driving his flocks to their new pastures. He could of course have waited until morning and set off then, arriving home only the next evening and losing a whole day in the process, something he could not afford. Furthermore, there was hardly anyone left at the winter camp besides Gulyumkan and the boy and one other family, also waiting their turn to be transported by truck to the summer camp, and there were no men at all.

Boston was therefore in a particular hurry that night, urging on his Donkulyuk, who moved quickly and with a confident stride. He was making good time, and was pleased with himself. Donkulyuk sped through the night, his golden ears and mane gleaming in the moonlight and the taut muscles on his rump rippling like the surface of water at night. The weather was neither hot nor cold, with the scent of grass in the air. Boston's rifle hung across his back: no knowing what might happen at night in the mountains. Once he was back home again he would hang the gun in its place, unloaded, and with it a full clip of five rounds.

Boston reckoned on reaching his camp by daybreak, towards five o'clock, and by all the signs this was likely to be the case. During his night ride he was aware again of the strength of the ties which bound him to his wife and son: only a day apart and he was already missing them. What worried him most as he rode was that Akbara might start prowling around their hut and set up her fearful howling, terrifying both Gulyumkan and Kenjesh. Boston had to keep reminding himself that the she-wolf had stopped her visits since the death of her mate, or at least was no longer to be heard. There was no particular reason for concern.

As he rode, Akbara crouched in the Bashat gorge and wailed her lament to Byuri-Ana by her old lair. Even if she visited Boston's camp she would not have bothered anyone – after Tash-Chainar's death she did no more than listen dolefully to the voices that wafted across to her from the human settlement. Finally that fateful day arrived . . .

By the time Boston woke the sun had climbed high in the sky: having arrived at the first light he had slept for about four hours. He would have slept longer but his little son roused him. Despite all Gulyumkan's efforts to keep Kenjesh away from his father that morning the moment came when, busy with packing, she took her eye off the boy for a moment and Kenjesh, chattering to himself, tapped his father smartly on the cheek. Boston opened his eyes grinning and gave Kenjesh a hug, aware of a surge of tenderness towards the child. He was so happy to see the boy, his own flesh and blood, growing up so healthy and active, proving at less than two years of age to be so bright and showing that he loved his parents. In his looks and character he was like his daddy, except that his gleaming eyes, as bright as two blackcurrants, were his mother's. The boy was a favourite with everyone, and as he gazed at him Boston could not but feel proud to have such a delightful son.

'What is it, son? Time for me to get up? All right, pull me up! Pull my hand, there's a good boy! Ooh, what strength! And now give me a big hug!'

Meanwhile Gulyumkan had brewed up her husband's favourite drink, a thick Kalmyck tea with roast poppy seeds, milk and salt, and since not only the flocks but all the livestock, even the dogs, were far away in the mountains the Urkunchievs were able for once in their lives to enjoy their tea in peace and quiet, without any interference. Few people can realize how rare such relaxation is for the shepherd and his family. His animals require constant attention, day and night, every day of the year, and when the flock is one thousand strong, or fifteen hundred counting the new-born lambs, such carefree mornings are beyond the dreams of a shepherd's family. They sat there relishing their inactivity before getting down to the business of packing up for the entire summer. The truck was expected by midday, and by that time all their household effects had to be ready.

'My, it's too good to be true,' repeated Gulyumkan. 'Such bliss, such peace and quiet! I don't know about you, but I don't want to leave. Let's just stay here. Kenjesh, tell your daddy that we're not going.'

Little Kenjesh babbled some nonsense, climbing first into his father's lap, then his mother's, and Boston good-humouredly agreed with his wife.

'Good idea! Let's stay here all summer!'

'You say that now,' laughed Gulyumkan, 'but after one day you'd run off back to your flocks so fast that even Donkulyuk couldn't catch you!'

'Quite right!' replied Boston contentedly, and stroked his bristly moustache, a sign of contentment.

They drank their tea sitting on the floor at a low, round table and the boy scampered around them. The adults wanted to feed him, but the youngster was particularly mischievous that morning, running around and playing pranks. It was impossible to get him to sit down and eat. The doors were thrown wide open – it would have been too hot with them shut – and Kenjesh periodically darted outside, running round the yard, chasing the fluffy young chicks that foraged on the ground round their mother hen. The hen belonged to their neighbour, the nightwatchman Kudurmat. Kudurmat himself had already moved to the summer camp, while his wife Asylgul planned to travel in the truck with the Urkunchievs. She had already popped in to see them, telling them that she was ready except for putting the hen and her chicks in a basket, but she would be able to do that when the truck came. For the time being she planned to do some washing. The morning passed, and soon the noonday sun was beating down. Everyone was busy. Boston and his wife were tying bundles and wrapping up crockery. Asylgul was doing her washing, emptying her basin of soapy water out of the door at intervals. Little Kenjesh was left to his own devices, and he ran in and out of the house and chased the chickens.

Meanwhile the mother hen led her chicks away from the house and round the corner, where they could scratch undisturbed in the ground. The boy pursued the chickens and, unnoticed by the adults, they ended up behind the window-less wall of the barn. Here, in among the burdock and sorrel plants, it was quiet and summery. The chicks cheeped noisily as they pecked in the rubbish and Kenjesh laughed softly as he chatted to the chickens and tried to stroke them. The hen was not in the least afraid of Kenjesh, but when a large grey dog suddenly appeared close at hand, stalking quietly towards them, she squawked angrily and led her chicks away. Kenjesh, however, showed no fear of the big grey dog with its funny dark blue eyes. She gazed meekly at the small boy, wagging her tail in friendly greeting. It was Akbara, who had been prowling round Boston's camp for some time that morning.

The wolf had dared to approach so close to human habitation because since the previous night the yard had been deserted, with no sight or sound of humans or dogs. Propelled forward by her unabating maternal grief and undying hope, she cautiously made the rounds of all the sheds, stalls and feeding pens, and finding no trace of her lost cubs she stalked right up to the humans' huts. Now Akbara stood face to face with the child. We cannot know what told her that this too was a child, a man cub, just like any of her own cubs, but born of man. When he stretched his hand out to stroke the nice doggy, Akbara's heart, already softened with grief, began to flutter. She walked up to him and licked his cheek. The boy was delighted at her caresses and, laughing softly, put his arms round the animal's neck. At this Akbara felt an onrush of tenderness, and lying down at his feet she offered to play – she longed for him to suck her teats, but instead he sat on her back to ride her like a horse. Then he jumped off and called her to him – 'Jur, jur! Let's go!' – with peals of happy laughter, but Akbara dared go no further, she knew that there were humans there. Remaining where she was the wolf gazed sadly at the little boy with her deep blue eyes, and he went up to her again and stroked her head, at which Akbara licked him all over, something he found the greatest fun. The she-wolf lavished on him all her pent-up tenderness, and breathed deeply of his own child's breath. How wonderful it would be, she thought, if this little man cub could live in her lair beneath the overhang.

Taking great care not to scratch his neck the wolf seized the lad by the collar of his coat and, with a sharp toss of her head, threw him across the nape of her neck, in the way that wolves carry off lambs from their flocks.

The boy uttered a piercing shriek, short and sharp, like a wounded hare. The nightwatchman's wife Asylgul, who was about to hang out her washing, rushed up to the barn on hearing Kenjesh's cry, looked round the wall in horror and, throwing the clothes on the ground, ran to Boston's hut.

'A wolf! A wolf has taken the child! Come quickly, quickly!'

Boston snatched his rifle hastily from the wall and hurtled forth from the hut, followed by Gulyumkan.

'There! Over there! There's Kenjesh! The she-wolf's carrying him off!' wailed Asylgul, clutching her head in horror.

'Stop! Stop, Akbara! Stop, I tell you!' shouted Boston with all the force of his lungs, and raced in pursuit of the wolf.

Akbara quickened her pace. Boston charged after her, brandishing his rifle and shouting in a voice that was distorted with panic, 'Leave him, Akbara! Leave my son! I'll never touch your kind again! Leave him, drop the boy! Akbara! Listen to me, Akbara!'

He forgot that words meant absolutely nothing to the she-wolf. His shouting and running in pursuit only frightened her, causing her to run the faster. But Boston continued to shout and chase her.

'Akbara! Leave my son, Akbara!' he implored.

A short distance behind ran Gulyumkan and Asylgul, wailing and keening in despair.

'Shoot! Quickly, shoot!' shouted Gulyumkan, though Boston could not shoot so long as the wolf was carrying the child on her back.

The shouting and panic behind her only spurred Akbara on, inflaming her wolf's instincts and strengthening her resolve not to release her quarry. Holding the boy in a mortal grip by the scruff of his neck, she ran determinedly forward into the mountains, and even when a shot resounded behind her and a bullet whistled past above her head she still did not drop her burden. The boy continued to cry, calling for his father and mother. Again Boston fired into the air, not knowing how else to frighten off the wolf, but the second shot, too, failed to scare her. Akbara retreated further in the direction of the screes where she would have no trouble throwing her pursuers off her trail and concealing herself from view. Boston was beginning to despair. How could he save the child now? What could he do? What had he done to deserve this monstrous punishment?

'Drop the boy, Akbara! Drop him, I beg you, leave our son alone!' he implored the kidnapper, panting and wheezing, like an overridden horse.

Boston fired into the air for the third time, and again the bullet whistled over the beast's head. The screes were getting closer and closer. Boston had only two rounds of ammunition left, and realizing that in another minute he would lose his last chance to rescue the child he decided to fire at the wolf. Dropping straight from a run on to one knee he took aim, his sights pointing at the legs, and only the legs. How could he ever aim straight? His chest heaved and his hands shook, refusing to obey him. He made a supreme effort to muster all his strength and, watching through the shaking slit of the gunsight the undulating motion of the wolf's stride, for she ran as if swimming through stormy waves, he aimed and squeezed the trigger. Missed. The bullet kicked up a puff of dust and passed beneath the wolf. Boston reloaded, packing the last round into the chamber, took aim again and without even hearing his own shot saw the wolf leap up and then collapse on its side.

Shouldering his rifle Boston hurtled forward to the wolf as if in a dream. He felt as though he were running in slow motion, floating slowly across a vast empty space . . .

Finally he reached the wolf and the world went cold, as if a hard frost had hit him. He hunched forward and tottered on his feet, his face twisted in a soundless cry. Akbara was still alive, but beside her his child lay lifeless, a bullet through his heart.

Suddenly, after all the commotion, the world around him froze, then faded and vanished altogether, its place filled by a raging, fiery darkness. Unable to believe his eyes, Boston bent over the body of his son, stained with its own crimson blood, lifted it slowly from the ground and pressed it to his own breast, then stumbled back, marvelling for some reason at the deep blue eyes of the dying wolf. Then he turned about and, numb with grief, moved towards the women who were running to meet him.

His wife seemed to grow larger as she ran, until finally a giant female form strode towards him with an enormous disfigured face and enormous distorted arms stretching out towards him.

He stumbled along like a blind man, pressing the body of the child to him. Behind him staggered Gulyumkan, wailing and keening, supported by the arm of her neighbour.

Deafened by his own grief, Boston heard nothing of this. Suddenly the noise of the real world broke through and submerged him, like the thunder of a waterfall, and he realized what had happened. Lifting his eyes to heaven he called out in a terrible voice: 'Why? What are you punishing me for?'

At home he placed the child's body in his cot, which stood ready for loading on to the lorry, and Gulyumkan threw herself at the head of the bed and wailed exactly as Akbara had wailed through those many long nights . . . Beside her on the floor sat Asylgul . . .

Boston now walked out of the house, taking his rifle with him. He fitted one cartridge clip to the magazine and stuck the other in his pocket, just as if going into battle. Then he threw a saddle on to Donkulyuk, leapt astride the horse and rode off, without a word to his wife or to Asylgul . . .

Once he had ridden some distance from the camp he gave the animal its head and the golden stallion galloped along the track to Taman.

He found his man easily, although he was prepared if necessary to leave no stone unturned and drag him back from the ends of the earth.

In Bazarbai Noigutov's yard, loading operations were also in progress: they too were dispatching their household goods to the summer camp. Occupied in this way, the men did not notice Boston appear outside the enclosure, then dismount, remove his rifle, reload it and remove the safety catch. They noticed him only when he came up to where they were working. Bazarbai leapt down from the truck and stared at him in astonishment. 'What do you want?' he asked, alarmed by the look in Boston's eyes. 'What are you doing here? What are you staring at?' he added with rising alarm, sensing that something was seriously amiss. 'About the wolves again, is it? Haven't you got anything better to do? They've questioned me at length about all that. I've made a written statement.'

'I don't give a damn what you've written,' retorted Boston menacingly, keeping his eyes fixed darkly on his enemy's. 'I'm not interested in that any more. I've come to tell you that scum like you should be wiped off the face of this earth, and I'm going to do it myself.'

Bazarbai did not even have time to duck. Boston raised his weapon and fired at point-blank range. Bazarbai staggered, as if to take cover behind the truck, but a second bullet caught him in the back and, spinning round three times, he cracked his head against the body of the truck and slid to the ground, scratching convulsively at the earth. It was so sudden that at first no one moved from where he stood. Only when the unfortunate Kok-Tursun threw herself wailing on the body of her husband did the others all raise a shout and rush to the dead man.

'Don't move,' ordered Boston loudly, looking around him. 'No one move from the spot!' he threatened, pointing the barrel of his gun at each of them in turn. 'Anyone moves and I'll give him the same treatment, so be warned: everyone stay where you are! I've got plenty more rounds, don't worry!' He patted his pocket. They all stood as if rooted to the spot, uncomprehending, all of them dumbstruck. Only the wretched Kok-Tursun continued to lament over the body of her hated husband.

'I always knew you would croak like a dog, dog that you were! Now kill me too, murderer!' she wailed, hideous in her misery, and hurled herself at Boston. 'Kill me like a dog. All my life long I've never known a moment of joy, so why should I live any longer?' She tried to scream something else about having warned Bazarbai that he had no business stealing those cubs and that no good would come of it, but that monster wouldn't stop short at anything, even stealing wild animals and spending on drink all the money he got for them, but she was grabbed by two shepherds who stopped her mouth and dragged her away.

After this Boston looked around him and said in a voice that was soft but severe, 'Now I shall go and give myself up. I'll do it alone. You are to remain where you are. Have you got that?'

No one uttered a sound. To a man they were totally dumbfounded by the shooting. As he stared into their faces Boston suddenly realized that from that moment he had crossed an invisible line of demarcation and now stood apart from the rest of his kind: after all, these were good friends who stood around him, people with whom he had earned his daily bread from one day to the next, year in, year out, but now from their faces he could tell that he was become a total stranger. From now on he was cut off from them for all time, just as if he had never known them, as if he had suddenly risen from the dead and for that reason alone his presence was a source of horror.

Leading his horse by the rein, Boston moved off without looking round, in the direction of the lake where he could give himself up to the authorities. He walked along the road, hanging his head, and behind him, limping silently and tugging at the rein, followed his faithful Donkulyuk. And so Boston's life drew near its end . . .

'So this is the end,' said Boston aloud, and a terrible realization dawned upon him: up until now, he had been an entire world, whole and complete within himself, a world whose story was now played out to the very end. Within himself he was both heaven and earth, he was the mountains, the she-wolf Akbara, and also the great Mother of all living things: he was Ernazar, abandoned for all time in the ice beneath the Ala-Mongyu pass, and his final incarnation – the child Kenjesh, shot by a bullet fired from his own gun; he was Bazarbai, spurned and destroyed within him, and everything, all he had seen and lived through in his days on this earth. All this was his own universe, had lived in him and for him, and now, although all would endure just as it had always endured, it would do so without him and become another world; meanwhile his own world, his unique, irretrievable, personal universe, was lost for ever and would never be born again in any person or any thing. The end of his world, its death-agony, was now upon him.

On the deserted open track that led to the lake Boston spun

309

round abruptly, threw his arms around the neck of his horse, and hung there sobbing inconsolably.

'Oh Donkulyuk, you're the only one who does not see what a terrible thing I have done!' he wept, his whole body convulsed. 'What can I do? I've killed my son with my own hands and now I walk away, leaving him unburied and my beloved wife alone.'

Then he tied up the leading-rein and secured the stirrups to the pommel of Donkulyuk's saddle so they would not bang against the animal's flanks.

'Go, go home! Go wherever you want!' he said. 'We shall never meet again!'

He slapped the horse on its rump with the palm of his hand to chase it away, and the horse, amazed at this sudden freedom, headed back to the camp.

Boston, however, continued on his way . . .

The blue expanse of Issyk-Kul came closer and closer, and he longed to melt into it, to disappear. He wanted both to live and to die. Just like the white horses on the lake – the wave surges up, dies away and then is born again out of itself . . .